Praise for Cold Waters

"A compelling story filled with evocative description, deeply drawn characters, and heart-pounding drama."

—Elle James, *New York Times* bestselling author

"Herbert's haunting language, gothic tone, and vivid portrayal of small-town southern life add layers to this intriguing suspense. I was hooked from the first word!"

—Rita Herron, *USA Today* bestselling author

"Herbert delivers a fast-paced mystery, where nothing is quite what it seems. Family secrets and a cold-case murder are at the heart of her compelling novel, where the author masterfully paints the canvas of a sedate southern town with intriguing characters and a crafty plot. Readers won't soon forget the chilling thrill of *Cold Waters*."

—Laura Spinella, bestselling author of the Ghost Gifts novels

"Small towns hide the darkest secrets, and Normal, Alabama, is anything but in this southern gothic thriller that will keep you turning the pages until the very last. A twisted, southern gothic family drama that will stay with you long after you've closed the book. A stunning, deftly written journey through the dark corridors of the human heart."

—Sara Lunsford, author of *Tooth and Nail*

"*Cold Waters* is an unforgettable suspense story steeped in decaying old houses, dark family secrets, and rumors in a small Southern town."

—Leslie Tentler, author of the Chasing Evil trilogy

COLD
WATERS

COLD
WATERS

DEBBIE
HERBERT

THOMAS & MERCER

Published by Thomas & Mercer, Seattle
www.apub.com

Amazon, the Amazon logo, and Thomas & Mercer are trademarks of Amazon.com, Inc., or its affiliates

ISBN-13: 9781542042482 (hardcover)
ISBN-10: 1542042488 (hardcover)

ISBN-13: 9781542042505 (paperback)
ISBN-10: 154204250X (paperback)

Cover design by Shasti O'Leary Soudant

Printed in the United States of America

First edition

To my husband, Tim; my sons, Byron and Jacob; and my father, J. W. Gainey

Chapter 1

VIOLET

The tingling in my ear was the first omen.

Everyone knew an itchy ear meant people were talking about you, so I glanced out of the corner of my eye at the few people leaving the bus station. I didn't want to be spotted. But they paid me no mind, casting anxious looks at the slate sky before scurrying away, eager to escape the impending summer storm. Thunder crackled from afar.

A crow cawed, and I sought its form. The bird perched on a power line, a sleek black silhouette against the heavens. A lightning bolt speared the sky, forming a chiaroscuro of gray and black shadows in its momentary flash. The crow cawed again, the cry raucous and haunting.

Most people would have counted this as the second omen, but I wasn't most people. I welcomed the storm and the darkness and the crow. It all served to divert the good folks of Normal, Alabama, from noticing me and possibly recognizing my face—which was eerily similar to my dead mother's.

Old Willie Crenshaw pulled up close to my bench in a battered Plymouth Duster. He rolled down the window and motioned for me to enter. It was a welcome stroke of luck that he had happened to be dropping off his grandson at the station. He was, perhaps, the only person in town who would pay me a kindness.

I gathered up the large box beside me with one hand, resting it against my right hip, and lifted my solitary suitcase with the other. I kept my face forward, not daring to veer it an inch to the right or left as others brushed past me. Quickly, I threw the luggage in the back seat and opened the passenger door, grasping the box in my hands.

"Hold on now," Willie cautioned. "Careful of that there spring." A wicked coil of metal stuck out of the faded, threadbare upholstery.

"Thanks for the warning." My left ass cheek would have been punctured without it.

"Been meanin' to tape that up."

Cautiously, I slid in and shut the door, holding the box in my lap. Its solid form, which housed its strange but precious contents, made me feel more secure.

"You've had this car forever," I noted. The vehicle had been ancient before I'd even left Normal. A miracle of engineering had kept the motor running.

Willie slapped the dashboard. "This thing'll be a valuable antique one day."

Was he joking? I suppressed a smile. "Right."

He threw back his head and laughed, a breathless rasping that shook his shoulders. "Your face," he managed to gasp. "The same look my Cora has when I say that."

"How is she?" I asked politely.

"Fair to middlin'. Like always."

Which communicated much of nothing. We fell into an easy silence as he pulled out of the station and onto the road, driving at least ten miles an hour under the already slow speed limit.

The second omen appeared as Willie crept the battered Duster through downtown. An ambulance rounded the corner from Barefoot

Avenue and pulled onto the main drag just ahead of us, lights blazing. I pinched my nose straightaway to ward off bad luck.

Less than a minute later, the third sign—everything always came in threes, didn't it?—occurred as his car rumbled over the railroad tracks. I lifted my feet and raised both arms to touch the car roof. For a split second, Willie did the same, as I'd known he would. You couldn't be too careful. I mean, nobody wanted to die young when you could have prevented it by merely lifting your feet while going over tracks.

He stole a glance at me. His weathered black face held both curiosity and compassion, just as it had in the old days when he'd done the occasional odd job around the house for my dad.

"I'm sure Delaney was puttering round the garden, and the time just got away from her," he said.

I bet. I hadn't believed him the first time he'd offered up that lame excuse. Delaney had left me stranded at the bus station. If Willie hadn't happened by and seen me sitting on the bench with my luggage, I might have lingered there another two hours or more, sending off increasingly agitated texts to my sister, who apparently wasn't carrying her cell phone.

My silence must have made him uncomfortable. "And yer daddy can't drive no more," he offered. "You'll find everything's . . . changed. That's why I wrote you. Figured you'd want to know."

His letter had been brief and to the point: *Your daddy is doing poorly. Might want to pay a visit while you can.* I'd debated for days over whether to return. I didn't have many fond memories of a loving father, but duty pressed its relentless grasp on my conscience, overriding my logical objections. Besides, this homecoming might help me address the two ghosts of my past that refused to stay dead and buried—Mom and Ainsley Dalfred.

"You did the right thing, Willie. Thanks. How'd you get my address?"

"Yer sister."

I squeezed the bloodstone clutched in my right palm. My thumb fit neatly into the indentation at the top of the tumbled rock, as if it had been custom fitted for my touch. The lady at the Green Fairy metaphysical store had promised it warded off negative energy. I needed all the armor I could get.

We passed by the old oak, whose canopy twisted sideways, reaching all the way to the other side of the road. Willie beeped his horn as we drove under the tree, so—as tradition mandated—I made a wish.

Don't let it be as terrible as I fear.

We'd be at the house in minutes. This called for a heftier charm. Trusting the old more than the new, I reached into my jeans pockets, tucked in the bloodstone, and replaced it with the glass chip I always carried.

When I was nine, the crows had brought me their first gift—this chip of cobalt-blue glass that had glittered in the dusk like a fairy bauble. Or maybe like a frozen sliver of ice from the sea. So blue it hurt my heart. That azure chip had stood out amid the ash-and-bone-colored landscape of home. A promise of a magical land where the muddy Alabama River flowed down to the Gulf of Mexico and transformed into a turquoise sea that lapped against sugar-white beaches.

My fingers brushed against its smooth, cool surface, and calm flowed through me like a slow-moving stream.

"Whatcha got there?" Willie asked, glancing sideways as he maneuvered the car down the bumpy dirt road.

I shrugged. "It's like a worry stone," I replied with elaborate casualness.

"You ain't got nothing to worry about. I know yer folks are"—he stumbled a heartbeat—"dying to see ya."

I cringed.

He blushed.

Yeah, *dying* wasn't a good word choice, considering my past history. My nervousness returned.

I held the chip in the hollow of my palm, wishing I were my fourteen-year-old self, who could trust that it was a magic talisman to keep me safe. But despite my compulsion to ward off bad luck, I didn't much believe in magic anymore.

A twist around the bend, where white oaks towered and the spanish moss waved in the wind like an old friend, and we were near. Excitement warred with my worry. This was home, after all. The only one I'd ever known.

There.

My heart thundered, and I leaned forward in the seat, taking it in all at once.

It was as familiar to me as my own face and had an eternal quality. Generations of the Henderson family had lived here. But where once it may have been just this side of majestic, its years were now showing like a matronly grande dame's. It was nevertheless substantial, with an air of decayed gentility.

Wisteria vines climbed on either side of its frame, the wild encroaching on the domestic shelter. The white paint had worn thin on the south side of the house, and the wraparound porch had a subtle sag in the middle. The windows were large and dark—no need to bother with curtains when there were no nearby neighbors. The haint-blue shutters—painted that hue to ward off evil spirits and ghosts—hung crooked and were missing a few slats. But at least the massive antebellum columns remained impressive.

The forlornness of the slightly shabby structure was offset by Delaney's gardens. Purple hydrangeas, azaleas, cemetery roses, confederate jasmine, and hostas lined the home's foundation as well as the driveway.

"Bet you're glad to be back, eh?" Willie stopped the car and openly studied me, his old, wrinkled fingertips tapping the steering wheel.

"Sure." I crammed the blue chip back in my pocket and opened my purse. "I really appreciate the lift. Thanks for—"

He held up a hand. "Keep yer money."

"But . . ." A twenty-dollar bill fluttered in my fingers. Willie and his family could use the money, unless their circumstances had vastly improved during my years away.

"No way," he insisted. "Glad to help out. Yer sister's got her hands full with yer daddy. You'll be a blessing to them."

I frowned and stuffed the money back in my wallet. "Okay, then." I took a deep breath and opened the car door, retrieving my suitcase from the back seat. Willie gave me an encouraging nod before I closed the door. I watched him drive off in a trail of red dust. If everyone in Normal were this friendly, coming home might not be so bad.

Perhaps time had softened their hatred.

My fingers clutched and unclutched the leather handles of the suit case that held all my worldly possessions. I wished I had more. I wished I had a hefty bank account and could live anywhere in the world but here. But wishes and magic had died for me eleven years ago, and the clean beaches of Gulf Shores were merely a spot on the map, as foreign as the Taj Mahal.

I slowly turned and walked to the house. Would have been nice if they'd at least been on the porch to greet me. Then again, Dad might be too feeble and Delaney too busy. I climbed the concrete porch steps, careful of the crumbly spots and cracks. At the door, I hesitated. Should I knock or just enter? It was my home, but one I hadn't visited—couldn't visit—for all these years.

A loud screech, and the door opened. The decision had been made for me. Through the screen, a gray-skinned and gray-haired man clad only in his underwear studied me with hostility etched in his heavily lined face.

"Dad?" I asked, uncertain. Of course, it must be, but the wrinkles and thinning silver hair threw me.

"Did ya bring me my Jack?"

I'd know that rough voice anywhere. It was him, all right. I stiffened. Should have figured that would be his first question.

"If you mean Jack Daniel's, then no, I didn't bring any." I took an involuntary step back, out of striking range.

"Hey," a voice called from within. "Get away from the door, Dad. Jeez." Footsteps clomped across the room, and Delaney appeared behind the screen. Her mouth opened and shut as she stared.

I shifted from one foot to another. "It's me." A heartbeat ticked by, and I hurried to fill the void. "Violet."

"Oh shit . . . I mean, sorry." Delaney shrugged and gave a breezy smile. "I was out in the garden, and the time slipped away from me. How did you get here?" She stuck her head out the door to peer at the driveway.

"Willie Crenshaw. I waited for two hours and sent you a dozen texts and phone calls." I couldn't help the accusatory note in my voice.

"Like I said, I was in the garden. I didn't think to bring my cell with me."

I pinched my lips together before I could say something I'd regret. I mean, seriously? She couldn't have missed one day of digging?

Delaney cocked her head to the side, studying me. "I knew you were coming, and yet it's still such a shock to see you. Imagine—after all these years, you're finally back home." She pulled open the screen door. "Come in."

Long thin arms embraced me, her warm hair pressed against my cheek, and I inhaled the clean scent of baby shampoo, lilies of the valley, and something herbal. A deep, unanticipated longing crept over me to be a kid again, talking and laughing with Delaney before the events of That Night.

She withdrew, and I stepped over the threshold. Large bouquets of flowers in crystal vases did their best to cheer the gloom of the old place and offset the underlying smell of sickness—a combination of disinfectant and urine and mentholated cream.

Dad, thankfully, had already disappeared, but I could hear him shuffling about upstairs, mumbling. I pointed to the staircase. "How bad is he doing? Dad didn't even recognize me."

She relieved me of my suitcase and shrugged. "Some days are better than others."

Which didn't tell me much. I suspected the bad days outweighed the good, and I wondered how she stood it.

Delaney maneuvered around me, heading for the stairs, the right side of her body slightly leaning from the weight of my suitcase.

"Let me get that." I tugged at her arm, surprised at the strength of her resisting, muscular biceps. Presumably earned from all the gardening, I guessed.

"It's no problem." Her voice was firm. A woman used to running a household and giving orders. "Besides, you've got that box to carry."

I followed her up the creaking stairs, past the familiar portraits of grim Henderson men and women of past generations that lined the right wall. Ours was not an inheritance of cheerful dispositions. I could see a resemblance in Delaney. My older sister was serious. Not glum, but calm and matter of fact, meticulous in her bookkeeping job and family responsibilities. Or so I gathered from her infrequent visits to me at my various hospitals.

"And here you are." Delaney entered my old bedroom and set the suitcase by my antique dresser.

My breath hitched. Nothing had changed, not even the early-teen pink bedspread with ruffled lace trim. Photos of ballerinas in pink and lavender tutus hung on the walls. I set my box on the dresser, walked across the walnut floor, and opened the glass french door to my balcony. Same old pecan tree I used to jump onto from the balcony deck. I'd shimmied down it many a night to go skinny-dipping in the river. The wrought iron bird feeder was still there. Did my old friends think I'd deserted them?

Sadness pinched my heart, and I hastily shut the door. "It's all exactly as I left it."

"I didn't know if you wanted me to redecorate or not. You can change it any way you'd like," Delaney said easily.

"This is fine." I wouldn't be staying long, anyway. Just long enough to get my portion of Mom's inheritance, which had been waiting for me unclaimed all these years. Now, I was finally ready. With that money I could start a new life somewhere far away.

Delaney plopped on the bed and patted the mattress.

I sat beside her.

"It's like old times," she said with a smile, running a hand through her sun-streaked locks and glancing at herself in the mirror. Tiny freckles dotted her nose and the tops of her cheeks like a faint sprinkle of pixie dust.

"Sure. Old times." I tried to match her light tone. But the long days and nights of my exile and the horror of our friend's disappearance weighted the time between us. The distance stretched as taut as a pulled rubber band, until I feared it would snap and sting me.

Her forehead creased. "Are you really okay? Will staying here be too stressful for you?"

"I'm not going to break." I stood and paced to work off my irritation. I had no right to feel indignant. She was only concerned, and with just reason.

"All right, then." Delaney stiffened and rose from my bed, her face averted.

I'd gone and hurt her feelings.

"Sorry. I'm fine, really. I wouldn't have come if my counselor had advised against it. She says I'm perfectly capable of handling whatever happens. She even thought returning here might help me." I rolled my eyes. "You know, confront my past issues."

Delaney regarded me soberly. "I hope she's right. It won't be easy. Folks around here have long memories and short fuses. They believe the worst."

"Let them," I said, lifting my chin. I reminded myself it would only be for a few weeks. Maybe less. There were only a few locals whose opinions concerned me. "Do you ever see Ainsley's parents?" My voice trembled, and I swallowed past the lump in my throat.

Her blue eyes softened. "They're . . . the same. Give them time."

"They'll never change." Even if they could forgive me, time would never alter the facts—I had been the last one to see their daughter alive, and I remained a person of interest in the open case.

"Well, *I'm* glad you're back. It's glum with just Dad and me in this huge house."

"You told me he was going downhill, but I thought he'd recognize his own daughter."

"You can't take it personally, Violet. His memory comes and goes."

"Is he still drinking?"

"No. But that doesn't stop him from trying. Every time he leaves the house, he wants to go to the liquor store. And he's convinced there're hidden bottles of alcohol around the house and grounds."

"Is he ever"—I faltered a heartbeat—"mean . . . to you?"

"No. Not too bad. He's shoved and slapped me a couple times and cussed me out, but nothing major. I've learned how to handle him when his temper flares."

I gaped at her and the casualness with which she'd said those words. "But you shouldn't have to put up with that. It's wrong."

Delaney walked to the mirror and dusted dirt from her T-shirt. "It's life. Besides, he can't help himself these days. It's the dementia."

Dementia, my ass. He'd always been a harsh, hard man, especially when he drank. I forced myself to recall more pleasant memories. When sober, Dad was decent. He used to take us to the Dairy Queen every

Sunday for orange Dreamsicles and had insisted one Christmas on getting us a puppy over our mom's objections.

The sound of smashing glass exploded from downstairs, followed by a loud curse. "Shit!"

"I'd better go clean it up before he cuts himself." Delaney hustled to the door and paused. "Rest up from your trip, and then we'll eat dinner. I have your favorite—baked chicken and corn bread dressing."

I blinked back sudden tears. She might not have bothered to pick me up at the station, but she had remembered my homecoming and had gone to some trouble to cook.

A better sister would have cleaned up the mess downstairs for her, or at least have helped. But I kicked off my shoes and lay on the bed. I *was* tired. Tired in the way that an emotional day drains your energy quicker than digging ditches. I closed my eyes and curled on my side, giving in to the lethargy. My breathing slowed, and my mind drifted to a numbing darkness.

The darkness melted to liquid that glistened and shimmered. It swirled and rippled and beckoned. I swung on the rope out over the river and let go—dropping into its inky promise of coolness on a humid summer night. Water engulfed my sticky-hot flesh in a baptism of relief. I broke through the surface, laughing.

Ainsley. Your turn.

Silence thickened in the waning-moon evening, and adrenaline pulsed through my body in waves of fear. My throat clogged, and I couldn't take a deep breath.

A sharp rap at the door burst the silence, and I jerked up, gulping oxygen. Deep shadows trembled in the dusk, and I shook my head, disoriented. This wasn't my bare little room at the Serenity Hills Halfway House for the Emotionally Disturbed. This was a huge princessy room with a girly bedspread and ghostly paintings of ballerinas in pastel tutus, all pale arms and legs contorted into impossibly graceful poses.

Ah yes, my old childhood bedroom.

The pounding began anew. *Bambambambambam.*

"What is it?" I stumbled out of bed, drunk with interrupted sleep and the nightmare's hangover. "I'm coming." I reached for the doorknob, but the door opened before I could grasp it.

Dad filled the entrance, and the wrinkles on his face deepened with his scowl. But at least he'd donned pants and a shirt. "Time to eat, Violet. You always holdin' things up for your mother."

Mom had been dead for years, but at least he recognized me now. The smell of chicken and pan dressing drifted up the stairs, and my stomach growled. "Be right down," I promised. I rushed to the bathroom, washed my hands, and ran a brush through my hair.

Downstairs in the formal dining room, Dad and Delaney were already seated, and I quickly took my place at the table. Second chair on the right—same as ever. Mom's pink cherry blossom plates were set out, along with the better serving pieces and real silverware. Delaney had made an effort to make the occasion special.

The moment I sat, Dad started eating at a fast and furious pace, as if afraid the food would be snatched away before he could finish.

Delaney touched his shoulder. "Stop. You know you have to take your medicine first." She picked up a tiny plastic cup by his plate and held it in front of him. The mixture of pills in different sizes and colors looked like a handful of M&M'S mixed with Good & Plenty candy.

In one expert thrust, Dad emptied the bottle into his mouth and washed it all down with a chug of sweet tea. I wanted to ask why he needed so much medicine but decided to ask Delaney when he wasn't around. Who knew how much he picked up from conversations around him? No need to make a bad situation more difficult for my sister. He took his meds willingly, and I had no right to start questioning things and possibly get him riled up. If anyone knew the importance of medication, it was me. I had my own pretty little prescribed pills stashed away.

Delaney lifted her glass of tea. "Here's to Violet's homecoming."

Dad stopped eating and looked up with raised brows. "What are we toasting *with*?" he asked hopefully. "Wine's traditional, but I prefer bourbon."

"Water," Delaney answered, lips pursed. "Plain ole water."

"Well, that's no fun," he muttered, setting back to work on the chicken.

She winked at me, and it felt like old times. Us against the parents and all their rules. I clinked my glass to hers. "To coming home."

Delaney dug a square of dressing from the pan and put it on my plate. Her charm bracelet tinkled and shone under the chandelier's prismed light. As did a huge honker of a diamond on her left ring finger.

"Are you engaged?" I asked, astonished.

She held out her left hand and splayed her fingers wide. "Almost a year now. His name is Sawyer Harris, and we'll be married next April."

Sawyer? What a prissy, preppy kind of name. I pictured a tall man with conservatively cut hair wearing polo shirts, tailored jeans, and dock shoes. Harris . . . the name didn't ring familiar. "He from around here? Do I know any of his family?"

"Don't see how. They live in Birmingham."

Over a hundred miles from Normal. "Why haven't you told me this before now? We've talked on the phone several times, and you never mentioned him."

"I wanted to surprise you and tell you in person."

She'd surprised me, all right. "But"—I nodded my head in Dad's direction, whose attention was focused on the meal, apparently unaware of his precarious future, then lowered my voice to a whisper—"who's going to take care of him when you get married?"

Delaney set her fork down with a bang, and I jumped. "I don't know, Violet." Her words were deliberate and edged with something dangerous. "But I've been taking care of him for years, with no help from anyone."

With no help from *me*. The accusation silently spun about the dining room, and my face warmed. Stunned shame twisted my gut. Not only had I never helped, but the idea of offering to do so had never occurred to me.

"Sorry, Delaney. I've been wrapped up in my own . . . problems."

Her features relaxed. "Never mind. I shouldn't have said anything. Of course you had to take care of yourself. I couldn't expect you to tend to anyone else when your own . . . health . . . has been so fragile."

Underneath the table, I made a sign of the cross for a blessing, then took a slow sip of tea and collected myself. "I'm stronger now," I said, hoping she didn't catch the tremble in my voice. I cleared my throat. "I'll take care of Dad some while I'm here. Give you a break."

"It's okay. I don't expect anything." She took a dainty bite of butter beans and chewed.

I spooned more dressing into my mouth, but my appetite had disappeared. Did she want me to help or not? Maybe she didn't think I was capable.

"Sawyer is amazing. He's an architect. We met at an art gallery in Birmingham, and it was love at first sight. He told me I was the most beautiful woman he'd ever seen." Delaney's eyes glowed, and she played with the emerald pendant on her necklace. "Spoils me rotten too. Takes me to the nicest restaurants and concerts, buys me whatever I want, and he's so—"

"What about Dad?" I interrupted, knowing that once Delaney got on the topic of herself, she could ramble on for an eternity.

"What about him?"

"Who watches him while you're out with your boyfriend?"

"Oh, that. I hire someone to sit with him. Anyway, Sawyer and I went to the symphony last weekend and had—"

I tuned her out. My spartan existence at the halfway house and her expensive dates with the perfect fiancé were so far apart she might as well be talking about living in a colony on Mars. I glanced over at Dad, who had finished eating and leaned back in his chair. His eyes closed, and I worried he'd fall asleep and keel over on the hardwood floor.

"Is it his bedtime already?" I asked.

"Actually, he usually takes a nap after an early lunch, but with the excitement of your visit, he stayed up later than normal. Plus, his medication makes him drowsy."

In other words, I'd disrupted their schedule. "I'll be glad to help while I'm here," I assured Delaney again. "Why don't you take tomorrow off? Maybe go to Birmingham for the day to visit Sawyer?"

"I'd love to—but are you sure you can handle it?" Hope battled with doubt in her eyes.

"Sure," I lied. "Piece of cake." I turned to Dad and saw that his eyes were half-open, and he was staring at me. "We'll be fine, won't we?"

He stood and pointed a finger. "Who are you?" he yelled, shaking with rage. "What are you doing in my house?"

"Calm down, Dad." Delaney stood and drew his attention. "It's Violet. Your daughter. Remember, I told you she was coming for a visit? It's time for your nap." She led him from the table, and I sat alone, wondering why I'd ever come home. I could have holed up at a cheap motel until Delaney mailed the inheritance money. No doubt my counselor would describe my return as some deep psychological need to find love and acceptance. And she'd encouraged me to come back and face my past.

But hope had been washed out of my spirit long ago. Seemed I was destined to end life like the long line of my grim, unsmiling ancestors whose portraits haunted the hallways.

After washing the dishes, I escaped to my bedroom for a few minutes and opened my box on the dresser. The largest item was the whittled bird that Seth, a fellow patient, had given me one Christmas at the Cottonwood mental institution. That went on my nightstand, where I could view it last thing at night and first thing in the morning.

Next, I removed a small metal coffee can filled with buttons that used to belong to my grandma. I gave it a shake for good luck and set it on top of my dresser. Finally, it was time to unpack my smaller treasures. I gave a silent thanks to Luanne, a kindly caretaker at Cottonwood, who had held them in safekeeping. Because of her tender mercy, they'd been protected from theft and curious eyes. Whenever I wanted to hold the mementos for comfort or luck, Luanne would unlock them from the cabinet and leave me with them for as long as I wanted.

Carefully, I lifted out the dozen plastic trays that held my crow keepsakes, the various gifts they'd bestowed on me when I was younger: paper clips, buttons, an earring, marbles, nails, bits of broken glass, shiny pebbles. I'd kept everything—except their occasional offerings of dead baby birds.

Frankly, the crows had first noticed me because I was a messy eater as a kid. We'd unload from the family station wagon, and crumbs from our fast-food forays would spill from my lap. The ever-watchful crows would swoop in and feast.

Some people said they were ugly, but I found their raven-black plumage—sometimes tinged with bright green or deep purple—fascinating. I had read up on them and taken to leaving shelled peanuts on my balcony for them to eat. In return, they'd brought me these bits and baubles. Our unusual friendship had gained such local notoriety that when I was ten years old, the *Birmingham News* had run a story on the crow gifts, and the article had subsequently been picked up by the Associated Press. Folks around Normal had called me the crow girl—until four years later, when everything had been overshadowed by the events of That Night.

Now, they called me a suspected murderess.

Chapter 2

VIOLET

July 2, 2007—eleven years earlier

Mud squishes between my toes as we pick our way through the swampy woods. Ainsley's hair, crow black as mine, melds with the July night. A sliver of moonlight illuminates the pale places of her body where the sun never shines.

The elliptical beam of the flashlight pierces the dark shadows. The limbs of the moss-covered oak form a webbed tangle against the moon. Skeeters and frogs roar in the night—insects on a bloodsucking mission and amphibians croaking their horny pleas.

"Here," she says, throwing her lemon-yellow T-shirt on the lowest branch of a white oak. It hangs like a tempting bit of citrus next to a grungy towel we keep here for our skinny-dipping soirees.

I throw my faded pink T-shirt next to hers, watching as she carefully knots her long hair into a bun at the top of her head. She arches a brow. "Aren't you gonna put your hair up?"

"Nope. No need."

I don't have to explain what that means. Ainsley has a pretty fair inkling of my homelife. Her parents observe every little detail about her, whereas mine are too busy arguing with each other to pay me much attention. Only Delaney will notice if my hair is damp in the morning. But my sister can hardly tattle, seeing as how she often joins us.

Tonight, I'm glad Delaney is home in bed and I have Ainsley all to myself.

I try not to stare at Ainsley's chest. Only one year older than me, and she's already developed boobs. Will I ever grow a pair?

I plunge into the water. It's as warm as a bath, but at least it's wet. Anything to escape the mosquitoes and wash off the film of sweat that coats me like armor the minute I step into the humid air.

A splash and then water rippling at my waist mean that Ainsley has followed me into the river. I dive under, reveling in its complete liquid caress. I pop up next to Ainsley, and she shrieks, yet a grin splits her face.

"Payback will be hell," she promises.

Laughing, I swim back to shore. "Only if you catch me," I tease. But I'm not worried. We're swamp mermaids. We have a secret bond out here in the wild darkness as we swim and play and explore.

This is our private world where no one can see us. A magic place where we can do as we please in these stolen night moments when we sneak out of our respective homes. The promise of summer stretches before me—full of excitement and just the teeniest bit of danger. But the danger is a spirited dance on the sharp edge of a knife.

It keeps us tingly and daring and alive.

Chapter 3

VIOLET

Present day

Piece of cake? I'd be eating humble pie by dinner. Dad was killing me. If I'd had any sense, I'd have waited a few days before volunteering to Dad-sit, given him time to get used to my presence.

I shook my head as he slipped out of my sight. Reluctantly, I left the back-porch shade and followed him through the yard as he muttered and poked with a broken tree limb among the flower borders. I twisted my long hair up on the top of my head and secured it with a hair tie.

"Are you ready to go inside now?" I asked for the gazillionth time. "It's hot out here."

He mumbled and didn't bother to look up, still thrashing the stick between plants and dragging deep lines in the dirt. He ritualistically etched these soil mandalas, yet they seemed to bring him frustration rather than peace.

"Delaney's not going to like you messin' with her flowers," I warned. "You're going to be in trouble when she gets back"—*please, God, let it be soon*—"and probably me too."

He muttered something that sounded like *sludge*, or it could have been *gludge*, or he could have been telling me to piss off, for all I knew.

I sighed as he headed for the old shed. "Not this again," I complained. Quickly, I stepped in front of him, blocking his path. No more asking him questions. Maybe if I was firm, he'd stop this ridiculous, fruitless search for God knew what. "Time to go inside."

Dad circled around me, muttering.

I raised my arms skyward and grunted in frustration. Once more, I scrambled in front of Dad and stood my ground. "Listen. I can guess what you're looking for, but I'm sure Delaney's already found all your old hiding places."

He paused and looked up, silent, eyes blank. He didn't remember me again, and I took it as a personal insult.

"The hooch is gone," I yelled, hands on hips. "Get it? Now we're going to march into that house right now before you suffer heatstroke."

His eyes narrowed, and he lifted his stick, pointing it at my chest. "Jezebel," he spat.

"No, Violet," I countered dryly. "Your daughter."

"Liar."

He swung his arm backward, preparing to haul off and hit me. The blue chip in my pocket radiated strength. It would protect me against this danger. I controlled the instinct to jump back. Instead, I clenched my jaw and grabbed his raised arm.

Alarm flickered in his faded blue eyes, and the stick fell harmlessly to the ground.

"Don't you even *think* about hitting me, old man. I'm not a kid anymore."

"I know who you are." A cagey expression flickered in his eyes.

"Oh yeah? Who?"

"Violet. The baby. Hyacinth's baby girl." A wistful note crept into his voice, and guilt twisted my gut.

I gently took his arm and guided him to the porch. Dad couldn't help the restless, pointless wandering. "Sorry I yelled at you," I apologized.

"Where's Delaney?" he asked, voice querulous. "I want Delaney."

Shit. I didn't want Delaney to come home and think I either had been mean or was incompetent. Maybe both. "She'll be home tonight." I thought fast. "How about we go to town, and I'll get us a milkshake?"

"Peach?"

"If they have it."

"Okay," he answered, docile as a scolded child.

Inside, I grabbed the Lincoln Continental keys from the fireplace mantel, hoping the ancient car still ran. Delaney drove a red Toyota but said she kept the Lincoln as backup for emergencies. As far as I was concerned, keeping Dad mellow was a family crisis of sorts. On the way out the door, I snapped a sprig of ivy from the vines crawling the porch columns. I'd stick it in the car's unused ashtray as protection against motor malfunctions. It would do until I could attach a bell somewhere inside the car. Hey, if it worked for Harley-Davidson bikers to ward off gremlins, then it would work for me as well.

Lucky for me, the engine cranked to life, and we were off in minutes. At the outskirts of town, I noted several pickup trucks parked at the Feed and Seed. On a whim, I pulled into the lot. "Stay here," I told Dad. "I'm running inside a minute."

I rolled down the windows, not daring to leave the AC and motor running in case he decided to take a spin on his own. On the porch, a couple of old men sat, dressed in overalls and playing checkers.

"Hey," I called, waving a hand as I hurried past them.

They regarded me quizzically. No doubt they'd expected Delaney to emerge from the car. Their gazes shifted from me to Dad, who was hunched in the passenger side.

The bearded one spoke up. "Are you——?"

"Violet." I smiled, faking a confident air. "The younger daughter."

Neither of them smiled back or spoke, and I turned away, face flushed from more than the heat. This had not been a good idea. I shouldn't have ventured into town alone without Delaney as a buffer.

I considered retreating to the Lincoln, but giving them gossip fodder about my cowardice would make things worse next trip.

Taking a deep breath, I opened the door and stepped inside, instantly familiar with the old smell of fertilizer and insecticide. At the bell jingle, all the customers glanced over and then stared, trying to guess who the stranger might be. With any luck, I could make my purchase and escape before they figured it out. Quickly, I shifted my gaze to the middle of the far-right wall, relieved to find that what I needed was in the same location it had always been. I walked straight over, avoiding eye contact as I lifted the ten-pound bag of shelled peanuts and hauled it over to the wooden counter in the middle of the store.

Still keeping my eyes downcast, I set my purchase down, dug a twenty out of my purse, and laid it on the counter.

And waited.

Large hands with hairy knuckles splayed on the ledge and made no move to collect my money. "How much do I owe you?" I asked, pulling out an additional five-dollar bill.

"22.95."

Of course. Inflation had done its work in the years I'd been away. I pushed the bills toward him, keeping my expression neutral.

He folded his arms across his chest and gave me the once-over. "Violet Henderson?" he asked, raising an eyebrow.

I nodded. From the corner of my eye, I saw a woman with black, silver-tinged hair making a beeline toward me. Her jaw was stern, back stiff, and tension rippled toward me like a tidal wave.

Fear prickled my spine.

I wasn't ready to face Ainsley's mom.

"So you've returned—" the clerk began.

"How dare you show your face here," Mrs. Dalfred's voice cut in, slicing me to ribbons. "They let you out of the crazy house?"

I winced but didn't dare defend myself.

"Why did you come back? Haven't you hurt our family enough?"

Hot tears clouded my vision, but not enough to obscure the blaze in her eyes or the fire in her fisted hands. Ainsley had possessed her mom's dark hair and delicate features. It felt as if Ainsley herself had risen from the dead to condemn me.

"I'm sorry," I whispered.

"Sorry?" She snorted. "You're *sorry*? My Ainsley is gone, and that's all you have to say?"

The air pressed down on me, and my peripheral vision faded and tunneled down to Mrs. Dalfred's face. It was like looking through a kaleidoscope—she appeared far away and fragmented into pixels of black-silver hair and burning blue eyes.

She grabbed my shoulders, her thumbs imprinting themselves in the tender pockets of flesh under my collarbones. Her face radiated an intensity that I'd only seen before on the faces of the truly mad. And I'd seen mad aplenty.

"Where's Ainsley?" she rasped.

Well, wasn't *that* the quintessential question that plagued my life. The one that had branded me inside and out until it had become the defining identity of Violet Henderson. The unsolvable mystery that had ruined my childhood and threatened to steal my future.

Panic kidnapped my lungs and heart, held them hostage in its pitiless grip.

"Where is she?" Mrs. Dalfred yelled. "What did you do to her?"

An awful silence descended, and I was aware of everyone's scrutiny.

She threw up her hands. "As if you would tell the truth. You lied about being with Ainsley the night she disappeared. The truth isn't in you."

I stumbled backward, grabbed the peanuts, and turned, carefully making my way to the door—willing my wobbly legs to support me and not daring to look back.

"Miss Violet? I have your change," the clerk called out.

If it were a hundred dollars, I'd have still kept walking. I exited the Feed and Seed hell and made it to the Lincoln, collapsing inside.

"About time. It's hot in here," Dad complained.

I started the motor, and cool air freshened my face and body. Quickly, I fished out the prescription bottle from my purse and dry swallowed two pills.

Deep breaths.

I forced my lungs to inhale and exhale—low and slow—as I leaned back in the seat, eyes closed. I willed my mind not to think of Mrs. Dalfred's attack. For now, I had to get myself together, get Dad his milkshake, and get home.

Three things.

If I kept my mind focused on executing those three tasks, I could function until I was safely home and the anxiety pills had had time to cast their calming enchantment. I backed the car out of my space and exited the parking lot. In minutes, I arrived on Main Street and drove past the familiar landmarks—Dixie Drycleaners; the imposing, baroque courthouse that dominated the downtown square; and O'Neil's department store, where Mom had taken me to buy my first bra.

I was glad to see that Ruth's still stood on the outskirts of Normal. Even more glad to note that the establishment had added a drive-through service, which meant I wouldn't have to leave the car and risk more public scrutiny. The fresh-faced teenager at the window had no clue who I was, and that suited me just fine.

"Hey, Mr. Henderson." She smiled, passing two plastic cups to me. "Where's your daughter?"

His brows drew together in confusion. "She's gone. I don't know where she runs away—"

"Keep the change," I interrupted, pressing some bills into her hand. The girl looked mildly alarmed, as if I might have taken the old man hostage or something.

I smiled, waved at the server in what I hoped was a reassuring fashion, and headed home. Dad had lapsed into silence, and I turned on the radio and sipped the creamy peach shake, allowing the sugar and the music to distract me from my disastrous first trip into town.

The Lincoln rattled and rumbled on the dirt road home. I gritted my teeth, sure that a muffler or a shaft or some such mechanical accoutrement would give up the ghost and drop off, leaving me stranded in a hostile town with no money and a crazy man on my hands. Before I set foot in here again, I'd find a bell to hang on the front mirror to ward off any motor gremlins intent on destroying belts, sparks, and whatever else kept an engine running smoothly. I breathed a sigh of relief when I pulled into the driveway and bustled Dad inside to the den, where I set him on the sofa and turned the TV to a John Wayne movie, hoping a western would keep him entertained until dinner and bedtime.

How did Delaney do it day in and day out? And still manage to run a bookkeeping business from home while taking care of him? I felt drained from the responsibility of Dad-sitting. Was this what new mothers felt when they watched over their infants? If only I could be more like Delaney.

I slunk to the kitchen and dug out leftovers from last night.

At last, a chemically induced mellow enveloped me like a warm blanket, drowsing my body to a slower heartbeat. My limbs and eyelids wanted to succumb to the gravitational pull to close shop and shut down. I ached for the blank void of sleep, but I had responsibilities—a new and unwelcome burden. Delaney was right—I'd done nothing for years but indulge in my own misery, in my trouble coping with Ainsley's disappearance.

Well, to be fair, Delaney hadn't outright accused me of all that. It was what I'd inferred from her complaint about handling the caretaking alone. But interpreting other people's emotions placed me on dangerous ground. That was what my counselors had warned, at any rate.

Calmer now, I allowed my mind to remember Mrs. Dalfred's fury. No interpretation needed there. She blamed me for what had happened to Ainsley. Always did, always would. It was another thing I had to live with. And I couldn't imagine the pain she'd endured these past years. Her accusations today hurt, but the meds kept me from panic attack mode.

The sounds of shooting and war yells erupted from the TV set, and I peeked in on Dad, glad for an excuse to keep busy. He lay on the worn leather sofa, looking vulnerable and harmless in sleep. He'd kicked off his shoes, and his white crew socks were halfway off each foot. I padded back to the kitchen and stuck the leftover chicken and dressing in the oven and made myself a cup of coffee. I hoped the milkshake and short nap before dinner didn't totally disrupt his nighttime routine.

Shadows deepened in the early evening, and I felt as wilted as Delaney's flowers in the garden. I sipped my coffee, willing the caffeine to counteract the sedative's effect. Grabbing the bag of peanuts I'd purchased, I climbed upstairs to my bedroom and stepped out onto the balcony.

It seemed hopeless that the crows would return—not that I doubted their memory or intelligence, but after all these years, surely they'd have figured I was never coming back.

I certainly had never thought I would.

Ripping open the bag, I laid a dozen shelled peanuts on the wrought iron bird feeder, which featured a long, flat platform that allowed several birds to feed at a time.

"Here's to nothing," I muttered. Maybe a new flock would notice the peanuts and become my friends. I could use a few, whether of the human or avian kind. I sat in the wicker rocker, gingerly placing my weight on the half-rotted slats, and propped my feet on the railing.

Waiting. Hoping.

A gray squirrel scampered along the branch of a nearby oak and regarded me soberly, nose twitching. He wanted the peanuts in a bad way, but the move to gather them was too risky with me so close by. I sipped my coffee and watched, allowing us to get the feel of one another. Grandma used to say that unexpectedly seeing lots of squirrels or having a close encounter with one was a reminder that we reaped what we sowed. Mom had always dismissed Grandma's sayings as nonsense, but not me. I totally bought into Grandma's view that even though the world was a mysterious and often dangerous place, the universe also spoke to us through signs—if only we were wise enough and patient enough to notice.

Given my past, I needed to be extra mindful. The squirrel reminded me that at age fourteen I'd screwed up so badly that I now needed to work hard and do right for the rest of my life, or I'd sow more destruction.

My spine tingled. From the dark shadows, I sensed a movement in black—the tiniest flicker of motion. Like a lifted wing or a beak scraping against oak limbs. A slight breeze rustled the dangling spanish moss, as if old men's beards were being tickled. Leaves quivered, and the freaked-out squirrel hugged the tree, gracefully exiting. He'd be back for the peanuts the moment I returned inside.

More whispers of movement floated from the darker tangle of pines past the yards and gardens. A crow—perhaps even a murder of crows—watched me. But if they didn't want to be seen, they wouldn't. Most people were clueless that these intelligent birds were everywhere, observing us, studying us. Or they were superstitious that the black birds were an omen of misfortune and death. Not to mention just a plain ole nuisance for gardeners.

I dug out more peanuts and placed them on the tray. Plenty for squirrels and crows alike. Headlights strobed through the tree line by the dirt lane, and Delaney's car turned into the drive at the very moment I smelled burnt chicken. Oh hell. I'd been so distracted that I'd forgotten to tie knots on my kitchen apron to protect the food I was preparing, and disaster had struck. I hurried downstairs, dismayed at the thick cloud of smoke emanating from the kitchen.

Dad.

The image of him in vulnerable sleep seized my mind. What if the smoke was too much for his old fragile lungs? And selfishly, what if I'd caused harm to yet another person?

You're toxic. Toxic, toxic, toxic.

With each heart-slamming step to the den, the words condemned me. A quick glance in the kitchen, and I was relieved to find there were no red flames blazing but merely smoke billowing from the oven. I ran through the smoke, opened a window, and turned off the oven before resuming my trek to the den.

Dad sat up on the couch, coughing and staring at the smoke in confusion. For the moment, he was fine. I took his arm, frantic to protect him from inhaling too much smoke. "C'mon, let's step out on the porch for some fresh air."

He pulled back. "I want Delaney."

"She's outside." I pointed at the window. "There's her car now. Let's go meet her on the porch."

That did the trick.

We were both coughing as I rushed us out the door and helped him into a rocker.

Delaney's car skidded to a sudden halt, and a car door slammed. "What the hell happened?" She ran across the yard, pointing to the kitchen window. "Is the house on fire?"

"We're fine. Thanks for asking," I said, rolling my eyes.

Her mouth tightened, and I remembered her infamous rages from our childhood. This would really set her off.

"I can see you're still breathing," Delaney snapped. She stomped up the porch steps and tossed her purse on the porch glider before marching through the door.

I sat on a chair next to Dad and placed my head between my knees, dizzy with relief that he was unharmed and that the house hadn't burned to the ground. Day two was wretched, not the fresh start I'd hoped for.

The screen door screeched open. "How could you forget dinner was in the oven?" she asked. "I leave you alone for one day. One day! And this"—she waved a hand at the smoke—"is what I come home to?"

I scuffed the concrete floor with the toe of my sandal. "I'm sorry."

"You could have killed Dad."

"It was an accident." As soon as I said it, I recognized it as a lame excuse for my incompetence.

Delaney threw up her hands. "Oh, well, then," she said snidely. "An accident. That makes everything okay."

"I'm just saying—"

"All you had to do was heat up leftovers. That's it! Is that too much to ask?" Delaney sank onto the porch swing and buried her face in her hands. Her shoulders shuddered.

Her sobs shook me more than the almost kitchen fire. Delaney never cried. Delaney was the strong one who took care of everybody.

Dad glared at me. "You made her cry."

"I'm sorry," I offered again. "Delaney, everything's okay. I'll clean up inside and pick us up some chili dogs and fries at Ruth's."

She looked up at me, tears streaming down her face. "I try to have a day off to spend with Sawyer, and it's like the gods are punishing me for it."

"That's not true. I screwed up, okay? It won't happen again."

Delaney snorted and swiped at her cheeks. "Damn right it won't. Because I'll never leave you in charge again. You can't be trusted."

"Suits me fine." I stood and walked past her, miserable and angry at her accusation that I couldn't be trusted, even if those words were true. I entered the kitchen and glared at the closed oven door, which still seeped smoke from the top and sides. I debated the best way to approach the job. "Screw it," I muttered, jerking on a pair of mitts and opening the oven door. The chicken was charred black, and its insides were lit like a glowing ember. Coughing, I grabbed the pan and ran out the back door, black smoke fanning my face, choking me.

I threw the offending bird in the garbage can, pan and all.

High-pitched laughter erupted behind me, and I spun around.

Delaney was bent over, gasping, clutching a hand to her stomach. "You . . . you . . . the ch-chicken . . ." She pointed at the garbage can.

I walked toward her, uncertain if she was laughing at me or merely on the verge of hysteria.

"You should see your face," she panted. "Soot and tear streaks all over."

"So you're not mad at me anymore?" I'd forgotten her volatile mood swings. Storm to sunshine in seconds.

She waved a hand in the air, dismissing the notion. "I was too rough on you. Can't expect everyone to manage work and caretaking like I can."

The tension whooshed out of my body. "I deserved it. I promise I'll be more careful in the future."

Delaney placed an arm over my shoulder. "C'mon. I'll help you clean up the kitchen. It's really not so terrible."

We returned to the house. Laughing, talking. Like real sisters.

At the back porch, I turned around, again sensing that I was being watched. A high-pitched laugh, identical to Delaney's, sounded faintly from the woods.

"Did you hear that?" I whispered to Delaney. I placed a finger to my lips, and she stilled, cocking her head to one side.

A few heartbeats passed, but only crickets and the buzzing of insects pierced the silence.

"I didn't hear anything," she said, wrinkling her forehead, searching my face with concern. "Are you sure you did?"

"Maybe not. Sometimes crows mimic our laughter, so it might have been them. Forget it."

"It must be stressful coming back here. Maybe you should call your doctor if you're . . . um, having problems."

My face and neck warmed. "It was nothing."

I followed her inside and paused at the doorway, searching the inky blackness before shutting the door.

I had heard something. I was dead sure of it.

~

Much later that evening, after hours of hearing more about Sawyer and all of Delaney's fun friends and her employer who raved about her bookkeeping skills, I'd slipped off to my room and fallen into a deep slumber, when the sound of a car door squeaking open awakened me. I hurried to the window, glancing at the time on my cell phone. 1:11 a.m. A repeating number—meaning the universe had sent me a wake-up call to notice what was happening. And I always paid attention to the signs.

Pulling back the lace curtain, I caught sight of Delaney removing handfuls of bags from the back seat of her car. What the hell was she doing? Had she gone back out at night for groceries? Nothing local would be open this late.

Delaney stepped under the porch light and quickly skipped up the steps. I read the bag labels she carried—expensive retail store packages and totes decorated with pink stripes and fancy logos. Things she must have picked up in Birmingham.

But why sneak them in so late at night? As if sensing my stare, Delaney turned her head, craning her neck upward. Swiftly, I dropped the curtain and stepped back, crossing my fingers that she hadn't spotted me. The front door opened and shut, and I scurried to bed, pulling the sheets up to my chin.

Footsteps on the stairs, and then her light tread in the hallway. She paused at my door, and my heart inexplicably pounded. The doorknob soundlessly turned, and I shut my eyes tight as her presence crossed the threshold and drew close.

"Violet?" she whispered.

I didn't respond, faking sleep, and seconds later she left, quietly pulling the door shut.

My heart's erratic thumping eased, and I drew a deep breath. So what if Delaney—and her fiancé—had gone on a shopping spree? She was perfectly welcome to spend her money as she pleased.

Yet it didn't sit right, and I couldn't say why. When my sister had entered my bedroom, my scalp had tingled as she'd stood watching me in the darkness.

Chapter 4

HYACINTH

Twenty-seven years earlier

My stepdaughter was always a sneaky little thing. I came so close to not marrying Parker because of her. If I hadn't been under so much pressure from Mom to make this match, I might have bowed out. After our wedding rehearsal, Parker brought her to Mom's house, where a few of us had gathered for an after-dinner coffee. At the time, Delaney was a cute little four-year-old with snow-white hair and large blue eyes. But often, I'd catch her giving me an odd look, a cold, calculating stare that had no place on a young child's face.

She's just nervous, I'd tell myself. *Naturally, she's afraid and jealous of me*, I'd add when I caught her lying to Parker, saying I'd been mean to her when I had not. *She's used to having her daddy all to herself*, I'd say when, yet again, Delaney manipulated something I'd said—as though I'd intended to hurt the child.

Yet I was determined to win her love.

Back then, I believed anything possible. Before Parker started drinking himself to ruin, before my stepdaughter proved to be as difficult as I'd feared, and before I wanted to leave Parker for another man.

But the first crack in my fantasy world was at my wedding rehearsal. My family and friends cooed over how darling Delaney was in her pretty dress as she sprinkled rose petals down the bridal aisle. And she *did* look adorable. But some intuition had me follow Delaney when she sneaked out of the room where we all sipped coffee after the rehearsal dinner.

I shadowed her down Mom's carpeted hallway. Delaney never looked back. She entered the guest bedroom, where my wedding gown was laid out on the bed. With no hesitation, the little hellion walked over to it and deliberately upended her glass of grape juice onto the white lace of my gown.

"What have you done?" I cried.

A smile tugged the corners of her mouth. "I don't want you to marry Daddy. I want you to go away."

I blinked back angry tears. This wasn't a child's temper tantrum or an angry outburst. This was . . . I wasn't sure what it was. But I didn't like the child's calm, calculated move.

Footsteps came rushing down the hallway and through the door. Parker entered first.

"What happened?" he asked, his face lined with worry.

As if on cue, Delaney burst into tears. "I'm sorry, Daddy. I came to look at Miss Hy's dress, and I accidentally spilled my juice." She hiccuped and rubbed pitiful little eyes that held no tears.

My mother rushed in. "We'll soak it in water right now and then rinse it with vinegar. It'll be fine." She slanted me a worried glance as she scurried to the laundry to try and fix my ruined dress. How I wished Dad were still alive. He'd see through Delaney's act in a heartbeat. But all Mom cared about was appearances, and she was determined I marry into Parker's highbrow family, whose ancestors had founded the area. Ridiculous to me, since we were far wealthier. But my mom believed the money Dad had inherited from his grandfather's moonshining had in some way tainted the family name. All that mattered to me were Parker's blond good looks and the way his touch lit me up.

Parker stared at me accusingly, at my flushed face.

He picked up Delaney and stroked her blonde curls. "It's okay. Hy understands you didn't do it on purpose. Don't you, Hyacinth?" His eyes held a desperate appeal.

What could I say? To tell the truth was futile. Delaney would give her four-year-old's innocent denial, and I would look like the typical coldhearted stepmother, so jealous of her husband's affection that she'd misconstrued a child's clumsy accident.

I swallowed my anger and considered my reply carefully. It wasn't too late to back out of the marriage ceremony. I wasn't legally bound to Parker. I could still leave him at the proverbial altar.

I suppressed my misgivings and bit back my words. I didn't want to live in my mom's cold house anymore with its stifling rules and rigid formality. And I did love Parker. Surely his daughter would come round eventually.

But going through with the wedding was my first big mistake in a long stream of misjudgments and foolish attempts to have a happy marriage and family.

Chapter 5

VIOLET

Present day

The whispering began the moment we entered the drugstore. I folded my arms under my chest and pretended to be absorbed in a display of bandages and laxatives. Delaney patted my shoulder—"You'll be fine," she breathed in my ear—and got in line to fill Dad's myriad prescriptions.

The morning had gone normally enough—well, as normal as it got in our household. Dad had muttered and grumbled, pretty much ignoring us, while Delaney and I had talked about the day's tasks ahead. What a drama queen I'd been last night over nothing. Everything appeared back to normal between us.

I shifted my feet from side to side and, from the corner of my eye, watched the lunch crowd as they stared and pointed. An older lady with a helmet head of permed curls approached.

Please don't speak to me, please don't—

"Violet? I can't believe you're home after all these years. It's me, Hattie Pilchard. Your English teacher from seventh grade."

Hattie had not aged well, and she'd never been a beauty to start with. Her skin was ruddy and her eyes myopic behind thick glasses.

She smiled, but I sensed the hateful tiger waiting to pounce. The woman had not liked me then, and I could only imagine her opinion of me now.

"Never thought you'd return to town. What gives?"

The room grew quiet. I frantically sought Delaney, but she was talking to the pharmacist, her back to me.

"Visiting family," I replied, almost coughing, my throat parched. Involuntarily, one hand reached into my pants pocket, and I rubbed the smooth glass chip.

Hattie's eyes gleamed. "Ironic, isn't it?"

I shook my head, sure my nervousness was making me thickheaded and slow. "What's ironic?"

"This."

She thrust a newspaper at me, folded open to the local section, and I reluctantly read the headline.

Hatchet Lake to Be Drained for Dam Repair

A black-and-white photo of the dam slammed into my brain. The print swirled, and I grew dizzy. I massaged my temples. I wasn't prepared for this violent, public reminder of the night Ainsley had disappeared.

"Wonder what they'll find?" Hattie continued, smirking. "Ainsley's skeleton?"

The tittering of the onlookers passed over me in a wave, and I swallowed hard. I wanted to run out of the store and lock myself in the car, but my legs and brain were disconnected. My mouth opened, then shut.

"You always were a hateful old lady."

For a moment, I wondered if I'd said my thoughts aloud—but no, the words came from a woman my age with purple-streaked, bobbed hair. She strolled over to us from one of the tables.

Hattie flushed and frowned at her. "You're as crass and cheap as ever, Libby. The worst student I ever had." She scathingly eyed Libby's outfit. She wore cutoff blue jeans that showed plenty of tanned thigh, and her hoochie-mama top revealed a wide expanse of both stomach and chest.

"Oh yeah?" Libby drawled, not put out at all. She gave an exaggerated sweep of her lashes, so long and dark that I concluded they must be extensions. "You're breaking my heart."

Something about the angle of her chin and features was familiar, although only the ghost of the plain, fresh-faced girl remained. "Libby Andrews?" I asked.

She nodded. "That's me."

Hattie gave Libby the cold shoulder and glared my way. "Keep the paper." She marched out of the store, orthopedic shoes squishing on the cheap linoleum.

"C'mon and sit over here," Libby invited, cocking her head at an empty table. "We'll be two outcasts together."

I threw another desperate glance at Delaney, who was still conferring with the pharmacist. The few customers standing nearby flicked their gazes back to the merchandise on the shelves, but I felt their intense interest and knew they still listened and watched.

Libby leaned toward me and lowered her voice conspiratorially. "Give a great big ole smile like you're doing just fine. They'll hate that." She raised her voice. "In case you don't remember, Walt's has amazing handmade chocolate malts."

I flashed a fake grin and mechanically followed Libby to a table, into the heart of the lion's den.

"Another malt," Libby called to the teenage server. He nodded, eyes lowering to her cleavage. Libby winked at him. "Thanks, sweetie."

I tossed the newspaper on the empty chair beside me. Libby drew a long sip of her drink, staining the straw with crimson lipstick. I folded my hands, bracing for an interrogation. There was no reason for Libby to lure me to her table, unless she intended to ask questions and probe the mind of Normal's infamous madwoman.

She set down her shake. "I remember the time Hattie read your poem in class and labeled it *hilariously bad*."

I blinked at the unexpected topic, my mind shuffling through memories of Ainsley, who'd sat beside me in English. My mouth curved in a tentative smile. "I'd almost forgotten that stupid poem."

It was my most cringeworthy memory of high school. My angst-ridden attempt at poetry had indeed been hilariously bad, in a typical teenage-girl kind of way. And I'd never have written it if I'd known Ms. Pilchard would read my creative-writing assignment aloud and ridicule me in front of my classmates.

"How did that poem go? I only recall rhyming lines with *rain* and *pain*, and *tears* and *years*." Libby threw her head back and guffawed. "I'll never forget how red your face was when she read it."

"Yeah, it was a hoot." Was Libby making fun of me or trying to be nice? At least Ainsley hadn't laughed along with my other classmates. She'd told the teacher she liked my poem. Even now, the memory glowed inside me.

Libby's laughter dwindled to a chuckle. "Pilchard still shouldn't have ridiculed you, though. She didn't read anyone else's work aloud."

"It didn't bother me all that much," I lied. "Nobody liked her."

I remembered that later, I'd casually mentioned the incident to my family at dinner. The next morning, Mom had confronted the principal and threatened a lawsuit if Hattie or any other teacher singled me out like that again. It wasn't the first time Mom had intervened on my behalf. I was considered odd by kids my age, but that was the first time a teacher had bullied me.

Libby eyed me curiously, and I hurried to fill the silence. "Mom threw a fit at school about Pilchard, and I received a very undeserved A in English," I said. After rushing home from school and shredding the remaining poems in my notebook, I'd vowed never to write another damn thing.

"You were always a strange one," Libby observed, fingers drumming the table. "Always in your own little world. A loner."

Our server arrived and set down my shake. The milk chocolate nearly frothed over the top of the thick glass. I took a sip and closed my eyes, feeling like a kid again. Mom, Delaney, and I used to come to Walt's nearly every Friday, celebrating the end of the school week.

"As I remember, you had the attention of all the boys," I said.

Libby snorted and waved a hand over her breasts. "That's what happens when you're the first seventh grader to grow tits."

I took another long draw of the shake, wondering what her life had been like since junior high. Wondered what a normal life entailed—dating, graduating, possibly marrying and having children, a career. My own life had been, in many ways, frozen and barren as I'd grappled with the mystery of my missing best friend and what role I might have played in her disappearance.

"So," I began, wadding up a napkin. Conversation had never been my strong suit. "What have you been up to all this time?"

"The usual boring story." She shrugged. "You know, married right out of high school, got a divorce six months later. Managed to get an LPN license and then had a kid." Libby rummaged through a purse and then stopped abruptly, gripping the edge of the table. "Walt hasn't let anyone smoke in here for years, but I still reach for a cigarette. Old habits."

"How old is your child?" I asked in a diversionary tactic, afraid she'd ask questions about where I had been and what I'd been doing.

"Just turned four." A gentleness softened her features, and she looked like a young teenager who'd played in her mom's bag of makeup with a heavy hand. "His name's Calvin." She scrolled through her phone and showed me a photo. "The cutest kid you've ever seen."

I obligingly studied the photo. He had curly dark hair and a wide grin that made me think of Opie from Mayberry. "Cute," I agreed.

Libby stared expectantly.

"Very cute," I elaborated, shifting in my seat. Truth was kids all pretty much looked the same to me. I must have missed some vital nurturing gene.

Libby put her phone away and observed me sharply. "How's the homecoming been?"

I hesitated. "Subdued."

"Yeah, your dad's pretty bad off, and he keeps your sister running."

I looked over my shoulder, observing Delaney, at last, paying for the medicine. I hated that everyone knew our family's business, but at least it kept explanations to a minimum.

"Hand me your phone," Libby demanded suddenly. "I'll give you my number."

I slid it across the table, and she punched in data.

"Why would you do that?" I asked, genuinely confused.

"Because I think you might need a friend," she replied, sliding it back to me. "Small towns can be lonely places."

The only friends I'd ever truly had were Ainsley and my sister, and those relationships had been complicated. I'd never phone Libby. Still, she'd been kind, so I merely nodded at her comment.

The smile slid from Libby's face as the faint scent of lily of the valley announced Delaney's arrival. She sidled up to the table and gave a stiff nod to Libby. "Ready to go?" she asked me in a crisp voice that smacked of disapproval.

"You haven't finished your drink," Libby pointed out. "I can run you home later if you want to stay."

I stood, eager to leave, conscious of everyone watching us. And no sense adding fuel to the fire with Delaney—our truce was too new. I well remembered her tantrums when she didn't get her way about something. After yesterday's fiasco with the burnt dinner, I was on thin ice. "Thanks, but I better run."

Delaney was already several paces ahead of me, her back ramrod straight and nose in the air. I gathered the newspaper and my purse, fumbling with my wallet.

"It's on me." Libby waved her hand. "Better hurry if you want to catch up with Delaney."

I thanked her again and hurried after my sister, careful not to step on the sidewalk cracks. *Step on the crack, break your mother's back.* Didn't matter my mom was already dead; bad luck should be avoided no matter what.

Delaney didn't speak until we were ensconced in her car. "Libby Andrews isn't the kind of . . . person . . . you want to associate with. She's trashy."

"Don't be such a prude," I snapped. I could take her potshots at me, but Libby didn't deserve that. "Libby was nice to me. The only one in there who was, by the way."

"So you'll be friends with anyone who's the least little bit friendly? That's really smart. Are you that desperate?"

"Yes, I am." Perhaps I did need a friend after all.

She pursed her lips and frowned, backing out of the parking space. "Am I going to have to take care of you too? I have enough to do without managing damage control over your choice of friends."

"What's that supposed to mean?"

"You hang around Libby, and people will talk." She hit the accelerator, and we began zipping home at least ten miles an hour over the speed limit.

Her snobby attitude floored me. Our father was an alcoholic, and I was generally believed to either have murdered my best friend or be in some way responsible for her disappearance. At this point, my choice of friends hardly mattered. "As if they don't talk about us already? At least this would be a distraction from worse gossip."

"That's my point. Our family's been through enough. I'm tired of it. Don't make life harder for me, Violet."

The car hit a pothole on the dirt road. The vehicle lifted and landed with a thud.

"I'm not trying to make things harder for you. All I did was talk to someone who was nice to me." I'd had no intention of calling Libby, but Delaney's objection made me itch to do so. "Look," I said, lowering my voice, striving for calm. "You aren't my mother. And stop thinking of me as your little sister who needs protecting. I'm a grown woman now, capable of making my own decisions."

Her eyes slid sideways at me. "Are you really?"

There. She'd cut right to the quick of the matter. I inhaled sharply, gathering my wits. My counselors and psychiatrist had deemed me capable of functioning in the real world, but I couldn't help my own self-doubts. They pecked away at my core in a constant drumbeat of anxiety. I didn't answer and turned my face to gaze out the window. The green-and-brown landscape grew wilder as we approached home.

"You don't need to worry about me, Delaney," I said at last. She remained silent, so I tacked on my usual "I'm sorry."

We pulled into the drive, and she cut the engine, then placed a hand on my arm. "I'm the one who should be apologizing. I didn't mean to imply that you're, um, unwell. I'm just worried about you. Coming back here must be tough. I only want you to be careful in your choice of friends. Trust me—Libby Andrews is bad news. How about we forget her?" Delaney's smile was gentle, and it appeased my ruffled feathers. "Now help me bring in the bags, and let's check on Dad."

"You sure it was okay to leave him alone?"

"He's fine for brief periods at a time," she assured me.

I dutifully filled my arms with groceries and other supplies from town, and we made several trips back and forth to haul them inside. In the kitchen, Dad rummaged about until he found a bag of chips, settling in with the newspaper as Delaney and I put food up in the cabinets. Damn. If we'd gotten home ten minutes earlier, I could have thrown the newspaper away before he read it.

With every paper rattle, I cut my eyes to see if he'd read the article and would comment. I knew the instant he found it. His hands trembled, and he dropped the paper to cradle his head. "Damn it to hell," he muttered. He stood, voice rising. "Damn, damn, *damn.*"

"What is it?" Delaney rushed from the kitchen. "Calm down. Everything's all right. Why don't you lay down and take a—"

"Don't tell me what to do, young lady," he bellowed.

Delaney grabbed the bag of prescription meds and nodded at me. "Bring a glass of water."

I hurried, my pulse racing. How bad did he get these days? His temper had been a thing of terror, but he was older now, thin and a bit feeble. I handed Delaney the water, and she held a small orange pill in her right palm, at the ready.

Dad frowned. "I ain't taking one of them things."

"You know what happens when you refuse to take your medicine," Delaney said calmly.

Something—unease?—flashed in his cloudy eyes, and he docilely swallowed the pill.

Dad must be like me. If I didn't take my medication at the first onset of anxiety, my mind and body plummeted into a vicious spiral that was difficult to pull out of.

Delaney guided Dad by the arm. "Now, let's go have a nice nap."

Alone, I picked up the paper from the floor and started reading. Hatchet Lake would be drained by the end of summer, and the extensive dam repairs would be completed over the fall and winter, allowing the lake to be filled and ready next spring for the townsfolk's recreational pleasure.

What would they find when the water was drained and the earth laid bare?

Ainsley's body?

No, at this point there would be no body, only a skeleton. If it was there.

Fear clogged my throat. What did all this mean for me? I wasn't sure I wanted anything found. For years, I'd clung to a dream that Ainsley had been kidnapped, escaped her captors, and returned to Normal, unscathed. Then we could all move on with our lives, however damaged from the past.

And if her bones were discovered?

It would kill my dream, but maybe there would be a clue as to what had happened. They could finally find the guilty person.

Or they could arrest me.

But even that possibility wasn't my worst nightmare.

"Any idea what set him off?" Delaney asked, returning alone.

I shoved the newspaper her way, and she sat down and spread it open. I couldn't stand watching her face when she read the news, so I paced by the kitchen windows. Guilt weighed on my heart, as if every bad circumstance in our lives was my fault.

At her sharp intake of breath, I faced her. "What do you think? Good news or bad?"

The paper was clutched to her chest, and her eyes were every bit as wild and fearful as Dad's had been. "I-I don't know what to think."

"Same here."

The refrigerator hummed, and the disembodied noise from the TV continued, everyday sounds that gave no indication that our lives may very well have changed forever. My family might be concerned about their reputation, but my stakes were much higher. Yet again, I apologized. "I'm sorry," I said softly, as if I were responsible for a matter out of my control. Was it truly a coincidence?

She nodded absently, staring out the window. My mind pulled at the notion of swallowing a pill and taking a nap like Dad.

No. Bad idea. I'd taken two yesterday and had been cautioned to only use them sparingly. But I couldn't stay cooped up inside the stifling kitchen either.

"I wonder if there's a connection between your arrival and the dam repair," she said, tapping her index finger on her lips.

It was as though she'd read my mind. "How could there be?" I asked, quick to deny any link.

"They've been talking about those repairs for years, but the county commissioners kept claiming it was too expensive. Funny how all of a sudden they found the money."

"Still don't see the connection."

"I bet the Dalfreds raised a stink after seeing you. They don't want you here. While you were away, you were out of their minds. Your homecoming was a slap in the face. More than ever, they want Ainsley's remains found and to have you charged for murder. Get you out of their lives for good."

The truth of her words hammered stakes in my heart. I had to get out of the house and breathe fresh air. "I'm going for a walk," I announced.

Upstairs, I transferred a few handfuls of shelled peanuts to a lunch bag, and then I headed out. The late-afternoon sun scorched my fair skin, but as I entered the woods, the shade made the heat tolerable. I trod the old dirt path, crushing pine needles and twigs as I wove around the familiar twists and turns.

And tried not to remember the last time I had walked the trail. Or think of poor, butchered Irma.

The scent of water hung in the air, refreshing and alive. Of course I'd been drawn to this place, as painful as I knew it might be to recall the night Ainsley had vanished. Without a sound. Without a trace.

I remembered that we'd collected our stashed flashlights from the shed. I had tried to be extra careful that night, since I hadn't invited Delaney along. I'd wanted Ainsley all to myself without my sister's dampening influence. She'd enjoyed the stolen swims as much as we had, but I had occasionally needed a break from her constant demands for attention.

How was I to know that night would be any different? There'd been no premonition of evil. We'd laughed, stripped down to nothing, and swung out on the rope, over the running river. Back and forth, wild and free.

Until Ainsley had landed on the other side of the river and never come back. I hadn't even heard the sound of water splashing. Instead, there'd only been a terrible silence. At least, I *thought* that was how it had happened. We had climbed the cliff together to swing on the rope, and then later there'd been an ominous, profound silence.

Even the crickets and frogs and owls had been mute. Local myth claimed that this eerie quiet preceded a visitation by Irma. As if the insect and animal worlds were steering clear of her dangerous aura.

Ainsley? Where are you? I'd searched, finding nothing out of the ordinary—the extraordinary was in what was *not* there. I'd kept calling, each time more frantic and bewildered. *Ainsley! This isn't funny. Stop hiding.*

Something terrible had happened. I'd wandered the woods for what had seemed like the entire evening—although the police report estimated it had likely been only two hours—before my mother had found me. When we had arrived home, I hadn't gotten the beating I'd expected from Dad—there had been too many cops swarming the house and grounds. That would come later, after the police stopped dropping by and before I was diagnosed with a dissociative fugue. That was the first of several mental health labels once I was sent away for treatment, but it was the most important and the one that eventually stuck.

I sat on a nest of pine needles and stared at the sun reflecting off the water's wide expanse, imagining what secrets lay hidden beneath. No telling how many skeletons might emerge from the lake's muddy depths. Maybe even Irma's ghost would be set to rest.

Caw caw.

I raised my head sharply and searched the shadows, spotting a tiny patch of white. Disbelief rumbled in my chest. It couldn't be.

Tux?

I didn't dare make a sudden move, afraid he'd fly off. I mentally calculated. He'd been a baby eleven years ago when I'd left. Considering the life span of a wild crow could last two decades or more, it was entirely in the realm of possibility this was Tux.

No mistaking that triangular patch on his right breast, like a white handkerchief sticking out of a black tuxedo—hence the name. I smiled, wondering over the flock's choice to make Tux their solitary sentinel with his unique marking. He didn't blend into the shadows as much as an all-black crow. Still, if he hadn't wanted to be seen, I'd never have noticed him watching me.

As slowly and quietly as possible, I opened the lunch bag and threw out a handful of peanuts. Before I'd left years ago, Tux and his family would have flown over at once. I had lost that honor. But maybe, with time, I could regain their trust.

I rose to my feet, scattering the rest of the peanuts from the bag.

Tux never moved from his perch several trees over.

"Enjoy, little one," I said aloud. I left, knowing that he and the rest of the nearby crows would be enjoying the treat as soon as they judged I'd gone a safe distance.

Ridiculous, but my heart was a little less heavy with the appearance of Tux. Around the bend, I sneaked a peek behind me. Three crows were underneath the tree where I'd sat. They returned my stare, unmoving and silent and always watching.

Smart birds. *Freaky*-smart birds.

Bet they'd witnessed what had happened to Ainsley.

Chapter 6

VIOLET

Present day

The smell of grilled burgers and onions greeted me as I stepped into Walt's Drugstore. Libby was already seated, and I was relieved to see she'd chosen a booth at the back where no one else was around. Avoiding eye contact with anyone, I hurried over and slipped onto the worn red vinyl seat.

Libby winked. "You scurried over here like a little mouse."

"Didn't realize I was that obvious."

"It's okay. Understandable after that earlier bout with Hattie Pilchard." She slid a laminated menu across the table, and I scanned it quickly. "Have to admit I was a little surprised you called," Libby said, pushing back an errant purple lock of hair. Despite the colorful highlights, she looked almost conservative this morning in her work uniform.

"Me too," I admitted. "You were right. A friend would be nice."

Not only that, but it was secret spitefulness on my part. Delaney had warned me to stay away from Libby, and I was determined not to let her have her way about every damn thing. This meal out would consume almost the last of my measly cash, but I had to get out of the house and away from Dad and Delaney.

"How's your morning been at work?" I asked, eyeing her pink smock and the medical ID tag hanging from her neck: **LPN LILIBETH ANDREWS.**

"Busy," she answered. "Two births already this morning, and a new mother in labor admitted to our wing."

I envied her. How paltry my own life was by comparison. All I'd managed to accomplish was an associate degree and a résumé of various minimum wage jobs that barely covered my modest expenses at the halfway house.

"What about your morning?" Libby asked.

I was spared telling her about my dreary morning of household chores when the server arrived to take our order.

I gave him mine without looking up. "A grilled pimento cheese sandwich, fried pickles, and a Coke."

"Cheeseburger, french fries, and a chocolate malt," Libby said, gathering the menus and handing them over.

"What have you been up to?" Libby asked again when the server walked away.

"Cleaning," I admitted. "Delaney's decided to put me to good use giving the whole house a deep scrub. Not that I mind," I added quickly. "She has her bookkeeping job, after all."

Libby's eyes narrowed. "What bookkeeping job?"

"She works from home, keeping books for a couple of local doctors. I believe one of them is named Ed Jemerson."

"Eddie?" Libby threw back her head and laughed. "Good one."

"What's so funny?"

"Eddie's one of her . . ." Libby tapped a fingernail against her chin. "What should I call them? Lovers? Sugar daddies?"

I blinked. "Maybe in the past, but she's engaged now. Some guy in Birmingham named Sawyer Harris."

"What kind of a bullshit name is that?" Libby snorted. "I don't believe it. I just saw her last night when I got off the late shift. She and Eddie were leaving the pub together."

My mind puzzled out that bit of information. I had gone to bed early last night, dead exhausted from going through boxes in the basement, discarding old papers, ruined clothing, and other junk Delaney had never gotten around to sorting in years. She'd been home when I'd gone to bed, but this morning, she'd entered the house while I'd been cooking breakfast, claiming she'd popped out to run an errand. Had she been out all night with Eddie instead? And I had to admit that I never once saw her crack open a computer and do any real work. All her time was spent in the garden, dispensing pills to Dad, or leaving to go visit Sawyer.

"Even if that's true, it's her business," I said slowly.

"Sure, it is. Long as she doesn't lie about working all the time and guilt you into waiting on her hand and foot."

Bingo. That was exactly what had happened. Libby had Delaney nailed. "Do you know my sister very well?" I asked. "I didn't get the impression you were friends."

"I know her well enough. I see things, hear things. Word gets around in a small town."

"Don't I know it," I muttered.

"Here you go." The server handed us our food and drinks, his eyes lingering a second too long on me. I ignored him and jerked a couple of napkins from the table dispenser. "Need anything else, let me know," he added, and I relaxed when he left.

"Must be tough on you," Libby said, eyes full of sympathy.

I shrugged noncommittally and placed my hands under the table, unobtrusively making the sign of the cross to bless my food and drink. I wasn't religious, but the ritual soothed me when eating in public. I sipped my soda. "Not like I come into town too often."

She took a huge bite of her cheeseburger and glanced at her cell phone lying on the table.

"Lunch hour passes by quick," I noted.

Libby took a long draw of her malt. "Why did you call me? I mean, I'm glad you did. But I am surprised."

"You were right," I admitted. "I could use a friend. Get out of the house a bit."

"How long you plan on staying?" She dipped a fry in ketchup and munched away.

"Good question. I hadn't planned on staying long. I'd intended to get the money my mother left for me in her will and then leave at once."

"So what's stopping you?"

Libby sure was direct. I wasn't used to that. I held up a finger as I finished chewing a bit of my sandwich. Should I tell her the truth? What could it possibly hurt? Not like I'd be staying in Normal much longer. I swallowed, then gathered my courage. Yes, I'd arranged to meet her for all the reasons I'd stated, but I also wanted the gossip on Delaney.

"No money to leave, for one thing. Seems like Delaney evades me or picks a fight whenever I ask her about the inheritance waiting on me."

"Do you think she's spent it?" Libby asked bluntly.

"No," I said quickly. "Surely not. She and Dad were well provided for, and that old house is paid off. And it's not like there was a huge amount left for me. But it would be enough for me to get my own place and start life over somewhere new."

"Then you need to go down to the bank and set matters straight," Libby said firmly, pointing a ketchup-laden french fry at me.

I dug back into my sandwich. Libby didn't have much of a lunch break, and I didn't want to eat alone if she had to cut out. I contemplated her advice. Should I go to the bank? I hated drawing attention to myself, but I needed the cash. I was well past twenty-one now, and the State of Alabama had officially declared me mentally competent and free. There should be no legal issues withdrawing the money. Twenty minutes or so of being scrutinized by employees, and I'd leave the bank with enough dough to find my own place to live, buy furniture, and get a used car, maybe even splurge on a decent wardrobe.

"I suppose I should check on the account," I said slowly. Tiny bubbles of suspicion about my sister frothed at the back of my mind.

"What are you afraid of?"

"That you're right. That the money's all gone." I thought of the night Delaney had sneaked in those bags of designer merchandise. Admitting the bald truth made my stomach flip.

"Maybe the bank's kept your money protected. Was it saved in a trust account?"

"Yeah, but I'm worried that Delaney could have withdrawn the money, saying that the withdrawals were made on my behalf." I cleared my throat and looked away from Libby's bright, kind eyes. "Since I was, you know, not mentally competent to handle my own affairs."

Libby took a long swallow of her drink and then forcefully set it down. "Did she ever do a damn thing for you while you were there? Visit you? Bring you gifts or presents?"

"No. She only came to visit about four or five times."

"A year?"

"No. The whole time I was gone. The few times she came were only because Dad wouldn't visit and my doctors wanted to try family therapy."

"Then if she's made false claims or submitted false receipts to make withdrawals on your account, she's committed a criminal act and should be prosecuted."

The thought of police and lawyers made me cringe. And then the possible publicity . . .

Libby leaned over the table and softened her voice. "Everything might seem overwhelming right now. Just take it one step at a time. And the first step is to get to the bank and find out the truth. If the money's there, then all's well and good. If it isn't, you need to either confront Delaney and have her pay you back or press charges and force her hand."

I sighed. "You're right. Time to start acting like a responsible adult."

"Damn straight." Libby downed the last of her fries, tucked her phone in her purse, and stood. "Do this again sometime? Maybe come over for dinner one night, and we can talk more. I don't have much free time or money to be hiring babysitters."

"That would be great," I said in a rush, also rising from the booth. "I have to run too. Delaney's going out, so I'm Dad-sitting."

We paid the cashier and headed out the door. Blistering heat covered me in waves.

"Later," Libby said, waving and heading to her car. "Let's get together later in the week."

I waved and then walked in the opposite direction, careful to avoid the sidewalk cracks. *Step on the crack, break your mother's back.* Having avoided the bad luck, I stepped off the curb and prepared to climb into the sauna of my car's interior. I'd rolled down the windows of the ancient Continental, but it would still be unbearably sticky.

"Violet Henderson?"

I jerked my head to the side and studied the tall, lanky man dressed in a worn gray suit.

Detective Kimbrel. I'd remember him anywhere. His dark hair was peppered with gray now, and his skin sagged slightly at the jawline, but it was him, all right.

I stiffened but forced my voice to be civil, if not friendly. During the investigation into Ainsley's death, he had always been kind to me. Hell, he'd even been with my mom when she'd found me wandering the woods that night. "Detective Kimbrel," I responded with a polite smile.

He stuffed his large hands in the pockets of his trousers. "Heard you were back in town."

"Just a brief visit."

He nodded and studied me. A prick of unease shivered at the nape of my neck as I recalled that the work to drain Hatchet Lake had begun. If Ainsley had died there, they'd find skeletal remains. Would this same man be the one investigating me all over again? Maybe this time even charging me with murder?

My hand clenched the car keys so hard I felt the metal ridges burn into my palm. I had a mad urge to rush to the bank, demand my inheritance, and take the first plane to the Bahamas. I wiped a bead of perspiration off my upper lip. What if the seasoned detective could read my thoughts—see right through me?

"How are you doing?" he asked, squinting in the sunlight. "Plan on staying in Normal for long?"

Damn. The questioning had already begun. Did this mean he was going to warn me not to leave town next?

"I don't really have any plans yet," I said past the dryness in my throat. It was the truth, even if it sounded evasive.

He shuffled from one foot to the next. "How are your sister and father?"

"Fine."

I could almost swear he seemed as nervous as me, although I must have been imagining it. What did he have to be nervous about?

"Good, good," he muttered.

An awkward silence gathered between us. "Guess I'll be moving on then," I said lamely.

"Okay. Good to see you. And here . . ." He pulled a card from his pocket and held it out to me. "If you ever need anything, call me. I mean it."

His kindness touched me and made me uneasy, all at the same time. I stuffed the card in my purse. "Thanks."

"My pleasure."

I felt his eyes on me as I walked away and climbed into my vehicle. The ivy sprig in the ashtray was brown and crumbly. I made a note to myself to replenish it when I got home, perhaps adding a pinch of basil and ginger to the mix for even more protection. Once driving down Main Street, I glanced back in my rearview mirror. The man still stared after me, and I licked my dry lips. I had a hunch this wouldn't be the last I saw of Detective Boone Kimbrel.

Chapter 7

BOONE

Present day

I stood on the sidewalk feeling as though I'd been mule kicked in the stomach. Violet, with her heart-shaped face and large soulful eyes, was Hy all over again. Not a trace of Parker Henderson to be found—damn it. Although perhaps it was for the best. Nothing for Parker to be suspicious of, since Violet was the spitting image of her mother. If there was anything of me in my daughter, it was her long fingers, which I'd noticed as she'd taken my business card, and her above-average height.

Hyacinth. The woman I'd never forgotten in spite of every vow and good intention to do so. I remembered every kiss, every stolen, illicit moment of the past.

Mostly, I led a contented life. Ellie was a decent wife, and our two boys were fine, if somewhat distant, young adults. They'd both ended up taking jobs in Atlanta after college. We were disappointed, but who could blame them? More opportunity there than in a small town. My job was steady and secure and afforded us a solid middle-class existence, same as the three generations of my family who had lived in this town. But often late at night, as Ellie softly snored beside me, I played the *what if* game. What if I had run away with Hy all those years ago when she'd discovered she was pregnant? What if I'd raised Violet with her? Perhaps that terrible tragedy by the river would never have happened.

"Hot damn, who's the looker?"

Josh Adams, my partner, was suddenly by my side.

Thirty years my junior and new to the job, Josh managed to grate on my nerves even after two months working together. I gave him a stern look. "The young lady's name is Violet Henderson."

"Any relation to Delaney Henderson?" he asked with interest.

"Sisters. How do you know Delaney?" Josh had transferred over from the Huntsville Police Department upon his promotion from a beat officer to detective and—lucky me—had been assigned to be guided on detective work under my senior experience. I didn't expect him to be familiar with any locals.

Josh winked at me. "C'mon. You're not so old you haven't heard the rumors around her? The easy chick who likes rich, married men? The nymph of Normal?"

"Didn't take you long to get wind of local gossip."

"Part of the job."

I followed him into the patrol vehicle and let him drive. My thoughts drifted as we traveled through town. Delaney. Hadn't thought much of her over the years, despite the raised eyebrows in some circles whenever her name was mentioned. Hyacinth had certainly never cared for her stepdaughter. According to Hy, the girl was a born liar and manipulator.

"What other gossip have you heard about the Hendersons?" I asked, curious if he'd heard news about Violet.

"Something vague about possible murder being associated with that family. What's the deal?"

Might as well tell him. Hatchet Lake was being drained as we spoke. Soon—very soon—they would in all probability find the skeletal remains of one Ainsley Dalfred. A knot of dread in my gut had been my constant companion ever since I'd heard news of the dam repair job. What was this going to mean for Violet?

"Eleven years ago, a young girl, age fifteen, went missing," I began. "The last one to see her alive was Violet Henderson."

Josh's young face lit with curiosity. "That chick I just saw, huh? She must have been pretty young when this happened."

"Violet was fourteen. The girls had a habit of sneaking out of their homes late at night and meeting each other down by the river. They lived only about a quarter mile from each other."

"What were they doing out there? Partying?"

I stifled a sigh. Josh always had a hundred questions. But I had to admit curiosity was an excellent trait in a detective.

"Apparently, they liked to skinny-dip. Some of their clothing was left behind when Ainsley disappeared. That's how we knew exactly where they were that night."

Josh's mouth curled. "What was their deal? Were they meeting guys there?"

I shifted in my seat, uncomfortable with the question. "It means they were young and thought it would be fun to go swimming. Don't always jump to conclusions," I warned.

"Right, boss," he said in a tone that let me know he believed me an old fuddy-duddy who knew nothing about teenagers and sex.

"Anyway, I received a call late one evening from Violet's mother, concerned—"

"Hold on." Josh lifted a hand from the steering wheel and shot me an incredulous look. "Why call you? Wouldn't she have called the police department or 911?"

"We didn't have a 911 system out here until six years ago. This isn't Huntsville."

"So why not call the police station directly?"

Josh was sharp and not easily evaded—I'd give him that. "I'd been out to their house before on a domestic-dispute call. Mrs. Henderson didn't press charges, but she did accept my business card. Seems she'd held on to it in case she changed her mind or needed assistance without having to state her business with a dispatcher."

I hadn't thought about that first night we'd met in ages. By the time I'd arrived at their house, fear had sobered Parker, and Hyacinth had been more embarrassed than hurt. She hadn't wanted the gossip that would follow after filing a report. Both her and Parker's families ran in exclusive sets.

And here we were, decades later, and I'd also palmed my business card off on her daughter.

Our daughter.

"Quite the family. I get the picture," Josh said with a nod. "Go on. Mrs. Henderson called you because . . ."

"Violet was missing. She woke in the night, checked in on her, and found her bed empty. Delaney tattled and told where Violet often met Ainsley by the river. Mrs. Henderson walked down there and found one of Violet's sandals and Ainsley's shorts and T-shirt, but both girls were gone."

My voice trailed off as we crossed the bridge, and I gazed into the swirling Alabama River. How many lives had the water claimed? Probably twice the number of bodies found or that we even knew of had been swallowed in its secret depths.

"That's odd."

I furrowed my brow and frowned at Josh. "Of course it's odd. We're talking about two missing teenagers."

"Not that part." Josh waved a dismissive hand. "I meant about her mom checking in her room during the middle of the night. Violet must have caused Mrs. Henderson lots of trouble for her to be so suspicious."

I shrugged and attempted to strike a casual tone. "Meh, just the usual teenager stuff."

"If you say so. How long did it take to find Violet?"

"Almost two hours. We found her wandering barefoot in the woods, dazed and confused. Couldn't even remember her own name and didn't recognize her mother."

"Is it possible both girls were hurt by some perverts? Or maybe they'd hooked up with some guys for a party, and things turned rough?"

"Violet wasn't physically injured, other than a few scrapes and cuts that appeared to be caused from roaming the woods. We later had her tested, and medical personnel determined that there were no signs of sexual assault. Some of her memory returned a few days later. She remembered meeting Ainsley that night for a swim. But nothing after that."

"How convenient," Josh said dryly.

"Again, don't jump to conclusions." It was hard, but I kept my tone mild. Wouldn't do me any good to show a personal bias toward helping the person of interest in this case. "At first light, we assembled a search team. We discovered a large amount of blood on a rock where the girls swam. Turned out to be Ainsley's blood. Divers were called in, but she was never found. The prevailing theory is that Ainsley swung from the rope on the cliff above, hit her head on that rock, and drowned. The current must have moved her body toward the lake."

"But the victim could have been pushed from the cliff, correct?" Josh pressed. "Or maybe even stabbed or shot by the murderer. With no body to examine, anything could have caused that spilled blood."

"There's no proof that Violet, or anyone else, caused the victim's death."

"That loss of memory—it's too convenient."

I took two slow, deep breaths. "If it was fake, she managed to fool a team of state psychiatrists who questioned her for the courts," I pointed out. "And there was no motive. She was best friends with the victim."

"And what's the school of public opinion say?"

"Most Normalites would say she's guilty," I admitted. "But that doesn't make them right."

"Or wrong."

"Look, Violet had severe PTSD or something after the incident and spent most of her adolescence and young-adult life cooped up in mental health facilities. She's suffered enough without the town's blame and suspicion."

"You like her," Josh accused. "Maybe that's clouded your judgment."

"I have compassion. And my mind is sound."

He shrugged. "Touché."

This old case might mean nothing to my partner, but it consumed me. That night, and all its secrets, would haunt me forever.

Chapter 8

VIOLET

Present day

The scent of fried chicken sent a pang of nostalgia through me as I remembered many a Sunday afternoon eating it at church socials. Nobody, and I mean nobody, could fry chicken like the old ladies of the church. There was some kind of hoodoo magic in those battered breasts and wings that no restaurant fare could touch.

Too bad that the price of such a treat came at the expense of a visit by the church hospitality committee. An unannounced house call to welcome me back into the community.

Some welcome.

Ruby, Shelby Jean, and Dixie—the Burkhardt sisters—could scarcely contain their avid curiosity about me. I stifled the urge to jump out of my seat and yodel at the top of my lungs like the crazy person they believed me to be. Crazy or a murderess—perhaps both.

"We're so glad you've come home," Ruby said, sipping her glass of iced tea. "After all these years. Imagine."

Shelby Jean ripped her gaze from me to Delaney. "You must be so pleased to have her back."

"Of course." Delaney bestowed a sweet smile upon me, appearing angelic and poised. She'd washed up from working in the garden and donned fresh clothes. I was all too conscious of my grimy T-shirt and jeans from scrubbing floors all morning. I scrambled to my feet, eager to escape their circling around me like a flock of birds. That matronly threesome of old biddies wanted to peck away at me, as if I were on trial at a crow tribunal. Much as I loved my corvid feathered friends, I knew that they were notorious for occasionally murdering one of their own.

Despite the sunshine, a sudden outburst of rain erupted, pelting the roof and front windows of the house. From a distance, thunder rumbled. But we were in no danger from the storm. I'd placed an acorn on every windowsill of the house to keep out lightning.

"Devil's beating his wife and making her cry," Ruby observed.

"Oh dear," Shelby Jean said with alarm. "I didn't even think to bring an umbrella."

"It will probably blow over shortly." Delaney offered a soothing smile. "You know how these sudden summer showers are. If it doesn't stop, you can borrow one of our umbrellas."

Shelby Jean patted her fluffed curls. "You're always so thoughtful." Her gaze slid past me in what I fancied to be a silent rebuke.

"I'll take that platter and put it up," I said, taking it from Dixie. In the kitchen, I picked out a wing from the mound of fresh chicken and bit in. Mmm . . . as good as I remembered. I finished it off and helped myself to another. The less time with the Burkhardt sisters, the better. The low drone of conversation continued in the den, and I sighed. If I didn't return shortly, it would be rude, and Delaney would scold. Reluctantly, I shoved off from where I leaned against the counter and washed my chicken-greasy fingers. In the hallway, I paused in front of the mirror to run a hand through my tangled hair.

"Hope you don't mind our asking," Dixie said, her voice now intelligible. "Has Violet been . . . you know, well? Is she still . . ."

I held my breath, wondering how my sister would respond.

"Hard to say," Delaney began. "I'm truly worried about her. She has nightmares most nights. I've been awoken many a time to blood-curdling screams."

"Poor thing," Shelby Jean commented. "Has she said what the nightmares are about?"

"No, but last night when I entered her room, she was tossing and turning, and I heard her saying *Ainsley* over and over."

A chill ran down my spine. Liar. I hadn't had that many nightmares, and I'd slept like a log last night, thanks to my sedatives. Why would Delaney say this?

"Perhaps it's a guilty conscience," Ruby breathed.

I couldn't see the sisters, but I could picture their bright, snoopy eyes taking this all in and preparing to spread rumors across town.

"Perhaps," Delaney agreed. "But no matter what, Violet's my sister. I'll look out for her, just like I do for my father."

"Poor girl," Ruby clucked sympathetically. "It's not fair that some-one as young and pretty as you should be so burdened by family."

"I only do what anyone would do in my circumstances. Besides, my fiancé, Sawyer, insists that when we get married, I won't have to take care of anybody but him. He hates to see me working so hard all the time."

The self-righteous tone in her voice was maddening. She didn't have to "take care of me," and if Dad was so much trouble, she could put him in an assisted living facility. I tamped down my anger and strode into the room, determined to do damage repair.

"Didn't realize I was such a burden," I said dryly, resuming my seat. "Matter of fact, I thought I'd been a help to you watching Dad and doing housework."

The three old ladies swung their gazes back and forth between us, eyes as bright and curious as those of a stray dog circling a fresh treat.

Delaney didn't blink. "Of course, you've been trying your best to help me." Her voice dripped with sweetness, and I wanted to smack her.

"It's not your fault you almost set the house on fire when I visited my fiancé. Poor Dad was so upset. But I should have realized not to expect too much too soon."

I swallowed back a retort. Nothing I said would help the situation or make the old biddies believe I was as sane as them. I stood and addressed the sisters. "We don't want to keep you. I'm sure you're all busy visiting folks. Thanks for the chicken."

All three immediately fluttered to their feet, and in a swirl of powdery perfume and swishes of floral-printed dresses, they beat a hasty exit. Delaney escorted them to the door, again thanking them for being so thoughtful. But once the door closed, she turned on me.

"You were rude," she accused. Her eyes raked over me. "And why didn't you wash up? I told you they were coming this afternoon."

"No, you didn't."

"I mentioned it twice at breakfast," she insisted.

She hadn't, but I let that go. "Why did you tell them those lies about me having nightmares?"

"They weren't lies. Every night, you scream in your sleep."

My anger went down a notch. Was she telling the truth? I shook my head. "If I had nightmares, I'd remember."

Delaney arched a brow. "Do you always remember your dreams or wake up from a bad one?"

"No, guess not," I had to admit. "Do I really call out Ainsley's name?"

"You do. Repeatedly. Last night and most every night."

This looked bad. As if I were sleeping fitfully because of guilty memories. Maybe I really *was* responsible for Ainsley's death. Normal people didn't have nightmares every time they slept. There was something about that night I couldn't quite remember, a black abyss in my mind that allowed no entrance of light. Despite years of therapy and hypnosis, I couldn't account for what had happened to Ainsley, or the hours afterward when I'd roamed the woods until Mom and that detective had found me.

The two had coached me to say nothing to anyone about that night, and then they'd put me to bed. Might have worked, too, if the search and rescue team hadn't found one of my sandals and my friendship bracelet by the river, along with Ainsley's clothes.

And then there was that large rock stained with blood . . .

I mentally shook myself and thought longingly of the pill bottle on the bedside table upstairs. I was going to need one or two to calm down. My eyes stung with tears. "But you didn't have to tell the Burkhardts about the nightmares and the burnt food."

"I'm not going to lie for you," Delaney said quietly. "It all happened just like I said it did. Are you calling me a liar now?"

"No." I stiffened and drew my shoulders back. Since she was already upset, I had nothing to lose bringing up the issue of my inheritance. I'd skirted around it ever since I'd arrived, afraid of coming across as cold and callous. Time to finally broach the matter. "Didn't know I was a burden to you. Maybe it's time you gave me my portion of Mom's estate, and I'll be on my way."

Dead silence greeted my words. The grandfather clock ticktocked the seconds. From the corner of my eye, I spotted Dad walking out of the barn, a shovel in hand.

"Your plan is to take the money and run?" Delaney said at last, her eyes and voice flat. "You're always running away. And now you want to grab what's left of our money and leave me here alone to deal with Dad and this house that's falling apart? That's hardly fair."

I drew a shaky breath. When she put it like that, it did make me sound shallow and cruel.

"Coward," Delaney whispered.

My heart pounded, and the air pressed in on me. I couldn't breathe. I had to get out of the room. Had to take a pill and try to think rationally. I skirted around Delaney and raced up the stairs. Making a beeline to the bedside table, I grabbed the pills from the top drawer and shook two out. I dry swallowed them and then stepped out onto the balcony, intent on enjoying a little fresh air before the peaceful drowsiness set in.

Bright sunlight stung my eyes. This was my least favorite time of the day. I much preferred the gentle, fading light of evening with its promise of sleep and oblivion around the corner. Directly beneath me, the patio cement was blinding in the sunlight. Like everything else about the house, it was in a state of mild disrepair. *Patio* was too fancy a word for the slab of concrete now cracked and crumbling in places where weeds shot through the holes. The only furniture out there was an old Plexiglas-and-tile table sporting a weather-beaten, ratty umbrella that rose in the center from a rusted metal pole. Before she'd died, Mom had fussed at Dad about renovating that sorry excuse for an outdoor living area. She'd wanted to enclose it and make it a sunroom, and he'd insisted that would be a waste of time and money. Like everything else between them, it had turned into a huge bone of contention, and nothing had been done.

At least my balcony deck remained, although it was in need of repair as well. I walked to the far end by the iron bird feeder and toed a couple of loose planks. A few of the boards were half-rotten. Wouldn't take that much money to hire Willie to come out one afternoon and replace the rotten pieces, maybe even give the deck a good sanding and stain the old wood.

But I had no intention of sticking around for long, not to mention I didn't have a dime to my name.

Delaney was already outside, pulling weeds. Bet she wasn't in nearly the agitated state that I was.

The bird feeder was empty. I went in my room, grabbed a handful of peanuts, and returned outside. Would Tux and the others come closer today? I dropped the nuts in the feeder, sat in the rocker, and waited.

Within minutes, a flock of crows flew over the garden. Delaney shook her fists at them and screamed, "Get out of here!"

They cawed, and a couple of them swooped close to her before flying skyward again, as if taunting her. There was no love lost between my sister and the crows who disturbed her garden. They flew to a nearby oak and perched, observing me.

Delaney also watched me, hands balled on her hips. Her irritation was evident from the downward pull of her mouth. Well, let her be pissed, then. I wasn't going to give up feeding the crows. They were the only friends I had in the world.

Ever since Ainsley had disappeared.

Chapter 9

VIOLET

Present day

"Where have you been?" Delaney bounced out of the den before I even had time to shut the front door behind me.

"Out." No sense riling her up about my lunch meetings with Libby.

Her face flushed. "Why didn't you tell me you were leaving the house? I have things to do."

I took in the flowered sundress and gold hoop earrings. Her long hair was curled in loose waves, and her face was made up. Meeting Dr. Eddie, perhaps?

"And what do you mean by *out*?" she continued. "You don't have any friends here. And you hate going into town. So where were you!"

I hesitated. I didn't want to argue, but she might hear from someone else that I had been with Libby. "I had lunch with a friend. I do have one."

She cocked her head to the side. "Who? You've been away for years, and you hardly ever go out. Oh, wait." She scrunched her face like she'd bitten into a sour persimmon. "Let me guess. Libby Andrews."

"Speaking of going out . . . before I came home to visit, who watched Dad whenever you left the house?"

"I'd hire a neighbor. Are you really complaining about watching the old man? It's the least you can do after all the years I've done everything by myself."

I nodded toward the den, where the low drone of the TV sounded. "Can't he hear us?"

"He's half-asleep. I gave him his meds, and now he's taking his usual afternoon nap." Delaney pushed past me. "Gotta run. Try not to burn down the house."

She never let me forget my one slipup. "When will you be back?" I called after her.

At the bottom of the porch steps, she paused a moment. "I don't know. Probably late."

Delaney was up to no good. I just knew it. "What about Sawyer?" I asked.

Her brow furrowed an instant. "Who? Oh, Sawyer. What about him?"

"What should I tell him if he calls?" I asked sweetly.

"I have my phone. There's no reason for him to call the landline." The sun shone on her golden curls as she walked to her car.

So much for my plans to find my legal paperwork and head to the bank that afternoon. But maybe this was for the best, after all. Talking with Libby had helped me to see things more clearly. There was so much I questioned about this household, and it was time I found answers. Resolutely, I went to the den, where Dad was sprawled on the couch, his mouth slightly open as he lightly snored. His hands were folded on his stomach, and dirt was caked on his knuckles and under his fingernails. If it weren't for his constant digging, he'd have no hobby, no life at all.

Satisfied he was in a sound sleep, I returned to the kitchen and opened the cabinet where Delaney stored all his pill bottles. There were over a dozen of them, and the labels indicated that he had more than one doctor, most of whom were from Huntsville and not local. I took photos of each bottle label.

The prescription drug names meant nothing to me, but Libby would know. And if she didn't, she could refer me to a doctor or pharmacist to see if Dad was being overmedicated. I didn't have much fondness for him, but it seemed wrong that he slept so much. And the larger red flag was how Delaney always reached for the pills when he was being difficult, or when she couldn't go off gallivanting and leave him home because he was awake.

Pictures taken, I climbed the stairs to my room. While Dad slept, I could read over the letter and will I had received from an attorney years ago, informing me that I'd inherited a modest sum from my mother.

I entered my room and stopped three steps in. Something felt wrong. A faint scent of lily of the valley lingered. Why had Delaney been in my room? On the surface, nothing appeared out of order. I went to the dresser and opened the first drawer, where I kept my underwear.

Neatly folded tank tops and shorts greeted my eyes. What the hell? I opened the second drawer and found pajamas—but again, not where I had originally placed them.

"Control freak," I muttered, marching to my closet. What had been hanging on the left was now on the right, and vice versa.

Why? What possible difference could it make to Delaney how I stored my clothes?

I stood in the middle of my bedroom and looked around, spotting my desk in the corner. Had she messed with it as well? Quickly, I crossed the room and began opening drawers. My personal effects appeared in order. I opened the box that held all my neatly sorted gifts from the crows and immediately saw that they were precisely arranged in reverse chronological order. The plastic compartment that should hold one of my first gifts—a bit of red string—now housed a dull green marble, the very last gift they'd brought me.

Anger stiffened my spine. I didn't let anybody mess with this box of gifts. Ever. All through the communal living at the state facility and then the halfway house, everyone knew to leave my box alone. I didn't have much, but what was mine was mine, and I guarded that box like the Hope Diamond.

I rummaged through my papers for the copy of the will, determined to take it to the bank first thing in the morning.

It wasn't there.

Incredulous, and with mounting unease, I searched again. Nothing. Delaney had taken it. That was the only explanation. Again, the question was *why*. Had she tossed it because the money was gone and she wanted to prevent me from discovering the truth?

Dread weighed down on me like a wet blanket, and I sat in the desk chair, absorbing what it all meant. If the money was gone, there went my hopes for a shiny new start in life.

No. I couldn't, I wouldn't, stay in this house and this town. Even if it meant living at a rundown shelter and working a minimum wage job until I could get on my feet. Slowly, I rose from the chair. Here, in my own bedroom, I felt violated. Delaney had seen and touched everything I owned. It wasn't that I had any secrets, but still . . . I valued my privacy. It had been a rare commodity where I'd spent the last few years.

Libby's suspicions about Delaney played in my mind like a tune that stayed with you once you heard it. Without debate or a conscious plan, I marched to Delaney's room and entered.

It was opulent and huge. She'd taken over the master bedroom and shunted Dad to a small bedroom downstairs. A four-poster bed, dresser, and armoire, all carved mahogany, had originally been used by our parents. Another reminder that at one time, our parents had been quite wealthy. What had happened to all the money?

Libby's knowing grin at the mention of Delaney's job gave me pause. If not a job, then she at least had money coming in. It made me uncomfortable to think of my sister accepting money from men, but who was I to judge? What was the harm in it as long as she was happy? Being confined so much to this house taking care of Dad must have been lonely and unrewarding. Surely she deserved her secret pleasures—as long as they didn't come at my own expense.

I went to the walk-in closet and flung open the door. It was packed with clothes and shoes. Dozens of shoes, many of them still in their designer boxes. Shirts, pants, and dresses hung color coded, and I couldn't help comparing the sheer amount and quality of these clothes with my own shorts and mostly worn-out jeans and T-shirts. As for myself, I'd always thought four pairs of shoes more than enough—one pair of sneakers, one pair of dress shoes, a pair of sandals, and a pair of earth-brown casual shoes.

As I walked deeper into the closet, my fingers trailed along the quality fabric of her clothes. I shook my head at the many items that still had price tags dangling from the sleeves. How many of them had been earned from sugar daddy money, and how many of them might have been purchased from my trust fund?

I paused near the back, catching sight of the familiar peach-sequined ball gown, which still sported the white silk banner embroidered with coral text, proclaiming Delaney the "2004 Miss Normal Peach Queen." That title meant the world to her. A twelve-by-fourteen-inch photograph from the winning moment was framed and mounted near her dressing table.

Leaving the closet, I proceeded to the dresser and opened the large leather jewelry box. A rainbow of colors gleamed against the black velvet lining . . . clear gems, reds, greens, blues, pinks, and all hues in between. Whether they were expensive gems or fakes, my inexperienced eye couldn't tell. I closed the lid and glanced at her dresser drawers. *Turnabout is fair play.* She'd had no qualms going through my possessions and even rearranging them to suit her own fancy. No harm in me doing the same.

The first drawer contained lace and silk panties. I smiled wryly at the contrast to my utilitarian cotton panties straight off the shelf from Walmart. And so it continued as I went through all the drawers, finding more and more expensive, first-class items. I'd half expected to find my copy of the will tucked in with her lingerie or hiding between folded sweaters, but there was nothing.

I proceeded to the master bathroom, which smelled of lilies and lavender. On a dressing table, she had a variety of cosmetics spread out. All of them name brand, of course. I picked up a tube of red lipstick, painted it on my lips, and then preened in front of the mirror.

The sophisticated color made me appear more adult and the resemblance to my mother even more striking. She'd favored red lipstick and a sophisticated perfume that smelled like magnolias.

If only Mom were still alive.

If only Ainsley were still alive.

My reflection blurred from my tears, and I grabbed a wad of tissue and angrily swiped the lipstick off my lips. *Don't look back.* That was my steadying mantra when the past threatened to smother the present. And if I couldn't manage that by the sheer force of my willpower, there was always a little pill with my name on it.

Abruptly, I left the bathroom and headed back downstairs to check on Dad. He was in the kitchen, pouring a glass of iced tea.

"Finished your nap, I see."

He startled, and tea sloshed over the side of his glass. His usual glare morphed into dismay.

"Dad?"

He took a step backward, and the drink crashed to the floor. "Hy? Wh-what? How?"

"No, it's me. Violet, your daughter." I grabbed a dish towel and began mopping up the spilled tea and shards of glass. I saw he was barefoot, so I guided him by the arm, steering him clear of the mess. "Go back in the den while I clean this up. I'll fix you another glass."

His face flushed an angry red, and his eyes narrowed to mean slits.

I recognized that look. My stomach flipped in the old way I remembered from childhood.

"You ruin everything," he accused. "Why, I ought to—"

"Calm down," I ordered in a firm voice, pushing down the fear of my little-girl self that wanted nothing more than to run away to my room.

"Don't you tell me what to do, Hy. If I wanna—"

"I'm Violet. Your daughter." I pointed at the broken glass on the floor. "Do you want to slash your bare feet open? Huh?"

He glanced down, and the fire went out of his eyes. I drew a deep breath and rose to my feet. "Go on now," I said.

Thankfully, he became docile and ambled to the den. I returned to the kitchen. What had set him off this time? Sudden realization struck. The lipstick must have left a stain, and he'd noticed my resemblance to Mom. He must have thought she'd somehow returned from the dead.

I finished cleaning the floor and idly picked up one of a dozen mason jars Delaney had sitting on the counter. Each contained crushed dried herbs from which she often made tea. I opened the jar lid and inhaled the bracing green scent of rosemary. In spite of her crappy moods and domineering attitude, I still wished Delaney loved me half as much as she loved her garden.

Chapter 10

HYACINTH

Twenty-five years earlier

Anniversary-cake frosting stuck to the roof of my mouth like sugared glue, tasteless and gooey. I took an unladylike gulp of iced tea to wash it down and then set my plate on the coffee table.

"Is that all you're going to eat?" Mrs. Henderson asked, brow raised. Her tone, as always, implied some subtle wrongdoing on my part.

"Watching my figure," I lied. My lips involuntarily curled upward at the irony.

"Seems like just yesterday you and Parker got married," my mother-in-law replied, taking another bite of cake.

Seemed more like ten years instead of two. I glanced at Parker, who sat in his leather recliner, sipping a double bourbon and Coke. He'd wait until his mother left before he started the serious guzzling. He raised his crystal tumbler an inch. "Another year of wedded bliss," he muttered.

Per her usual fashion, Mrs. Henderson turned the conversation around to herself, launching into tales of her country club set. Who was traveling where, who was rumored to be in financial trouble, who was seeing whom. People I couldn't care less about.

All I cared about was Boone.

Heat flushed through my body in a fever as I recalled our last rendezvous. Boone's expert hands and lips touching and probing me, thrilling me in a way Parker's drunken fumbles no longer did.

Never thought I'd be the kind of woman who cheated on her husband. But then, I'd never thought Parker would turn into a mean alcoholic either. His descent had been rapid, but looking back, the warning signs had been there all along, and I'd blindly overlooked them.

"Excuse me," I murmured, picking up the plate of sliced cake.

Neither acknowledged me as I went to the kitchen and began scraping the rest of the leftover cake into the trash can. It was nothing but garbage to me, same as my marriage.

Delaney was suddenly beside me, her elbows jutting into my side.

"Stop. I want another piece."

I half turned, blocking her grab. "No," I said firmly.

Her lips flattened, and her eyes turned cold, the way they always did when she didn't get her way. "Why not?" she demanded.

"Because you've already had two pieces, and sugar keeps you awake at bedtime."

"I'm telling Dad you're being mean to me," she threatened.

I'd had it. Sure, I could blame my annoyance on hormones, but in a flash, I realized I couldn't take it anymore. Not my farcical marriage, and certainly not this ungrateful, manipulative stepdaughter. I slammed the trash can lid shut. *I'm telling Dad.* How many times had I heard this same refrain?

"Go right ahead," I snapped, barking out an angry laugh. "Nothing he can do about it now, is there? The cake is all gone."

Delaney's eyes widened at my unexpected defiance. "You'll be sorry."

Like hell I would. I watched as she marched into the den, complaining loudly. "Mom's being mean to me." Her voice hitched, and I pictured Delaney's fake look of hurt, the pouting lips and stooped shoulders. "All I wanted was a piece of cake, and she said no and then threw it away."

"Hy," Parker called out. "Why the hell did you do that?"

He always took her side. Sighing, I entered the den and folded my arms. "She'd already had two pieces."

"Nuh-uh. Only one," Delaney lied, with a pathetic swipe at her tearless eyes.

"Really, Hyacinth," Mrs. Henderson said with an imperious lift of her fat chin. "Was it necessary to—"

"Yes," I interrupted. "You two spoil Delaney rotten, and you're not doing her any favors."

My mother-in-law's outraged gasp didn't bother me in the least. She'd never warmly embraced me into her son's life—instead, she idolized Alyssa, Parker's first wife, who had died of cancer years ago.

What did concern me was Parker's reaction. He carefully set down the tumbler and rose, his eyes flashing a warning. I stood my ground. Would he really hit me in front of his mother? I didn't think so. And if he did—well, let Mrs. Henderson see her son in his true colors.

He stood an arm's length away. "Apologize to Delaney."

"For what? I haven't done anything wrong. Now, if you'll excuse me, I have to run to the pharmacy before it closes." I grabbed my purse from the chair and turned toward the door, half expecting him to grab my arm.

He didn't.

I walked out the front door and scurried to my car like a prisoner set free on furlough. Once in, I locked the doors and headed straight to the Dixie One-Stop to make my call. I hadn't seen Boone in two weeks. He'd been either busy with work or busy at home. Tonight, he'd have to make time for me.

At the general store, I hurried to the pay phone in the left front corner and dropped a dime. A male voice answered, but it wasn't Boone. One of his sons, then. It could have been worse—his wife might have answered. And if she had? I was past caring. Once I had Boone on the line, I hurriedly told him to come meet me straightaway.

My heart raced the whole car ride to our spot. I was near to burst with my secret. Finally, I pulled onto the lonesome back road.

Boone stood by the old oak tree, his dark-blue sedan almost hidden behind a copse of pines, our place for spur-of-the-moment trysts. Soon, we wouldn't have to hide in dark, out-of-the-way corners.

I got out of the car and ran to him, throwing my arms around his neck, and cuddled into his broad chest. He waited a heartbeat and then stepped back. "What's wrong?" he asked.

"Nothing. Everything. I can't live with the two of them another minute. Parker's abusive, and Delaney deliberately causes trouble between us and makes it all worse."

"That's nothing new. I've encouraged you to divorce your husband many times. You aren't safe," he said gently. "Still, I've never seen you this upset before."

His brown eyes were kind and warm. How could I bear another minute of Parker when I loved Boone? He'd shown me what true love could be between a man and woman. Now I couldn't bear to endure a loveless marriage. Boone had to feel the same.

"Let's run away together," I said rashly. "Leave this place and never look back."

Something I couldn't identify flickered in his eyes. My throat tightened as I waited for his response.

"Run away," he said slowly, running a hand through his thick, dark hair. "We're not carefree teenagers, Hy."

"It's not too late for us," I insisted. "Why should we both stay in loveless marriages?"

"I have kids. A job. I can't walk away from all that."

"You can get another job. Have your children on weekends. People divorce all the time."

"I'm not the weekend-dad kind of guy."

Oh, but you're the kind of guy who fools around on his wife. I didn't say it out loud, but something of my sentiment must have shown.

"I don't expect you to believe me, but you're the only woman I've been with since I got married. It was wrong of me. I see that now. You know how guilty I've felt this whole time."

A buzzing pounded inside my brain. He'd picked a hell of a time to develop a sense of guilt. "Are you—breaking up with me?"

Boone hadn't been busy these past two weeks. He'd had a sudden attack of conscience.

"I'm sorry, Hy." Awkwardly, he patted my shoulder. "You're special to me. You know that. And I'll probably always regret not starting a new life with you. But—"

"You bastard." I slapped his hand away and took a step back. "I thought you loved me."

His eyes held pain, but determination too. "I did. I do, but it's not enough."

The buzzing in my head grew louder, a rumbling that shook the base of my world. I rubbed my temples. I had loved him so much, had trusted he would always be there for me, no matter the circumstances. Now what the hell was I going to do?

"Hy, stop it. What we had was great, but we need to move on with our own lives. Forget"—he pointed between us—"whatever this was. Forget me."

I placed a hand on my stomach. "Forget?" I spat out a harsh laugh, wanting to hurt him as much as he'd hurt me. "Not hardly. I'm pregnant, Boone. With your child."

His face turned ashen. "How do you know it's not Parker's?"

"Because you're the only one I've slept with in the past six weeks."

Boone dropped his face in his hands momentarily and then took a deep breath, facing me. "Under the circumstances, you don't want to keep it, do you?"

I'd thought I knew pain in all its violent and subtle forms, but nothing could have prepared me for this moment. I turned away and stumbled toward my car.

"Hyacinth," he called out. "Wait. What are you going to do?"

I squared my shoulders and faced him one last time. I still had my pride, my dignity, and that counted for something. "Have this baby. Don't worry; I won't ask you for anything."

"At least let me quietly pay you child support."

I got in the car, slammed the door shut, and then rolled down the window. "I don't want a damn thing from you."

I drove away, trying to quell my panic. I wasn't the first woman who'd ever been in this situation. I'd try to make it work with Parker again, at least until the baby came. The man was so tipsy in the evenings he wouldn't remember if we'd made love or not the past few weeks. I patted my stomach, vowing to protect my unborn child.

The baby was all I had left of Boone.

Chapter 11

VIOLET

Present day

"Next."

The bank employee gave me a welcoming smile, and I followed her to the desk in the main lobby. I would have liked more privacy but was too intimidated to ask for it. I'd arrived as soon as the bank had opened at nine o'clock and had only had to wait for one other person to complete their business.

The banker looked to be in her midthirties and wore a navy suit and matching wedge pumps that clicked smartly on the linoleum. She motioned for me to have a seat and then went around her large, gleaming desk and sat across from me, her hands folded on the paper ledger. "How may I help you today?" she asked crisply, coming directly to the point.

"My name's Violet Henderson. It's my understanding that my mother, the deceased Hyacinth Henderson, set up a trust fund account for me at this bank. I'd like to view the balance."

"I'll need your identification, please."

"Of course." I dug my wallet out of my purse and handed her my driver's license.

She turned to the computer screen and clicked away on the keyboard. I held my breath. After a few moments, her lips pursed, and her fingers paused. "There's been no activity on this account in years," she said.

I hoped that was a good sign. "Could you provide me a printout of the balance?"

"Certainly."

A few more taps on the keyboard, and the printer whirred. She picked up a piece of paper and pushed it across the desk.

This had been easier than I had imagined. Eagerly, I glanced down at the numbers. My eyes scanned the top line and drifted downward, noting there had been a large number of withdrawals. At the ending balance amount, I drew a sharp breath.

One hundred eighteen dollars and thirty-five cents.

I felt dizzy. The numbers grew blurry and my eyes unable to focus. I was conscious of the banker watching me. Fear clogged my throat.

"But . . ." My lips felt numb and dry. "There must be a mistake," I sputtered. "I've never withdrawn any money."

She turned back to the screen and clicked away again. "There's another name on the account, Delaney Henderson. It appears that she has legal authority to draw from this account."

"I never gave permission for that." This was the worst possible news, my biggest fear confirmed.

Her face drew up in concern. "Let me have the manager look into this. One moment, please." She printed out more papers, gathered them together, and rose, towering above me. "Excuse me."

Discreetly, I removed the blue glass chip from my purse and rubbed it between my thumb and index finger. Even though I'd taken my anti-anxiety meds before coming, my heart still raced. Outside the lobby window, cars drove past, and I imagined the drivers as everyday folks carrying out everyday business in a comforting routine. Lucky bastards.

This was taking forever.

There went my dreams of having the cash to start a new life. I crossed my legs, and my right foot bobbed up and down.

"Ms. Henderson?"

I swiftly jumped to my feet and faced an elderly gentleman with silver hair, dressed impeccably in a gray pinstriped suit. His smile was gentle and his blue eyes warm. He looked like the kind uncle I'd always wished I had.

"Come to my office, and we'll get this sorted straightaway."

"Yes, sir."

I slipped the blue chip back into my purse and followed him. Privacy at last. His office was huge, and his massive desk was situated in front of a large bank of windows. My serviceable but shabby shoes sank into the deep plush carpet. Everything—desk and shelves and cabinets—gleamed a dark-walnut color, and framed certificates of achievement dotted the walls. In short, everything one would expect in a bank manager's office to provide the comforting illusion of safety and stability.

"Earl Tottle," he said, holding out his right hand.

I shook it. His grip was firm and reassuring.

"I knew your mother. So sorry for your loss."

"Thank you, sir. It was a long time ago."

I settled into the dark-brown leather chair across from his desk and kept my purse in my lap. Placing it on the floor would be disrespectful of the money it housed. Grandma had always warned that setting a pocketbook on the floor meant you'd go broke. Today I was especially heedful of her warning as I waited expectantly.

Mr. Tottle sat down and opened the file on his pristine desk. "Your mother left forty-five thousand dollars in a trust fund for you. At the time this was set up, you were a minor. As such, your father had control of the money until you turned twenty-one. The terms of the trust did specify that any money needed for your . . . special care . . . could be withdrawn on an as-needed basis."

"My special care?" I asked.

He looked up from the paperwork. "While you resided at the mental health facility, the trust specified that you were to be provided whatever wasn't covered by their regular fees."

"Such as?"

"Trips, toiletries, clothing, gifts, et cetera."

Dad and Delaney had never brought me gifts, and I could count on one hand the number of times they had visited me. The only money I'd ever received were the annual deposits, which shouldn't have made a huge dent in the trust.

Mr. Tottle glanced down at the file again. "For the first year of the trust, no money was withdrawn. Then your only sibling—Delaney Henderson—was placed in charge of the trust after your father—Parker Henderson—was declared mentally incompetent."

Delaney had blown through the money left for me. My face flushed with anger. "The withdrawn money was never spent on my care."

Mr. Tottle frowned and rifled through the papers in the file. "Each withdrawal was accompanied by a written receipt, and the money was spent in accordance with the trust terms. Would you like to take a look?"

Would I ever.

He handed me the papers, and I scanned the receipts. There were extensive trips across the country, expensive clothing, furniture, and other odds and ends. Each lavish purchase was accompanied by a check with Delaney's signature.

I swallowed hard and faced Mr. Tottle. "I never went on any of these trips or received any of these purchased items."

His kind face expressed even more compassion. "This is disturbing news, indeed."

"Is there anything I can do?" I whispered.

"I'd suggest getting an attorney and pressing charges. Perhaps he can sue the party responsible for damages, and you can recoup your losses."

Was there any money left in the family estate? I had my doubts. This money was lost forever.

He stood, and I understood he was finished with me and my problem. I rose on shaking feet. "May I have a copy of that file?"

"Certainly. I wish you well, and I'm sorry for the disturbing news." He thrust the file into my hands and guided me out the door, gently yet firmly.

I stepped outside into the blazing heat, clutching the handful of papers.

One hundred eighteen dollars and thirty-five cents. I doubted that would even pay an hour of a decent attorney's fee.

I'd been royally screwed.

Chapter 12

VIOLET

Caw caw caw.

The crows' cry and a cacophonous flapping of wings alerted me to trouble. What had Delaney done now? They had a mutual hate society operating. It infuriated Delaney that they messed with her garden, and they in turn had declared her public enemy number one because she used to throw stones at them while trying to protect her seeds and produce.

Crows never forgot a face. They'd even pass information on an enemy down through the generations in their sophisticated Corvidae language.

Don't ever anger a crow.

I got out of the car and ran to the backyard in time to witness Delaney lift a large rock and raise it in her right hand. Over a dozen crows flittered above my sister, raucously cawing. Dad was farther back in the yard, digging holes and ignoring the drama.

"Stop it!" I yelled. "You promised!" She'd vowed years ago to never harm them again when I'd caught her throwing stones.

Delaney cast me a brief glance and then threw the rock at one of the scolding crows that was swooping low. Her missile brushed the edge of its black wing.

Tux? I anxiously searched for a patch of white on its breastbone, relieved to see nothing but black feathers.

"Stop it, Delaney." I planted myself in front of her, hands on hips.

Her face flushed red, and her chest rose and fell with heavy breaths.

"They keep eating my new tomato seeds." She threw her head back and glared at the flock.

"Calm down. They'll go away as soon as you get ahold of yourself and leave them be."

She swiped her forehead and shut her eyes for a moment, evidently getting herself in check. "Stupid birds," she mumbled. "I oughta get a pellet gun."

"Leave them alone," I snapped. "So what if they got a few seeds? They're just following their instincts and trying to survive."

"Wish they'd survive somewhere else. But no, you encourage them by setting out peanuts all the damn time. I'll never get rid of them."

As if sensing the danger had passed, the crows flew en masse to the woods. But I had no doubt they were still watching us. They observed everything from the dark shadows of their lairs, their black feathers and eyes blending in the darkness, unseen by us while they spied and cataloged our deeds, good or bad, as they affected their territory and helped them understand human nature. It was my personal belief that this went beyond mere instinct and intellect. They were generally curious about us.

"Forget them. We need to talk."

She huffed. "I suppose I could use a break. Hot as hell today."

Everything had to be on Delaney's terms. She was only talking to me because *she'd* decided it was time for a break. Her manner had bothered me as a kid, but I'd put it down to older-sister bossiness. Yet maybe it went deeper.

"Hey, Dad," she yelled. "Time to go in."

To my surprise, he dropped the shovel and walked toward us.

"Meet you inside," I said. No way I was confronting Delaney without ammunition. "I have to get something out of my car first."

Her blue eyes grew speculative. "Sounds mysterious. What's up?"

"You'll see." I left her then, unwilling to give her an opportunity to mount a defense or attack by tipping her off on the subject matter. I felt the scrutiny of her gaze on my back as I returned to the car for the bank file. Petty or not, a rush of satisfaction made my step lighter. Let her wonder what was up and be off kilter for a change. I considered putting off the discussion until after dinner and letting her stew a bit more, but I was too angry. And truth be told, a little fearful that if I didn't speak up now while adrenaline energized my anger, I never would. That I would bury my fury and disappointment and be engulfed entirely by the force of her strong will.

File in hand, I returned to the house, where Delaney sat at the kitchen table sipping a drink.

"For you," she said, pointing to another glass on the table. The crystal tumbler glowed with a maroon liquid bobbing with ice cubes that glittered like quartz crystals. "Raspberry-and-rosemary mint tea. Made with fresh herbs from the garden. Super refreshing."

My mouth watered, and I became aware of my parched throat. The unexpectedly nice gesture on Delaney's part was probably calculated, but that didn't mean I had to go thirsty. I picked it up and gulped half of it down at once. It was delicious. "Where's Dad?"

"Watching TV. What's up?" she asked, eyeing the folder.

I remained standing while she sat. "I went to the bank today."

The silence gathered, and I let the tension build, closely observing her face for signs of guilt or fear. Delaney met my gaze head-on, unflinching.

"So? Go on," she urged, taking another sip of tea.

"I know what you did."

"And what would that be?"

Her question was laced with amusement, and I flushed with anger all over again. I raised my voice. "You stole from the trust account Mom left me. It's almost all gone."

"Steal? I did no such thing."

Her calmness turned up the heat of my fury. I slapped the file on the table, and the papers spilled out. "Yes, you did. It's all here, Delaney. Every withdrawal. All the fancy trips and clothes and jewelry and God knows what else. I never got anything, and you never *ever* took me anywhere. Not even out to a McDonald's for a damn cheeseburger."

I might as well have lit a match. Delaney rose to her feet and glared. "You're accusing *me* of profiting from all the money in the family?" She gave a bitter laugh. "That's hilarious. You've ruined us, Violet. In every way—financially and emotionally. You and your mother ruined the Henderson name."

Even though I was taken aback in disbelief, I caught that she'd said *your* mother, instead of *our*. We were half sisters, but it wasn't something we ever mentioned. I never even thought about it much. Delaney had always been in my life, and my mom had married Dad when she was only four years old. My mom had raised her—the only mother that Delaney had ever known since her biological mother had died when she was two years old.

"Leave Mom out of this. How dare you spend my trust fund?"

"Why shouldn't I? I deserved to have at least a little fun in life. I worked my fingers to the bone all day, every day, for over a decade while you sat on your ass at that expensive, private mental house."

"I wasn't sitting on my ass. And that private place was only for two years; then it was the state hospital. Hardly idyllic. But you'd never understand."

"Only two years? That place cost a damn fortune. And I'd take weaving baskets any day compared to what I've been through. *I'm* the one who had to make the funeral arrangements when she died. *I'm* the one who's had to take care of Dad. *I'm* the one who takes care of this old house. *I'm*—"

"Stop it," I said through clenched teeth. "If I could have helped, I would have."

"Right. Easy for you to say that now."

"I needed that trust money, Delaney. It was going to help me start over in life. Someplace where people don't know me."

"What about me?" She thumped her chest. "You're leaving again, and I'm stuck. It's not fair."

I tried to reason with her. "You're getting married and moving to Birmingham. I'd call that a new start."

"Do you know what's left of our family's supposed fortune? Almost nothing."

Typical of Delaney to switch topics. My head spun at the news we'd lost everything. "Nothing? Where did it all go?"

"Your mom didn't have as much as we all thought she did. She led us on. Once we paid her burial fees and set aside for your trust fund, everything else went into paying for your care. She'd stipulated in the will that it be earmarked just for you. All she cared about was seeing that you were provided for, and the hell with me and Dad."

I sank into a chair and dropped my head into my hands. Mom. How different my life would be had she lived. I wouldn't have made it if I'd been thrust into the state system right after Ainsley's disappearance. When I'd left the private facility and been placed in a state one, my quality of life had plummeted.

"You told me the private place was too expensive, but I didn't know it put such a burden on the family. When I was forced to transfer to state care, it felt like I was being punished. Only I didn't know what I'd done."

Delaney sighed and sat back down as well. "I wasn't going to tell you, but when you started screaming at me, I lost my temper."

"I'm sorry." I wouldn't have believed it thirty minutes ago, but I was apologizing. Again. No matter what happened, everything turned out to be my own fault. I laid my head on the table, on top of the bank statements. The numbers blurred and squiggled, and I shut my eyes.

"You're forgiven." She patted my arm. "Looks like you're all tuckered out."

Her words seemed to come from the bottom of a well—deep and distorted. I felt a pressure near my elbow and then a tug.

"Why don't you go lie down a bit on the couch?"

A solid wrench shot through my arm and shoulder, and I was lifted from the chair. I roused myself.

"This way."

More pressure across my shoulders and the nape of my neck. So heavy I wanted to melt into the floor and curl up in a little ball.

"C'mon. One foot in front of the other."

Stumbling, I made it to the couch at last and fell into its soft, worn fabric, as exhausted as if I'd completed a triathlon. A pillow was tucked beneath my head, and seconds later, the pinch in my feet released. Dead weight plopped onto the pine flooring—once, twice. My shoes? The thumps echoed in the deep recesses of my mind.

My thoughts drifted into a gray void, but I couldn't quite slip into the comfort of sleep. Straining, I opened my eyes. Delaney's face swam before me, shifting and wavering, as if I were viewing her from underneath a layer of clear water. Wind rippled the surface, distorting her features—the blue eyes framed with blonde lashes, the Mona Lisa smile curling the edges of her full lips. A smile that I could never interpret. Was it kind or condescending? Tendrils of honey-colored hair tickled my neck and cheeks.

"Whaaat?" My tongue and mouth were lazy, unable to form distinct syllables. Both my upper and lower lips were numbed, useless dead appendages.

"Shh." Delaney's index finger touched the cupid's bow of her lips.

Mesmerized, I trailed the trajectory of her finger as it—ever so slowly—left her mouth and traveled toward me.

"There's a good girl," she whispered.

The tip of her finger brushed against my mouth—shockingly cold. I shivered and closed my eyes, unable to deny my body's urgent need for sleep. Or maybe it was an instinct to shut out Delaney's image.

The gray void morphed into a black abyss. Currents of raven-colored water flowed against my bare legs. My eyes scanned the darkness, searching. A few feet away, the inky water churned and bubbled, as if a river monster stirred.

With a great splash, the surface erupted. Ainsley's head and shoulders bobbed up from the frothy depths. Her sly smile and teasing eyes pierced me. A hand lifted from the water, and she crooked a finger at me.

Come here to me.

I'm coming.

But my legs were thick and heavy as tree trunks, dead weight that could not move against the raging current. Ainsley slowly sank back into the river.

Don't leave me! Take me with you!

In reverse motion, the churning waters stilled, and the bubbling subsided. The last air bubble burst, and once again, I was alone in the world.

Ainsley. My forever-vanished dark mermaid.

Chapter 13

VIOLET

July 2, 2007

"Come back," Ainsley calls from the dirt shoreline, and I return to her as best I can under the sliver of moonlight. Its beams cast shimmering glitter across the muddy river water, as if strewn by some careless god.

Ainsley's long black hair slips from the loose bun and falls, covering her shoulders like a veil of midnight. Just as mine does. We could be sisters and not just best friends.

She wiggles out of her shorts. No panties. She tosses the shorts onto the limb of a nearby oak, and they land next to her yellow T-shirt.

I almost catch up to her, but she slips out of my grasp at the last second.

A tease.

Sometimes I think I hate her. No, that's not true. I love her.

Ainsley splashes into the water and dances to some unseen music. Mud oozes between my toes as I navigate the river's unpredictable bed. I try not to think about snakes.

"Pssst." Ainsley crooks and then flicks her fingers at me like a striking rattler.

"You don't scare me." I creep forward and gasp when my foot strikes a sharp rock.

"Stop being such a baby."

I suck it up, swallowing huge gulps of humid air.

"Let's take a dive," she says, and I limp along, following Ainsley up the well-worn dirt path to the cliff. It's only about twenty feet up, but compared to the rest of the flat Alabama countryside, it seems mountainous.

At the top, Ainsley flies across the red dirt, grabs onto the frayed rope dangling from an oak, and swings Tarzanlike across the river, letting go once she's a safe distance from shore. For three seconds, she's suspended between air and water. A flash of pale skin followed by a streak of black hair that breaks free of the bun and whips about her head like a dark cloud.

A shriek and a splash, and Ainsley quickly surfaces.

"Your turn, kid."

Irritation prickles the back of my neck. Only a year older than me, and she thinks I'm a baby now. Ever since she turned fifteen last month and started dating that Sammy Granger, she acts like a Miss Know-It-All.

She slings me the rope, and I catch hold of it on its knotty end. My hands are slick with perspiration, and it almost slips through my fingers. Then I'm flying, body tense, anticipating the drop. I let go and hit water. The water might be muddy, and it isn't cold in the summer, but it's wet, and I'm grateful for small mercies. A whoosh, and the perspiration is washed from my body.

Ainsley laughs and splashes me. She's close, but just out of touching range. I wonder if Sammy has ever seen her like this. I don't want to think of Sammy.

I splash her back. Ainsley grabs my arm and pulls me to her. I hardly dare breathe. She stares at me with the strangest flicker of emotions dancing in her gray eyes. Anger, no. Humor, maybe. Pity, yes. Affection, a touch. Exasperation, loads.

A roar of crickets and skeeters drums in my ears, loud as a marching band. I can't think, can't react.

"Little Violet," she murmurs, cocking her head to the side.

I've just opened my mouth to argue when I notice her gaze has shifted to some point beyond my shoulder.

"What is it?" I ask.

"I thought I heard something."

My skin tightens with fear, and I resist the urge to glance back. Hatchet Lake is so named because of a 1941 murder when one winter Jed Isaack caught his wife, Irma, meeting another man by the lake. In a rage, he picked up a nearby hatchet, whacked Irma to death, and then threw her body into the cold water. Ever since, people claim that Irma, wearing a tattered, bloody nightgown, roams the nearby woods of both the lake and the river feeding into it, crying for her lover to save her from Jed.

Tonight wouldn't be the first time that Ainsley or my sister has frightened me by pointing at the woods and screaming, "There's Irma!" They know I'm a sucker when it comes to ghost tales.

I lift my chin. "Liar. You're just trying to scare me."

"No, really. I heard a twig snap, then a rustling through the pine trees over there."

I jerk my head around and peer through the inky blackness. The pines across the river are the same as ever. Nothing emerges from their dark shadows. We both stand still, waiting. We've sneaked out of our houses to meet here late at night, and if we get caught . . . well, it doesn't bear thinking about.

There is no sound, which should be a comfort. But the air seems to compress around me. I want to shrink into the hot night, dissolve into a thousand tiny black particles that would render me invisible.

No one walks out of the woods. "We're safe," I whisper.

But I don't believe it.

Chapter 14

VIOLET

Present day

A staccato machine-gun percussion exploded between my ears, and a blinding whiteness seared me like an angelic beam.

Or an annihilating nuclear blast.

Hard to tell with dreams. And it *was* just a dream. The veins in my temples pounded hard, as if they wanted to splinter through my flesh. I massaged them, hoping to ease the pain enough so I could return to sleep. But it was no use. Disoriented, I stretched, and my feet hit against the arm of the couch. Moonlight beamed through the den's window-panes. Remembrance flooded—the awful news at the bank, Delaney's anger, and my shame.

I was unsure which was worse—the day's reality or the evening's nightmares. It had been one dream after another, and they'd all been about Ainsley. Thirst and an overwhelming need to down a couple of aspirins drove me to my feet, and I walked to the kitchen. Was the rest of the household asleep? I poured tap water into a glass, shook out a couple of pills, and shuffled into the dining room as I downed the medicine.

Something shifted in the shadows outside the window, and I squinted, trying to make out what moved in the night.

Dad was bent over at the waist, digging with the shovel. I set my glass on the table and hurried out the back door. His obsession was unhealthy, and I was shocked at how deep it ran.

"Dad! What are you doing?" I cried as my feet flew along the dew-covered grass. I drew up next to him, panting. Newly planted roses and tomatoes lay uprooted in Delaney's neatly lined garden, and I gasped at the damage. "Oh, *Dad.* Delaney's going to be epically pissed."

He looked up at me, his wrinkled face and midnight-blue eyes as lucid as I'd seen since returning home.

"Maybe this is a payback. She's always mad about something and yelling at me. Might as well do what I want."

Unexpected laughter tumbled out my throat. "I can't argue with that."

He continued with his work, and I watched, unwilling to interrupt. As long as he seemed in his right mind—well, as sane as you could be digging up a garden in the moonlight—I wanted to take advantage of it.

"What are you trying to find?" Delaney and I assumed it was alcohol, but maybe it was something altogether different.

"Confederate money."

Blow me over with a feather. "What makes you think there's any buried in our backyard?"

"Old Henderson family legend."

I stifled the bubble of laughter that threatened to spill from my chest. Every old southern family claimed there was buried treasure hidden in their property, but it seemed highly unlikely to me. I felt compelled to reason with him while he was in this coherent state.

"Any old paper money or stocks that were buried will be worthless or rotten," I warned. "Doubt you'd get much cash for them, even as a historical artifact."

"Ain't looking for paper. My great-granddaddy claimed there were gold bars and valuable coins. Had to hide them from the damn Yankees."

"Even if that were true, I'm sure it's long gone by now," I said gently. "There might be a few scattered coins, but you can't dig up every inch of this land, you know."

He mumbled something incoherent, and I feared I might be losing my one shot at a real conversation. "You do know who I am, right?" I asked quickly.

He stopped and stared at me again. "You're Violet. My baby girl."

My heart pinched, and an unaccustomed tenderness for my father overwhelmed me. "I'm going to get a job, Dad. Soon as I can, I'll buy you a metal detector."

"I'm tired." He ran a dirty hand through his gray hair, and his lips trembled.

I took his shovel and placed my hand by his elbow. "Time for you to get some rest. Let's go inside."

Slowly, we picked our way through the yard. Out of the corner of my eye, I caught movement by an upstairs window. The lace curtain in Delaney's room rippled softly, as though recently brushed back by an invisible hand.

Dad laughed, for no apparent reason. And I wondered—who was the crazy one here? Perhaps we both were. I glanced up at the dark window of my sister's bedroom. And if that were the case, I'd have to diagnose Delaney as suffering a similar condition.

From afar, I sensed that she watched us, as silent and hidden as the stealthiest of crows. The night air had helped clear my fuzzy head, and I couldn't help but wonder if she had put a little something extra in my drink. I'd been on psychotropic medications way too long not to notice that today's sudden sleepiness and strange dreams had a chemical root.

But why would Delaney do that?

I puzzled over the question as I ushered Dad inside, turned on the lights, and guided him toward his small bedroom. It seemed that the discussion of money had shaken Delaney. Had she somehow guessed that I'd been to the bank before I confronted her? And had she decided to drug me to try and keep me from asking where my money had gone? But if we were broke, there was nothing she need fear any longer—she'd already admitted the painful truth.

Unless . . . she was lying again.

"Wash your hands and go to bed," I urged Dad.

He turned, hand on the bedroom doorknob, and regarded me with sharp, flashing eyes. "Don't drink the tea again. *Ever.*"

I blinked, and he was gone, softly shutting the door behind him. Fireworks sizzled my mind, little seizures of *aha*s. I flipped off the light switch and started up the stairs, only to gasp and halt abruptly.

Delaney stood above me near the top of the staircase. The night-light in the hallway illuminated her silhouette, clad in a pink satin nightgown, and backlit her long blonde hair like a halo. But the expression in her narrowed eyes and the hard set of her jaw were far from angelic.

My hand flew to my neck, and I gave a weak laugh. "Delaney, you scared me."

"What were you and Dad talking about? Why did he dig up my roses?" Her voice slashed at me like a knife, triggering childhood memories, the bad kind. It was the same spiteful voice that used to taunt me the moment my parents had left the room and we were alone.

Mom and Dad hate you.

You're ugly. Stupid.

You're not one of us.

We wish you were dead.

Slaps and pinches would ensue, followed by threats of more dire punishment if I tattled. Dad always believed his little princess. I think Mom knew—she rarely left us alone together.

But I was no longer a child. I shrugged and answered her question. "We weren't talking about anything in particular. I happened to see him outside, brought him in, and told him to wash up and go to bed."

I took a deep breath, summoning bravado, and continued up the stairs. Delaney didn't budge from her spot, blocking me from continuing. "Move," I ordered, using the same cold, flat tone she used with me.

She arched a brow. "Say *please.*"

"I don't have time for your games. Get out of my way."

She stepped to the side and broadly swept an arm upward, a queen bestowing permission. "Go."

I made my way around her, breathing in the scent of lilies. God, how I hated that smell. My legs practically melted with relief as I passed her, and I grabbed the railing for support. The immediate danger had passed.

"Do you remember what really happened that night?" she asked softly.

The whispered words hurt like a gut punch, but I instinctively knew better than to show weakness. Slowly, I turned and faced her. "No."

"Well, I remember. Everything. I heard you sneak out of the house to meet Ainsley. I knew y'all were up to no good."

She's just guessing. Flinging implications and lies to see what stuck. I kept my face impassive. "You don't know shit."

Delaney gave a tinkling laugh that doused my skin like ice water. "And you were angry with Ainsley that night, weren't you?"

I ground my teeth together to stifle my shock. "What's your point?" I snapped.

"And I remember afterward. When Mom and that detective brought you home, all wild eyed and dirty, claiming you were lost and had no memory of what happened."

"I didn't remember. And still don't."

Delaney hiked up one step and leaned into me, her face inches from my own. "Dissociative fugue, my ass. Of course you remember. Later, after everyone else had fallen asleep, I climbed into bed with you, and you told me what really happened to Ainsley."

My lungs squeezed tight, and I couldn't breathe. Lying. She had to be lying.

My sister's mouth twisted into a mocking smile. "Remember now?"

I shook my head. *No.*

"It's okay, little sis." She gently ran the tips of her fingernails down my arm, which still clutched the railing like a lifeline, and I shivered. "Your secret's safe with me."

I backed away from Delaney as though she were a rattlesnake coiled to bite. "No. I never told you anything because I don't know what happened to Ainsley. You're lying."

"Am I?"

The question hung in the air. I didn't have the means to answer it, and Delaney was well aware of my predicament. That night was a void, and at times like this, I preferred to keep it that way. What was done couldn't be undone. Ainsley was forever gone.

Chapter 15

VIOLET

March 2009

Cottonwood Specialized Care Facility, a.k.a. State of Alabama Institution for the Mentally Ill, a.k.a. the Nuthouse

I hated it here. Hated every friggin' detail of this place. The ugly concrete walls and institutional green paint, the metal cots spaced so close together I could reach out an arm on either side and touch the thin mattresses of my cellmates. Yes, I said *cellmate*. *Patient* is a euphemism.

And don't even get me going about the food here, or the monotonous daily schedule of working the laundry room, watching a small noncable TV in the cafeteria/rec center, and attending the occasional group therapy sessions.

The quarterly team psychiatric meeting I'd just attended had been chaired by an old bald man in a rumpled suit and a bored female who had taken notes and avoided eye contact. I'd glanced at the nameplate on his desk—**DR. LESLIE CARRINGTON**—as he'd read over my paperwork from Pine Ridge Treatment Clinic, the private center that my dad, apparently, could no longer afford. Mom would never have agreed to this transfer if she were alive.

"You'll find Cottonwood quite different from your previous digs," the doctor had commented with a thin smile.

Digs? I pegged him as an aged hippie. Had he once sported long, flowing hair and tie-dyed T-shirts? He'd prescribed more sedatives to help with this "transitional phase" as I adjusted to my new existence. I wasn't ungrateful for that mercy. He'd quickly dismissed me, and as I'd headed out the door, I'd overheard him remark to the woman whose name and function I was never informed about, "Dissociative fugue? Sounds more like selective amnesia, if you ask my opinion."

They'd both snickered.

Bastards.

I walked the long hallway back to Dorm E West Wing, taking my sweet time. It was fairly deserted and quiet in the large dorm rooms. Most everyone was busy with their "corrective care work therapy." In my case, that meant four hours a day in the sweltering heat of the laundry room. I figured I could waste another twenty minutes before the laundry supervisor sounded an alarm to round me up.

At the last room on the right, I entered my dorm and paused, surprised to find two women hovering by my bed. One of them reached into my nightstand and pulled out an object, holding it up to the fluorescent overhead light.

The broken Christmas ornament glimmered, an ovoid length of pink-and-white glass etched in a snowflake pattern, clinging to a metal filament and bulb. One of my sacred crow gifts.

Anger scalded my veins, and I ran at them. "Put it back!"

Startled, the woman dropped the ornament, and it splintered on the concrete floor in a tinny splat. I stared at the ruined shards, my temples pounding.

"It was broken anyway," the thief's companion said with a shrug. "What's the big deal?"

I grabbed the collar of her shirt. "It was mine. Mine! Don't you ever go near my stuff again. Got it?"

Her eyes widened, and her gaze shifted past my shoulders. Too late, I heard the footsteps from behind.

"Let go of her shirt," a deep voice boomed.

I did, but my nails raked into her exposed collarbone as I stepped back, breathing hard.

"What's going on here?"

I recognized the voice—a Cottonwood employee, Luanne Smithers, watcher of loonies.

I bent down, picking up the ornament base and tiny slivers of pink glass. Blood oozed from my fingertips, and the sharp slices of pain interrupted my rage. I surreptitiously swiped at the tears running down my face. I wouldn't give those women the satisfaction of seeing they'd gotten to me.

"She's gone off about nothin'," one of them said. "Crazy lady."

"Look a-here. She scratched me."

"That's what you get for taking somethin' that don't belong to you," Luanne said. "Now both of you git back to work afore I call a counselor to write up an incident report."

Tweedledee and Tweedledum left without another word.

"Here ya go, honey." A tissue was tucked into my hand. "Leave that mess alone. I'll sweep it up."

I arose on shaky feet and sank onto my bed, staring numbly at my bloody fingers. "They had no right to go through my things."

"'Course not."

Luanne sat beside me, and the cot creaked under her considerable girth. I'd seen her around. She was some sort of assistant counselor. Which meant that she was an omniscient presence in this wing, overseeing patients and keeping the peace.

"Was that somethin' special they broke?"

"Yes. It's from a collection." I didn't elaborate on the details.

"There's more in your nightstand?"

I nodded. By the time I got out of here, every last piece would be stolen or broken. None of the crow gifts were worth anything, but they'd be pilfered out of pure meanness—because they meant something to me, and now those women knew it.

"Let me take a look."

I opened a drawer, and Luanne took a quick peek. I expected her to laugh at the menagerie of worthless trinkets, but she didn't.

"Put them in a bag and follow me. I'll stow them in safekeeping for ya."

I blinked at the unexpected kindness. "You will?"

"You bet. Come to my office, and I'll clean those cuts, too, while we're at it."

What do you know? One of the lowest-paid employees here seemed more concerned about me than that stupid doctor. Quickly, I wrapped my collection in a spare pillowcase, also throwing in sprigs of dried magnolia leaves and blossoms that retained a trace of the sweet scent that always reminded me of my mother. Seemed every time I went into the hospital yard, they appeared nearby. Maybe it was crazy—maybe *I* was crazy—but it felt like Mom was still with me, watching over me from afar.

I followed Luanne to her office in the common area. Inside the spare, minimally furnished room, she locked up my goods in a metal cabinet and then withdrew a cotton pad soaked in alcohol. Like a child, I laid my hands on her desk, palms up, as she gently swiped away the blood.

"When you get angry, honey, take three deep breaths and *think.* Don't do nothin' stupid. In a few years you'll either be released, or you can transfer to a halfway house."

I blinked, wondering what all she knew about me. "What makes you say that?"

Luanne bandaged my cut fingertips. "I read the case files. Helps to know everything about the girls under my care."

Her care. My eyes watered again, but not from anger. I cleared my throat. "So you read about . . . why I'm here."

"Uh-huh." She returned the bandage box to the first aid kit and placed the kit in a desk drawer.

My entire body tightened, bracing for the inevitable snide remark over my convenient memory loss. Folks back home were plenty upset I'd been "let off the hook" in a legal arrangement my attorney had arranged with the DA. Once I turned twenty-one, I was free to walk out the door, providing the psych doctor signed off that I was normal.

"Those girls give you any more trouble, you come to me, and I'll take care of it."

"You will?" My eyes narrowed. "Why?"

"Because no one deserves to be mistreated." Luanne rose from her seat. "Anytime you want to check on yer stuff, let me know, and I'll unlock the cabinet."

"Thanks. Really, thank you."

A gentle smile tugged the corners of her thick lips, and she patted my arm. "Everything's going to be all right, darlin'. Just hang in there. I'll help you."

"Yes, ma'am." I jumped to my feet. "Guess I better get back to the laundry room."

Luanne glanced at her watch. "No need. Your shift ends in thirty minutes anyway. Just chill, and I'll cover for you."

Hope unfurled in my chest, a tiny seedling grasping for light. Thirty minutes to myself before group therapy. I'd go out for a walk in the yard and enjoy the sunshine. With a lighter heart, I left the office.

A guy walked out of Dr. Leslie Carrington's office, a scowl distorting his features. There was no employee name badge clipped to his T-shirt. He was one of us, but I'd known that the moment I'd laid eyes on him. Something about the disheveled hair and slump in his shoulders.

Normally, I kept to myself, but today—bolstered by Luanne's unexpected kindness—I spoke.

"I saw the doc today too. Man's a real downer, isn't he?"

The scowl melted from his face, and he grinned. His features were well defined and strong, his green eyes bright and lit with amusement.

"Yeah, Doctor Care Less."

Unaccustomed laughter bubbled from me.

He held out a hand. "I'm Seth."

I took his hand, felt the warmth of real human contact for the first time in ages. My stomach lurched and cartwheeled in a way it hadn't since . . . I tamped down the memory and spoke. "Violet," I answered, hoping my body's waves of warmth didn't scorch him.

"Violet," he murmured, still holding my hand. "That's a pretty name. It fits you."

He released me, and I nervously stuffed both hands in my jeans pockets, feeling awkward and shy. What did I know of guys? I'd never even been on a date.

Seth cocked his head toward the door at the far end of the back hallway. "I was going for a walk. Want to join me?"

You betcha. I followed behind him, grinning. The year stretch at Cottonwood had just gotten a lot more tolerable.

A nurse sat at an old battered desk at the end of the hallway, stationed like a prison guard at the exit door for the yard. But she let us through, and I closed my eyes, gulping large breaths of fresh air. The fall sky was pewter and the air pregnant with rain. I didn't care. Anything was better than being stuck inside, where ugly concrete seemingly rose from the cold floors to form walls and ceilings. My body tensed, straining to hear the distant rustle of birds and animals.

"This place isn't all bad, you know."

My eyes popped open. I'd forgotten Seth. "Don't tell me you like it here."

"*Like* isn't the term I'd use." He shrugged, and my gaze caught the vulnerable slope of his hunched shoulders as he zipped up his sweatshirt jacket. "After you get used to the routine, to the rules, it's . . . peaceful."

Seth colored slightly as I gaped at him in surprise. We began walking the perimeter of the flat expanse of lawn encased on all three sides of the building by a thick tree line of pine and cypress, a living fence between the normal and the crazy, the free and the incarcerated.

But of course, it wasn't as simple as that. Life couldn't be so easily defined and categorized.

"Peaceful, huh?" I prodded. "In what way?"

"Everything's decided for you. When to get up and eat, what to do at what time of the day."

I tried to see it his way. What I saw as a lack of freedom Seth viewed as freeing his mind from a myriad of decisions.

"Go on."

His eyes shuttered, became guarded. "No confrontations with my dad here. No more trying to hide crazy thoughts like suicide. Instead, the staff urge me to open up more."

I tried not to wince. What had been so terrible in Seth's life that he wanted to die? But it was much too soon for me to ask him such a thing. I didn't want to share my own private mental hell. Yet I admired his courage in sharing his thoughts with me.

Touching was discouraged here between patients, but I needed to touch Seth. I slipped my hand in the pocket of his jacket, and his large hand wrapped around mine like a warm glove. I squeezed his fingers, and we furtively clasped hands as we strolled the yard.

I had a friend. Maybe more than a friend. Suddenly, I had to know. I cocked my head toward a nearby pine and tugged at his hand. Seth followed me as I rounded the tree and then pressed my back against rough bark. "Kiss me," I demanded.

He did.

My body sang with excitement. It thrilled me—and terrified me, all at once. Seth must have sensed my hesitation. He pulled away and smiled gently, running a hand through my tousled hair. "Guess we should head back."

"Right."

I pushed away from the pine and glimpsed the unblinking stare of a perched crow only a few yards away. A guardian angel feathered in black, watching over me.

I'll be back. With food, I silently promised the crow. Wind rustled the pretty, dead leaves, and several fell down my cheeks, gently brushing my skin like a caress.

Mom. She was still with me—always would be. My heart refused to believe the news of the fiery car crash that had ended her life less than a year after Ainsley's disappearance. That news had spiraled me into a regression I was just starting to emerge from.

Now was a season for new friends, new experiences, no matter the circumstances.

We finished our walk, hands still secretly joined inside his jacket. My fingers curled around a slip of paper in the bottom of his pocket. Before we returned to the building, I slipped the bit of paper into my own pocket.

"See you tonight in the rec room?" Seth asked before we continued on our separate ways.

"Yes." I felt foolishly excited at the prospect of sitting around with the other patients watching an old movie. But I'd take my moments as I could. Back at my own dorm, I withdrew the paper scrap I'd filched, curious what it might be. It was only a piece of a gum wrapper, but I carefully tucked it into my nightstand drawer.

Some girls had corsages or movie tickets as souvenirs of their first date, their first boy kiss. I had a gum wrapper, but it would suffice.

Chapter 16

VIOLET

Christmas 2012

Cottonwood Specialized Care Facility

The crow swooped down, grabbed the peanut in its beak, and flew off. "Ingrate," I called out with a laugh. What I wouldn't do to see Tux's friendly face once again. My breath created wisps of chilled smoke, and I shivered against the nip in the air. Time to head back. I couldn't wait to meet Seth and give him the Christmas gift I'd bought.

I slanted my head down, fighting the wind, and ran to the door. Inside, Cottonwood was as cheery as one could expect at a mental hospital during the holidays. Still, I'd managed to carve out a bit of happiness for myself. And just two weeks ago I'd been relieved to find that several hundred dollars had been anonymously deposited in my personal account at Cottonwood. Every year, like clockwork, the money would come around the holidays, and I scrimped by and made it last as long as possible. I couldn't imagine who'd been so kind. Dad or Delaney? That didn't feel right. They obviously didn't care much about me, but perhaps the money was to soothe any guilt they might harbor about forsaking me to state care.

I put the matter out of my mind, and with a quick backward glance to make sure no one was watching me, I scurried downstairs to where, hopefully, Seth awaited.

He didn't disappoint. The utility room door was ajar, and I spotted his auburn hair in the semidarkness—a flash of bright color, like a burning ember in a gray ash pile. Heart near to bursting, I ran to him, dangling a twig of mistletoe above his head. I'd pinched it from the Christmas wreath on the rec room door and had eagerly anticipated sneaking away to meet Seth here in the basement. Our place. To outsiders, it might appear sordid and gross, but to us it was sanctuary.

"Kiss me," I commanded, and he willingly complied. A gentle kiss, the kind that made me all gooey inside.

"You smell good," he said roughly in a husky voice.

"Courtesy of Luanne's gift," I said, extending the inside of my wrist for him to smell it better. "A bottle of perfume." It had a strong top note of magnolias, which reminded me of Mom. I marveled at how my friend always managed to know just the right thing to make me happy.

From above, a Christmas carol blared, followed by a stampede of foot stomping.

"What the hell?" Seth half rose from our seated position on the floor and gazed at the ceiling, as if afraid it was in danger of caving in on us.

I doubled over laughing. "It's the local cloggers," I explained.

"The what?"

"Cloggers. You know, those hillbilly dancers that wear gingham skirts and bloomers. It's like tap dancing on steroids."

"Sounds like we're missing a cool party," he joked. He sat back down and pulled something from his jacket. "For you. Merry Christmas."

Grinning, I accepted the small box wrapped in red tissue and dug into it. Inside was a hand-carved wooden baby bird.

"I whittled it," he said, his face slightly red. "It's not much, but I know you like—"

I wrapped my arms around him and gave him a fierce kiss. "It's perfect. Thank you." I laid my head on his shoulder, and the tears flowed. How was I ever going to say goodbye to Seth?

"Whoa, there. What's the matter?" he asked.

I couldn't tell him. Instead, I reached in my back pocket and pulled out a folded sheet of paper and handed it to him.

Seth read the short note and then looked up. "This is great news. It's what you've wanted, isn't it?"

"Yes, but . . ." I drew a deep breath. "The halfway house is in Montgomery. We won't see each other again."

"We knew this day would come. I have news of my own. I'm being released next Friday."

"But . . . how? Are you going back home?"

Seth had told me his story. He'd been depressed after the death of his mom and had taken one of his dad's hunting guns, intending to take his life. When his dad had tried to stop him, Seth had turned the gun on him. Seth had never intended to actually shoot his father, but his dad had involuntarily committed him anyway, claiming Seth was a danger to himself and others.

"Hell no. My old man has got nothing to do with it. Dr. Care Less finally decided I'm no longer a threat. My brother got me a job lined up working the oil rigs."

"Th-that's wonderful."

Seth drew me into his arms and kissed the top of my scalp. "We're both going to be okay, Violet. You'll see."

These stolen moments had never been meant to last. He'd be free, making new friends . . . new girlfriends. I wanted that for Seth. I wanted his life to be easy and filled with friends and a special love that provided unconditional acceptance and support. He deserved that. Some woman would be lucky to have such a patient soul. He'd certainly let me open up to him at my own turtle's pace and never complained.

I clasped the wooden bird to my chest and tried to be happy for both of us. Forcing a brightness that I didn't feel, I cleared my throat and presented him with a small wrapped box I'd hidden in my jacket. "I have something for you too."

Seth opened the box and lifted the silver chain and medallion. "What is this?"

"A Saint Christopher medallion." Suddenly, I felt the gift was all wrong. Neither of us were religious. It had been an impulse purchase from a catalog.

"It's supposed to be for protection and blessings," I explained. "Kinda lame, now I think about it. If you—"

"Know your problem? You think too much." Seth kissed my forehead and then slipped the chain around his neck. "I'll always wear it and remember you, Violet."

Chapter 17

DELANEY

Present day

The image of my upturned roses and the secret whisperings between Dad and Violet set my temper sizzling. I stared at Violet. The dark changeling child had been foisted upon me when I was six years old, and now she'd returned, all these years later, insinuating herself back into my life. It wasn't fair. Her mother was long dead, and Dad didn't recognize her half the time. Did she really think she could just show up as an adult and claim an inheritance? Take over the Henderson land and family house? Disrupt my routine and order?

In the faint hallway light, her almost black hair blended into the shadows and accentuated the pale, heart-shaped face that framed her blue-purple, almond-shaped eyes.

Violet was exotic and striking, all the more so because she didn't recognize her own beauty. The *shrinking violet* stereotype fit her—or at least it had when she was a child. Now I wasn't so sure. Her name was more like the color than a flower—a confusing mixture of red passion and blue frost.

We couldn't have been more different, and she'd never felt like a true blood sister. I blamed Hyacinth for that. The woman had taken an irrational dislike to me from the start—*me*, not even old enough to be in kindergarten when Dad had first introduced us. And now Dad and Violet were getting chummy? I wouldn't be crowded out again.

What had they been whispering about downstairs? The startled, guilty flash on her face when she'd spotted me on the landing had been undeniable.

Violet broke away and entered her bedroom, closing the door. A metallic click signaled she'd locked it. How dare she? What was that all about? This was my house, after all, and she was merely a guest.

I stomped down the stairs and flung open Dad's bedroom door. He didn't so much as twitch at the noise and kept one side of his face smashed against a pillow, eyes tightly shut, and a blanket pulled up to his chin. I wasn't fooled.

"You know better than to get out of bed at night and go outside. You better not have destroyed my roses again."

Why did he have to dig up my roses? I worked so hard on them, trying to beautify our lives. I got no thanks for my gardening or for any of my efforts and caretaking. And now Violet came home and they were all tight—leaving me out of things. He couldn't have secrets with Violet. *I* was his favorite daughter. The one he loved most and preferred, even over Hyacinth, when she was alive. Hurt fizzed through my veins at his betrayal. Wasn't it bad enough my biological mother had died before I'd ever had the chance to know her? Bad enough that my stepmother and Violet had always been close and had denied me entry into their tight bond? At least I used to mean something special to my dad.

"I'm sorry. It won't happen again," Dad said in that whiny twang that grated on my nerves.

"What were you and Violet talking about?"

"She asked why I'm always digging—that's all."

I clicked my tongue in frustration. "There's no treasure—or whiskey—buried in the backyard. All you ever do is destroy all my hard work."

And if there was any money, it'd be all mine. But no point getting him riled. I eyed the dirt-sprinkled sheets. Which meant even more housework for me tomorrow. "Go wash up before getting back in bed. You're filthy."

He obeyed without protest, and I left, slamming the door on the way out to punctuate my displeasure. Apparently, I was the only one in this house with all their brain cells functioning normally. I frowned as I passed my sister's door and then entered my bedroom.

Violet was becoming a problem. Bad enough she'd gone poking around at the bank and made friends with Libby after I'd told her not to. But if she thought she could form an alliance with Dad, I'd need to step up my game. Rearranging her stuff to keep her off balance was child's play. Tonight, I'd hopefully stirred a memory in Violet's mind about her role in Ainsley's disappearance. How much did she remember? How much was she faking about a memory loss? Violet was no innocent angel, as I well knew. Somewhere deep inside, she knew it too.

I wanted her out of here. Out of my house with all her meddling and self-righteous attitude. But I'd have to show some patience while driving her away, or everything could blow up in my face.

I took down the photo hanging on the wall and quickly tapped out the safe's keyboard code. Inside the small compartment, my fingers grasped a small velvet pouch, and I made a fist around the smooth fabric that housed my most secret possessions. How many times had I started to throw these away over the years? Holding on to the trinkets was dangerous. Yet here they remained. I sat on the bed, untied the pouch strings, and let the contents tumble out.

Hell yeah. This was my big gun. If needed, I could use this against Violet.

Chapter 18

VIOLET

Present day

For weeks now, Delaney and I had settled into a truce of sorts as we each went about our lives. Between the somewhat-settled tension at home and a new job, my days were full and left me little time for brooding.

At work, I still wasn't used to the manual labor. I placed both hands on my lower back and stretched, easing my strained muscles. My position at the Whispering Oaks Nursing Home required lots of bending and stooping. Most of my eight-hour shifts were spent emptying bedpans, helping patients in and out of wheelchairs, stripping beds, and other such glamorous duties. Not that I was complaining. It was steady pay, and with my first paycheck tomorrow, I planned to open my own checking and savings accounts. My freedom accounts, as I'd privately labeled them.

Despite the backbreaking work I was damn grateful that Cora Crenshaw, Willie's wife, had informed me of the opening. She supervised this shift, and I couldn't ask for a more understanding boss.

Entering room 429, the last room on the hall, for my last task of the day, I wheeled the meal cart next to Mrs. Emmeline Upchurch's bed.

At the sound of the squeaking wheels, she turned from the window and faced me with rheumy pale-gray eyes.

"It's you, the new girl," she said in her shaky old-lady voice. "What's your name again?"

"Violet." I never offered my last name, just in case anyone's memory here remained intact. I rolled her to a seated position and lifted the top from the steaming tray.

Her face scrunched, and she gave a delicate sniff. "What's this?"

"Roast beef, mashed potatoes, carrots, and peas, with lime Jell-O for dessert," I answered cheerfully, setting a glass of iced tea and eating utensils by the tray. "Hope you enjoy."

I beat a hasty retreat, eager to punch the time clock and hit the road. Libby and I were going out for pizza tonight. When she'd first suggested it, I'd immediately said no, but she'd insisted it was time for me to get out more. "You stay in that old house of yours too much," she'd argued. "And then you work all day in the old folks' home. It's time to live it up a little."

I knew Libby meant well, but truthfully, I felt more comfortable at my job than any other place in town. My cheeks still burned when I thought of my encounter with Ainsley's mother at the Feed and Seed, and then Hattie Pilchard's pettiness at the drugstore. What if I encountered more of the same tonight?

Cora walked out of room 341, and we nearly collided in the hall.

"Oops, sorry," I mumbled.

"Not your fault, honey." She fell into step beside me. "Job getting any easier for you?"

Cora was as nice as she could be, same as her husband. But I couldn't help the blush that heated my cheeks and neck—couldn't stop the uncharitable thought *Look how far the Hendersons have sunk.* Our former cleaning woman, who used to scrub our house every week, was now my boss. It made me uncomfortable, like I had done something wrong. As if I were personally responsible for the collapse of the family name.

"Everything's fine," I answered, keeping my attention on rolling the cart. "My back's bothering me a little, but I'm sure I'll eventually get used to it."

She gave a booming laugh. "At least you're young enough that it's not killing your feet. Walking on concrete all these years has done a number on mine."

"Yes, ma'am." I stopped abruptly by the kitchen. "Going to turn this in. Excuse me."

She laid a warm hand on my shoulder. "Wait. We need to talk."

Startled, I searched her suddenly sober eyes, and my heart skittered out of control. A patient or one of their family members must have recognized my name. They were going to ask me to leave. I was an unsuitable employee. A liability. A potential public relations disaster if an irate client complained to the media that a suspected murderess roamed their halls.

Of course, I'd only been a person of interest in the disappearance of a teenage girl years ago, but I knew what Mr. and Mrs. Dalfred and the Hattie Pilchards of this town thought of me.

Guilty. Secretive. Dangerous.

"Follow me," Cora said, heading to a small room across from the nurses' station.

My hands began to shake, and I swallowed hard. I actually *liked* this job. I felt anonymous. The elderly patients didn't much notice or give a fig about me. They were involved in their own daily—often painful—struggles just to survive. I was only an employee like any other who came and went during the long years as they lay mostly bedridden within this brick building with its institutional green walls and utilitarian linoleum flooring.

Cora shut the door and stared at me intently. "Is everything okay?"

"Yes, ma'am."

"Do you really want to keep this job?"

"I do." Time to eat humble pie. "I need the money."

"There are other jobs."

Was she asking me to quit? I swallowed hard. "Has someone complained about me?"

"No. You work hard and mind your own business. There have been no complaints."

Relief washed over me until her next unexpected announcement.

"I talked to Delaney yesterday." Cora hesitated a heartbeat. "She's concerned about you."

"She is? Why?" I'd had no idea the two had kept in contact.

"Says you have nightmares and suffer from the depression."

Not again. "I don't have that many nightmares," I assured Cora. "And I'm not depressed."

"She also says that you've been forgetting things."

"Like what?"

"Little things. Like where you've placed belongings and recollecting people's names and such."

I shook my head. "That's not true. I promise I'm fine. I'll continue to do a good job." I drew a deep breath and blinked back the hot, angry tears. Now was no time to collapse into a weepy mess. It would only serve to make Delaney's claims more believable. And it certainly was no time for pride. "I really do need the money, Cora. Please."

She patted my hand. "Okay, honey. But if this work becomes too much for you, I hope you'll tell me. Your health's more important than any minimum wage job."

"Yes, ma'am."

Cora opened the door and left. Alone, I mulled over what she'd revealed. Maybe there was a kernel of truth in my sister's claims. I *had* been misplacing stuff—keys, purse, books. But I'd been half-convinced it was because of Delaney's need to put away whatever was lying about in her obsessive zeal to control everything in her environment.

But maybe the explanation was darker and deeper. Was I losing it again? Was my mind slowly spiraling into a downward slide, unable to cope with the stress of the outside world?

Black pinpricks swarmed my vision, and a roaring filled my ears. I gripped a shelf lined with cleaning supplies to keep from falling. *Get it together and get out.*

Whispering Oaks, with its institutional smells and contained suffering, wasn't an ideal working environment. It was too much like that awful state place where I'd lived, a lovely brick building that resembled an antebellum home on the outside. But on the inside, we'd shuffled about like zombies, lining up in the pill line in the morning for our antianxiety meds and again at night for more tranquilizers. Days had become weeks, then months, then years . . . all lost in a monotonous, numbing existence that was only one notch above the pain and fear that lay outside the walls. If it hadn't been for Luanne and Seth, I would never have made it out of Cottonwood.

No! I wouldn't—I *couldn't*—go back there and return to an anesthetized subsistence. I'd worked too hard for this chance at freedom—for the right to walk out in the sunshine whenever the mood hit me, to sit with my crows, to make my own food and eat whenever I fancied, to decide how late to stay up at night or sleep in the morning. Whatever happened, my place was in the real world now, and that meant earning a paycheck.

Drawing my shoulders back, I headed to the lobby to collect my purse.

~

Sheila's Pizza Den was noisy and packed, but it did have the smell of pepperoni and sausage going for it. I searched the crowd for Libby and spotted her in a corner booth, already drinking a beer. She waved at me, and I made my way over, slipping into the booth with its cracked red vinyl seats and a scarred wooden table. Nothing had changed at Sheila's in my time away. I took a small comfort in that knowledge.

"You're late," Libby said by way of greeting. "I went ahead and ordered a large pizza with all the toppings. That okay?"

"I'll eat anything but anchovies." I pictured Emmeline Upchurch's dinner tray with its disgusting glob of lime Jell-O. Poor lady. But I'd suffered those institutional meals for years myself, and these days I was determined to enjoy real food.

"Want a beer?" She signaled to a server.

I'd never even had a sip of beer. I opened my mouth to protest, then snapped it shut. Why not live a little?

A tall, slim teenage girl with a blonde ponytail stepped up to the table. "Whatcha need?"

Libby nodded her head my way. "A beer for my friend."

"I'll need to see your driver's license," the girl said.

"No problem." I dug out my wallet and opened it. The cellophane slot where my license normally appeared was empty. I frowned and checked the other wallet compartments. What the hell had happened to it? Frantically, I searched the rest of my purse on the off chance it had fallen out.

"Problem?" Libby asked.

"I can't find my license." Cora's words swept through me in a panic. Was Delaney right about me? Or was my sister trying to mess with my mind?

"No alcohol, then," the server said. "Want something else to drink?"

"Diet Coke."

I threw my purse on the seat beside me. Elbows on table, I rested my head in my hands.

"It'll turn up," Libby said. "Don't get upset. Happens to me all the time."

"Easy for you to say." I placed my hands in my lap and leaned back in the seat. "I seem to be misplacing everything lately. Or so Delaney says."

"So what? Not like you're used to having to carry around ID and keep up with so much."

"True." Everything had been taken care of for me for years.

"Even if you can't find it when you get home, you can get another made at the DMV."

Libby made everything seem so simple. No wonder I liked her.

She drummed her fingers on the wooden table, and her brow creased.

"What is it?" I asked.

Libby took another sip of beer before answering. "I'd debated bringing this up, but I ran into Delaney yesterday at the drugstore, and we had a chat."

"That's strange." Delaney didn't approve of my friend. What could she possibly want to talk with her about? Unless . . .

"Yep. Bizarre, even. Your sister claims that she's concerned about you. That you're under a lot of stress."

I groaned, wondering how many people Delaney had contacted with the same song and dance. "She called my boss and said the same. Did she tell you I've been depressed, having nightmares, and misplacing stuff?"

"That pretty much summed up our conversation. I told her to go screw herself."

"Bet the word is all over Normal that I'm a nutcase—though they probably all thought that anyway."

"Well, *I* certainly don't think so. If anyone's crazy, it's Delaney. Have you seen that mysterious fiancé of hers yet?"

"Nope. She says Sawyer's busy preparing for a big trial in Birmingham next month."

"Uh-huh. You even seen a photo of this"—she raised both hands and finger quoted—"Sawyer Harris?"

"Not yet. But Delaney said they'll be taking engagement shots soon, and then I can see how handsome he is."

"You ever talk to him directly?"

"He's called her a few times when I've been home, though I haven't spoken to him." Delaney had always left the room after his call, a dreamy smile on her face. I'd never questioned that, naturally assuming that she'd want to speak to him in private.

"Riiiight," Libby drawled with a smirk.

With an effort, I put aside embarrassment about my family and Delaney's lies. This was one of Libby's rare weekends without Calvin. His father had picked him up after her day shift had ended. She could let loose for a few days, and I wasn't going to be a downer. "Thanks for inviting me for pizza. Let's forget about my sister for tonight."

"Good idea. How's the job going?"

"I like it. Thanks again for providing me a reference."

Libby waved off the thanks. "You really like it? Not exactly glamorous or high paying."

"Okay. Let's say I like getting paid, then."

The server set my soda on the table, and I raised my glass to Libby's. "Here's to earning a paycheck and to relaxing weekends."

She laughed and gulped more beer.

Someone passed close by our booth, and I idly turned to the side. A table full of couples my age stared at us. One of the guys gave me a goofy grin and then placed a hand by the side of his head, twirling his index finger in a circle—the universal sign for *crazy*.

All of them erupted in laughter.

I swung my head back to Libby, and she squinted at me. "What's wrong?"

"Just some jerks. Forget it."

"Hell no." She slammed her glass down and glared at the bullies.

I kept my eyes lowered and didn't watch their reactions to her anger, but the guffaws reduced to a few snickers, then stopped. The server slid our pizza on the table.

"Don't let those idiots spoil a perfectly good pizza," Libby said.

We dug in, and I let the pepperoni goodness do its job in lifting my mood. Halfway through, I remembered one reason why I hadn't canceled dinner tonight when I'd wanted to. I wiped my hands on a napkin and pulled out my cell phone.

"Not trying to ruin a good time here, but I need your help with something. Figured with your nursing background, I'd get your medical opinion." I pulled up my photo gallery and then frowned.

Dad's prescription-bottle photos were gone. Every single one.

Could I have accidentally erased them? I was no tech whiz, but it seemed like if I'd touched a wrong button, it would have deleted all my photos. But my crow pictures remained. There was Tux with his little patch of white, and there were a couple of other pictures I'd shot of crows perched on my balcony railing, waiting for their daily peanut treat. Unease prickled down my spine. Had Delaney managed to guess my password and tamper with my phone? It was the only logical explanation.

"What's wrong?" Libby asked.

I threw my cell phone back in my purse and helped myself to another slice of pizza. I'd take more photos later.

"Nothing. I'll ask you about it another time. Was Calvin excited about seeing his dad?"

As I expected, Libby's face lit at the mention of her son, and she plunged into a long story about all the cute things Calvin had said about the upcoming visit. It struck me that Libby never mentioned the father's name or why the two had broken up, but we all had our secrets.

I only half listened to my friend, anyway, consumed with the implication of the missing photos.

Was Delaney overmedicating Dad so that he was easier to control and take care of?

I couldn't decide if she was a concerned daughter and caretaker for Dad, or something else entirely.

Chapter 19

BOONE

"What we got happening today, boss?"

Josh Adams strolled to my desk, rubbing his hands together, and I suppressed a sigh. Had I ever been that enthusiastic and green? These days, I welcomed slow periods on the job, using the downtime to file and take care of admin tasks that I'd put off while focused on a case.

I lifted a stack of papers in my inbox. "Go through these and either file what needs to be kept or toss out what's already been handled."

He snickered as if I were trying to pull a fast one on him. "You're kidding me, right? I mean, come on, we're living in the digital age. Who keeps paper?"

"Old shit-for-brains like me, evidently."

I didn't trust a computer to safekeep important documents or anything I might need to reference in the future. Setting the pile back in my inbox, I mulled how to get Josh off my back. I could offer to let him streamline the admin work, but he'd just annoy me later, pestering me to learn some new process or a new computer operation, and I sure as hell didn't want that. I'd gotten along perfectly fine in the twenty-plus pre-Josh years of my employment.

Brilliance struck. The light from my bright idea practically illuminated the gloomy room with its gray walls and small windows covered with grimy old miniblinds. "Fine. You want real detective work; I've got it." I spun around in my chair and opened the tall filing cabinet behind me.

"If we went paperless, we could get rid of old behemoths like that cabinet," Josh offered helpfully. "Open up this space more. A new coat of paint on the walls wouldn't hurt either. Something a little more cheerful. Know what I mean? I've been thinking—"

"Always dangerous." I grabbed the entire row of hanging files that lined a drawer and plopped them on my desk. "Here you go. Cold case files dating back ten years. Impress me with your newly acquired detective skills."

"Glad to."

But instead of picking up the files and heading to his own desk, Josh skimmed the tab headings.

"Looking for something in particular?" I asked curiously.

"The Dalfred disappearance."

The casual mention of that name punched me in the gut. "Dalfred?" I repeated stupidly.

"Yeah. The one you told me about a few weeks ago when we bumped into that hot chick on Main Street. She was the last person to see the missing teenager alive, right?"

"As far as we know." The lie felt heavy even as it slipped off my tongue.

"Here it is." Josh pulled the file from the rest of the stack and headed back to his desk, which sat only eight feet away from mine.

I cleared my workspace and methodically worked my way through the first couple of memos cluttering the inbox, but my pleasure in the routine task of organizing was shot. Some brilliant idea *that* had turned out to be. Carelessly handing over the Dalfred file was going to bite me in the ass; I just knew it. I found myself sneaking glances at Josh, who had spread out everything in the file on his desk. I might give him grief about his newbie status, but the young man was sharp. Would he find some incongruence in the photos and statements?

Stop it. He might be clever, but I'd had years of experience in covering my ass before Ainsley Dalfred had gone missing. Abruptly, I rose and walked to the break room—more a closet than a room, if truth be told. A cup of coffee would be a welcome diversion. I stepped into the room and halted, blinking at the counter where my trusted old coffee machine had once squatted. In its stead was some modern red contraption.

"How do you like the new Keurig?"

I practically winced at the sound of Josh right behind me. "The what?"

"Keurig. It makes individual cups of coffee. Here, I'll show you." He pushed his way in front of me and pointed to a stack of tiny containers. "You've got a choice: french roasted, decaf, flavored coffees, and even tea. What's your preference?"

"For God's sake, I just wanted black coffee," I grumbled, returning to my desk. I stared down at an old report, but the printed words didn't register. Again, I recalled Violet's wary expression as she'd regarded me on the street. To her, I was nothing but a stranger, one bound up with old, bad memories.

The familiar *what ifs* plagued me. Could I have prevented this tragedy if I'd run off with Hyacinth years ago? What if Hyacinth had never called me when she couldn't find Violet in the woods that night? What if she'd found Violet earlier and had merely ushered her daughter to bed without involving me?

Nothing had ended well for any of us. Hy was long gone, and Violet had suffered to the point that she might always live a haunted life. As for me, life had lost all its zest and flavor when I'd said goodbye to Hyacinth.

She may never have believed it after I'd reacted so badly to the news of her pregnancy, but I did love her. Always would. Even though our affair had only lasted less than two years, and despite everything that had happened.

The scent of vanilla and coffee invaded my rambling mind. A brewed cup steamed beside my elbow. "Here you go, old man. Give it a try."

I picked up the mug and sniffed. "What is this fancy-shmancy crap?"

"French vanilla and cream."

I took a cautious sip, and creamy sweetness enveloped my mouth. This might have been the best coffee I'd ever tasted, not that I'd tell Josh.

"Well?" he asked.

"It's passable."

"Damn straight." He returned to his desk and became absorbed with the Dalfred file.

The kid thought I was archaic and dull. Wouldn't he be surprised if he were aware of how much I really knew about the case—down to the exact details of most of what had transpired that night.

Details that would never be filed in an official report.

Details that could get my ass fired—and that would be the mildest of the possible repercussions if those details ever came to light.

Hot liquid splashed onto my shaking hand.

Play it cool. No one had ever so much as raised an eyebrow at my report. Josh Adams wouldn't uncover anything earth shattering either. Only my guilty conscience foresaw trouble. *Do you really expect to keep everything secret forever?*

The cell phone on my desk rang, vibrating the wooden tabletop like a Mexican jumping bean cranked on steroids.

Bad news?

The question bitch-slapped me as it always did when my phone rang or the boss called me into his office. *This is it—this is the day,* it would taunt me. *Gonna all explode in your face now. And it would serve you right.*

I answered the phone.

Dan Thornell's booming voice sounded, loud enough that Josh overheard. "Get in my office right away," he ordered. "I have big news."

"Should I bring Josh?" I asked. Not that I wanted my partner in there, but the kid would hound me for every detail if he didn't hear the big news directly.

"Sure." The phone clicked off. Dan, the police chief and my boss for nearly a quarter of a century, was an impatient man, although a decent person. He was a straight-to-the-point kind of guy who saw everything in black and white. Suspects were either guilty or innocent. Extenuating circumstances and shades of gray weren't entertained. The son of a Baptist preacher, he had an unambiguous moral compass.

We entered the room, and he pushed back in his leather chair, his pale-blue eyes lit with grim satisfaction. He pressed an intercom button on his large landline phone, which harkened back to a 1980s version of high tech. If Josh thought I was archaic, Chief Thornell was still in the Dark Ages when it came to technology. "Alice, bring me the Ainsley Dalfred file."

I'd been expecting those very words every day for eleven years. And still, my gut nosedived.

Josh rose. "It's on my desk, sir. I'll go get it."

At Dan's raised brow, I filled him in. "Josh just started reviewing cold cases. This is the one he picked."

Of course he had—it was the biggest unsolved mystery in Normal. Solve that, and he'd slap a gold star on his rookie résumé.

I gripped my old, familiar coffee cup in both hands, sending warmth to my numb fingers. "What's up?" I managed to ask casually.

"Construction workers found the skeleton of a young female at the bottom of Hatchet Lake. Her skull was crushed on one side. Harris was on patrol near the area, so I sent him over to the scene. They're waiting for John Hill to arrive."

Hill was the county coroner. He'd bag the remains and make a positive identification.

"Got to be the Dalfred kid," Dan said. "Now that we know where she is, we have to figure out how she got there. The big question is whether her skull was intentionally bashed by someone before she entered the water or if she hit it against a rock when she went swimming."

"Hill's good, but it's doubtful he can make that determination after all these years."

Dan rose. "Word's already leaked to Ronnie Lynn with Channel 12. She wants an interview ASAP. The Associated Press wants an interview as well. Meanwhile, I need you to notify Mac and Janine Dalfred about the discovery."

Right—I got the fun job while he talked to the media. But I had to hand it to my boss—he'd been chief for a long time and knew how to keep his job safe from the interlopers who cropped up after every election, eager for a public position in return for their campaign contributions.

"I'll take care of it immediately," I promised.

Josh gave me a nod. "I'll go with you."

Dan's walkie-talkie crackled. "Harris reporting, sir. Wanted to let you know a couple of cement blocks are located near the skeleton."

Dan and I stared at one another grimly. "Ten-four," he said, stuffing the device back into the case on his belt.

"We might have a murder case," Dan said. "Those blocks must have been used to keep the victim's body from rising to the surface."

"Unless the blocks were trotline anchors left behind by fishermen," I suggested.

Josh snickered, and I wanted to kick him.

"Highly unlikely," Dan said. "The Dalfreds are going to be out for blood now. They were sure this would happen. Raised one hell of a stink with me and the mayor last week, insisting the lake finally be drained."

Alarm jangled my gut. "You met with them and didn't even tell me about it?"

"Didn't think the meeting would amount to much. Their displeasure with our investigation has never been a secret. But this time, the mayor finally put pressure on the utility company, and they agreed to proceed with the much-needed repairs."

Dan shrugged into his suit jacket and placed his uniform cap atop his thick silver hair. The official attire made him look more imposing and authoritative than usual. The reporters would eat it up.

I headed to the door to proceed with my unpleasant task.

"Boone, stay a moment."

I turned and faced him while Josh stepped ahead of me and shut the door on his way out.

"Let your new partner go over everything from the past. Fill him in on all you remember. Adams came highly recommended from the Huntsville police chief, and I'm optimistic he'll invigorate our department. Bring in fresh ideas. With any luck, he'll pick up some detail on the case that we overlooked."

That *I* had overlooked, he meant. His words stung. Reinvigorate, my ass. Quickly, I tamped down the resentment. My pride wasn't important at the moment. I had to face Ainsley's parents again. While I was out, I'd also swing by Whispering Oaks and speak with Violet. I wanted her to hear the news from me first, and I wanted to prepare her for what was to come.

I dug my keys from the desk drawer and left the room. In the hallway, Josh called, "Where are we going?"

"Thornell's headed to a community club meeting. Just go back to your desk and review your case."

"Why did the chief want to speak privately with you?"

Did he not understand the meaning of the word *private?* "Nothing important."

"I'll go with you to see the victim's family."

"No. I'd rather do it alone."

The corners of his mouth tightened, and he stiffly took a step back. "Fine. Whatever you say."

I'd hurt his feelings, and some mean part deep inside of me was smug about it. But I'd deal with Josh later. Right now, I had to keep moving, keep thinking ahead to the next step.

Because if I stopped, I might surrender to a crippling paralysis. Guilt and fear nipped at my soul, snarling twin wolves that smelled an opportunity to take me down. But I couldn't let that happen. I'd made a promise to Hyacinth that I'd always protect Violet.

Whatever it took, I'd make sure Violet wasn't blamed. She'd suffered enough.

Hell, it was the least I could do for my daughter.

Chapter 20

VIOLET

July 2, 2007

"I don't have time for you anymore," Ainsley says. "Sammy's touch turns me on like yours never did and never could."

"Why?" I cry, unable to hide my anguish.

"Oh, come on, Violet. Don't take this so hard. We had a few good times, didn't we? It was like an experiment. But now the real thing's come along. I came tonight to tell you that. I'll never meet you like this again."

Never again. I'm horrified.

"What did I do wrong? Please tell me. Whatever it is, I'll change. I promise." I have no pride. Without Ainsley, I am nothing. As soulless and unimportant as the sand beneath my bare feet. I grab her arm. "Please," I say again.

"You've done nothing wrong. I'm sorry. Really. I didn't know you took this so . . . seriously. We can still be friends. Just not . . ." Her voice trails off, and she points between our naked bodies. "Not this. Not anymore. Okay?" Pity flits across her face, and she begins to inch away from me, eager to bring this—bring *us*—to an end. And still I am begging. I fall to my knees and wrap my arms around her legs.

"Stop it," she says, a hint of impatience in her voice. "What's wrong with you?"

I stumble to my feet. Pity mixed with annoyance shines in her eyes and pushes me off an edge. *Make it stop. I have to make the pain stop.* Without thought, I strike at Ainsley. A primitive animal reacting blindly to pain. The crisp smack of my palm against her cheek startles us both. I step back, stunned.

Now Ainsley is the wild beast, a black crow of vengeance. I see it in her flashing eyes and the outraged furrow of her brow. She hurls her body at me, her black hair lifting and rippling in the air, hands outstretched and fingers curled like talons. She means business.

Without conscious deliberation, I raise my own hands, palms up, prepared for the onslaught. The rip of nails slashes the side of my neck and shoulders. My palms land on her shoulders. I push her.

Push her with every ounce of strength in my body.

Chapter 21

VIOLET

"Violet Henderson, report to the front desk."

The disembodied voice over the Whispering Oaks intercom set my heart pounding faster, an unfortunate conditioned response that I'd developed. Friendless and practically without family since I was fourteen, when I was summoned, it usually meant bad news, never anyone wanting to chitchat or ask how my day was going.

Not only that, but a black cat had crossed my path this morning when I'd driven past Ruth's. It had darted underneath the Continental's wheels in a mad dash to get to the dumpster, where an employee had been emptying trash. Protocol had demanded I return home and start the trip over to avoid bad juju, but doing so would have meant arriving late to work. I had driven on. All morning, the image of that scrawny cat had festered in the back of my mind. Should I have returned home and started the journey over? Was I about to be punished?

I left the room I'd been cleaning and hurried down the hallway. Patients in wheelchairs lined the walls as they waited for the cafeteria to open for lunch.

Had I done something wrong? I mentally reviewed the four hours I'd worked so far. I'd reported on time and performed the usual duties without incident. Still, the feeling of guilt and foreboding stayed with me as I approached the receptionist in the front lobby.

"You called me. Violet Henderson."

The middle-aged woman intimidated me with her perfect bouffant and the icy, precise manner in which she routed incoming calls and bossed everyone around—visitors as well as staff.

"I know who you are," she said snippily, as if I'd insulted her competence. "Visitor for you."

"Me?"

She pointed a bony finger, with its red-lacquered fingernail, to the corner of the lobby.

Detective Kimbrel rose from one of the well-worn upholstered chairs. His tall presence dominated the room, and he walked toward me, his expression solemn and searching.

"Miss"—he glanced at the receptionist's nameplate on the desk—"Flanders. Is there someplace I can talk in private with Miss Henderson?"

"Down the hall to your right. Third door on the left." With that, she resumed clicking away at her keyboard. We'd been dismissed.

He swept a hand, indicating that I should lead the way. I marched forward, conscious the entire time of Detective Kimbrel behind me, observing my every movement. At the designated door, I entered. Every wall in the residents' library was lined with used paperbacks, mostly romance, medical, and self-help books—all used and hopelessly out of date. A large conference table dominated the center of the room, and I took a seat, folding my hands on its smooth wooden surface.

Kimbrel seated himself across from me. "Sorry to disturb you at work, but there was an important discovery today in the Dalfred case." He paused, letting his words sink in. "Thought you'd want to hear it from me first, before it's broadcast all over the news."

A tightness squeezed my chest. *Ainsley.*

Somewhere in the bowels of the facility, a dinner bell rang, followed by the sound of dozens of squeaking wheels. Another day, another meal in their long lives. It was all so ordinary and so wrong. I broke his gaze and stared down at my clenched hands. They were the hands of someone twice my age—red and calloused from scrubbing all day, every day. My "work therapy" at the state-run mental hospital had consisted of handling wet clothes in the laundry room and wiping down cafeteria tables. It had prepared me well for this job. The psychiatrists and social workers might even call me a success—that is, if their aim for patients was set incredibly low. I'd certainly hit such a target.

Not that any of that mattered.

The detective hadn't come to deliver good news. My old, sweet fantasy that Ainsley was alive died, right here in the library with its musty books. Printed relics that no patients ever bothered to check out.

He spoke again, abruptly shattering the silence. "After the lake was drained, construction workers—"

"Stop! Please. I can't bear it." I jumped up, and the wooden chair toppled to the ground. I walked to the small window on the back wall and stared out into the bright sunshine. Just a few more seconds alone with my delusions of reuniting with my childhood friend. But his voice cut into the brief silence.

"They found a young girl's skeletal remains. Forensics hasn't yet confirmed that it's Ainsley Dalfred, but I have no doubt that it's her."

A garbled sound erupted from my throat. Of course it was Ainsley. I closed my eyes, conjuring her laugh, her smooth, sleek body as she swam in the moonlight. All gone forever.

Had I done this? Had I killed Ainsley?

Surely not. I had loved my best friend.

Oh, but you were so angry with her that last night. And what about all those lost hours when you roamed the woods? You must have killed her. Murdered your best friend, and when you realized what you'd done, you became so traumatized that you erased it from your brain. Locked it up tight and buried it so deep that you've lost the memory forever.

Damn it. I wanted to remember. I wanted to know if I was a monster or a victim of some bizarre circumstance.

The scent of leather and soap drew near. Detective Kimbrel was beside me. He reached out an arm as if he wanted to place it over my shoulders and comfort me, but then he let it drop by his side.

"Have you told Ainsley's parents yet?" I asked.

"Yes. I stopped in on the way over here."

"Do they . . ." I bit my lip to stop the tremble. "Do they think I'm responsible?"

"They're grieving right now. Angry too. Give them time."

He'd skirted my question, but his meaning was clear. "They think I killed her," I said dully.

"Does it matter what they think?"

I stared into his dirt-brown eyes, trying to understand him. Shouldn't cops be suspicious and probing? Hell, I found it suspicious that he *wasn't* suspicious. It made me uncomfortable, as though he had some secret knowledge I wasn't privy to, seeing as how I must surely be a person of interest in the case. "You've always been kind to me. Thank you."

"I've never thought you killed that girl."

"Why?" I asked abruptly. "Seems like I'd be your most logical suspect, since I was the last one to see her alive."

"There's no motive," he pointed out. "And it doesn't fit with what I've observed of your character."

"But you don't know me," I blurted. "Not really. You interviewed me as a child, after I'd experienced the worst trauma of my life. Hardly the basis to make such a judgment."

"I knew your mother. And I've consulted with your treatment staff over the years."

That took me by surprise, and not in a good way. "I thought my medical records were confidential."

"They are. But they did let me know you were well behaved and cooperative. No record of violence."

Me and the rest of the patients were mostly too overmedicated to get riled enough to fight. But if the reports were a check in my favor, I wouldn't argue against it.

"Plus, look at you now," Kimbrel continued. "You're working at a nursing home, helping the elderly. To me, that shows you have a compassionate nature."

"It's a job," I remarked dryly. "Helps pay the bills."

"Your supervisors say you do an excellent job here and that the patients like you."

"You've been questioning Cora about me?"

"Only once, yes."

Anger and humiliation washed over me. I'd considered Cora a friend, or at least thought she liked me well enough, since she used to work for my family. She also had known me as a child before this black cloud of doubt had stained my reputation. An even worse thought struck. "Why are you really here?"

"I told you. I didn't want you to hear the news from television."

"Got to be more to it than that. Isn't now about the time you warn me not to leave town?"

"It probably would be for the best."

I'd had no plans to leave Normal until I'd saved money and knew Dad's medications were aboveboard. Still, I'd liked having my options open.

I paced the room.

"What's the problem? You weren't planning to leave soon, were you?" he asked.

"No. I just don't relish the possibility of being put away again. I spent too many years of my life under forced confinement. Yeah, you can call it treatment instead of jail, but the fact is I couldn't make my own decisions, not even something as simple as what I wanted to eat for supper. And I couldn't leave either. So you can see why any threat to my freedom scares me, Detective Kimbrel."

"Understandable."

"Do you think there will be new evidence? Is there any chance I'm in danger of arrest?"

"We're unlikely to uncover new clues after all the time that's elapsed. But like I said, I never believed you guilty of murder. From all accounts, you two were close friends."

Had he never worked crimes involving betrayals of family or friends? I brushed the unbidden thought aside. If he considered me innocent, then lucky me.

"Were her remains . . . I mean, was there much left of it? Was everything intact? Are you sure it's Ainsley?"

"Forensics will confirm from her teeth, but that's only a matter of time. All that remains is the skeleton, and there's evidence of blunt-force trauma to her skull on the right side. Far as I'm concerned, that doesn't necessarily spell murder. She could have accidentally hit her head on a rock when diving and lost consciousness, and then the current dragged her body out from the river to where it empties into the lake."

"You make it all sound so . . . simple. So cut and dry." I returned to my chair and crossed my arms and legs. "Anything else I should know?"

He hesitated. "Cement blocks were found near her body. That's problematic."

"Why?"

"The body might have been weighted down."

His words drummed through me. I couldn't have gone to such elaborate, calculating lengths, could I? If only I could remember. "What do you think the town's reaction will be when word gets out?"

"Not going to lie. Everyone will be talking and speculating. Might be rough for you for a few days or weeks."

"Or forever. If I stayed. Even if the coroner rules it an accidental death, people in Normal will always speculate that I killed Ainsley."

"Then leave." Kimbrel rose to his feet. "There's nothing to tie you down here, is there? Your mother's dead, your father's mind is gone, and your sister . . ."

"What about Delaney?"

"Like I said, I read some reports from your hospitals. Family visits were rare. It's not like you're close with the two who remain."

I followed him to the door on shaky legs. In the hallway, he faced me. "Didn't Hy—didn't your mother leave you any money? Rumor had it that she inherited a nice sum after her parents died."

"It's all gone. Well, I take that back. There's less than a hundred and fifty dollars remaining in the trust fund account she left me. But the money went to my care, and other things." I was sure my bitterness must have shown.

"What other things?"

"Personal care items, trips." My lips pressed together. I was talking too much. Wouldn't look good for me to complain about my lack of money, considering the news he'd just delivered.

"What trips?"

I considered his question. Not a smart idea to lie. "Look, I'm not going to cover up for my sister. Delaney spent a lot of my money on herself. Clothes, jewelry, vacations—it all added up."

We reached the lobby, and he stopped abruptly. Anger flashed across his face. "Hy intended it for you. Not only is what Delaney did immoral, it's illegal. She must have falsified receipts. I can speak to the bank manager on your behalf."

"I've already spoken to him. Let it go," I said dully. "I don't have money for a court battle, and even if I did, the trust money's gone. My sister has had a lot of stress over the years taking care of our dad alone and keeping up that great big ole house. Hardly fair for me to show up and expect an inheritance."

"If your mother only knew, she'd—"

"Forget it." The news of Ainsley's death was too fresh for me to quibble over the lost money. It was gone, and I'd have to make a fresh start in life using my own wits.

He extended his hand. "This all must have come as a shock. Why don't you leave work early today? Prepare your father and sister."

No sense in preparing family. Dad was wrapped in his own world, and Delaney thought the worst of me anyway. Yet I hesitated. Could I really do that—take an afternoon off just for me? It seemed so decadent. I wasn't worthy.

"Go on," he urged. "Ring your boss. It's worth a try."

"Maybe." I slanted my gaze toward the receptionist, whose hands had stilled on the keyboard. Old witch was listening to every word.

"I'll call you if there are any developments." He reached into his pocket and pulled out a business card. "If you need me—"

"You already gave me one."

He tucked it back in his pocket. "Ah, right. Goodbye, then."

I watched as he exited the building, trying to pinpoint why he disturbed me. His appearance was like any other middle-aged man I'd ever met—except for his long legs, which placed him head and shoulders above most people. His manner was also common in older southern men—formally polite in an old-fashioned way.

I shrugged and returned to my duties. Fine for someone in his position to spur-of-the-moment ask for an afternoon off, but my job was still too new, too vital, for me to risk any type of censure. I loaded steaming trays onto the meal cart and then began my familiar lunchtime duties, delivering them room by room. On the surface, the routine provided a modicum of comfort for the underlying turmoil churning in my gut.

She's dead. Dead, dead, dead. With every squeaky turn of the cart's wheels, the refrain spun in my mind. It rutted into the deep recesses, impressing the finality of the situation to my brain and heart.

Room 429, Emmeline Upchurch. The last delivery. In thirty minutes, I'd repeat the whole procedure in reverse, collecting trays and returning them to the cafeteria for washing.

"Good afternoon, Mrs. Upchurch. Hope you're hungry." I pasted on a polite smile and placed the steaming silver tray on the table by her bed.

Her faded gray eyes narrowed at me as she roused herself to a seated position. "For this rubbish? Not particularly."

"Should be something there you'll like. A buttered roll, maybe?" Her complaints didn't faze me. I heard a variation of the same from most patients. I lifted the top of the tray and started unwrapping the cellophane covering the Jell-O.

"Don't touch that!" Mrs. Upchurch scolded. "I don't want the likes of you handling my food."

What the hell? I stepped back and faced her. Complaints I was used to, personal insults not so much. The woman was perpetually unpleasant, but not at this level of nasty. Maybe she was just a germophobe, though, and didn't mean it personally.

"Is there a problem?" I asked, keeping the polite, though forced, smile on my face. "I can assure you, I washed my hands prior to touching the trays."

She glared at the plate of roast beef and potatoes. "For all I know, you might have slipped arsenic in them mashed potatoes."

I snorted. Mrs. Upchurch was too ridiculous to take offense with. Poor lady must suffer from dementia, same as my dad. I kept my tone reasonable and cajoling. "Why would I poison you? Go on and eat your food." I reached for the tray top. "I'll leave you to it."

Mrs. Upchurch delivered a sharp slap against my knuckles. I pulled my hand back and shook out the sting. The old biddy was surprisingly strong. Pretty feisty for a ninety-two-year-old woman who must weigh all of 115 pounds.

"Don't eat it, then. Your choice."

I spun on my heel and grabbed the cart. Disproportionate anger blazed through me like a burn. Best thing for me to do was get out of there quick, before I said or did something that spelled trouble.

"Hey, you! Miss!" Mrs. Upchurch called out. "I saw you on TV. Right before you came in. I know who you are now."

I slowly turned around to face her.

"Thought yer name sounded familiar. Violet Henderson. You was the last person who saw that little girl alive. Alice, was it?"

"Ainsley," I whispered past the burn in the back of my throat.

"She ain't nothing but a bag of bones now." Her crusty lips twisted in malicious pleasure.

Horror pinned me to the spot, rooting my feet into the cheap linoleum flooring.

"What'd you do to yer supposed friend? Hold her head underwater until she couldn't breathe no more?"

This wasn't happening. This crazy ole witch wasn't spewing evil accusations. Mrs. Upchurch licked her dry lips, as if she could taste my fear.

"Or were you two fighting over a boy, and you knocked her upside the head?"

A boy. Sammy Granger. Black floaters whirled across my eyes. My peripheral vision narrowed until Emmeline Upchurch became a tiny pinprick figure. She was so very far away from me, and I was alone with the encroaching darkness.

I curled my fingers into my palms and made tight fists. Nails dug into flesh, until the pain grounded me to the moment. The here and now. Room 429. Emmeline Upchurch.

Go.

I left the cart in her room. In the hallway, I strode past the rows of doors, many of them open to reveal droning television sets. Before, it had been merely background noise, but today I imagined some well-groomed reporter saying my name while images of a barren lake and a body bag whisked into a state vehicle played in the background.

Detective Kimbrel had been right. I should leave work at once. My legs broke into a sprint as I headed to the break room to gather my purse. I took deep breaths, but my lungs were a sieve that couldn't hold oxygen. I bit the inside of my mouth, again concentrating on the pain. Get to the car. Take an anxiety pill.

In the lobby, the receptionist frowned at me. "Where are you going?"

"Family emergency," I lied. "Tell Cora I'm sorry." More deep breaths that couldn't fuel my racing heart. "Gotta get home."

Outside, I scrambled to my car, locked myself in, and dry swallowed two pills. Cool air-conditioning blasted my face. I leaned back in the seat and shut my eyes, forcing myself to take long, slow breaths. I don't know how long I sat there in the car's safe cocoon, but eventually, my body calmed, and lethargy set in.

On the downside, I didn't want to move, much less drive anywhere. My temporary home held no joy for me, and I couldn't go back to work and face Cora yet. Dispiritedly, I pulled out of the employee parking lot. With any luck, Delaney would be out, and Dad would be napping. I'd love a nap myself before delivering the news to them about Ainsley's remains.

Delaney was going to throw one helluva screaming fit. Might even throw me out on the streets.

The way I felt, I wasn't so sure I'd oppose being kicked out of the house.

Chapter 22

VIOLET

Present day

The house was, thankfully, cool and dark and silent as a graveyard at midnight. I slipped inside, shutting the door softly behind me. Dad was asleep on the couch. I tiptoed to the back window and spotted Delaney weeding her herbs and vegetables. My shoulders sagged in relief. I'd be able to sleep off the effects of the anxiety pills before the evening news, and then, with any luck, I'd calmly tell her about the detective's visit.

I started past the kitchen door, then stopped. Now would be as good a time as any to take new photos of Dad's pill bottles while Delaney was occupied. Quickly, I opened the top-right cabinet drawer.

They were gone.

Nothing remained except a few odds and ends. I checked the drawer beside it, scrambling through more junk. Still nothing. Systematically, I checked every cabinet drawer and even opened the cookie jar—but Delaney had moved them. They could be stored anywhere in the damn house.

I couldn't deal with that right now. One problem at a time. I trudged up the stairs and then sank onto my bed, not even bothering to kick off my shoes. A familiar drowsiness settled into my body, and I gladly surrendered to the void of sleep.

~

Bam bam bam.

I startled awake at the pounding on my bedroom door. A second later, it flew open, slamming into the opposite wall so forcefully that the knob tore a hole in the drywall.

Delaney's eyes were wild as lightning, and her hair was frizzled into a tangled mess. Fury emanated from every inch of her taut body. "*You,*" she said in a loud, deep voice. She pointed a finger at me, advancing slowly toward the bed.

I clutched a nearby pillow and drew it onto my lap. "Wh-what?" I asked.

"You could have warned me. I heard that a cop visited you at work today."

I glanced out the window and saw that the sun had set low and the shadows had lengthened. "Guess you've already watched the evening news."

Delaney brushed aside my comment. "But no, you don't say a word. You come home early and creep into bed. Just left Dad and me to hear it announced to the world."

"Sorry. I wanted to tell you before the news came on, but I overslept and—"

Delaney stalked over to the bed and towered over me. Her index finger jabbed at the air, only inches from my face. "You're nothing but a selfish bitch."

Her lips spittled my face, and I scrambled backward. But I wasn't quick enough. She tried to grab my arm, and I slapped her hand away. Again, Delaney came at me, and I shoved her. She fell against my nightstand on the tumble down. Blood dribbled from a cut on her forehead, and she dazedly touched the wound, the blood coating her fingers.

"I-I'm sorry," I stammered. I hadn't meant to hurt her; I'd only wanted to protect myself.

I wasn't sure my apology even registered with Delaney. The dazed look on her face was replaced by one of righteous anger. She rose and came at me again, grabbing a handful of my hair. My scalp burned, and I screamed in pain. Delaney let go and placed her hands on her hips, still clenching a clump of my hair that hung from her right hand.

Angry tears tracked down my face, and I swiped them away as I stood. "Don't you ever raise a hand to me again. You got that?" My voice choked on a sob. I sounded like a pathetic wimp, not someone to be taken seriously.

"You started it," she said, pointing to the blood on her forehead. "And if you don't like it, get the fuck out of my house."

"It's not *your* house. It's Dad's," I shot back.

"Fine. You want Dad to be the one to throw you out? I'll have a little chat with him."

Her threat brought me up short. A little chat? In light of the huge quantity of pills and Dad's warning of her herbal teas, I had no doubt that Delaney thoroughly controlled our dad. If I left him alone with her, how far would she go to finally own the house and all that was left in the bank? For all I knew, she might even have arranged an insurance policy as a bonus.

I couldn't leave him alone with her. He hadn't been a great father, but he was still my dad. I'd gather information about all the damn medicine she gave him, and then I'd have him evaluated by another doctor. I stifled my pride.

"Give me the rest of the summer, Delaney. I need to make arrangements. I need to draw a few paychecks. Then I promise I'll leave here and never come back."

She glared at me, her chest still heaving in anger. "You're an embarrassment to me. Always have been. You and your damn crows and all your sneaking out into the woods to meet Ainsley."

I lifted my chin. "I've done nothing to be ashamed of."

An ugly smirk twisted her lips. "We both know that's a lie. You got into an argument with Ainsley, and you killed her."

"Stop saying that! I don't remember what happened that night."

"But *I* do. You confessed to me that you did it."

Not this again. My ears burned, and a loud ringing echoed inside them. "You're lying. Trying to poison my mind."

"Am I?"

I stared at her, shaking with frustration. Had I killed Ainsley? *That* was the question that haunted my nights, and Delaney damn well knew my vulnerability.

A beating of feathers rustled near the balcony. At the door, three crows cawed, and one of them tapped his beak on the glass pane.

"It's time for their night feeding," I noted woodenly. I started to the door, hoping she'd go away, but Delaney grabbed my arm.

"Is that all you care about? Those damn crows? I'm trying to talk to you."

I snatched my arm out of her grasp. "There's nothing more to say."

"What are we going to do about the gossip? Now that her skeleton's been found, everyone will be talking about that girl again. Dragging our family name through the mud."

"This is about me, not you and Dad. I'm the one they'll gossip about. If we're lucky, it will blow over eventually."

Delaney snickered at my half-hearted lie and began pacing my room, plucking at the frayed hem on the bottom of her shirt. She mumbled under her breath, the sounds so soft and garbled that I couldn't understand her words. I wished she would just go. All I wanted was to feed my birds and be left alone. Suddenly, she halted and gave me a peculiar look.

"What?" I asked warily.

"I have a solution to our problem. Let's sit down and talk."

Delaney again sat on my bed and patted the mattress, placating me with a smile. "Sorry. Just had to vent some. I'm not mad anymore."

Would I never get used to her mercurial mood swings? Delaney of the sunshine and the storms. I rubbed my aching scalp where she'd pulled out a chunk of my hair. No way I was getting in striking range again.

"Ah, c'mon," she urged. "Don't you want to hear my great idea?"

Not really, but she obviously wasn't leaving until she'd had her say. I dragged the chair from my vanity and plopped it a good six feet from where she sat. I folded my arms across my chest. "Shoot."

"Okay. First, after all these years, if your memory hasn't returned by now, it's not happening."

"That's not true. My therapist told me that coming home, where the trauma occurred, might help jog my memories. Sometimes, all it takes is for one of the senses to be reawakened—a certain smell, or a shifting of light, or the texture of an object. And then all the pieces of the puzzle come together in one fell swoop."

"And has that happened?" she prompted.

"Only a few bits and snippets of memory," I admitted. "But I have hope."

I pictured Doctor Lipscomb in her navy suit jacket and matching pants, the thick glasses that had sat upon her small pug nose. *A remembered sensation can spark a whole series of minirecalls*, she'd explained. *It's possible that you might one day recover all or partial memory of what occurred in your fugue state.*

She'd gone on to explain that it was more likely I'd never remember the lost hours, but that fact was none of my sister's business.

Delaney gave me a pitying smile. "Maybe it's for the best that you never recall all the details of that night."

"I want the truth," I insisted.

She didn't answer me, and the silence thickened between us. The crows outside cawed louder, signaling their impatience.

"Even if the truth means knowing you killed Ainsley?" she asked.

A pressure tightened my chest. "Yes," I answered, the single syllable strangling my lungs.

"I'll tell you what you said to me that night."

Doubts suddenly assailed me, but I pushed them aside. It was time. "Go ahead."

"After Mom and Dad had gone downstairs to talk to the police, you slipped into my bedroom and stood by my bed. Mom had insisted you shower, and you'd changed into your nightgown. You stood there staring at me with these huge, sad eyes." Delaney paused a heartbeat, as if reliving the moment. "Then I asked, 'Did you do it?' I didn't think you were going to answer at first, but you whispered, 'Yes. I hate Ainsley.'"

"No!" I jumped out of the chair. "I wouldn't have said that."

Delaney rose and came to me, drawing me into a quick embrace. I pushed her away.

"Oh, Violet. It's okay, honey. You were a child, and you acted in a moment of anger." She stroked my cheek, and her cold fingers trailed down my face and neck. My nerves tingled as if a cluster of spiders was crawling my flesh.

Again, I took a step back.

"Think about what I told you," Delaney said sympathetically. "Maybe that will help your memory."

I wouldn't—I couldn't—stand another minute of this conversation.

"I have to feed my birds," I said abruptly, striding to the corner of my bedroom and scooping a large quantity of shelled peanuts from the bag I'd purchased at the Feed and Seed store. I walked toward the balcony, holding the silver scooper of peanuts in one hand.

"Don't you want to hear my idea?" Delaney asked.

I'd have no peace until she spoke her mind. I unlocked the french doors and silently waited.

"The best solution for all of us is for you to speak to that detective again—what's his name? The one that visited you today."

"How did you know he came to see me?"

"I know everything that happens around Normal. Most people do. It's how a small town operates."

I sighed. "His name's Boone Kimbrel. What's your big idea?"

Her eyes widened, as if I should have figured out her meaning. "To confess, of course."

"Confess to a murder I don't remember committing?"

"You don't have to decide tonight, but think about it."

"And how does this help *you?*" I asked dryly. "Wouldn't it just be more bad publicity involving the family name?"

"Yes. It'd be hell for a few weeks or months, depending on how long it took for a new scandal to happen. But eventually, it would be over. Mystery solved. Everyone could move on with their lives."

"You mean you could move on with me locked up and out of your hair."

"Not at all. You'd be getting treatment again. And surely you wouldn't have to stay long? You were a minor when this happened. And really, it was all so long ago."

"No," I ground out.

"Think of the relief it would be for Mr. and Mrs. Dalfred to finally know the truth."

That was a low punch to the gut. I worked my mouth, but no words escaped.

"It would all be for the best," Delaney insisted. "You'd serve a year or two at some treatment facility, and then you wouldn't have this hanging over your head anymore. Once released, you could move somewhere far away. Make a fresh start in life."

A hot darkness exploded within me, and I lifted my hand, slinging the scooper of peanuts at Delaney. "I did *not* kill Ainsley!"

My shout echoed in the room, and even the crows stopped their squawking.

Delaney calmly shook out a couple of peanuts that had landed in her thick hair. "Temper, temper," she chided. "Better keep it in check, Violet. You get angry enough, I'm afraid you might commit murder." She paused a moment. "Again."

Delaney left me then, turning away and sauntering out the door.

I sank to my knees among the spilled peanuts and buried my face in my hands. A soft peck sounded beside me, breaking through my haze of grief. Lined along the bottom of the french doors, six crows intently regarded me. A reluctant smile turned up the corners of my mouth. Each had their head cocked at a slightly different angle, as if, as a collective, they could piece together what was happening.

Or it could be they just wondered why their meal hadn't been delivered yet.

Chapter 23

VIOLET

Present day

Of course, now I couldn't sleep. Not after that long afternoon nap, and not after Delaney's "helpful" suggestion that I turn myself in for murder. Gingerly, I touched the bald spot on my scalp where she'd ripped out a chunk of hair.

I opened my nightstand drawer and picked up the amber bottle of sleeping pills. Did I really want to do this? Spend my life doped up just as I had in the mental health facility? I flung the bottle to the floor. It was two a.m., and if I took them now, I'd be groggy at work tomorrow morning. Best to just ride out the insomnia. Go to bed early tomorrow night and get back into a normal routine.

The long night stretched before me, hours of alternating boredom and worry. Stupid me; I'd thought it'd be a relief knowing whether Ainsley was dead or alive. I hadn't been prepared for this profound shock and grief from the news of her death.

The lavender walls and little-girl-style bedspread weighed on my nerves. They were reminders that, in some ways, it was as if my own life had stopped the night Ainsley had disappeared. I opened the french doors and stepped out onto the balcony. The night air was fresh, with a light breeze, and the full moon beckoned—a lime orb set against a black velvet sky littered with diamond stars. The constellations were brilliant and clear here without the town's light pollution.

What a shame the crows couldn't keep me company in the lonely night. It would be hours before they stirred at dawn. My gaze drifted from Delaney's well-tended garden to the dark silhouette of the tree line. Although it wasn't visible from my perch, I knew the Alabama River ran just past that copse of trees. I imagined the sound of its rushing water, the damp-earth smell of its shore, and the feel of its liquid caress on my hot skin. It tantalized me like the memory of a sweet dream that slipped away from consciousness seconds after awakening. A dream forever lost.

It taunted as well as tantalized. The place where one life had ended and another had become stunted. The place I'd roamed in those few hours that had altered the course of my life—and I couldn't remember a damn second of what had transpired. How could I ever know and accept myself without knowing if I were a murderer or a victim of some bizarre accident? Heat pressed into my palms as I gripped the iron railing.

The black void beneath tugged at me like a seducing demon. Topple over into the darkness and end it all. My third-story bedroom was plenty high enough, and the ground below a hard cement slab of a patio. I pictured my body flying in the air, three seconds of descending terror, a flash of pain, and then . . . nothing.

I backed away until cool glass pressed against my thin pajamas, bracing my dark fancies. Jump from a three-story house? I'd likely end up cracking my spine and then be forced to endure the mercy of Delaney's care. That hadn't worked out so well for Dad, and he used to adore her, the precious older daughter born from his beloved first wife. In his eyes, Delaney had shone like a rare jewel—sunny and bright, the child of his true love. And toward the end, he'd increasingly alienated himself from me as his and Mom's fighting worsened.

No good came of reliving those memories, and I returned inside, away from the balcony's dizzying height.

As if being pulled by invisible marionette strings held by some cruel god, I stuffed my feet in a pair of slippers, walked out of my room, and crept down the hallway and stairs. The house was dark and creaky, as though it were a sentient beast that lay sound asleep and snoring. I grabbed the flashlight we always kept on the dining room chifforobe and quietly let myself out. The grass was sleek with dew. I passed the vegetable-and-herb garden and kept walking, a sleepwalker drawn by the magnetic pull of her subconscious. The droning and chirruping of insects grew as I entered the woods, a loud static, a monotone that fueled my brain's plodding insistence. The rush of water roared in my ears now, a waterfall of doom. I heard and smelled it before I reached the cliff's edge. Silver glinted and flashed on the moonlit river. I arched the flashlight's beam across the canopies of trees and saw that someone had cut down the dangling rope we used to swing on. Only a short coil of rough hemp remained on the oak limb to mark where it had been.

Whoo whoo. A barred owl screeched once and then followed that with the classic hooting call that repeated twice and for all the world sounded like a human calling, "Who cooks for you? Who cooks for you?"

Rage. Remembered rage vibrated my cells. A dissonant piano note struck over and over and fevered my brain. I gasped and clutched my temples with both hands as a memory sliver resurfaced from some dark crevice in my mind.

~

Adrenaline spikes my blood, and I ache for release from a terrible anger and hurt.

Ainsley's hand latches onto my right forearm—she wants to talk more. Fury consumes me, as if I'm a wounded wild animal that's been cornered. She spins me around, and with my free hand, I slap her face. Hard.

She gasps and lets go of me, taking a step backward. Surprise and then anger play across her face, and she comes at me, intent on retaliation. I don't think; I act. Her body shoves against mine, fists flailing in hammer blows.

"Get away from me!" I scream.

~

As suddenly as the memory resurfaced, it stopped—as if someone had pressed the off button on a television set. Click. My mind was a gray static of nothingness. I squeezed my eyes shut, trying to sink back into that awful night's replay, but it was no use. The curtain had been drawn, leaving more questions than answers.

We'd gotten into a physical altercation. But why? What had happened next? Evidently, I'd been the clear victor, as there hadn't been any significant bruises or scratches on me in the following days.

What more had I done to Ainsley?

Chapter 24

HYACINTH

July 2, 2007

Some faint scratching noise pierced my light sleep, and I turned on my side. I regretted this immediately as I caught a whiff of Parker's bourbon breath. He was dead to the world, as usual, after a round of after-dinner drinks. At least he wasn't physically abusive anymore when drunk. Scared the shit out of him that time I'd called the police. We'd established a truce, Parker and I. We stayed together for the money and reputation.

But I wasn't sure how much longer I could stand living here. Delaney only grew more troublesome with age and showed no signs of maturing into a decent, self-sufficient young lady. I feared how she might influence Violet, who was going through a bit of a bumpy adolescence. To my mind, she was too sensitive and intense about her attachment to the crows and to her best friend, Ainsley. Her only friend, as far as I could tell. My Violet was a loner, and that concerned me.

I rolled onto my opposite side and scooted to the edge of the mattress, as far away as possible from my husband. Sighing, I plumped my pillow and tried to drift back to sleep, but it was useless. Sleep eluded me. Might as well go downstairs and read a bit; sometimes that helped these restless nights. I arose, making no attempt to keep quiet, and slipped into the hallway. The floorboards moaned and creaked in the usual places. One day, I'd leave this place, and when I did, I wanted a sleek, modern apartment in a large city. Or a beach cottage in an exotic location. In other words, the total opposite of my current life.

Halfway down the stairs, I paused, listening to the night sounds—the hum of the air conditioner, Parker's snores, a branch scraping against a window. Nothing out of the ordinary, and yet unease prickled the nape of my neck.

Better take a quick peek at Violet. Just two weeks ago, I'd caught her trying to sneak out of her bedroom by climbing down her balcony. She'd claimed she was only going to investigate a shiny object she'd seen on the ground nearby. True, the crows might have dropped another gift for her, but that was hardly unusual, and Violet could have waited until morning to look. I had my suspicions. There'd been various other signs of sneaking out—a window not fully closed, a nightgown with mud on the hem, or damp hair in the morning when she came downstairs to breakfast immediately after waking.

I hated being the suspicious sort of mother who snooped around her children's business, but lately, Violet was being difficult. That's what came of hanging around Ainsley Dalfred. I'd never liked that girl. She was sly and fast.

As quietly as possible in our old house, I retraced my steps, proceeded down the hallway to Violet's room, and gently turned the doorknob.

A shaft of moonlight through the half-open window spotlighted an empty bed. I flipped on the light switch and marched over to her bed, drawing back the lavender-and-pink quilt as if she were still a small child I might find curled up at the foot of the blanket. My worst suspicions were confirmed. Violet had indeed sneaked out of the house, and I would bet it wasn't the first time either.

Fueled by anger, I marched to Delaney's room and opened the door without knocking.

"Wh-what—" came her drowsy voice in the darkness.

I switched on the light. "Do you know where Violet is?" I asked without preamble.

Delaney slowly rose up on one elbow and yawned. "She's not in her room?"

"No. Do you know where she might have gone?"

A mischievous gleam lit her eyes. "Maybe she slipped out to go meet someone."

"Who?"

"Someone she wanted to meet in secret."

I didn't care for the smirk that hovered on my stepdaughter's mouth. "If you know something, spit it out. I'm in no mood for your games right now."

"Ainsley Dalfred. Who else?"

I tried to absorb the implication of Delaney's sly manner but came up empty. This was merely Delaney being her usual undelightful self, spreading lies and discord in the path of anyone unfortunate enough to be nearby. A pied piper of mischief and meanness.

"Any idea where they might be?"

I hated the thought of calling Ainsley's mother at this ungodly hour for help. Actually, I hated the thought of communicating with Ainsley's family at all.

"Maybe. But I don't want to be a tattletale." Delaney said the words sweetly, but I knew the venom behind her every word and action. As a child, she'd constantly reported Violet's least little wrongdoing, always trying to make herself look good and Violet look like the naughty one. Parker might not see his daughter for who she truly was, but I damn sure did.

I grabbed Delaney's arm and shook her as hard as I could. "Tell me, damn you."

"Okay. Let go of me." Delaney jerked her arm away, and we glared at one another, each of us breathing hard.

Our hatred had never been so open.

"I know where she might be," Delaney said at last. "Down by the river at the swinging rope. They meet there sometimes."

I knew that spot exactly. It wasn't far from our backyard. When they were young, I used to take the girls there on summer afternoons for picnics and a swim. I spun on my heel and headed to the door.

"I wouldn't go down there, if I were you," Delaney called out in a singsong voice. "Might see something you shouldn't."

My palms itched to slap Delaney, but what good would that do? She was past disciplining, always had been since I'd known her. Besides, I had to find Violet. I slammed the door behind me and heard her laugh.

Forget her. Find Violet and bring her home.

Quickly, I returned to my bedroom and dressed. Parker never stirred. Not that I expected any help or concern from that quarter. I'd never confessed that Violet wasn't his child, but he had plenty of suspicions. I rushed downstairs. What else would I need? A flashlight and a cell phone.

The humid air wrapped around me like an invisible wet blanket. Mosquitoes and gnats buzzed and nipped at exposed skin. I'd flipped on the back-porch light, so now I marched into its yellow beam and followed it out until the air was again a curtain of darkness. Turning on the flashlight, I continued forward, mindful of snakes that might suddenly dart onto my path.

The anger and initial adrenaline rush flushed out of my body, leaving me tired and worried. Was Violet okay? Delaney's malicious insinuations taunted me, and I feared what I might find when I arrived. If Delaney was right, what would I say? What would I do?

I stopped abruptly and trembled as I considered my course. Should I keep going and discover the truth? Or return home and wait for daylight before calling the cops and neighbors? But no, I knew my duty. My child needed me. Again, I marched forward.

This was merely a teenage prank. A lark. Just two girls out for a little fun. They were probably having a good old time swimming.

Violet was going to be in so much trouble when I got ahold of her.

Chapter 25

VIOLET

Present day

"It's raining."

The little boy stood at Libby's front door, a red lollipop clenched in one hand. He regarded me solemnly after that rather obvious weather pronouncement. His brown hair curled in adorable ringlets, and his round, bright eyes were curious.

I bounded up the last couple of porch steps and set my umbrella against the wall.

"So it is. You must be Calvin."

"Calvin Donnell Andrews. I'm this many"—he held up four fingers—"years old. Mommy's in the bathroom," he added.

I bent down on one knee and held out a hand. "Nice to meet you, Calvin. I'm—"

"*Vi-let.* Mommy's friend."

"Right."

Calvin stuffed the lollipop in his mouth and offered me his hand—all red and sticky with sugary goo. Laughing, I ignored the outstretched hand and shook the relatively clean one by his side. "Nice to finally meet you, little man."

I stood and slipped out of my dripping rain jacket.

"Calvin! Where are you?" Libby's voice drifted toward the open door. She appeared two seconds later, hair wrapped in a towel and a harried expression on her fresh-scrubbed face. I blinked, startled at the contrast with how I usually saw her, sporting heavy eye makeup and red lipstick.

She ushered Calvin back through the door and waved me inside. "I saw that look on your face." She grinned. "All my careful artistry takes time."

"You look nice either way—just took a sec to take in your natural beauty."

Libby snickered and scurried to a small kitchen table, where she plucked a wipe from a plastic bin and scrubbed Calvin's sticky fingers and mouth. "Just gave him a bath. You should have been here five minutes ago; he was clean as a pin. Go have a seat in the den. We'll be right there."

Libby's house was small and in an older neighborhood, but I loved the old-fashioned vibe of the architecture, which contrasted with her eclectic, modern style. The sofa was red leather and positioned atop a black shag rug. Bold abstract paintings brightened the walls, and Calvin's photos were proudly displayed among them. A few of his toys lay scattered on the floor, and a pile of women's magazines was stacked on a glass coffee table.

It had a homey, comfortable feel. A place where you could put your feet up and relax.

I'd no sooner settled on the sofa than Calvin ran across the room and plopped beside me.

"You wanna read me a story?" Without waiting for my answer, he picked up a children's book from the coffee table and handed it over.

"I'd love to."

Libby touched the towel turban on her hair. "Sure you don't mind?"

"Positive."

"Okay, that'll give me a chance to comb out my hair. Back in a few."

Calvin cuddled his miniature body against mine. He smelled of soap, shampoo, and a faint trace of sugar. Five pages in, his eyes began to droop closed. It was clearly bedtime, but he fought the good fight against that trap of resting. I remembered that as a kid, I'd hated bedtime, too, convinced that the minute my body betrayed me and drifted off, I would miss all the grown-up fun continuing on without me.

The rain outside intensified, and the night grew darker. I stopped reading and played with one of Calvin's ringlets. His eyes popped open. "Read more," he commanded.

I did. Again, he nodded off. But minutes later, thunder rumbled, and he awoke once more, pulling himself to a standing position. He grabbed onto my hair like it was a pull bar.

"Ouch!" I winced and couldn't stop the gasp of pain.

"What happened?" Libby flew into the room. "Calvin, let go of her hair. You're hurting her."

"I'm sorry." He let go and patted my shoulder. "You got a boo-boo?"

"I'm fine." Involuntary tears ran down my face, belying my words.

Libby frowned and walked closer. "Let me see."

She'd leaned over and run her fingers through my hair before I guessed her intent. I hissed when the tendrils were stirred.

"What's this?" Libby cried. "You've got a bald patch of raw skin. Calvin, what did you do?" She dropped her hands and quickly scanned both her son and the sofa, evidently looking for a clump of my hair.

"Don't scold him. Calvin didn't do it; this happened last night."

"Was an accident?" he asked, again patting my shoulder.

"Right." I mustered a smile that pacified him, but not Libby, judging by her deepening scowl.

"Let me grab my first aid kit. Calvin, time for bed. Come along." She held out her hand, and Calvin sighed heavily before scrambling off the sofa. He recognized the firm command.

"Do I hafta, Mommy?"

"You hafta."

I chuckled as Libby scooped him to her hip, and they headed out. "Back in a jiff," she called over her shoulder.

My new friend was a good mother; that was plain. I couldn't imagine ever having a rug rat of my own. Had never even been on my radar. But a twinge of envy tugged at my heart. Unconditional love was an awesome thing to witness. Maybe one day I'd have that in my life again. When Mom had died, so had the one person who'd loved me in that no-holds-barred kind of way.

I walked to the window, enjoying the light display from distant lightning bolts. Storms intrigued and stirred me. I'd latch on to whatever random happiness came my way and celebrate it. Libby's unexpected friendship was one of those rare, undeserved blessings.

"Now tell me what really happened."

I whirled around, caught off guard.

Libby ran one hand through her still-damp hair and lifted the red plastic box she held in the other. "Time for a little TLC." She sat on the sofa and threw a floor pillow at her feet. "Sit down here, and let me have a look. How'd it happen?"

Sighing, I obeyed and settled on the large throw pillow. Might as well tell her the truth. She'd get it out of me eventually. "Delaney."

"What the hell?"

"I know. I'm still surprised. It's as if we were kids all over again. You'd think we'd have learned some restraint at our age."

"That's it. You're moving out of that house. You can't live with a maniac." Her hand rummaged in the first aid kit, and she pulled out a tube. "This might sting a bit at first, but it's an antibiotic and numbing cream. You'll thank me later."

Cold goop pressed on the burning, raw sore. "Ouch." I jerked out of Libby's grasp.

"All done," she pronounced brightly, handing me the tube. "Take it with you when you leave and reapply as needed."

"Spoken like the mom of a toddler and an experienced LPN." It *did* feel loads better, and I sighed in relief.

"Are you going to press charges?"

"What? No." The idea had never entered my mind. Besides, I had hurt Delaney as well.

"You should."

"I'd rather avoid the police right now, if you know what I mean."

Libby gave me an assessing look. "There's no reason to fear. You had nothing to do with Ainsley's death."

"How can you be so sure of that?" I asked, blinking back unexpected tears. Kindness always did me in, wrecked me deeper than any mean act ever could.

"Because you're a good person."

"But . . . maybe I wasn't always so good."

"We went to the same elementary school and junior high. I saw you around."

"Still . . ." That was hardly a ringing endorsement for understanding my true character.

"One time in elementary school, I saw you stick up for a special ed kid in the cafeteria. Johnny Nix and Carl Randall were making fun of the way he walked, eyes always peeled to the ceiling. The kid ignored them, so they blocked his path and pushed him. Everyone stood around watching. Except you."

I tapped my lip, thinking. "Oh yeah. That little boy who didn't talk and didn't appear to even notice anyone. I'd forgotten all about him."

"You told the bullies to leave the kid alone. His name was Eric . . . something. His family moved away a couple years later. Looking back, I realize he must have had autism. Anyway, I never forgot it—or you."

"Thanks, Libby." My words weren't enough, but they were all I had.

"Stop being so hard on yourself. Anyone who'd stick up for another kid like that—well, it showed me where your heart's at. I don't know what happened to you that night you were found roaming the woods, but I do know you couldn't kill anyone."

I stared down at my hands folded meekly in my lap. Those same hands had slapped Ainsley. What else had I done in my anger? And did I really want to know the truth? I looked up and faced Libby, wondering how much I could reveal.

"But not remembering what happened plays with my mind. I mean, we all have a dark side. Right? What if I were angry with Ainsley, and for, let's say, five seconds—I lost all my self-control? The logical, rational part of my brain might have been overpowered by rage."

Libby shook her head emphatically. "Nope. Don't believe it."

Because you haven't experienced a dark shadow side like I have. Libby was a better person than me, even if she hadn't figured that out yet. But I'd said enough. So I shrugged and summoned a smile. "You have more confidence in me than I have in myself."

"Now, if I'd heard that Delaney had been suspected of murder, I wouldn't be surprised. God, she's always been such a little diva."

I gave an uneasy laugh. "Thanks for staying my friend. It can't be easy with all the news stories and speculation going on now."

"How's everyone treating you?" Libby asked. "Everything okay at Whispering Oaks?"

I nodded. "Soon as I got to work this morning, Cora took me aside and told me not to worry about the news coverage, that I hadn't lied on my application, my references checked out, and staff and patients were pleased with my job performance."

"See? Everyone likes you."

"Not everyone"—Emmeline Upchurch came to mind—"but today wasn't near as bad as I'd imagined."

A few people had eyed me with a new curiosity after last night's news bomb about the discovery of Ainsley's remains. Emmeline Upchurch had turned her nose up whenever I'd entered her room, but the rain had kicked up her arthritis, and my murderous character hadn't been front and center on her mind.

"Seriously, Violet. You need to get out of that house. I don't have a spare bedroom, but you could sleep on the sofa until you find a place."

"I can't."

"Why not?"

Who would feed my crows? But that sounded silly—I couldn't admit such a thought. "It wouldn't be fair to you and Calvin if I stayed here."

Libby opened her mouth to protest, but I rushed on. "Besides, I need to find out if Delaney is overmedicating Dad. I wouldn't feel right leaving and not trying to help him."

"You could report suspected elder abuse to authorities."

I shuddered to think of Delaney's reaction if an investigator arrived on our doorstep.

"You're scared of your sister, aren't you?"

"Maybe a little," I admitted. "But her anger is usually short lived. And she can be nice sometimes too. This morning she apologized and fixed me breakfast."

"Big freaking deal."

"Yeah, but—"

"But what? Delaney attacked you. What was that all about, anyway?"

Heat chased across my face as I remembered I hadn't been entirely innocent in that altercation. "Delaney said I was an embarrassment to the family. Which is true."

"Your dad's past caring. All she's concerned about is herself."

I couldn't deny that truth. "Jeez, Libby. But she's my sister. You know? I do have some good memories of our growing up together. She and Ainsley and I used to . . ." I faltered.

"Go on."

"We had some good times. We'd sneak out of the house at night and meet Ainsley by the river." I thought longingly of those carefree summer nights—the utter freedom of escaping adult supervision and running wild under the moonlit skies. The scent of honeysuckle and the kiss of cool water on bare skin.

Libby's sharp voice interrupted my reverie.

"Was Delaney with you the night Ainsley disappeared?"

"Huh? No. At least . . . no, she must not have been. I do remember being found by my mom and the detective. They led me back to the house. Dad and Delaney were already there, waiting on us."

"Doesn't mean they were home all that night," Libby pointed out.

"But—wait a minute—what are you saying?"

"Hasn't it ever occurred to you that maybe you weren't the last person who saw Ainsley alive?"

"No," I whispered. That wasn't entirely true, though. Early in our rendezvous, I'd heard something . . . a rustling in the distance. A snapped twig and then eerie silence that had prickled my skin. I dismissed this chain of thought. The woods were full of deer, foxes, rabbits, and other roaming creatures. To bring it up only sounded like a lame attempt on my part to cast suspicion on others.

One coral sandal had been found less than six feet from a blood-splattered patch in the sand. Blood had also been found on a boulder in the middle of the river.

Ainsley's spilled blood.

My sandal.

The only physical evidence and clues of what had happened.

"What if Delaney followed you out of the house and you didn't notice? Or your dad might have—"

"Leave my dad out of it," I snapped. He might have been a mean drunk, but to cold-bloodedly track us down and kill . . . no, I couldn't see it.

Libby threw up her hands. "Just throwing out possibilities. Something spooked you that night. Could have been an unexpected encounter with a dangerous man or some punk guys. Lots of people went to that same swing by the river."

"The police looked into that, even had me medically examined to see if I'd experienced any sexual trauma. There was nothing to indicate rape." I shifted in my seat, uncomfortable with the memories of that hospital visit and staring into the overhead fluorescent light as a doctor did something down *there*, where I wouldn't look. Bad enough to feel the cold metallic instrument probe.

"It was so long ago," I said at last. "We may never know what really happened."

"What if there was a way?"

I threw up my hands. How many times had I tortured myself over the years trying to remember what I'd seen that night? What little I remembered, the argument and my push, only damned me further.

"I've tried everything. Different therapies and drugs, hypnosis, revisiting that area in the woods, dream analysis—"

"I'm not talking about your memory."

"Then what do you mean?"

Libby leaned forward. "Have you ever heard of *gaslighting?*"

"Yeah. I've seen that old Bette Davis movie where her cousin tries to drive her insane."

Libby raised her brows. "Can't you see the parallels in your own life? Delaney's trying to make you think you're either mentally incompetent or guilty."

"Maybe." I couldn't deny that my sister had a dangerous temper. But a deliberate, prolonged campaign to drive me insane? Did she really hate me that much?

Libby ticked off incidents on her fingers. "She steals your money and gets you to accept her crime without reporting it. She guilts you into practically being her slave and has you watch your dad in almost all your free time. And then, to top it all off, she tells you to confess to a murder you don't remember committing. And all those misplaced items of yours? The nightmares she claims you have? The way she talks behind your back and lets everyone think you're not quite right? She's gaslighting you, babe."

Rain slashed against the den's bay window, and I startled like a baby bunny rabbit. "An organized campaign to drive me bonkers? Why would she do that?"

"Money."

"We can't have much left, so—"

"You sure about that?"

"I haven't seen a bank statement," I said slowly. "But they don't live like they're wealthy. The house is old and needs work, their cars are old, and they don't ever go anywhere."

The list of Delaney's extravagances spent from my trust fund came to mind. Whatever traveling Delaney had enjoyed had come at my expense.

"Exactly." Libby slammed a hand down on her chair's arm. "Bet she's hoarding every penny of the estate, along with your dad's disability checks. And who knows how much money her lovers slip her on the side?"

I hugged my arms around my knees, drinking in her theory. "So you imagine she wants to have me put away. That way she doesn't have to share any money with me." I placed a hand on my chest and felt comforted by the steady beat of my heart.

"Yep. Prison or the mental home. Either works."

"Come on. A bit far fetched, Libby." But even as I outwardly denied her theory, doubt assailed my mind.

"Money is a powerful motive; don't discount it. Delaney might be gaslighting you so that you appear guilty of the crime. As if you're a mentally unstable person who can't handle the real world because of a secret shame that eats away your sanity. Isn't that what a desperate, greedy woman might do to preserve her way of life?"

Inwardly, I winced. *Secret shame.* A montage of wrongdoing squirmed like a rumba of rattlesnakes in my belly, all roused for a lethal strike—my angry hands jabbing at Ainsley, screams absorbed in the malignant night.

"You've watched too many old movies." I gave a weak laugh and stretched out my feet, crossing them at the ankles. "And even if you're right, it doesn't help solve the mystery of Ainsley's murder. Don't worry about me—I can handle Delaney until I get the opportunity to move out. Can we drop all this and play cards or something?"

"First, hear me out. I have an idea."

How could I graciously refuse? "Go on," I said reluctantly.

"Reverse gaslighting."

I blinked at the fervent gleam in her eyes. "Meaning . . . ?"

"Give Delaney a taste of her own medicine. See if you can rattle her, expose her darkest secrets."

"You're assuming she has some."

"Don't we all? If she knows something about the murder, you can shake it out of her. I wouldn't put anything past your sister. For all you know, she might have killed Ainsley."

I let Libby's words absorb into me and weighed their truth. Delaney was a lot of things—but a murderer? "You're forgetting the most important point here," I said slowly. "Delaney had no motive to kill Ainsley."

"That you know of."

A hollow laugh rattled in my throat. "This is ridiculous."

"Isn't it worth a shot? What have you got to lose?"

I gently patted the bald patch on my scalp. This was what happened when you crossed Delaney or didn't jump to do her bidding. How far would my sister go if she discovered I was deliberately trying to sabotage her plans—if she indeed harbored such a scheme?

"Come on, Violet," she said gruffly. Libby's fingers dug into the chair's armrests, and she watched me with an unnatural intensity in her heavily mascaraed eyes.

Suspicion skittered down my back. Slow I might be, but I eventually caught on. "What do you have against my sister?"

"Nothing." Libby shrugged, but I caught the flash of guilt in her eyes.

"Out with it."

"Okay, okay. She might have stolen an old boyfriend. But that was a long time ago. I'm over it."

Libby had a personal agenda. *That* was why she'd befriended me so quickly and unexpectedly that day in the drugstore. *That* was why she fed me misgivings on Delaney's character. And *that* was why she wanted to turn me away from my sister.

I rose. "No, you're not over it. Never were. You're trying to use me to get back at Delaney."

"That's not true. I swear it isn't. Okay, maybe at first, but not now."

I grabbed my purse and rushed out the door. On the porch, I picked up my umbrella but didn't bother opening it. What did I care if the rain soaked me through and through? Maybe a good soaking would wash away some of my stupid.

"Hey, don't leave like this, Violet." Libby followed me out to the porch. "Come back, and let's talk."

I trudged to the car and got in without a backward glance. Should have known from the get-go that Libby's sudden friendship was fishy. I was a damn pariah in the town. Nobody wanted shit to do with me. I gunned the car's motor. Through the windshield wipers, I spotted a glimpse of Libby standing on the porch, arms wrapped around herself, staring forlornly into the darkness.

A momentary twinge of sympathy surged through me, but I suppressed the urge to return to Libby's house with its offer of false comfort and false friendship.

Tires squealing, I peeled out of her driveway, reckless as the storm. Was it possible Delaney had killed Ainsley? If so, why? Pure meanness? Images of my sister exploded in my mind in a dizzying series, illuminated like flashbulbs against a black canvas—Delaney holding out a pill bottle to Dad, handing me the glass of herbal tea, the rage in her eyes as she'd grabbed my hair, sneaking in shopping bags from her trip to Birmingham, throwing a stone at the crow. Suspicion unearthed something dark and long suppressed within me. The string of tiny bells dangling from the front interior window jangled like a warning. The windshield wipers swished to and fro, *split* and *splat*. I fell into a mild road trance.

Split splat. Get Delaney back.

Splat split. Give Delaney fits.

Whatever else I thought of Libby, she was right. I was sick of playing the pawn in my sister's schemes and had been pushed to my limits. Time for a little pushback. In psycho-speak, time to sharpen my assertive skills. Who knew what buried secrets might be unearthed? Delaney was a well of deception.

Mind trickery. After all my years living with Alabama's most crazy, this should be a snap. I'd break Delaney like a twig and pry the truth from her lying lips. If she was the one who'd really killed Ainsley . . . I'd make her pay. Serve up my own dish of southern-fried justice.

And I knew just how to start the process.

Chapter 26

BOONE

Present day

This was a fool's errand Josh and I were on. In his zeal to solve the Dalfred case, Josh had insisted we drive out to question an old suspect in the disappearance.

Unless he'd moved without notifying local law enforcement—which in itself was a parole violation for sexual offenses—Gerald "Dinky" Stedmyer still lived at the end of a pothole-riddled dirt road that abutted the Alabama River. The farther Josh and I drove, the narrower the road became, until low-lying tree limbs scratched the vehicle. The high-pitched grating of metal chafed my already dour mood.

"You sure you know where you're going, Kimbrel?" Josh asked, frowning as he looked out the passenger window.

"Lived here all my life," I muttered, swerving to avoid a pothole large enough to do serious fender damage. This road was even worse than I remembered. That, or time had deteriorated the already appalling road conditions. Moss-laden trees encroached upon the area, and the packed dirt of the road had eroded to the point that it was almost unnavigable.

"How much further? Maybe we should ditch the car and walk the rest of the way."

"Can't stop now," I answered, not without a bit of petty satisfaction. "No way to turn the car around until we reach the clearing by the river."

"How much further?"

"Can't rightly say. Could still be a ways to go." I glanced at Josh, who was sharply dressed for fashion and not for comfort. "This was your idea," I reminded him.

Now that Ainsley's remains had been found and Josh was reviewing the old files, my rookie partner was insistent on becoming a hero and solving this case. I suspected that meant pinning the blame on the most convenient target. Which was why I found myself on this ridiculous drive. Josh had leaped at the theory that Dinky Stedmyer was a prime candidate for the murder. Upon learning of a recently released sexual offender around the time of Ainsley's disappearance, Josh had seized on the notion that I had been incompetent in my initial interviews with the suspect and had overlooked some vital clue that would establish his guilt.

"Yeah, yeah. Rub it in about my suit." Josh shrugged out of his jacket and undid another button on his neatly pressed oxford shirt.

It had been all I could do not to grin outright when Josh had arrived at the office this morning, eager for his first murder-investigation interview. Instead, I'd merely quirked a brow at this rookie behavior. "You going to be mighty hot and uncomfortable before the day's end."

Ker-thunk.

My stomach dropped as if I'd nosedived on an amusement park ride. The unmistakable sound of scraping metal followed the thump. Our fender was toast. "Shit!"

"Sounded bad," Josh offered unnecessarily.

Well, now, wasn't my partner the observant one?

"Want me to get out and take a look?"

"No point. Car still runs." Dan Thornell was going to have a fit when the automotive-repair bill crossed his desk later.

Carefully, I rounded a bend in the path—it could hardly be called a road at this point—and abruptly landed in a small clearing. An ugly cement block house awaited us. It was painted a garish turquoise that was covered with large splotches of mold. Its dark windows winked at me like giant black eyes. An old fishing boat lay partially covered in weeds. Rubbish was strewn willy-nilly about the place, and a rusting Chevy truck was parked by a haphazard plywood structure. "What the hell," Josh mumbled. "Didn't know outhouses even existed today."

"You're the one who wanted to interview Dinky," I reminded him.

"Yeah? Well, if I'd known he lived in squalor, I'd have summoned him to our office instead of driving out here."

"You think this is bad—wait until you get a gander inside the place. That is, if anyone still lives here."

Without waiting to hear Josh's response, I got out of the car and walked to the door, kicking junk out of my path as I went.

A car door slammed behind me, and Josh momentarily appeared at my side, a bit breathless. "If he's home, maybe we should conduct the interview outside. Might be more sanitary."

Ignoring his helpful suggestion, I knocked on the door. "Mr. Stedmyer?" I called out. "We're with the police department. Open up."

A stirring sounded behind the entryway. I concentrated on the rustling noises, trying to ascertain if it was scampering rats or a human shuffle. The door squeaked open, and it took all my resolve not to take two steps backward at the stench.

I looked down. Gerald Stedmyer wasn't even five feet tall, and I barely recognized him from my encounter with him eleven years ago. He hadn't looked chipper then, but now his skin was deeply wrinkled and an unhealthy ash color. Open sores marred his face and arms. He threw a hand up over his eyes, squinting as if he hadn't seen the sunlight in quite some time.

"Whadda ya want?" He sounded more bewildered than disturbed to find us on his doorstep.

I flashed my badge. "Officer Kimbrel. Do you remember me? We spoke years ago about a young girl's disappearance near here. Ainsley Dalfred."

"Dunno her."

At my nod, Josh opened a folder and pulled out an old black-and-white photo of the victim. Rather than stepping forward and offering it to Dinky, he held the photo at arm's length. "Does this jog your memory?" he asked.

"Nah. Never seen her."

Josh's face hardened. "Look again."

Dinky leaned toward the photo. Josh's mouth slightly dropped open, and his nostrils pinched. I hid a smile behind my hand. The kid was trying not to breathe through his nose.

"Dunno her," Dinky repeated.

"Mr. Stedmyer," I interrupted. "This has gone from a missing persons case to a murder. Ainsley Dalfred's remains were found a couple miles from here, at the bottom of the lake."

"Why ya asking me 'bout her?" He glanced back and forth between us, apparently befuddled.

"Why do you think?" Josh snapped. "You're a registered sex offender on parole for raping a thirteen-year-old girl."

Dinky cowered against the doorway. "That was a long time ago."

"Once a pervert, always a pervert," Josh said, carefully returning the photo to his folder.

He whimpered like a scolded puppy. "I been good."

"Then you won't mind if we search your house?" I asked.

"I-I don't like people messin' with my stuff."

"Just a quick walk-through, then. What do you say?"

Dinky shrugged and moved away from the entry, waving us inside. "I guess that'd be all right."

Josh slanted me a "You've got to be kidding" glare. With a sweep of my arm, I gestured to the open door. "You first."

I thought he'd refuse, but he took a deep breath, as if about to dive underwater, and then plunged inside. I followed, similarly bracing myself.

"It's kinda messy in here this morning," Dinky warned.

The stench of rot was strong but not unbearable. I'd expected worse. Like its owner, the place was old and falling apart. Cheap, worn pieces of furniture—obvious dumpster finds—were strewn helter-skelter, and piles of dirty, chipped dishes lined the tables and floors.

Dinky hurried by me, gathering up a stack of magazines from the frayed couch. He stuffed them under a chair, but not before I had a chance to see the covers. Some type of nudie mags. Dinky gestured at an old chair with a suspicious yellow stain on its seat cushion.

"Wanna have a seat?" he asked in a surprising show of hospitality.

"That's okay. We'll just do a quick walk-through, if you don't mind."

"I guess not." He shifted his feet from side to side, clearly nervous.

It took all of thirty seconds to walk from the main room, through a kitchen, and then to a bedroom. I took only a cursory glance at the stacks of junk. After all this time, there would be nothing here to implicate Dinky in the Dalfred murder, even if he had been the killer. Which I knew was impossible. The only item Stedmyer could possess that would allow us to bring him in would be an object physically linked to Ainsley—such as a piece of the clothing she'd worn the night she vanished, or the missing necklace and braided friendship bracelet her parents claimed that she'd always worn.

None of that had been found with the girl's remains. The clothes and the bracelet would have disintegrated long ago from water, but the necklace had never been recovered. Most likely the current had washed it away, or the cheap metal had rusted, broken off, and sunk deep into the lake's sediment.

This whole trip was a pointless waste of time.

Josh picked up a piece of cardboard on the kitchen counter, disturbing several cockroaches, which scurried to the nearest crack in the wall. He squealed like a girl, and this time I couldn't suppress a chuckle. He shot me a dirty look and strode back to Dinky, who rubbed his arms like he was under siege from scurvy.

"You want to finally come clean, Dinky?" Josh asked, jabbing his finger near the man's chest. "Set your conscience straight after all these years? Must be unbearable to carry so much guilt for so long."

"I ain't done nothin' wrong."

"Ah, c'mon." Josh brandished his folder in the air. "I got your rap sheet right here. You've been in and out of one institution or another since age eleven, when you inappropriately fondled your six-year-old foster sister."

Stedmyer swallowed hard, and his crusty lips trembled. But to his credit, he didn't try to defend himself.

"From there you moved on to other young girls, until it finally escalated to kidnapping and rape."

"I done served my time fer it."

Josh made a move as if to step forward but abruptly changed his mind—evidently not wanting to get too near the possibly disease-ridden Dinky.

"If you did this—and we *will* get to the bottom of this matter—we'll show no mercy. Unless, of course, you want to confess and cut a deal now."

Dinky whimpered, and tears spilled down his filthy cheeks. "I don't wanna go back to prison. They were mean to me."

I shuddered to imagine how the other felons had preyed upon the man. Inmates were reputed to hold a special hatred for child molesters. That, combined with Dinky's small size and his obvious mental disabilities, made him the perfect target for the more sadistically inclined prisoners.

Josh pounced on Dinky's vulnerable admission. "Confess, and I'll try to arrange matters so that you don't get sent back there. If you're declared mentally incompetent, the judge can send you to a psychiatric hospital."

"But I ain't crazy neither."

Josh smiled with no humor. "Your record says otherwise. And take a look around this place. It's disgusting. Unfit for human habitation. No person in their right mind lives like this."

His lips wobbled. "But it's mine. I come and go as I please."

"Wouldn't you rather live in a nice room with your own TV? Where all your meals are delivered and your every need is met? Plus you'd be around others and have people to talk with."

"It do get a mite lonely out here," Stedmyer agreed in a small voice.

My annoyance with Josh grew to an active dislike. He was too ambitious. He'd reviewed the Dalfred files and fingered the weakest link in the chain, the one person he might manipulate into a confession. Wouldn't surprise me if he had a statement already printed and in his folder, ready for Dinky's signature.

"What do you say we end this charade, right here, right now? Tell us how Ainsley ended up at the bottom of Hatchet Lake, and I'll do everything I can to help you."

Dinky cast me a desperate look. However reprehensible I found his character, the man was innocent—of this crime, at least. I couldn't stand by and watch my partner browbeat him into a false confession.

Or could I?

The possibility sparkled in front of me like a shiny Christmas package, wrapped and delivered. One that would solve all my problems. It meant Violet would be free of the dark cloud that plagued her mind and heart, and her reputation in the community restored. And the biggest blemish on my career—never capturing Ainsley's abductor and killer—would be wiped clean.

All I had to do was keep my mouth shut and let Josh reel Stedmyer in.

"What do you say, Dinky? Have we got a deal?" Josh extended his hand in a show of affability.

Dinky's right arm twitched by his side, as though he was seriously considering shaking Josh's hand and agreeing to a verbal deal.

I stepped between them. "No dice. Thanks for letting us look around. We'll be going now."

Dinky collapsed on the sofa and pushed his long, ratty hair back from his face. His relief was palpable. On the other hand, I felt the heat of Josh's glare as I walked past him and stepped outside.

I breathed in great gulps of pine-scented air and strode to the rear of my police vehicle to survey the extent of the fender damage.

"Why the hell did you let him off the hook?" Josh bellowed from behind.

I shook my head at the sight of the twisted metal and then got in the car.

Josh entered, slamming the passenger door. "What the hell?"

"Watch your mouth," I answered calmly, though I was stewing inside. "I'm your supervising officer, and I won't stand for it. You want a letter of reprimand in your file?"

Josh's lips thinned to a straight line, but he shut up and buckled his seat belt. The little shit wanted no blemish on his record, nothing to slow his chase to the top of the law enforcement hierarchy.

I started the motor, and cold air blasted from the vents, chilling the sweat on my arms and forehead. Dinky appeared in the doorway and waved at me. I rolled down the window. "What is it?"

He motioned me over. Probably wanted to speak with me alone and be reassured he wasn't going to be arrested and hauled off to the county jail. I exited the car, leaving the motor running. Josh opened his door, and I shook my head, gesturing for him to stay where he was.

Josh scowled and slammed his door shut. It was going to be a long ride back to the office.

I walked to Dinky, stopping several feet away from where he stood.

"Didn't want to say nothin' with that other feller listenin'."

"Go on."

"Maybe I do recognize that girl in the picture."

This wasn't what I'd expected. "How's that?" I snapped.

"She used to meet up with some other girl near the river. They favored each other a bit. Both had long black hair and skinny little bodies . . ." He abruptly clamped his mouth shut, as if realizing he'd incriminated himself.

"How do you know what their bodies looked like?" I asked stiffly. My early sympathy for the man had been misplaced. Once a sex offender, always a sex offender. After all these years, I should know better.

"Well, er, I mean, you can tell they was skinny girls just by seein' 'em with their clothes on."

He was way too obsessed with their bodies. With my *daughter's* body. "You ever speak with Ainsley Dalfred?"

He shook his head, long tendrils of matted gray hair flapping against his cheeks. "Nah, I just seen them together a few times at night." He shuffled his feet. "Skinny-dipping."

Fucking pervert. "Let me get this straight. You'd hide out behind some tree and watch them strip down and go swimming."

"I weren't hurtin' 'em," he whined.

This Peeping Tom had seen my daughter naked. Many times. My hands tightened to fists. Then an even worse thought struck me. Only years of training kept my face neutral and my voice flat.

"What else did you see out there in the woods?"

"One night I heard 'em fussin'. Weren't close enough to make out the words. They climbed up the cliff, still snappin' at each other. I figured they was headin' on home since they weren't havin' no fun. So I left. They ain't never come back again after that night, neither."

I hardly dared breathe as I studied his face. Was he telling the truth? Because if he'd seen something he shouldn't have, this was a big problem.

"You sure you didn't see anything more?" I pressed. "Was anyone else out there in the woods besides the two girls?"

"No, sir. And now I done told ya the truth. The whole truth. I never laid a hand on them girls."

I studied him. Fool me once . . . "Maybe you're telling the truth. Maybe not. Don't leave town, Stedmyer. You understand?"

"Yessuh." He nodded vigorously.

I strode back to the car and wordlessly buckled my seat belt.

"What did Dinky want?"

I didn't answer right away, wondering the best way to play this. "What do you think?" I said at last. "The guy wanted an assurance that we aren't going to return later today with an arrest warrant."

"If you'd let me have my way, I might have gotten him to confess."

"It would never hold up in court. You know that."

A confession that would never stick. There was no physical evidence to tie Stedmyer to the murder. If only.

Back down the dirt road we went, bumping and careening every inch of the way. At last, we left the backwoods behind and pulled out onto a paved county road.

"You shouldn't have interfered," Josh said flatly, staring straight ahead at the road.

"You're still pouting? Gerald Stedmyer had nothing to do with that girl's death."

"You can't know that for sure," he argued. "I'd say there's a high probability he did do it. For God's sake, Kinky Dinky is a convicted sex offender, and as the crow flies, his cabin is less than a quarter mile from the Dalfred and Henderson houses."

"Which makes him a suspect, but we've no grounds to arrest him. If I'd known you were going to harass the guy, I wouldn't have humored you by driving you all the way out here. Now just look at our car."

"Humor me?" Josh gave a bitter laugh. "You're jealous because Chief Thornell asked me to step in and review the old investigation."

I neither denied nor confirmed his accusation. At the moment, the rookie's opinion of me was the least of my problems.

"It almost seems as though you don't want this case solved," he continued.

My fingers clenched the still-hot metal steering wheel, and I kept my eyes focused on the road.

"Are you protecting someone? Like that Violet Henderson woman?"

I didn't dare answer. If he ever guessed Violet was my daughter, I'd lose any shot of protecting her from suspicion.

"There've been rumors about the Henderson family. The dad's a mean, crazy alcoholic; the oldest child, Delaney, has a wild, slutty reputation around town; and Violet's evidently as nuts as her father."

"Considering the short amount of time you've lived here, you've managed to pick up quite a bit of gossip."

"I've heard even more," he bragged. "A few people have speculated that Violet and Ainsley's friendship was too intense to be platonic. Did you consider that angle when Ainsley Dalfred first disappeared?"

"Of course. You're not telling me anything new."

"It's really weird," Josh continued, drumming his fingers on the file in his lap.

He left it at that, and the silence got under my skin. I finally broke down and asked, "What's weird?"

"The mother—Hyacinth, was it?—dying so soon after the scandal. There's been talk that she was having affairs and was about to leave her husband."

Holy crap. My gut twisted, as if I were walking along a cliff, inebriated and clumsy, in danger of tumbling off the edge. I ground my teeth together, bracing myself in the here and now. "So what? Shit happens. Sometimes a cigar is just a cigar."

"And sometimes it's an overlooked clue. You never considered that Mrs. Henderson's husband might have rigged her car to catch fire?"

"There's no evidence of that." I had to throw him off course. Quick. "Believe me, every angle, every possibility, was thoroughly explored. The chief asked that you look over the case with fresh eyes. Doesn't mean he expects a rookie to waltz in and solve it. Trying to strong-arm Gerald Stedmyer into a false confession was a dick move."

Josh stiffened, his face and neck exploding with crimson. He had much to learn about patience and self-control. I pulled into the station and navigated into the reserved spot marked **INVESTIGATOR**. Before I came to a complete stop, Josh huffed out the passenger side, slamming the door. By the time I exited the vehicle, he was already in the building.

Fine by me.

I should have simply put my foot down when Josh had insisted on interviewing Stedmyer. It had been a fool's mission from the get-go. Humoring the rookie had certainly done me no favors. With any luck, my trainee partner would leave after his six-month probationary period, seeking better grounds for advancement in a larger city. The only other investigative position in Normal was mine, and I had no plans to leave. Although I met the age requirement for retirement, I needed to work at least ten more years. We'd finished paying off our house last summer, which had allowed me to squirrel away more money for retirement. After all the shit I'd put Ellie through, she deserved the tropical travels of her dreams one day.

I took a quick photo of the damaged fender and trudged into the station, not looking forward to writing the incident report on the vehicle mishap. Andy Bushnell, the department's procurement officer, laughed his ass off when I showed him the photo.

"What the hell? I'd expect this out of some new guy, not you, old man," Andy said, typing away on the keyboard. "What was the approximate time of the accident?"

"About ten fifteen a.m."

A few more cursory questions, and he rolled his chair back as the printer churned. "Done," Andy pronounced, picking up a stack of paper. "Sign and date the forms in triplicate, and email me that photo on your cell phone."

"You got it. Thanks." Overall, that had been painless. I'd drop off the completed report on Dan's desk whenever he left for lunch.

"How's the new partner working out?"

"Hmm," I replied, reviewing the report.

Andy laughed. "That good, huh?"

I merely shrugged. Andy was a friend, but I'd been around long enough to know that walls had ears. Anything said in the station was liable to be repeated to everyone.

He winked. "Better stay on the good side of the kid, considering Thornell is his great-uncle."

His what? My face must have betrayed my surprise.

"You didn't know?"

"Nobody ever said a word about it."

"I think they were trying to keep it on the down low, but I heard it from Glenna, who heard it from Margie in Personnel."

And didn't that just explain so much? "Thanks for clueing me in, buddy. Want to grab a burger in an hour or so?"

"Yup. Ring me when you're ready." Andy picked up a file and set back to work on whatever he'd been doing before I'd interrupted.

Back in my office, I kicked up the computer and set to puzzling out my latest problem. Could this day get any worse? At least, for the moment, Josh wasn't at his desk, and with any luck, he was off on his own, pursuing another futile tangent. That or he was holed up somewhere on his cell phone, already speaking with Thornell about our disastrous morning with the fender damage and the failed interview with Dinky. Thank God that Stedmyer hadn't mentioned his Peeping Tom activity in front of Josh. As things stood now, Josh thought I had been too lenient with the suspect, too soft in my approach. It was in my best interest that both continue to harbor that belief. Footsteps echoed in the hallway, and I guessed it was probably Josh returning to his desk.

Quickly, I placed a call to the social service worker our department worked with from time to time, inquiring how to aid a mentally ill person who was, essentially, homeless. As Josh entered and slipped behind his desk, I made no effort to hide my notes or disguise my business.

"Appreciate your recommendations," I told the social service worker, scrawling down names and numbers. "Most likely, this person will refuse to leave his run-down shack of a home. I get that. It's his, and he enjoys the isolated location. Still, he obviously suffers from mental health issues, and he should have the opportunity to decide between his current residence and a state facility where he'd be provided sanitary conditions and three square meals a day."

I didn't have to look up to know that Josh stared at me in outrage. I felt his burning glare like the sun's rays blistering my skin. After exchanging a few pleasantries with the social worker, I hung up the phone.

"What the hell? Now you're trying to help Dinky get in a nuthouse? He gets declared mentally incompetent, and our number one suspect is out of reach."

"He might be your number one suspect, but he's not mine."

Josh pursed his lips, as if to cut off a further outburst, and cut his gaze to the paperwork on his desk. He had plenty to say, but evidently, he recalled my earlier warning about crossing the line and acting with insubordination. Of course, I'd threatened that before I'd known his connection to the chief.

As if on cue, Thornell's door opened, and Josh went to him, saying something in a low voice that I couldn't overhear. Josh shook my boss's hand, and I caught the conspiratorial understanding that flashed between them. Hell, now that I looked closely, I saw the similar coloring and a certain something about the mouth and jaw that marked them as kin.

Josh returned to his desk, shooting me a smug smile. No wonder he was so confident. Must be nice having an uncle in the chief's position.

"A word with you, please," I said to Thornell, picking up the vehicle incident report and walking around my desk. I needed his signature on the report to facilitate getting the repair work done quickly.

He frowned and glanced at his watch. "I was about to head out."

"This won't take but a minute." I strode into his office, determined to have a word in private. The man was always leaving the office for some Rotary Club meeting or what have you. Good thing he was a mere figurehead, because politicking left him little time for real work.

Thornell shut the door behind me and then sat across his desk from me, a jovial smile pasted on his face. "What can I do for you, Boone?"

"Sign off on this." I shoved the report across the desk. "I'm sure your nephew has already clued you in about the accident."

"Ah, so you heard." He signed his name with a flourish and then leaned back in his chair, steepling his hands together.

"C'mon, Dan. It's only a matter of time around here before news like that slips out. Why didn't you tell me to start with?"

"Wanted to give Josh an opportunity to prove himself on his own merits. How's he doing?"

What was I supposed to say? Tell my boss that his nephew was an arrogant kid who was more concerned with making an arrest than seeking the truth? I saw now where Josh got his ambitious streak. Besides, anything my partner had reported on our strained relationship was bound to portray me in an unflattering light.

"He has a lot to learn."

"Of course. We all start green. And it will do us good to have a young person employed with a fresh perspective."

What a crock.

"You know, Boone . . ." He leaned forward with the affable, practiced smile he flashed at his numerous public speaking events. "You and I are getting on up there in age. It's our responsibility to train those who'll take our place one day."

"Plenty of time for that. I don't know about you, *Dan*, but I plan to stick around at least another ten years or more."

His smile wore thin. "That long? At your age, you're already eligible for retirement."

"Sorry to disappoint you." Ellie and I had started relatively late in life having children, but I'd never regretted waiting until we were more financially stable, even if it meant another decade dealing with Dan. Josh—not so much.

"I see," he said slowly. "Well, you never know. If the economy improves, maybe the county could offer you an early-retirement incentive package."

Now that was a deal we could both appreciate.

I nodded. "Sounds good."

I was almost out the door when Dan spoke up again. "Train him well, Boone."

"Yes, sir." He couldn't have made his position more clear. He wanted me out and his nephew in. I was to teach my replacement how to fill my shoes, and then my services were no longer wanted.

"And Boone?"

I stopped, one hand frozen on the door handle.

"You do think my nephew has got a ton of potential. Right? Josh was an honor roll student at Alabama, majoring in criminal justice. Plus, he got a good report from his internship at the Tuscaloosa Criminal Justice Center, and also at the Huntsville Police Department."

"There you go, then."

With that ambiguous answer, I left. At my desk, I collected my car keys.

"Going somewhere?" Josh asked.

"Lunch."

I didn't invite him to come along.

~

The conversation with my boss weighed on me all afternoon. Despite the dangling carrot of early retirement, I was edgy and moody. Josh and I sat at our respective desks, not saying a word to one another and avoiding even accidental eye contact. The moment I could make my escape, I did, arriving home a good two hours earlier than usual.

Snappy music hit my ears as I crossed the threshold. From the TV set in the den, a breathless voice urged viewers to *burn those buns* in an annoying, high-pitched tone that exuded fake enthusiasm. Ellie halfheartedly kicked her legs in time to the beat. Her shoulder-length hair was pulled back in a ponytail, and her slightly oversize hips were stuffed into a pair of old gym shorts. A ring of sweat stained her white T-shirt, an old castoff of mine that no longer fit.

"Ellie?" I called out.

Her head snapped around. Surprise widened her dove-gray eyes. She gave a self-conscious laugh and wiped a hand across her sweaty brow. "What are you doing home so early?"

Her annoyed inflection subtly communicated that she'd rather I weren't. I'd messed up her routine. Usually after an hour of dancing to an aerobics tape, she'd shower and then start putting supper together.

"Nothing much shaking at work. Keep going," I said, nodding at the TV.

She grabbed the remote and shut it off. "Never mind."

"No, really. I'll get out of your hair . . . I can hop in the tub and read the paper."

Oh shit. I'd said exactly the wrong thing in mentioning the newspaper. Every day, it was full of stories on the discovery of Ainsley's remains and the reopening of the old disappearance case, now upgraded to a murder investigation.

"Oh, sure! Read all about the Henderson case."

Ellie marched to the sofa, grabbed the paper, and practically stuffed it in my gut. The bold-font headline jumped out: **Speculation Increases on Old Mystery of Teenage Murder**. I folded it in half, a late, futile attempt to evade the subject.

"Thanks."

"And don't use up all the hot water." Her lips compressed into a thin line, a sure sign she was upset.

"Honey." I laid a hand on her shoulder. Her muscles tensed beneath me, and she shrugged off my contact. The reopening of Ainsley's case had apparently dredged up old hurts. "This will all blow over eventually," I offered.

"Like hell it will. It's starting all over, a repeat from eleven years ago. You're obsessed with the case again, obsessed with *her*."

I, of course, knew immediately that by *her*, my wife meant Hyacinth. The person who must not be named.

"She's dead," I stated flatly. "And I'm not obsessed with the case. I'm home early, aren't I?"

Ellie did a slow clap. "First time in your career."

"Don't exaggerate."

Unwittingly, I recalled the early days of my career. Before children, before Hyacinth. I'd rush home as soon as possible after work and sometimes even come home for lunch. And by lunch, I meant having a quickie with my hot wife. What had happened to us?

"It's not like you want me hanging around anyway," I ruefully noted.

"Not true."

"Then let me make you ecstatic. There's a possibility I could be offered an early retirement."

"What? When?" As I'd suspected, she wasn't overjoyed. Merely curious.

"Another year or year and a half. I can buy out the time I briefly worked for the state before becoming a cop."

"Can we afford it? Money's tight after paying for Brad's and David's college degrees."

"Let me worry about the money."

"I could go back to work. Just temporary until we've saved more money."

"No." Ellie was unhappy enough in our marriage without returning to the old job she hated. If it came down to that, she'd become even more resentful and snippy.

Ellie folded her arms and drew a deep breath, as if gathering her courage. "Is she yours?"

My ears rang. Not now. Hadn't I suffered enough crap in one day? We hadn't discussed this issue in ages. "What are you talking about?" I hedged, gathering my wits.

"You know damn well what I'm talking about. The woman at the center of controversy again. Violet. Your lover's daughter. Is she yours as well?"

My denial was swift and automatic. Why reverse course now? "No."

"Why should I believe a damn thing you say?" Gray eyes filled with angry tears.

"How many times do I have to tell you that she isn't?"

"Until I'm satisfied you're telling me the truth."

"In other words—never."

"If that Violet's not your daughter, then why did you send money to her through the years?"

Paralysis cemented me to the floor, and my lungs seized.

"Yeah, that's right. I know about it. Close to five thousand dollars slipped to her using prepaid credit cards." Ellie huffed out of the room and stomped up the stairs.

It hadn't been my money. Not most of it, anyway. I'd merely been the channel to funnel funds. But I could hardly tell her that, either, without raising more questions.

Alone, I didn't know quite what to do with myself. Follow Ellie upstairs and continue lying as I had all these years? Or tell her the truth and risk losing everything?

In the end, I did what was convenient and least emotionally taxing.

I opened my cigar box and pulled out a Montecristo, then poured a glass of whiskey. Carrying both vices outside, I sat on the porch and lit my cigar, studying the cherry tip as it glowed. Another night of *un*marital bliss at Casa Kimbrel.

All my fault. I readily acknowledged my guilt.

A strange feeling tore at my gut. I felt as though I were wavering on a precipice. One day soon, I'd have to pay for my many sins. I might have avoided a crisis this evening, but it was the proverbial calm before the storm. You couldn't do the terrible things I had done and not expect to pay the price.

Secrets and lies would always catch up to you, no matter how hard you worked to keep them hidden in darkness. And when they did, the truth would forever destroy my life.

Chapter 27

HYACINTH

July 2, 2007

A length of thick, frazzled rope hung from an oak limb. I'd been here thousands of times, even as a child myself, and had nothing but fond memories of jumping in the water to cool down from the blazing 'Bama heat. But tonight, the hanging rope appeared ominous. It twitched in the night breeze like a venomous snake.

I rubbed the goose bumps on my arms.

"Violet," I called, "where are you?"

Only the rush of water against rocks answered me. Maybe she was afraid to speak. Or maybe Delaney had sent me on a fool's errand.

"You're not in trouble. I'm worried. You there?"

Still nothing but the water and a cacophony of insects. I walked to the cliff, observing the fresh set of bare footprints in the moist ground. About the right size for Violet. At the embankment's edge, I looked down. Moonlight sparkled like quicksilver on the dark water below. My eyes searched and located a lump of pale . . . something. It lay against a boulder, unmoving. Probably a piece of abandoned junk. And yet I felt compelled to get closer. Reluctantly, I picked my way downhill, descending into the liquid darkness. The slightly musty scent of water and mud, mixed with the sound of the rushing river, flooded me with memories of carefree summers as a kid. I pushed the nostalgia aside and concentrated on finding my child.

In the flashlight's path, more footprints dotted the shore. Barefoot impressions in the sandy soil. Flashes of yellow and pink cloth flapped on a tree limb. I made my way over and shined the light. Two T-shirts. The pink one I immediately recognized as Violet's. I untangled it from the limb and held the soft fabric to my face. It still smelled of Dreft laundry detergent and the faint musky-sweet scent of my daughter. I wasn't sure if finding her shirt was a good or bad sign. I turned my attention to the yellow shirt, picking it up and shaking it out. It was the right size and style for a teenage girl, presumably belonging to Ainsley.

I shined the flashlight's beam underneath the brush and found three sandals, one of them a familiar coral shade, bedazzled with pink and purple crystals. My heart beat faster. Unmistakably Violet's. I searched a few more minutes but found nothing else. I draped the T-shirts on my arm and held the sandals in one hand, their straps interlaced in the crook of my fingers, and kept walking the shoreline.

"Violet!" I called out again. Then, "Ainsley! Anyone there?"

The tall sweet gums guarded the far side of the river like secretive sentinels of doom. Again, I had to shake off the dread. Violet was fine—probably home in bed by now. When I got ahold of her, she'd be grounded for at least a month for scaring me like this.

But fear trumped anger as I again spotted something not quite right, that strange bundle of paleness that lay midway in the river. I kicked out of my sodden slippers and plunged in. Warm water flowed against my ankles, then my calves, as I gingerly walked atop bits of sharp pebbles and mud. A few more steps, and I was thigh deep. I raised my arms, keeping the T-shirts and sandals dry as I walked in up to shoulder level. I'd no clue why I'd brought the found items with me or why I felt it was important to keep them dry. Should I return to shore and leave them where I'd left my flashlight and cell phone?

No, finding clues to Violet's whereabouts was urgent, and I wouldn't waste time. Another step, and my foot found no purchase on the river floor. The sudden deepening here was what made the rope-swinging dives possible, as shallow water would be much too dangerous.

The pale form was only a dozen or so feet away, but I still didn't recognize its shape or identity. I'd have to swim farther. I dropped my arms—to hell with keeping the shirts and sandals dry—and swam until I came to the boulder. I clung to the rock, my breath loud and labored, as though I'd run for miles.

The thing was before me. Horror bubbled inside me, and I gasped for breath. *It can't be. It can't be.*

But it was. The pale, naked torso of a young girl lay against a boulder, face pressed against its hard surface, the rest of her body still submerged.

Not Violet. Dear God, not Violet.

But I couldn't be sure. The hair was wet and matted. I forced myself to lay a hand on her cold, wet shoulder. Slowly, I eased her body over, searching for familiar signs of my Violet as the girl's face flopped into view.

A long nose, oval face, and full lips. It was a familiar face, all right, but not my daughter's.

"Ainsley," I breathed. Dark blood ran down her right temple from a jagged cut. I shook her shoulders. "Ainsley! Wake up! Where's Violet?"

Her head lolled to one side, her neck as weak and useless as a newborn baby's. The eyes never opened.

She must have swung out on the rope, misjudged her landing, and hit her head on this rock. Somehow she must have managed to cling to the boulder. And now she was dead.

I released Ainsley and searched the darkness. If Violet had run home for help, she would have had to pass by me in the backyard. And she hadn't. So where the hell was Violet?

Chapter 28

VIOLET

The knock at the front door caught me by surprise. Dad continued eating his macaroni and cheese, unperturbed by the unexpected knock.

I strode to the door and opened it.

Purple hair glowed from the sun that backlit the tresses, rendering them as colorful as a mermaid's tail.

Libby met my gaze, chin lifted in determination and a squirmy Calvin wiggling on her hip.

"Let me down," the little boy demanded, breaking the silent deadlock between Libby and me. He slid out of his mother's hold and dived at my knees, wrapping his small arms around my legs.

I patted his dark curls and smiled. No fair of Libby, bringing Calvin along. He'd melt the coldest of hearts.

"Couldn't get a sitter," she volunteered, as if reading my mind.

Before I could even invite them in, Calvin streaked past me and ran into the living room.

Dad blinked and stared at the child as if he were an alien dropped from outer space. Now would not be a good time for one of his profanity outbursts.

"I'm hungry," Calvin said, scrambling onto the couch next to my father and pointedly staring at his food.

"Come on in the kitchen, and I'll fix you a bowl," I said.

They both followed me to the kitchen. I nuked a serving of leftovers while Libby settled him into a chair.

"Your dad's not looking so hot," she said in a low voice, coming to stand near me.

"He's getting old and has dementia."

"True. But still, his skin's really gray. You ever find where Delaney stashed his prescriptions?"

"No. I've looked everywhere."

"Huh." Libby tapped her chin, thinking. "So how does this work out when Delaney leaves you alone to take care of him? It's dangerous not to take the same meds at the same time every day."

I opened the nearest kitchen drawer and held up three plastic baggies. Libby peered at the array of pills lining the bottom of each. "She puts these together. One each for a.m., midday, and p.m., with only one dose per bag."

"Your sister really doesn't want you to know what he's taking."

"Claims it's because she's concerned I'll either forget the meds or screw up the dosages and timing."

I took the plate from the microwave and handed it to Libby. "What does he drink? I have water, iced tea—"

"Water's fine. Thanks, Violet." Libby stood still and smiled at me, a tentative upturn of her lips.

I knew the question behind the smile and the stare. But I wasn't ready to play nice and say everything was fine between us. If she'd betrayed me once, how could I be certain it wouldn't happen again?

I stared back, unsmiling.

"C'mon, Violet. It's true that at first, I might have only seen you as an opportunity to get under Delaney's skin, but I've gotten to know you and really do like you. Okay?"

I folded my arms and considered her words. "Why?"

Confusion clouded her eyes. "Why what?"

"Why would you befriend someone like me?" I asked flatly.

"Seriously?" A snort of disbelief. "Is your self-esteem so low you don't believe you're a likable person?"

"Actually, yes."

No one in Normal had ever thought of me as friend material before. Not after the business with Ainsley.

I turned and opened a cabinet, retrieving a small plastic cup. "Go feed Calvin," I said gruffly.

A warm hand pressed down on my shoulder. "I like you because you're a good person, Vi. Remember what I told you about watching you stick up for that kid in special ed? That's the truth."

I swallowed hard, and the cup trembled in my hand.

"Hurry up," Calvin called out.

Libby chuckled. "Besides, you like my son. Anyone who cares for Calvin is gold in my eyes."

A whoosh of relief swept through me as I poured Calvin a glass of water. I hated conflict, and I did need a friend, rusty as I was on how to act with one. "Back in a minute," I told them. "Going to check on Dad."

Quickly, I stepped into the other room. "Dad, you okay . . ."

He was gone.

I stared stupidly at the empty sofa and the abandoned bowl of food on the tray. What the hell? He must have slipped out the back door.

He's fine, I kept assuring myself as I walked across the pine floors to the window.

His stooped figure was huddled under the large pecan tree, a shovel in hand.

Not again.

I'd have to get him cleaned up before Delaney got home—whenever the hell that would be. Every day, her absences seemed to grow longer and more erratic. She'd turn up, breathless and mussed, talking a mile a minute about meeting Sawyer or getting together with friends.

"Dad? What are you doing?" I called to him, rushing out the door.

He didn't bother looking up, just kept trying to shovel dirt between the knotty pecan roots. His face was set in that stubborn look I'd come to loathe. I placed a hand on his shoulder. "Dad?"

He scowled and shrugged me off, mumbling incoherently as he thrust the shovel into the unyielding red clay.

"Everything okay out here?"

I turned to find Libby and Calvin a few feet behind.

"Isn't this just jim-dandy," I muttered, running a hand through my hair. I pasted on a smile. "Everything's fine. Y'all go on inside."

Calvin's face lit with excitement. "Oh boy! Are you digging for treasure? I wanna dig too. Can I?"

Libby winked at me. "That sounds like fun. Let's all dig for treasure. Got any more shovels?"

Wordlessly, I pointed to the half dozen shovels leaning against the house.

"He's going to have a blast with this," Libby said. "We'll make it an adventure."

An adventure. What the hell. I laughed, glad to not be alone with Dad. Glad to make a game out of an embarrassing situation.

Glad to have a friend.

"Let's do it."

Libby gazed at me, a brow raised. "What do you imagine we'll find?"

"Old whiskey bottles, most likely."

"What's whiskey?" Calvin asked. The kid was all ears.

"A magical golden elixir," I said ruefully.

Dad looked up, regarding us all with surprise, as if he'd just noticed he wasn't alone. "Whatever we dig up is mine, ya hear?" he said, eyes narrowing. "This is my property. Generations of Hendersons have lived here and worked this soil."

"Yes, *sir.*" With that, Calvin plopped down and set to work, his tongue slightly sticking out of his mouth as he concentrated on the task.

In the deep gloaming, under the old pecan tree that had provided bounty for an untold number of pecan pies and Christmas fruitcakes, the four of us set to digging. Peace settled in, the likes of which I hadn't felt since childhood.

Why hadn't I ever thought to join Dad in his hunt? So much more peaceful than fighting him like Delaney insisted on doing. I didn't care if he got dirty. Digging gave him some exercise, a little healthy outdoor air, and a whole lot more purpose in his dwindling world.

Metal clinked against roots, and the air grew cooler.

"How about I make us all some hot chocolate?" I proposed. "Or bring out a pitcher of iced tea? There's a bowl of fresh-cut watermelon in the fridge too."

"Yippee!" Calvin flung down the garden trowel and ran to the porch. Apparently, the thrill of the treasure hunt had already ended.

"Sure. But we'll have to eat and run. It's getting near his bedtime." Libby dusted her hands on her jeans and waved to my father. "Nice to meet you, Mr. Henderson."

Inside, it was dark enough that I needed to turn on the lamps and dining room chandelier. Warm ambient light glowed in pools of gold, and above us prisms of lights twinkled like fireflies. Magical. Like a swarm of fairies sprinkling pixie dust. As a kid, I used to lie on the wooden floor in the middle of the room and stare at the light, trying to make out the detail of their fairy wings.

Fairies. I laughed out loud. That memory hadn't crossed my mind in years.

I opened the fridge and took out the bowl of happy-pink watermelon chunks. "Iced tea or hot chocolate?"

"Tea. Mister Big Ears has enough energy without laying on the chocolate."

Calvin scowled and slapped his hands over his ears. "Not big," he said with a huff.

My mouth opened, and just as I was set to laugh, the flash of headlights in the driveway choked away my mirth. Doused it quick as a match dropped in water.

"Must be your sister. Fun time's over," Libby observed. "We'll take a rain check on the refreshments. Calvin, time to go."

He stomped his feet. "Nooo."

I winced at his cranky wail, then tapped him on the shoulder. "How about I fix you a bowl of watermelon to take home?"

The tears dried up immediately. "Okay."

Libby rolled her eyes. "Hurry. Delaney and I . . ." She cocked her head at Calvin, unwilling to elaborate.

"Right. I'm on it." Quickly, I scooped up some chunks in a take-home plastic container. But I wasn't quick enough. Already, Delaney was walking up the lighted path, running fingers through her tumbled hair and then swiping away smudged red lipstick with the back of one hand. Her jaw was set and her stride determined. Which probably meant she'd recognized Libby's old car parked in the driveway.

Libby took the container and steered Calvin to the door.

The door flung open, and Delaney exploded into the room, a blonde cyclone—one pissed-off psychotic storm.

"What are *you* doing here?" she roared, pointing a wobbly finger at Libby. Calvin cowered into Libby's legs, hiding his face.

"I invited her," I said with false bravado, but my face heated with shame. Libby would never, ever come back to visit our crazy house.

Libby's lips pursed, and her eyes flashed. She wasn't a bit scared of Delaney, but she did have Calvin to consider. "We came unannounced. If you'll step aside, we'll go."

"We?" Delaney glanced down, eyes widening as she caught sight of Calvin. "Harley Simm's son. Look at those dark eyes and hair. It's him all over again."

So that was the name of Calvin's father. I thought hard but couldn't place a face to the name. I'd always been a loner at school.

Libby stiffened at Delaney's words and stepped around her, gripping her son's hand. Calvin turned his head back sharply, gaping at my sister. "You know my daddy?" he asked.

"Do I ever!" She lifted her chin and gave a loud, high-pitched laugh, a fake falsetto that razored down my spine with each note. I couldn't imagine how it must have grated on Libby. Delaney went down on one knee, her face level with Calvin's. "Next time you see your daddy, you tell him that Delaney said hello and to give me a call. Can you do that for me?"

Calvin glanced back and forth from Delaney's teeth-exposing grin to his mom's flushed face and frowned. "You mad, Mommy? Is she a bad lady?"

Nailed it. My hand involuntarily swung forward to give him a high five, but I caught myself in time and pressed it against my side.

This time it was Libby unloosing a brittle laugh. "Manners, Calvin. Let's get a move on."

I also stepped around Delaney and followed them down the porch steps, intent on apologizing for my sister's rudeness. Calvin's little legs raced to catch up to Libby's angry stride. He stumbled on the driveway, and the container of watermelon chunks flew out of his hand and spilled onto the gravel. Luckily, he avoided scraping his knees, but the wailing of a tired, cranky four-year-old began again in earnest.

"Sorry about that," I told Libby.

"Not your fault." She ushered him into the car and buckled him in with efficient, practiced movements. "Calvin, honey, hush. We're going home, and you're going to bed."

I patted his hand. "Next visit, we'll eat first," I promised.

His full lower lip stuck out in an adorable pout, and he sniffed and hiccuped in the way children do after the storm of their tears has passed.

Libby shut the passenger door and walked around to her side of the car, her eyes peeled on me and avoiding Delaney's gaze. "Your sister still outside?"

"Yep. Standing on the porch, arms folded and smirking." I hesitated for a heartbeat. "I've never seen you so upset."

Libby stared straight ahead into the darkness, car keys dangling at her side. "He was Calvin's father," she said at last. "I was eight months pregnant when he moved out of our house and returned to his own place, where they practically lived together. In the end, Delaney didn't even want him. They broke up weeks later."

How could my sister have acted so callously? It was one thing to hurt me, but another to hurt my friend. Anger roiled in my gut. "And in the meantime, I gather that you gave birth by yourself and are raising a child alone."

"I don't regret having Calvin," she said quickly. "And Delaney isn't entirely at fault. Harley didn't have to be a shithead."

"Of course."

"I do hate her, though."

Astonished, I saw Libby swipe at her eyes.

"You still love that idiot?" I asked.

"What can I say?" She laughed feebly. "He's my fatal weakness. And don't you dare feel sorry for me. You have your own problems."

I glanced back over my shoulder to where Delaney stood in a pool of light, one leg crossed over the other and idly twirling her long blonde curls as she watched us. A golden angel of destruction.

I'd never been so angry with her.

"About that reverse gaslighting—" I said.

"Huh?" Libby took a deep breath and exhaled, apparently reining in her emotions. "What are you talking about?"

"At your house. You mentioned serving up some of Delaney's own medicine to her. Call her bluff, so to speak."

"Exactly. Time for you to make a stand. She treats you like shit and makes you, and everyone else who'll listen, believe you're crazy."

"And from there it's only a hair's breadth to jump from *crazy* to *crazy murderer*." Something about the cover of night made it easier to tell another person of my secret torment. I plunged on. "She told me that I killed Ainsley, that I confessed everything to her the night it happened."

"No. You couldn't kill someone. I refuse to believe it. Delaney's just poison."

A sharp rap sounded from inside the car, and we both jumped. Calvin knocked on the windshield again. Libby held up a finger. "One minute, Calvin."

"I want to rattle her cage," I said quickly. "See if I can get Delaney to admit her lies. Find out the truth."

Libby nodded. "I'll help."

I didn't know if Libby's alliance came from her belief in me, her hatred of my sister, or some combination of both. Whatever the reason, I was merely grateful.

"What did you have in mind?" she asked. "Maybe start with photos of her and Doc Eddie together? We could mail them to his wife."

We both stared at Delaney, who'd settled into the porch glider swing with crossed legs, swinging her top foot back and forth, looking idly amused at having upset my friend and her young child. "I thought I'd start with her most obvious lie, the one most easy to expose."

Libby quirked a brow. "The stolen money from your trust fund?"

"No. The fiancé."

"Ah, okay. Count me in. Call me later, and we'll figure something out."

I stood in the driveway, watching as Libby pulled onto the road. And I kept watching until the blip of red taillights disappeared into the night. I longed to go with them, ached to go anywhere, really, other than back into my own home. Reluctantly, I walked to the porch and tried to skirt around Delaney, who regarded me with an ugly smile. A blonde troll guarding a bridge, a monster that I knew would extract a hefty price for stepping into her lair.

"You really shouldn't have let Libby and her brat into my house," she said. Her words were delivered in a sweet and calm manner, but I wasn't fooled.

"He's not a brat, this is not your house, and I can have friends over if I want."

"Libby's a slut. Everybody knows that."

"Maybe she'd be married and respectable in your eyes if you hadn't hooked up with her boyfriend."

"Is that what she told you? If it hadn't been me, he'd have found someone else. Harley wasn't going to stay with that whore for long."

"Stop calling her that! You've got some nerve. Sitting there with your tousled hair and smeared lipstick and reeking of liquor."

One moment Delaney was on the glider, looking smug as a cat full of tuna, and the next moment her claws came unsheathed. Her blue eyes blazed as she sprang up and grabbed my arm. "Don't you ever speak to me like that again," she said with a hiss.

I twisted my arm, and she held on tighter, her fingers bruising the soft flesh of my forearm.

"Let go of me."

"Do we have an understanding?" she asked.

"Please. You're hurting me." I despised the tremble in my voice and the burning tears that gathered in my eyes.

Delaney gave a slow smile. "That's better. Now go get Dad cleaned up and put in bed."

Abruptly, she let go, and I leaned against the house, rubbing my abused arm. Despite my pathetic plea for mercy, I was even more determined to extract revenge and somehow save myself and my father from her tyranny. Slowly, I pushed away and opened the door.

"Murderer."

My head snapped back around to where Delaney had repositioned herself on the swing, fanning her flushed face with one of the discarded magazines she kept on the glider. She wasn't even looking at me. Her head leaned back against the metal swing, and her eyes were closed.

"What did you say?" I asked.

Her eyes popped open. "Nothing. What are you talking about?"

"Did you just call me . . . a . . . a . . ." I couldn't say the vile word.

"I didn't say anything. You must be hearing things." Her eyes widened, and her lips turned downward. "Poor Vi. I didn't realize hearing voices was one of your, um, symptoms."

I stared at her—hard. Hearing voices? No. It had never happened before. She was playing head games with me again.

But even after I'd coaxed Dad inside and assisted with his bedtime ritual, even after Delaney had retired to her bedroom, and even after I'd bathed and lain in bed, my mind raced.

Murderer.

Over and over and over, the word bounced around in my brain, ricocheting into every twisted nerve and synapse. Three guttural syllables of condemnation. It had to stop. So I did the only thing I knew to do. I opened the nightstand drawer and took two antianxiety pills. When the alarm rang in the morning for work, I'd have hell to pay. But groggy and grumpy I could handle. A sleepless night questioning my sanity—and my basic human decency—was far, far worse.

Another thirty to forty minutes before the medicine took effect. I kicked off the bedsheets and turned on the lamp for my nightly reading. I'd read until the words ran together and my eyes itched with fatigue. In the open nightstand drawer, I scrounged for the paperback Cora had loaned me.

It wasn't there.

I was almost positive that was where I'd left it, same place as always. Maybe the second drawer. I knelt on the floor and went through my assorted odds and ends—a few crystals, a deck of angel oracle cards, tissues, a notebook. The book was jammed in the back, a string of polished silver draped between its pressed pages. I opened it up, and a necklace slid into my lap. My pulse quickened, and my arms tingled with numbness, although I couldn't say why the necklace filled me with dread. With trembling fingers, I held it to the light.

A small cross dangled from the end of the chain. It swayed back and forth in my shaky fingers, a pendulum of calamity. I knew that cross, this necklace. I'd remember it if I lived to be one hundred. The way it perfectly fit into Ainsley's cleavage, the petite design drawing attention to her firm, rounded breasts. A symbol of purity juxtaposed with the flesh-and-blood reality of lust.

But what was it doing here?

I clenched it in my fist, the cross digging into my palm. I upended the drawer, strewing its contents across the floor.

Where had this come from? It hadn't been there when I'd moved in weeks ago and unpacked my meager belongings. I was sure of it. Had Delaney planted it there? And of course, if so, that begged the question of how it had come to be in her possession.

A strange noise filled my bedroom, and it took me a moment to realize it originated from me. A low, keening moan that vibrated in my chest. I clutched my stomach to press against the twitching pangs. I unclenched my fist and stared at the metal cross. A last, tangible connection with Ainsley. I remembered how it had glowed against her pale skin on that dark night. Grief consumed me, a black chasm that sucked me in with the weight of its powerful gravity.

Chapter 29

HYACINTH

July 2, 2007

I stared at the battered body. Ainsley Dalfred. Brazen, daring, and always pushing boundaries—precociously sexy. Everywhere she went, the girl flung pheromones willy-nilly. But now, naked and stripped of makeup, she appeared young. Vulnerable, even.

Delaney's innuendos ate at me, poisonous as hemlock. Violet and Ainsley's friendship seemed too intense. I suspected Ainsley was a bad— even dangerous—influence on my daughter.

"Violet!" I called again. Where had she gone?

The night's silence mocked my cries. I couldn't do this alone. Parker was dead-to-the-world drunk and Delaney nothing but a nuisance. I left Ainsley and swam back to shore.

I dropped the T-shirts and shoes as though they weighed a ton, then sank to my knees and dialed the old familiar number. Dear God, let it still be a working number. By the third ring, a desperate sob escaped me. It was no good. I was alone. No one to help me, no one . . .

"Hello? Who is this?"

His voice was rough with sleep and his tone impatient. Yet it still stirred all the love for him that I'd denied and suppressed. Even now, in the swirl of a crisis, Boone's voice touched me like an intimate caress. Our affair had ended before Violet had even been born, but I'd never stopped loving him.

"It's me." I didn't even bother saying my name; he'd know it was me.

"Second," he mumbled.

I waited. I'd wakened him from a sound sleep next to his wife, and he was hurrying into another room to talk, not wanting to wake Ellie. Didn't matter to me if I'd interrupted the woman's sleep or if the call had angered her. I was past tiptoeing around their marital relationship. Let her think what she would. Ellie could do nothing to harm me, and Boone's problems with her were his own business. Parker had guessed about my affair, but considering his own many indiscretions, he could hardly claim outrage about my infidelity.

"Hyacinth? What's wrong?"

"It's Violet." Silence strummed through the line. "Your daughter," I added unnecessarily.

"Go on."

"She's missing."

There. I'd said the words aloud. The unthinkable had happened.

"For how long?"

His voice was sharp and authoritative now; he'd been roused to full cop mode.

"I last saw her when I went to bed three hours ago. But she's not in her room now." I could hardly breathe, and my voice rose into a full-blown, high-pitched panic. "I can't find her."

"She's a teenager. Most likely she's slipped out to meet a boy. Does she have a boyfriend?"

I wished. If only it were that easy. I rushed to explain, a waterfall of words tumbling from my mouth. "No. You don't understand. There's a body. Ainsley's not moving, and I-I don't—"

"Body? Who's Ainsley? Take a deep breath and slow down."

I drew a ragged breath. "I think Ainsley might be Violet's girlfriend; at least, that's what Delaney implied. But you know how she is. Can't be trusted for shit. So I came down here, to the river, and—"

"You're babbling. Get off the phone with me and call the station. They'll make a report, then notify me, and I'll come straightaway, along with the other cops. We'll do a thorough search."

"No! No cops. Just you."

"But—"

"No cops," I insisted. "Didn't you hear me? There's a dead body."

"All the more reason—"

"Violet's your daughter. For once in your goddamn life, get over here and help her. It's the least you can do."

"Sec."

A muffled, garbled voice in the background. Ellie must have walked in on him.

"Yes, ma'am. I'll be right over." I recognized that official tone. His wife was standing nearby, all ears. "Your address?"

I gave a short, hysterical laugh. "Cut the act. Park your car nearby, and walk out of my backyard and then down to the rope swing by the river. You know where that is, right?"

"Ten-four."

"Don't let anybody see you or your car. I mean it."

"Right. We're on our way."

"And Boone? Hurry!"

The connection went dead. My shoulders slumped, and I dropped the phone. Loud, wrenching sobs shook my body. Whatever had happened here tonight was bad, very bad. My life had been touched by evil, and it would never be the same.

Dear God. Please help us find Violet. Please let her be okay.

Time ticked by, slow and deadly as the unsuspecting *Titanic* ship advancing toward a glacier. Despite the heat and humidity, chills spasmed through my body. Shouldn't take more than ten minutes for him to arrive, but I took little consolation in that fact. I'd never felt so profoundly alone. Draped on a boulder amid the rolling river, Ainsley's body lay lifeless, a monument to some terrible violence.

A sickly yellow light strobed through the tree trunks. The ground slightly rumbled, and limbs and leaves fiercely snapped under the weight of car wheels.

Boone, at last.

I lurched to my feet and ran toward the fog light. Seconds later, the light extinguished, and I hesitated. What if it wasn't Boone? What if it was a murderer returning to the scene of the crime? Quickly, I ducked behind a tree, hardly daring to draw a breath.

A flashlight shone through the darkness, its beam scanning up and down, left and right—advancing in a slow, methodical search.

Chapter 30

VIOLET

Present day

A black void coated my mind, a rip in the thread of my memory.

I dropped Ainsley's jewelry and crab crawled backward on the hardwood flooring. The necklace glittered against the dark wood like a harmless little doodad.

I rose unsteadily to my feet and shoved it under my bed. Then I paced the room, trying to put the final pieces together. What else had I done to Ainsley that night while I'd lost all control? How had her jewelry ended up in my possession? Damn it, empty pockets of memory still eluded me. I could only recall fragmented sensations from much later that night—the slap of shrubs and tree limbs, the loud sound of my breath wheezing in and out of my chest, sticky sweat falling from my forehead to my eyes.

Later, Mom and Detective Kimbrel had found me wandering the woods. But I couldn't decipher the precise point where my memory returned, as opposed to what I imagined had happened next based on what others had told me. That fateful evening was followed by days in bed where I didn't want to awaken to the hushed house. Mom would bring me in bowls of soup and iced tea. I didn't want to see anybody.

Detective Kimbrel had come once, gently asking a few questions and taking notes. Dad had stood in the doorway, frowning and watchful. Neither he nor Delaney had visited my room.

Occasionally, I'd hear loud arguing down the hall between Mom and Dad. I'd bury my head in the pillows and drown them out. I had done my best to keep myself shielded, wrapped in a cocoon. But it didn't, couldn't, last.

Red eyed and pale, Mom had entered my room one day and announced that I needed help. And by *help* she'd meant to get out of the house and leave. I'd arrived at the mental health facility shell shocked and depressed, a transplanted stranger in an alien world of other lost souls. A universe of zombies tucked away in a lovely redbrick building that more resembled a Georgian mansion than a prison.

Stop the self-pity. I had to decide what to do next. Until I formulated a plan to deal with this new development, the first order of business was hiding Ainsley's necklace. No matter how much Delaney pushed, I'd confess nothing. I wouldn't go back to Cottonwood. Not voluntarily.

My eyes scanned the dim room. Where could I stash this that would be safe from Delaney's prying? No dresser drawer or closet would do, and under the mattress or bed would be the first place she'd search for possible hidden secrets. The burlap bag of peanuts in the corner caught my eye. Perfect. Delaney hated the crows and would never think to feed them. I grabbed the necklace and hurried to the corner.

My bare feet tingled as the floor slightly vibrated beneath them. I froze, hardly daring to breathe. The vibration paused, then returned, and paused and resumed again. Footsteps. The pulsing grew stronger with each footfall. The doorknob slowly turned.

My eyes darted from the bed to the burlap bag as I debated what to do. Jump under the covers with the incriminating evidence in hand, or stuff the necklace in the bag? That moment's hesitation cost me.

Delaney poked her head in my room and then entered. "I saw your light on. What are you doing?"

I fought the impulse to jam my hands behind my back. Instead, I turned my back on her and got back into bed, drawing the sheets over me with one hand and with the other dropping the jewelry beneath the covers. I sat with my back propped on pillows against the headboard, hands folded in my lap. "Don't ever come in here without knocking," I said with a calmness I was far from feeling.

"Just wanted to make sure you were all right. I heard noises." She pointed to the unfastened drawer and the mess on the floor. "What happened here?"

"I was looking for one of my crystals that's gone missing. Not that it's any of your business."

We eyed one another, the silence glutted with suspicion. Her lily of the valley scent perfumed the air, cloyingly sweet.

Delaney eased onto my bed and crossed her legs, then leaned sideways, her right hand pressing down on the mattress, right where Ainsley's necklace lay hidden. I swallowed hard and kept my gaze on her face, determined not to betray my anxiety by looking down at her hand.

"You still believe in magic crystals?" She laughed. "Those aren't going to save you."

My heart beat faster. Did she know what lay beneath her fingertips? I couldn't help myself. My eyes darted to Delaney's hand, where her long, elegant fingers tapped against the sheets.

"Save me from what?" I asked, firmly facing her once more.

"Yourself."

"I don't know what you mean. I'm just fine."

"You look . . . scared. Like you've seen a ghost."

Oh, Delaney knew about the jewelry, all right. Which meant she'd orchestrated tonight's discovery. I saw it in the half-turned curl of her lips and the gleam of amusement in her slightly narrowed eyes.

She extended her index finger and ran a long, pink-tipped nail down my arm. My skin tingled all over, and not in a good way.

"You've got goose bumps," she said in that soft, trilling voice I despised.

"I was chilled."

"In the middle of an Alabama summer? I think not."

I folded my arms across my chest, and she withdrew her hand.

"You're still mad over my run-in with Libby."

"Of course I am. You have no right to attack my friends, especially when a child's present."

"I was kindness itself when it came to little Kenny."

"Calvin."

"Whatever. Just so you know, Libby's the one who started all the drama between us. Not my fault she doesn't know how to hold on to a man."

"You didn't have to start seeing her boyfriend. She was pregnant—"

"We're blood. You don't choose friends over family."

Some family. "I owe you nothing," I said flatly.

Delaney's eyes darkened to a midnight hue, the shade of a moonlit night swirling with black storm clouds. "You owe me everything. We both know you murdered Ainsley."

Automatically, my mouth formed to deny her accusation. The tip of my tongue pressed the ridge behind my front teeth, and my lips pursed to say no.

She arose slowly, pointedly glancing down at the upturned drawer by the edge of the bed. "There's evidence against you."

I steeled myself, tamping down my heart's violent pulse. If I showed any weakness, she'd pounce on me like a starving jaguar. She'd planted the necklace here. It had to be her. I didn't know how, but she'd managed it. I, too, glanced at the dresser and then shifted my gaze back to Delaney. "What evidence? Nothing incriminating down there."

"God, you're stupid. You think that's it? There's more where that came from."

I couldn't help my quick intake of breath. *More?* What else could there be? "How did you find . . . what . . . I don't . . ." My brain felt fuzzy as cotton, and I couldn't form words out of the chaos of questions she'd ignited.

"I warned you before." Her flat, dead voice stabbed with every word. "Go confess to the detectives investigating the murder. Don't put us, or yourself, through a trial."

"But—"

"It'll be much easier on everyone that way."

She turned in a flurry of pink silk and strolled away. At the door, Delaney glanced back over her shoulder, spearing me with stern eyes.

"Do it by the end of the week. If you don't, I'll tell them everything myself."

Panic tightened my chest, burning my lungs. The bottle of anxiety pills in my purse tugged at me with a sudden riptide of need. But no. I'd already taken some medicine. Could I really pull off what Libby had suggested? I had to try. I thought of the years I'd spent pulling off a tough-girl act at Cottonwood. Around the women in my dorm, I'd never let them witness any weakness or vulnerability. I'd kept my sorrow and worry contained until either it was lights-out at night or I was able to walk about the closed-in yard and listen to the birds flying freely above and around me.

I'd done it before. I could do it again.

Chapter 31

DELANEY

Present day

What would it be tonight—diamonds or pearls?

My fingers hovered over the velvet-lined jewelry box, then plucked up the diamond stud earrings. After my most-anticipated dinner with Normal's newest Peach Queen beauty pageant contestants, I'd meet Eddie for a night of dancing in Huntsville. It beat our usual date, which consisted of drinking wine out of plastic cups at the local Foxy Lady motel, followed by a satisfying fuck, after which he returned home to his wife. Not that I cared. I didn't want Eddie's name or devotion, only the monthly check he deposited into my bank account. And truthfully, he was a good companion on those nights when the loneliness and isolation out here became more than I could bear.

I put on the earrings and then turned sideways, checking out my profile in the full-length mirror. The expensive cocktail dress accentuated my curvy hips and legs, while my gold necklace, with its diamond carat, nestled snugly in my cleavage. That would draw a few eyes. My lips curled as I imagined attracting a new lover. Sex with Eddie was okay, but I wanted someone new and exciting. A big-spender type of guy who liked a little kink with his sidepiece of ass. A type of guy who let me call all the shots and stay in control. I would never let any man boss me around the way Dad had my stepmother. The way he'd ruled over all of us. I might have been his favored daughter, but I didn't always escape unscathed from his drunken tempers.

"You're all gussied up. Got big plans tonight?"

Violet lounged in the doorway, wearing cutoff shorts and a tank top, her hair pulled up in a topknot, the way she wore it to work. Loose tendrils of her dark hair had fallen, framing her delicate facial features. She was tall enough and striking enough to be a damn model. Without even trying, Violet exuded sexiness with a natural, exotic beauty that outshone me. And didn't that just piss me off. The stupid witch didn't have a clue how to use her wares.

"This little dress? Eh, I bought it at Walmart." I whirled back to the mirror and fiercely brushed my carefully curled hair.

"I've never found anything that nice at Walmart."

But Violet didn't need designer outfits to draw attention to her striking beauty, whereas I needed all the help I could get. I watched through the mirror as she leisurely strolled across my bedroom. Violet casually pulled off the elastic holding the bun, and her hair cascaded down past her shoulders in perfect waves.

"Nice jewelry too," she commented.

I flashed a wide smile. "The wonders of cubic zirconia."

"Is that so?" Violet perched on my bed, crossing her long legs. Dark eyes assessed me.

I flung the brush on my dresser and slipped into a pair of strappy, sequined sandals. With heels, of course—my own short legs needed enhancement to give the illusion of height that Violet possessed by birth. I'd hated Hyacinth, but I wouldn't have minded inheriting her looks. The Hendersons had a certain blond appeal, but the beauty of fair skin and light hair was also known to fade early.

"Did those come from Walmart too?" Violet asked, pointing at my feet.

I couldn't quite place her tone or mood. She wasn't confrontational, and yet unease rippled the nape of my neck. The Violet seated on my bed was a far cry from the whimpering, confused Violet I'd browbeaten so many times. "You sure are chatty this evening."

"We haven't talked much lately. I've been either busy working or out with Libby."

Libby. That weirdo still held a grudge against me for stealing her boyfriend. I'd told Violet to stay away from her, and she'd completely ignored me. That grated.

"I wouldn't trust that woman."

Violet surprised me. "Actually, you were right about Libby. Not good friend material at all."

"What happened?"

Violet shrugged. "She wasn't the person I thought she was."

"That's clear as mud."

I picked up my fancy purse and dropped in a tube of lipstick, powder, and my cell phone. Checking my reflection again, I cocked my head and studied my outfit. Could use a little more bling. I pulled out the second drawer of the jewelry box, which held all my bracelets.

Gleaming pearl necklaces nestled inside. Must have opened the wrong drawer . . . but no, this was the second drawer, right where I housed my bracelets. I jerked open all five drawers and stared, befuddled. Gold now mixed with silver, and the gems were no longer sorted by color. What the hell?

"Someone's been messing with my jewelry."

"Why would anyone do that?"

Again, that tone in Violet's voice. I faced her. "You must have done this."

Impossibly deep-blue-purple eyes widened. "Me? Why would I do that?"

"Certainly wasn't Dad. He knows better than to come in here."

"I remember when this used to be Mom and Dad's room." Violet recrossed her legs, left over right this time, and nonchalantly swung the top leg up and down. "Maybe he got confused and wandered in."

"That doesn't explain my stuff being rearranged."

"Anything missing?"

"Not that I can tell."

"No harm, no foul, then." Violet rose and stood beside me, gazing at my jewelry box. She gave a low whistle. "This is quite the collection. Must have set you back a fortune."

"Most of it's costume," I lied. Hastily, I closed all the drawers. Various lovers had gifted me expensive pieces over the years, but most I'd purchased myself. And why not? I deserved a few nice things in life.

Violet strode over to the opened walk-in closet. "And look at all these clothes . . ."

"Help yourself to a few things if you'd like," I offered quickly.

"That's so generous of you."

Okay, that was definitely a snarky remark.

"You must spend all of your paycheck on this stuff," Violet noted. "And yet I never see you working."

"What's that supposed to mean?" I snapped.

She faced me with that fake-innocent demeanor. "Nothing. Just wish I could find a job like yours. Instead, I work my ass off at Whispering Oaks for minimum wage."

"You're jealous."

"A little," she admitted. That pleased me.

"If the stress is too much, you can always return to the mental hospital," I hopefully suggested once again. "Confess everything and go back for treatment."

"I'm not leaving."

"Was that place so bad? I'm sure it's better than prison. Confess, and they might go easier on you, agree to let you return for more treatment."

"But I didn't do it."

Despite the bravado, I caught the flicker of doubt in her eyes before she dropped her gaze. Thought she could beat me at my own game? She was a fucking neophyte.

"Yes," I said gently. "You did."

I thought of my hidden treasures behind the portrait, a photo that captured me winning the beauty queen title. My eyes involuntarily darted there.

"So you say."

I sucked in my breath at her outright defiance. "How dare you accuse me of lying!"

"Right. You never do any wrong, do you? The golden child prized by Dad." She paused by my treasured photo mounted on the wall and ran a finger along the frame.

If she took it down, or if it fell . . . I rushed over and clasped the frame. "I can't stand a crooked frame on the wall; you know that."

Violet gave me a wide berth as she walked by. At the door, she paused. "By the way, I forgot to mention it last night, but your cell phone rang while you were in the shower. I answered it for you. Hope that's okay."

"Who was it?"

A mysterious smile lifted the corners of her lips. "Your fiancé called."

She swept out of the room, leaving me alone with my spinning thoughts. My fiancé had called? Why had she lied?

Violet must have discovered my little fib. Best to let the fiancé scam die so she couldn't throw it in my face again. I rushed to the door and spotted her at the bottom of the stairs.

"Not that it's any of your business, but Sawyer and I recently broke up," I explained coldly. "I didn't say anything, hoping our fight would blow over. It hasn't. If he calls again, just hang up."

Without waiting for her reaction, I slipped back inside and locked my door. Whatever Violet was up to, I didn't like it, and I needed to regroup. It felt like my sister had thrown down a gauntlet of some sort. I'd been lax lately, confident that she'd come round to do as I said. Bet anything that Libby was somehow behind Violet's new attitude.

I found the key to my jewelry box and locked it. Violet wouldn't get her hands on my gems anymore. Again, my eyes strayed to the framed photo. Time to up my game again. I lifted my smiling, victorious photo from the wall, opened the built-in safe, and gathered my lethal treasure. Carefully, I unwrapped the yellowed paper covering it.

Worthless or not, the filched trinket always excited me, reconnecting me to the moment I had made it mine. Reluctantly, I put it back into safekeeping and hurried out to my car. I was running a little behind schedule, but it never hurt to be fashionably late.

~

By the time I arrived, the Miss Normal Peach Queen Beauty Pageant dinner was well underway inside the festively decorated Veterans of Foreign Wars building. Peach-colored balloons and crepe paper hung from the ceiling. Metal-and-laminate tables were pushed together to form a twenty-foot-long row, which was covered with white tablecloths. Peach napkins were set beside each plate, and white vases filled with peach roses dotted the row in six-foot increments.

As one of the former beauty queen winners, I sat near the head of the table, presiding like royalty in my silver tiara that glittered with bits of peach citrine crystals. Normally, the tiaras were passed down from winner to winner every year, but I'd been determined not to relinquish my crown to another woman. Keeping the tiara had meant sleeping with Buddy Jenkins, the 2004 pageant director, but it had been totally worth the effort. The other former pageant winners kept shooting dagger glares at my crown during dinner, much to my secret amusement. Every year, it was the same old jealousy and sour peaches, which I found invigorating. It meant I was still attractive and powerful. A force to be reckoned with.

Tonight's dinner featured chicken with peach sauce, chargrilled peaches mixed with green beans, and a peaches-and-red-potato stir-fry—all entrées designed to showcase the versatility of our Alabama peach crop. Thankfully, the peach-cobbler dessert was familiar. Didn't have to stretch so far there to tout the fruit's sugary appeal.

I brushed back carefully lacquered tendrils of blonde locks, drawing attention to my perfect spiral curls shellacked with hair spray. What I lacked in my sister's natural beauty I artfully compensated for with careful attention to my hairstyle, makeup, and wardrobe. My half-up, half-down coiffure felt more like twisted straw than spun silk, but it was damn beautiful, and that was all that really mattered. My hand casually drifted down my neck and cleavage, long red fingernails tapping against my gold-and-diamond necklace and showing off my one-carat diamond ring accented with emeralds.

My engagement ring.

I'd described Sawyer in such glowing terms tonight that I'd started to believe in him myself. Now, I got excited as I described the upcoming nuptials at our destination wedding in Aruba.

"Aruba?" Sue O'Neill, seated to my right at the long dining table, grimaced. "You don't want to go there. It's too dangerous. Besides, after what happened to Natalee Holloway, I think all Alabamians should boycott that place."

Smug cow. She may have been Miss Normal a full five years after my 2004 crown, but she looked at least ten years older than me. Her coral cocktail dress was a shade too gaudy, and she was a good thirty pounds too heavy for the curve-clinging, cheap-nylon confection.

I flashed Sue my sweetest smile. "And where was your wedding and honeymoon, hon?"

"We got married right here in town and honeymooned at Gulf Shores." Her chin jutted out, and she patted the arm of the man beside her, a balding paunch of a guy that I remembered had played high school football. No prize there.

"That sounds absolutely adorable." My tone said the opposite, as I'd intended, and the other former queens around us snickered, even though I suspected they despised me as much as Sue did. Teach them to ever cross me like she'd dared.

"Where'd you get your dress?" asked Tiffany, last year's queen, eyeing my designer dress with envy.

"The Velvet Pumpkin. It's a little boutique in Birmingham."

I twiddled with the green silk ribbon of my shoulder strap. While everyone else was dressed in various peachy shades, I'd selected a rich emerald green that was a beautiful contrast to the other gowns.

Mary Ellen Smithers, this year's pageant director, stood and clinked her iced-tea glass with a silver spoon. Conversation dwindled to a twitter and then to silence.

"While we enjoy our desserts baked with Crenshaw County–grown peaches, the best in the country, our former queens will each stand for a moment and say a few words."

I sipped my iced tea, relishing the moment, almost here, to bask in everyone's attention. This year, I'd decided to make a public pitch to judge next year's contest. The five older women who had served as judges for the last twenty years needed to retire. If they had their way, the swimsuit contest would keep mandating one-piece outfits, and contestants with lame talents like baton twirling or reciting poetry would continue to win. I'd spoken to Mary Ellen a couple of times about my desire to judge, and she'd acted snooty about the whole damn thing. Well, that old witch didn't know it yet, but nobody held me down for long. I'd flirt my way onto the judges' panel if need be.

A couple of the former queens rose for a moment and made insipid remarks about the importance of the peach industry in our local economy. Mary Ellen looked my way and dipped her head in a regal nod. My turn.

Slowly, I set down my drink and scooted my metal folding chair back. Buddy Jenkins caught my eye and winked, taking a long swallow of his peach tea, which was no doubt spiked. I rose, conscious of the pretty picture I made—my tiara nestled in blonde curls and the green shimmer of my gown among the cheap orange getups of the other queens. I opened my mouth, but before I could speak I noticed dozens of heads had turned to the front door. A late arrival stealing my thunder?

A scruffy-looking young man with a red beard and longish, unkempt hair approached. He wore jeans and a faded AWOLNATION T-shirt. Hardly appropriate attire for the event. But what really threw me were his gray eyes, which relentlessly locked on me.

He didn't look to the right or left, just barreled forward with a determined gleam in his eyes and a slight smirk on his lips. An old lover? No, he didn't look even vaguely familiar. A disgruntled creditor? No, surely not. What was his game?

"Delaney?" he said loudly, sidling close to where I stood. He placed a hand on the small of my back, and I stood rigid with surprise.

"You look shocked to see me. Told you I'd do my best to make it." He waved at the crowd that avidly stared at us. "I'm Sawyer Harris. Delaney's fiancé."

I couldn't move, couldn't speak. Who the hell was this guy? Why was he doing this?

Someone fetched another folding chair, and he wedged a seat in between me and Sue.

"Go on, honey," he urged, slouching back in the chair with a big grin. "Make your speech. I'm all ears."

I jerked my gaze from the secret amusement dancing on his face, and my eyes swept the length of the table. "It's an honor to be here," I mumbled, quickly sinking into my seat.

"That's it?" Mystery man guffawed loudly. "I done come all the way from Mobile for one sentence? Stand back up and give them a speech deserving of a Peach Queen."

I rose unsteadily on my high-heeled feet, afraid to disobey. For once, I longed *not* to be the center of attention. My face, neck, and chest flushed with heat, and I licked my dry lips. Mary Ellen's face was scrunched in displeasure, but everyone else, particularly Sue, grinned with smug glee.

"I thought you were from Birmingham," Sue said, glancing back and forth between me and the imposter.

"As I said earlier," I rushed in, eager to stop the train wreck of a conversation, "being crowned as the Miss Normal Peach Queen was such an honor. It's a grand tradition of recognizing women right here in Normal, and I wish all of the new contestants much success."

Could that speech have been any more trite or insipid? But I couldn't think. Not now. Not while my mind and heart raced. I sat down abruptly.

My tormenter stood, clapping loudly and issuing a shrill whistle that for all the world sounded like a hog call. Amused titters arose, and it was all I could do not to bury my face in my hands. What an uncultivated asshole. Somebody was going to pay for this.

Violet? She had to be behind the imposter's appearance. I wasn't particularly well liked in town. Okay, several women flat out despised me for messing with their men, but Violet was the one who had practically declared war against me. Little sister was fighting back.

If this was how she wanted to play it, fine. She may have won this battle, but I would crush her in the end.

Finally, he sat down. My momentary relief was short lived when he draped an arm around my shoulders.

"You're an architect?" Tiffany asked, skepticism lacing her voice.

"Well, now, Delaney might have exaggerated a teensy bit there. I'm actually an architect's assistant. The gofer guy who fetches coffee and runs errands. Pay isn't all that great, but it beats the hell out of flipping burgers."

"You're the one being modest, Sawyer." I fought to keep my desperation buried as I faced down the sharks. "He's finishing up his master's degree in architecture next summer at the University of Alabama."

I leaned into him, whispering, "Whoever set this up, I'll pay you double."

"Deal," he whispered, picking up my glass of iced tea and waving it high in the air. "Roll tide," he said to our audience.

Half the people at the table muttered, "Roll tide" and sipped their drinks, while the other half mumbled, "War eagle." The usual friendly—and sometimes not-so-friendly—banter ensued between fans of the two state schools, and I began to breathe a little easier. I'd ride out this shit storm of a dinner and emerge unscathed. The man claiming to be my fiancé wasn't the prize I'd made him out to be, but he hadn't exposed me as a liar either. A few weeks, and I'd start spreading a story about breaking up with him. All was well.

No more taking chances. Violet obviously wasn't going to confess, so it was up to me to have her put away. She'd had her chance to take the route of claiming insanity, but no, she preferred playing hardball. I'd speak to Detective Kimbrel directly and provide him irrefutable evidence that Violet had murdered Ainsley Dalfred. He'd be praised for solving the city's oldest and most violent murder case, and I'd continue on as the sole heir of what remained of my parents' estate.

As the remaining queens gave their brief speeches, I sipped my iced tea. What I wouldn't do for a generous shot of vodka in it. I glanced over at Buddy, who smiled lecherously. I'd have to make my way over to him once I got rid of my pretend fiancé. I leaned into the stranger beside me, resting my head on his shoulder. "How much do I owe you?"

"One thousand bucks."

I didn't even bat an eye. "I'll write you a check."

Chapter 32

DELANEY

July 2, 2007

At the unmistakable squeak of the french doors opening, my fingers clutched the bedsheets in a death grip of fury. Violet was sneaking off without me again. Ainsley used to be *both* our friends, but something had changed this summer. They acted secretive, they ran off and did things on their own, and they whispered and giggled together and stopped talking when I got near.

Violet would pay for running off without me again. I sat up in bed, debating the best way to punish her. I could wake up Mom and Dad, saying I'd heard a noise and was afraid. They'd investigate and discover Violet was missing.

Or I could follow them, see what they were up to. It wasn't fair the way those two had cut me out. Hurt unfurled in my chest, hot and burning. No one wanted to hang out with me—well, no girls, anyway. Violet and Ainsley were younger than me, but at least they were fun at times. Tonight, they'd be down by the river, swimming and up to who knew what while I was here and all alone.

Quietly, I slipped on a pair of shorts and shoes and padded downstairs to let myself out the back door. I didn't know why Violet took chances leaping from her balcony to the pecan tree to sneak out when all you had to do was walk out the back door. Dad wouldn't be waking up until long after the rooster crowed, and Mom was too self-absorbed to notice what went on.

I waited until Violet vanished into the woods before I ventured out. She never looked back. I crept into the night's shadows as best I could. No need to keep her in my sight. I knew where she was going, after all. No surprise there. All I wanted was to hide in the bushes and listen to what they said. Something was amiss between the two. Once I knew their secret, they'd have to include me again—or else.

High-pitched laughter and splashes danced in the breeze, filtering down to my crouched position behind a large saw palmetto. Sweat trickled down my face, and the thin nylon of my pajama top stuck to my skin. Mosquitoes buzzed near my ears. I thought longingly of the cool water below. Damn my pride. I wanted to have fun too. And why shouldn't I? They didn't own the river.

I rose in time to see Ainsley pull off her shirt. Violet followed suit. Swiftly, I dropped down on all fours. Had they seen me? I didn't dare move.

More shrieks and giggles. I remained hidden. Skinny-dipping was a new twist. Before, we'd always just brought our bathing suits along and changed into them. But nudity wasn't that big a deal. Just because I put out for guys, though, didn't mean Violet was the same. Far as I knew, she'd never had a boyfriend. But you could tell at a glance that Ainsley was on the hunt for sex. Took one to know one.

It had gotten awful quiet.

I rose on my haunches, venturing a quick peek to see what they were up to.

They stood in the middle of the flowing river, their arms wrapped around one another, naked bodies and mouths pressing. I gasped and fell backward, underbrush crackling beneath me. Had they heard? It sounded loud as a firecracker explosion from my end. I flattened onto my stomach and peered beneath the fronds.

They stood apart, blankly scanning the dark night.

I considered popping up like a jack-in-the-box and screaming, *Surprise,* but frankly, my little sister had at last managed to shock me. And that took some doing. Besides, I needed to process this salacious discovery and consider the best way to work my knowledge of their secret to its best advantage.

Their playful banter resumed. The little traitors had decided no danger lurked here in the shadows. Maybe I should come back another night with my cell phone and shoot some video.

A faint rustling sounded to my right, and this time it was me searching the darkness. It had to be a deer or another largish animal. Who else would be out here this time of night?

Their laughing voices grew closer. They were coming this way to swing from the rope and dive into the water. Quickly, I darted farther into the woods, where the trees stood closer together. Soon as they'd both jumped back in the river, I'd make a run to the house to get my cell phone.

They started up the cliff, their voices louder with every step they climbed. It took me a minute to recognize the angry edge in their tone, and I still couldn't make out the exact words. Clearly, they were in the throes of a lovers' spat. I clasped my hands over my mouth to suppress a giggle. Catfight!

At the top of the cliff, they went at it. Screams and slaps rumbled through the humid darkness. I settled in to enjoy the spectacle.

Chapter 33

HYACINTH

July 2, 2007

"Hyacinth? Where are you?"

My knees jellied, and I clung to the pine's scratchy bark to keep from falling.

"Here!"

I left the protection of tree cover and squinted as the flashlight's beam pierced my eyes. The light shifted, lowering to the ground, shining on black uniform boots. Size 14. Strange, the tidbits of facts I remembered about my old lover. The freckles on the backs of his hands, his favorite old movie, the way his chest vibrated when he laughed. A sudden image: We are lying in bed naked, relaxing and teasing each other in that silly way we do after making love. He laughs at something on a vapid TV sitcom. My hand is lying on his chest in a mound of dark, curly hair. His muscles spasm beneath my palm, and I smile. At one with my love in one of those tender afterglow moments that bind couples.

Had Parker and I ever been that close—that happy? If so, it was hard to remember past the years of hurt and disappointment.

Boone reached my side. After more than a decade, he was close enough that I could touch him, smell him, be absorbed in the heated energy that crackled between us as I stared into his kind eyes. Alone, out here in the woods, we didn't have to hide our feelings. Instantly, I saw that he still loved me. And I must have been the worst mother in the world, because when he wrapped his arms around me, I sank into his strength, into his familiar smell and touch, and for all of two seconds, I was comforted, overwhelmed with love.

Strong fingers encircled my arms near the elbows, steadying me. Boone pulled away.

"Whatever's happened here tonight, we'll work it out," he assured me. "I'll find our daughter."

Our daughter.

In spite of everything, of all the anger and lies and years of going it alone, I was proud to have had a child with this man.

"Yes." I swiped a hand across my eyes.

"Where's the body you mentioned on the phone?"

"This way."

With one of his arms wrapped around my shoulders, I found the courage to backtrack through the woods and face the gruesome sight. I filled him in on everything I knew. Delaney's insinuations, the found clothing and sandals, my own suspicions of what might have happened based on Violet's recent rebellious behavior. The ugly suspicions crept out, surprising even me. But I couldn't afford to ignore my intuition. Violet's future hung in the balance, and I needed to discover the truth if we were going to be able to help her in the critical days ahead.

"You didn't really consider that someone other than Violet killed Ainsley?" he asked, all the time scanning the darkness, searching for Violet.

"Like who?"

"Could be anyone. Like maybe they came out here to meet some boys. Kids do that. They drink, get high, and do all kinds of stupid, foolish shit. A few beers, and they shed their clothes and decide to play Tarzan. Everyone round here knows this place is dangerous. The river's littered with sharp rocks and boulders."

"I didn't see any signs of a party. No beer cans or whiskey bottles."

We reached the water. "It's right through here." I pointed and started to wade the brackish water.

"Stay put. Every footprint could be important. We don't want to muck up an investigation."

An investigation. I shivered but didn't argue. I hugged my arms to my chest, watching his flashlight's beam shine on the lifeless body like a macabre spotlight. Boone returned to my side moments later, rubbing his chin.

"Where all have you searched?"

"Only right here near the shore. Should we divide up? Go different ways?"

"No. Stay with me. First place I want to look is by the swing."

I followed behind him, breathless but optimistic. Boone would know what to do. He'd find Violet. Any moment, I expected her to pop out of the shadows.

But she didn't.

Fatigue bore down on me, and my legs felt like wooden appendages. We trudged on, silent and relentless. A hint of morning crept into the lightening sky. His cell phone buzzed, and he turned from me, muttering crisp evasions to his wife about where he was and what he was doing.

That done, Boone stuffed it in his pocket. "Another ten minutes, and then I'll have to call in reinforcements."

I was torn. I wanted Violet found at once, to hold her in my arms and run my hands through her black hair, the exact shade and texture of my own. Yet I feared what would happen if she was found by a cop. Would they arrest her or be kind? She was only fourteen, still a child.

"Violet?" I kept calling her name, my voice cracking from wear and exhaustion.

Boone held out his right arm, blocking my path. "I hear something," he whispered.

I stopped, straining my ears. At last I heard it: muffled sobs. I circled in all directions, trying to pinpoint the source.

Boone jogged to the left, and I followed, adrenaline giving new life to my legs.

A tall, pale form shifted into focus. Violet, clad only in a pair of torn panties, stumbling about like a zombie. I ran toward her, then stopped when I came within arm's length.

My daughter looked right through me, as though I were merely an obstruction in her aimless, rambling path. I didn't know whether to shake her or gently take her hand. I took a tentative step forward. "Violet, honey, are you okay?"

I glanced at Boone, and he nodded. Afraid of spooking her, I ever so slowly reached out my hand and touched her arm. A flicker of awareness sparked in her eyes. "Everything's going to be all right, sweetheart. I promise you. Are you hurt?"

Violet just blinked, but at least she recognized me and didn't try to run off. My eyes quickly scanned her body. A few scratches on her neck and chest, but that was it.

"Mama?"

I pulled her to me in a fierce embrace. Her arms hung wooden at her sides. My baby took no comfort in my touch. I stepped back and swallowed hard. "What happened, honey?"

"Ainsley's gone." Her brow knotted in confusion. "I can't find her."

"We'll find your friend." I asked again, "What happened?"

"I pushed her."

The confession rang in my ears, upending my world. A pebble thrown in a lake spreading ripples as it sank and hit bottom. I sucked in my breath and glanced at Boone. The sharp angles of his face appeared even harsher than usual. It had hit him just as hard.

"She fell . . ." Violet's voice trailed away, and I remained silent, hoping she'd be more likely to continue without my pressure. Boone's hand, warm and strong, slipped into mine, and I squeezed it as though grasping an anchor in a stormy sea.

Violet turned toward the cliff. "Ainsley fell a long, long way down. And now she's gone."

Although I strained to hear her whispered words, they slammed into me with hurricane-gust strength.

I wrapped an arm around her bare, thin shoulders. "Yes, hon. She's gone. Now it's time for you to go back home. Mama will tuck you in bed, and then I want you to forget this ever happened. It's a nightmare we'll never speak of again."

Violet nodded, but she still had a vacant cloudiness floating in her eyes. I turned her to face me and cupped her chin in my hand, forcing her eyes to look directly in mine.

"Never, ever tell anyone you pushed Ainsley," I said slowly and carefully. "Do you understand?"

She nodded. Time would tell if I'd really gotten through to her or not.

I caught Boone punching numbers into his cell phone, the crisp keypad tones puncturing the air. "Stop it," I said with a hiss. "Don't call anybody."

His brows rose. "Got to notify Forensics to come get the"—his eyes cut to Violet—"get the, um, you know. Then I need to notify—"

"No. I mean it. Don't call anybody."

"Why?"

I grasped one of Violet's hands in my own. "I'm taking her in. Be back in five minutes. Please, Boone. Don't report this."

He opened his mouth to argue, but I turned away, rushing Violet to follow me to the house. She didn't resist but didn't attempt to match my faster gait or heed my urgent pleas to hurry either. Rather, she lumbered along like a docile sleepwalker in a semitrance. I couldn't worry about her emotional state. No time for that. Instead, my mind raced, thinking about what to do next. I'd need to devise a plan to protect my sweet Violet, and then I needed to convince Boone to go along with that plan. Inside the house, it was dark and quiet. Upstairs, a light shone from underneath Delaney's door. No doubt the little troublemaker had waited up to see what kind of trouble Violet was in. I wouldn't give her the satisfaction.

In the kitchen, I poured a glass of water and shook two antianxiety pills from my prescription bottle. Violet accepted the pills without question and obediently swallowed them. With any luck, tonight would only be a vague memory for her come morning. I popped a couple of pills myself and then, as quickly and quietly as possible, guided Violet to her room, dug a nightgown out of her dresser drawer, and slipped it over her head.

"Don't tell anyone about Ainsley," I whispered as she curled into a fetal position in her bed. I pulled the sheets up to her neck, and her vacant eyes met mine. I placed an index finger over my lips. "Shh."

The moment her eyes shut, I sneaked back down the hallway and paused at the top of the stairs. A snore rumbled from the master bedroom, and for once, I envied Parker the luxury of his drunken sleep. It seemed this night's horrors were unending. And it still wasn't over. I rushed downstairs and back out into the darkness. Somehow, I had to convince Boone to go along with my wild plan.

~

We oared the john boat, methodically slicing through still waters. Boone up front, me in the back, and our cargo in the middle. Cement blocks weighed the flimsy craft enough that black water crept over the sides. I stopped paddling and began casting out bucketfuls of water.

Soon, we left behind the river and entered the wide expanse of Hatchet Lake, the boat casting silent ripples behind us.

Irma won't be lonely anymore. The hysterical, inappropriate thought lingered. Poor Ainsley. Irma's death had been more painful and prolonged than Ainsley's had been, but at least Irma got to spend eternity in her white nightgown. Ainsley was as naked as the day she'd entered this world. Too late, I wished I'd dressed Ainsley in her discarded clothes I'd found.

"We should be out of hearing range now," Boone pronounced, dropping the oars inside the boat and pulling the cord to start the trolley motor. It sputtered to life, and we glided far across the lake.

Boone abruptly killed the engine. "This ought to do."

"If you say so." Here seemed as good a place as any. All that mattered was that the water depth be lower than any fishing rod line cast by fishermen. Too bad this crappy little dinghy didn't have a depth finder. But then again, I'd never expected to need such a fancy contraption, seeing as how I loathed fishing and anything connected with the water. I'd grown up with the lake practically in my backyard and yet had never learned to swim. Water terrified me—the sheer weight and mass of it felt oppressive.

Coral streaks of dawn slashed the sky. We had to hurry. Bass boats often launched at day's first light. All it would take was one random boat to spot us, and then we'd all be doomed.

I didn't want to look at the corpse, but I was compelled, drawn to the grisly specter of Ainsley's naked body and the smeared blood staining the delicate features of her face. Enough. I spun around on the boat's wooden plank seat and resolved to do what I must to protect Violet. I wouldn't look at Ainsley again.

My hands dug into the rough board planking by my thighs as Boone stood, violently rocking the boat. What if I fell overboard as well? Became tangled in the web of rope, body, and cement blocks?

Boone will protect me. I clung to that belief as his knees bumped against my back and he slightly grunted as he lifted the body. I braced my hands against the sides of the tiny craft, preparing for its final, brutal lurch when Boone would toss her body out into the water. I waited, sensing his hesitation.

"For God's sake, do it! Get it over with." I fought against the bile rising at the back of my throat. Our decision had been made over an hour ago after much debate—and then preparation. Parker kept his decrepit boat by the shed in our backyard, but finding the rope and blocks had taken a bit longer.

"I'm having second thoughts, Hy. The whole incident was an accident. Had to be. Violet didn't mean to hurt the girl."

"Doesn't matter. This will ruin our daughter's life. Do we really need to argue this point again?"

"I'll make sure Violet gets nothing stiffer than psychological—"

"No. Just stop." I fought to think of a new reason to keep Boone's silence. "Think of your career. Everything's bound to come out."

"I don't care. This is wrong."

"Then think of your marriage. Of your sons. You want to ruin their lives too? Because you will. Media and gossip will flay you alive. Not only for obstructing justice, but it will come out that Violet's your daughter."

His shoulders stiffened, and his mouth tightened. I'd hit home. But even then, I wasn't through. A deep-seated bitterness erupted to the surface. "What will your precious boys think then?"

"You leave them out of this."

Oh, hell no. He'd have left Ellie for me. I knew my power to entice and tempt Boone trumped the allure of his safe wife. Yet despite my knowledge of that power, I hadn't wielded it and pursued him over the years. Boone's sons needed their father, and I knew he'd never be happy with me for guilt of leaving them.

I didn't flinch from his hard glare. "If you don't do it, I will."

"Go ahead."

I dropped to my knees. With a rush of desperation and anger, I gripped under her waist with both arms and rolled Ainsley over the side.

Splash.

Rope swiftly followed the body down under, scraping against the boat's metal side, as if it were a live thing, frantic to escape its confines. I screamed and twisted to the side, desperate to evade its relentless plunge to a black abyss.

"Damn it, Hyacinth." Boone knelt beside me, tossing out the two cement blocks tethered to the rope around Ainsley.

They splattered into the water, creating a small eddy, which then flattened to the lake's original glassy surface. The sheer speed and utter return to normalcy belied the monstrous act we'd just committed. The lake had swallowed our secrets. Only now did I allow myself to feel a sliver of remorse for what I'd done. But to be honest, mostly what I felt was relief.

Boone's heavy breathing mingled with mine, and we sat unmoving. From far off across a field, a rooster crowed. It was a new day, a new era. Much as I wanted to stay here with Boone in the darkness with our secrets, I had a child at home who needed me. Somehow, I had to sweep this memory down to a dark place and keep on with my life.

"We'll never speak of this again," he said, picking up two oars and resuming his seat up front.

"Never," I agreed.

Chapter 34

VIOLET

Present day

Tux had returned.

I smiled as he cautiously inched closer, talons clutched around the thin metal railing of my balcony. I withdrew two shelled peanuts from my pocket and slowly laid them on the coffee table, a mere four feet from where I sat.

He cocked his head, one ebony eye fixed on me, unblinking and wary. I didn't move, didn't speak, curious if he would get any closer today than he had yesterday. This was a little kickoff to the game we played. A way to reclaim the old closeness. Every evening, I moved the treats closer to me, testing how close Tux dared come.

With an unnerving quickness, Tux dived for his treat and then retreated to the far end of my balcony, the treats safely tucked in his beak. As he crunched away, my mind returned to the niggling question of where Delaney had hidden Dad's pills. Day by day, he seemed to lose more verve. His digging attempts now amounted to little more than shuffling dirt back and forth with one of the stray fallen limbs of the pecan tree. The naps grew longer. Even now, he was half sleeping while watching television in the den.

I needed to find those pills and discover the truth about his mental state. I didn't trust my sister. As a precaution, I emptied out Delaney's herbal home-brewed teas whenever she prepared a jug and stuck it in the fridge. At least I could waylay those attempts to control us by sedation. Only last week, two bottles of my medications had gone missing, so I'd learned to keep my own prescriptions with me at all times, in case she decided to tamper with my drugs as well.

I'd already given the kitchen and dining room a thorough sweep. The den and Dad's room weren't ideal hiding places. Too much coming and going. The one time I'd snooped around Delaney's room, I hadn't found Dad's medicine tucked into a drawer. But I felt sure it must be there.

And Delaney's silence about her fiancé showing up at her beauty pageant dinner also unnerved me. Libby and I had paid one of her friends to act the part, and he'd assured us he'd done the job. Maybe I'd scared her into an uneasy truce of sorts. Showed her I was someone to be reckoned with, just as I had with those women at the state mental hospital.

"Back in a bit, Tux," I promised, setting out another handful of peanuts on the table. Delaney wasn't home today, so it wouldn't hurt to take another look around. Inside her room, the curtains were drawn, and the heavy mahogany furniture made me nostalgic. Many times I'd sat in front of that very dresser, Mom brushing my long hair and telling me some silly story from her childhood.

Now this area was a shrine to Delaney. She had a fortune lying about in antique perfume flasks, gold jewelry, and designer toiletries. Photos of herself were everywhere. I'd started to open a drawer when I noticed one of the picture frames was slightly off kilter—the Miss Normal Peach Queen photo.

Delaney was so particular about keeping everything just so. How had she missed this? I straightened it, frowning. A bolt of suspicion tingled from my fingertips and traveled up my arm. I had a sudden image of Mom lifting her wedding portrait from this very spot and opening a small safe to don a pearl necklace for a country club dance. I had forgotten all about it.

Was the safe still there?

Carefully, I lifted the photo and then blinked at the safe with its digital keypad. Dad's medicine was there, had to be. But I had no clue what the code might be. Half-heartedly, I entered her birthdate, but Delaney wasn't that stupid. The safe remained shut, its secrets locked up tight. Later, I'd ask Libby if she had any ideas for bypassing the code.

I returned to my balcony, but Tux had flown off with all the peanuts I'd left on the table. Settling back in my chair, I sipped iced tea and idly gazed at Delaney's garden in the backyard. A bit of something red sparkled like a ruby chip at the far end of the deck. I rose and made my way over, careful not to trip over a few of the old buckled boards. On the feeder lay a glass bead. I lifted it and held it up to the waning sunlight, where it glittered like iced sangria.

"Thanks, Tux," I called out to the wind, hoping my voice and meaning reached their intended audience. I had a feeling the old fellow was nearby watching as I claimed this latest gift. For most people, these bits and baubles would be no big deal. But for a mostly friendless woman whose only gifts for years had consisted of charity packages at Christmas—mostly socks, hard candies, and cheap bubble bath—these crow gifts were a sign.

I was watched.

I was appreciated.

My life mattered.

I tucked it in my pocket and tipped the feeder to one side, making sure my own secret remained hidden.

It was still there, the deadly treasure that I'd hid from my sister and the world. Ainsley's necklace sparkled for a brief moment before I laid the base back on top of the incriminating evidence. The smart move would be to bury the necklace deep into the earth, but I wasn't quite ready to part with this last physical link to Ainsley. Until then, I didn't think Delaney would ever think to search here.

I headed back to my chair. My toe caught beneath one of the buckled boards, and I plunged forward, my left arm catching most of the tumble as I hit the deck. I sat for a moment, assessing the damage. Nothing broken or strained by the feel of it, only scrapes and splinters bloodying one forearm. The deck really needed fixing. It wouldn't be that expensive. Since it was one of the few places where I could relax and unwind, it'd be worth it, even if I could afford my own place in a few weeks. I thought of Delaney's threat to kick me out by the end of the week if I didn't confess to murder. It had to be nothing more than idle bluster. She had no more claim to the house than I did.

I turned my attention back to the practical matter of the deck. Shouldn't be that difficult to pull up a few boards and nail in new ones. I'd watched Seth do it hundreds of times at Cottonwood. He'd worked in maintenance, and they'd once spent weeks building new cabinets and breaking down the old ones. The corners of my mouth turned up as I remembered Seth's wink and quick grin as he'd watched my first attempt to hammer a nail.

Full of resolve, I marched to the garage and returned with a hammer and tape measure. Tonight, I'd pull up the boards, and then on my way home from work tomorrow, I'd stop by the hardware store and have them cut a few planks to size. Determined, I squatted down and set to work, pulling up old rusty nails and rotted wood. I was slow and clumsy, but I could do it. To my surprise, the home-improvement labor felt empowering. If I could do this, take what was physically broken and fix it, maybe I could do the same with my circumstances.

I indulged in a delightful series of *what ifs*. What if Delaney and I could live in peace? What if Dad's health got better? I imagined the three of us a happy little family. What if . . . but there was no sense resurrecting the dead. Ainsley and Mom had no place in this rose-hued fantasy. I leaned against the railing, hammer still in hand, and rested.

Chapter 35

DELANEY

July 2, 2007

Violet shoved Ainsley away from her, and Ainsley stumbled backward off the cliff ledge.

A shriek and a splash.

Too funny! I doubled over, clutching my stomach as I tried to contain my laughter. Damn shame I didn't have video rolling to record this whole incident.

Violet stood at the edge, calling Ainsley's name at the top of her lungs. Over and over.

Go make up with your girlfriend, I wanted to shout. *Let me get it all on camera.*

As if she'd read my thoughts, Violet rushed down the cliff and ran into the river, prancing about like a startled pony. I didn't bother holding back the laughter anymore. As much noise as she was making splashing about, Violet would never hear.

"Ainsley! Where are you? Ainsley?"

Her sly girlfriend must be hiding about somewhere too. No doubt laughing her ass off at scaring my sister so bad. That's what I would do.

Another scream, but this one was different. A scream of absolute terror.

"No, no, no!"

And then came silence, more disturbing than any wail. Violet stopped her frantic prancing and stood in the cool, muddy waters, her hands plunged into her long hair, tugging violently at the dark tresses. Why? What had happened? I watched and waited. The sinister air thickened, and yet Violet remained immobile—like a wild, naked animal too stunned to move. At last she trudged forward, clutching her head in her hands as she staggered to shore. I almost felt sorry for her. I walked out from the trees and into the open, but she passed within six feet of me, staring straight ahead with dead eyes.

"Violet?"

She kept going, as though sleepwalking. Still naked. Curious, I waded into the water to find what had spooked her. Ainsley lay scrunched between two boulders. Had she really gotten hurt? I waded in deeper, the water swirling to my knees, then waist, then breasts. One side of Ainsley's face lay pressed against the unforgiving granite.

I stood over her.

"Ainsley?" I whispered.

No response, not even the barest twitch. Shock tingled down my spine. I figured she must be dead. That was some rotten luck, landing on the rocks like she had. Poor kid. She'd been a lot of fun to hang out with. Moonlight glimmered on the thin strand of silver around her neck. The attached silver cross pendant dangled off center of her cleavage. Without thinking, I reached for the necklace, unclasping the lock tangled in the wet, matted hair at the nape of her broken neck. I'd always admired the simple elegance of this necklace Ainsley wore all the time. I glanced down at her twisted, limp hand. The braided friendship bracelet Violet had made for her was there as well.

I took that too.

It was worthless, but I'd always had this silly longing to own one. The bracelets were all the rage right now between girlfriends, sisters, cousins, and mothers and daughters. But had Violet ever thought to make me one? No. And I deserved one more than the slutty Ainsley. I was her *sister*. That should mean something.

I gripped my prizes in my fist and turned away. Nobody would ever know I'd been here. Later, if anyone thought of the missing jewelry, they'd assume the river had washed it away.

What an exciting night this had turned out to be. My only annoyance was that my clothes were wet and dirty. If I'd been smart, I would have taken them off before getting in the water, like Violet and Ainsley. Which gave me an idea. Their dry, clean clothes should be around nearby. But getting rid of the filched clothes after I returned to the house could be a problem later. Best to keep on what I had and wash it out in the bathroom before throwing it in the laundry. Less risky.

Violet was going to be in so much trouble. Epic trouble. Possibly the put-her-away-for-life kind of trouble.

Two steps toward shore, and a faint moan wafted over the running water. Was it possible? I whirled around and leaned over Ainsley, mere inches from her pale, wet face. Her eyelids flickered with a beating pulse. Maybe she'd survive . . . maybe she wouldn't. That was Violet's problem, not mine.

I straightened, half turning to leave.

Ainsley's eyes opened to small slits, pewter-gray irises blinking. Did she recognize me? Her full lips wobbled, and a lone rivulet of water ran down her cheek. Whether it was tears or river water dripping from her scalp, I had no idea.

This was not good. Had she seen me take her necklace and bracelet? How would I explain my presence here to everyone?

I couldn't take a chance that she lingered and lived. For all I knew, Violet was already home, waking the parents and returning with help.

That would be just like my sister. Causing a major problem and then twisting circumstances so it would end up all my fault.

I couldn't let that happen. I ran back to shore and searched, quickly surveying broken bits of rock. It needed to be at least as round and heavy as a baseball, though jagged edges were preferred. Bending over, I scooped one up and considered its weight and shape in the palm of my right hand. This should do.

I returned to Ainsley's side and lifted the rock up high. Her eyes widened enough so that the glossy white of her eyeballs framed the pewter disks.

This is all on Violet.

My rock-laden hand whooshed down, a bird of prey diving in for the kill.

Chapter 36

BOONE

Delaney Henderson walked into the office, high heels pummeling staccato indentations in the old linoleum, whipping her long blonde hair like a weapon.

Trouble. It vibrated from her like a bad aura, infecting everyone in its wake. Her eyes darted from Josh's empty desk to me.

"May I help you?" I asked.

She hesitated, her red purse swinging against her legs, and then brushed past my desk to Dan's door. "This is a matter for Chief Thornell."

"He's not in."

This time Delaney didn't hesitate. She turned the doorknob and walked in—only to reappear in the doorway moments later.

"He really isn't here," she said, stating the obvious.

I pointed at the two folding metal chairs in front of my desk. "The chief and Normal's only other investigator are out for the afternoon. Again, may I help you, Miss Henderson?"

Delaney sat abruptly, clasping the red purse in her lap. We eyed one another uneasily.

"Detective Kimbrel. So you remembered my name after all these years?"

"Of course. What can I do for you?" My tone was polite . . . but barely so.

Her fingers twitched on the purse clasp, and then she flicked it open, withdrawing a manila envelope and pushing it across my desk.

I had a feeling I wasn't going to like whatever was in that envelope. "What's this?"

She nudged it farther toward me. "A bracelet. I believe you'll recognize its importance when you see it."

Bracelet? My thoughts tumbled over one another, racing to attach meaning to such an object. I turned the envelope upside down, and a small chunk of twisted leather plopped onto my office ledger, looking like a shriveled-up spider. A dead thing that could do no harm, yet it filled me with an unknown dread.

I quirked a brow at Delaney.

"Don't you see? It belonged to Ainsley Dalfred. It's the friendship bracelet Violet made her. She wore it all the time. All. The. Time."

And now I knew her game. Long ago, the Dalfreds had mentioned that Ainsley had always worn a cross necklace and this bracelet. It had been noted in the written interview as an interesting detail, should either ever appear one day.

That day had arrived. I leaned back in my chair, feigning innocence, the bracelet between us exuding danger. "What are you saying exactly?"

She rolled her eyes at me. Actually rolled her eyes. Easy to see why Hyacinth couldn't stand her stepdaughter.

"It belonged to a dead girl." She spoke slowly, enunciating each syllable, as if I were an imbecile. "A *murdered* girl."

"And how did you come into possession of this . . . thing?" I studied her face, the wholesome freckles that dotted a patrician nose, the sun-streaked highlights in her honey-colored hair, the wide, expressive eyes.

Somehow, they didn't combine to form an attractive woman, although they should have. Her face was a little too long, her chin a little too pointed, and the eyes a shade too calculating.

"I found it—"

"Around the wrist of the victim years ago? Are you here to confess?"

Outrage exploded from her eyes, and she jumped up so quickly that the chair clattered to the floor. She stuffed the bracelet back in the envelope with stiff, angry flicks of her wrist and fingers. "Of course not. How dare you! I came here trying to help in an investigation, and you accuse *me* of murder? I should have waited to speak with the police chief. You're clearly incompetent."

I met her gaze with dispassionate calm and spoke with an authority honed by years of police experience. No way I'd allow this woman to walk out of here with physical evidence in hand. "Sit down, Miss Henderson."

I opened a drawer, pulling out a small evidence container and an ID tag. Without glancing at Delaney, as though assuming she'd obey the command, I picked up a pen and scribbled on the blank tag.

"Humph." Muttering, she righted the chair and sat down with another huff.

I held out a hand and nodded at the envelope in her lap. "I'll take that."

She all but threw it at me.

"Let's start over, shall we? How did you come to be in possession of this item?"

"I found it in my sister's room. You'll remember Violet, of course."

The little snoop. "Naturally. When and how did you obtain it from her room?"

"I was cleaning. Violet's terribly messy. As if I don't already have enough to do, what with working full time from home and looking after our father."

"I see. And how did you know the significance of this particular piece of jewelry?" The missing necklace and bracelet was a detail we'd never released to the public.

Her mouth opened and shut like a fish out of water, gasping for air. "I-I just assumed . . . I mean, Ainsley's dead, and my sister had this hidden in a drawer in her room. Ainsley used to wear this all the time. Violet made it for her, you know. And there was the necklace, too, of course, that Ainsley always wore. It had a silver cross pendant with a diamond chip in the middle. Violet has that, too, the necklace. I saw it with my own eyes. Only now it's missing."

The pen clasped between my thumb and fingers trembled from the rage simmering within me. "You say you were cleaning and found this bracelet hidden in a drawer."

Delaney lifted her chin a fraction. "Okay. I wasn't cleaning. I'm not one to snoop or invade someone's privacy—"

Like hell she wasn't.

"But I've been worried about Violet ever since she came home from the mental hospital. She has nightmares, forgets things, acts strange . . . I'm afraid to even leave her in the house alone with Dad. Violet almost started a kitchen fire only the second day she was home. I barely got back in time to keep the house from going up in flames. So I went through her room, searching for . . . oh, I don't know what exactly. I guess clues to explain why she's so secretive, so full of guilt that she can't sleep at night."

Delaney stopped her rambling, reached back in her purse, and pulled out a prescription pill bottle. "I also found this in her room, and other medications too. Violet's on antidepressants and antianxiety and sleeping pills."

What a cruel woman. Throwing my Violet to the wolves like this. I sealed the evidence in the official police envelope and wrote the date and time on the tag. "What do your sister's medications have to do with anything?"

"Clearly, it shows she's unstable. A possible threat to herself and others. I'm worried about her, Detective. I've told her that if she needed help, it might be best to go back to the hospital. Or confess to y'all about her role in Ainsley's death. Might make her feel better to get this off her chest and finally begin to heal and move on with her life."

"Let me get this straight. You're only concerned with her well-being." I tapped the weighted envelope on my battered desk, struggling to maintain my temper.

"Of course." She met my gaze, straight-on sociopathic style, before fluttering her eyes demurely. "Okay, there's more, Detective." A tinny laugh escaped past her lipstick-stained mouth. "I *am* worried. I'm afraid Violet will kill me too. Just like she did Ainsley."

"Why? What would be her motive?"

"Money. Isn't that always the reason? Not that I'd presume to know the mind of a murderer."

That trilling laugh again.

"My family doesn't have much, but the house and land are worth something. And then there's Dad's social security disability and some money saved in the bank."

"You really think your sister would kill you for so little?"

"It's not easy for me to admit, but yes, I do. Just last week I woke up in the middle of the night, and Violet stood over me with the strangest expression on her face." Delaney shuddered. "Her eyes lacked all human warmth. It was chilling."

I didn't buy her story for a damn minute.

"You can ask our dad too," she threw in for good measure. "He's so afraid of Violet that he's taken to locking himself in his bedroom every night."

Parker Henderson had always been a chickenshit, unless it came to beating up on helpless women and children. I ignored Delaney's claim on that one. "By all accounts, Violet and Ainsley were best friends. So what's your theory on why Violet allegedly killed her?"

"Lovers' quarrel."

"I see. Do you have any other evidence to substantiate these claims?"

"Isn't this enough? You have the bracelet Ainsley wore the night she was murdered. And it was in the possession of the last person to have seen her alive. It's all there—motive and opportunity."

Delaney had watched too many police shows. "If you could find that necklace, it would really be helpful." I shoved one of my business cards toward her. "Call me right away if you do."

"Are you sure the bracelet isn't enough to go ahead and arrest her?"

"Maybe. But the necklace would be more incriminating." I needed that necklace. If someone else got to it first, Violet was in serious trouble. True, both jewelry items were only circumstantial evidence, but they would weigh heavy on jurors should the case go to trial. The prosecution would be sure to claim they were being kept as trophies by the killer.

"I'll try to get that necklace, then. This is disappointing, Detective Kimbrel."

Her gaze drifted once more to Dan Thornell's door. I couldn't have Delaney going to him or Josh with this matter.

"Tell you what," I said, leaning toward her conspiratorially. "I'll do what I can. Soon as the death certificate arrives from the department of public health, I'll arrest Violet on suspicion of murder. It should be any day now. In the meantime, you keep looking for that necklace. It'll strengthen the case against your sister."

She frowned, clearly unhappy I hadn't immediately rushed off to handcuff Violet and lock her in jail. I couldn't have an unhappy Delaney.

"Can't tell you how helpful this is." I held up the envelope and gave it a little shake. "Don't know if you remember, but I was the original detective on the Dalfred case. I've waited eleven years to solve this. No one wants to arrest Violet more than I do. No one. So you call me at once if you need me or find anything, and I'll contact you soon as I can move in for the arrest. How does that sound?"

"Perfect." She dropped my card in her purse and rose. "Let me know if I can help speed things up with the necessary paperwork from the state. A well-timed television appearance by me, crying over this stupid death certificate technicality, would surely spur them to action."

Technicality, my ass. I'd fabricated a quick lie, and it wasn't even a good one. Flimsy as it was, that lie bought me a little time to stave off possible disaster for me and my daughter. If she went to the news media, my career was toast.

"Don't go yet," I urged. "Give me a couple of days, and I'll make sure to set things right."

"Hurry. I, that is, we—Dad and I—don't feel safe in our own home. The sooner Violet is put away, the better. And whether that means the loony bin or prison, I don't much give a flip."

With that, Delaney marched out the door. I eased up from my desk, feeling as though I'd aged ten years in ten minutes, and then strolled to the window, which possessed a scenic overlook of the visitor parking lot. After watching her drive away, I returned to my desk and tucked the small evidence envelope inside my pants pocket. Soon as I got home I'd have to find a safe place to hide it.

How had Delaney ended up with that bracelet? Had Violet taken it from Ainsley after she'd died?

Maybe after the two had argued, Ainsley had taken off the bracelet and returned it to Violet. But Violet hadn't been holding anything in her hands that night we'd found her, and she'd been naked—so it wasn't as though she'd concealed it in a pocket either. And the necklace? If Ainsley had worn it swimming the night she'd died, I didn't recall seeing it.

Delaney knew something, had seen something.

That now made two people who might have witnessed Ainsley's murder that night, Delaney and Gerald Stedmyer. My fingers tapped a nervous beat against the envelope in my pocket. This wouldn't do. Not at all.

With shaking hands, I pulled up the contact list on my cell phone and made the one call I'd never wanted to make.

Chapter 37

BOONE

Present day

I'm afraid she's going to kill me, Delaney had said. *Dad's afraid too.*

I'd thought Delaney was lying when she'd spoken those words four days ago, but perhaps she was right, whether she recognized the real danger or not. Twigs cracked as I shuffled my old feet in the dirt. They were unaccustomed to standing for long periods. Surveillance was a job more suited for younger detectives. I kept the field glasses trained on the deck as I spied on my daughter from the safety of the woods located on the side of the Henderson property.

"Damn it," I muttered.

"What's Violet doing up there? Let me see."

I lowered my binoculars and stared at the stranger beside me.

Well, not really a stranger; I knew her body intimately. But so much time had passed. The woman beside me was still beautiful, even if wrinkles creased the corners of her eyes and forehead. Her hair was bobbed now, streaked with caramel highlights. And her skin was more olive than I remembered, as if the years spent in Portugal had baked an exotic hue over her curvaceous body.

Hyacinth.

She took the binoculars and focused on our daughter.

"She's tearing up floorboards on the deck." An indulgent smile flitted across the corners of her mouth. "Or rather, she's trying to. Why? Oh, Boone, look at her now. She looks so sad."

Even from our position, tucked inconspicuously within a copse of pine and oak, I saw what she meant. Violet sat on the balcony, head resting against the old rusted rails enclosing the deck. It looked like she was in prison, caged behind bars.

"I want to see my baby! Let me go ahead," Hy pleaded. "Delaney's not home."

"But Parker is. The light's still on in the den, and he's lying on the sofa. It's getting late. We'll just wait here until we see him retire to his room. Shouldn't be too long."

Hyacinth snorted. "Even if he saw me and told others, no one would believe that crazy old drunk."

"I'm not taking any chances. I have a career here, a family to think of. Not everyone can just pick up and run away from their responsibilities."

Hy was unrepentant. "And I'd do it all over again in a heartbeat. Thanks to me, Violet can leave this horrible town and live a comfortable life with me overseas, where no one knows her past."

"You haven't seen her in years. You can wait another forty minutes or so."

Bright, accusing eyes slammed into mine. "You should have called me the minute she came home."

"Maybe you should have kept better tabs on her whereabouts," I snapped. "After all, you're her mother."

"You think I don't know that? Okay, maybe I did get a little lax this summer keeping up with her progress, but she wasn't expected to be released until late this fall, at the earliest."

Despite Hy's defensive retort, a guilty flush stained her face and neck.

"Anyway, I'm here now, aren't I? I intend to make things right."

"How? By offering her money? You honestly believe that you can erase the years she spent without you? The pain she's suffered believing you've been dead? Still, if I had the chance to do it over, I'd have called earlier," I admitted.

"Why didn't you?"

"Because almost as soon as she arrived, it was announced the lake was being drained. Everyone was speculating that the Dalfred remains would be found and the case reopened. It would have looked suspicious if Violet had fled town. And frankly, I didn't want to ever see you again. You're poison. You ruin every life you touch."

She drew in a sharp breath, and pain lanced her features. "You could have called for Violet's sake, if not my own," she whispered. "Even if you hate me now."

I didn't hate her, but I couldn't let her know she still affected me.

"I wanted Violet to make it on her own, if possible. Might have been good for her to set old ghosts to rest. But your stepdaughter wasn't going to let that happen."

"I told you years ago that Delaney was manipulative. That one won't ever change. Best thing is for Violet to leave. Her real inheritance is waiting for her overseas. She can start a new life with me in Portugal."

"Money doesn't solve everything. And I bet she has no desire to live with you. Not after what you've done."

"Who the hell do you think you are?" she asked, folding her arms tight around her waist. "I never would have gotten away with faking my death if you hadn't helped. You're as guilty as I am."

What a fool I'd been. A reckless, besotted idiot. Hyacinth had come to me all those years ago with her tears, with her pleas. She'd overheard Parker tell Delaney that he planned to divorce her as soon as Hy's mother's estate was settled. Parker had bragged of bombshell news he could use against Hy in divorce court. That with a good attorney and a judge who was an old friend of his family's, he could get the majority of the money. In the end, Hyacinth had convinced me to act against everything I'd ever believed in—justice, faithfulness, even basic human decency. And not just once but twice.

You're as guilty as I am. Hy's words cannonballed through me. She was right. I'd been, in part, selfishly worried about the damage to my family and career if the truth came out about that night. At least Hyacinth had acted in the belief she'd be protecting Violet's future by setting up a safe living arrangement for the two of them.

So again, I'd helped Hyacinth when she was in need. Given my position as a detective, the faking part had been easy. A switch with another burnt corpse that was already too damaged for DNA testing. Then setting Hy's car on fire and writing up the fatal accident as the investigating detective of record. Hyacinth had already taken care of the detail work, slowly funneling funds from secret accounts in the States to an overseas bank and arranging a false identity and passport from an ex-con I'd recommended she contact. She'd vowed never to return to Normal, unless Violet needed her. Now her return might wreck my life and my career.

But the present circumstances justified Hyacinth's homecoming.

"Let's let sleeping dogs lie," I said, taking the binoculars and watching Violet. She'd returned to loosening nails, and a horrible possibility seized me. "Violet must realize Delaney's closing in on her."

"Why? What do you mean?"

"Maybe Violet's taking matters into her own hands. What if Delaney is telling the truth after all? Maybe Violet has snapped under all the pressure. Loosening those planks could set up a convenient accident. If Delaney fell, she'd hit cement. From that height, I don't think she'd survive."

Hyacinth shot me a reproving frown. "You're jaded. Violet wouldn't hurt her sister. Besides, there're too many variables in that scenario. Delaney would have to walk on the balcony, and then she'd have to fall, and even if she did fall, there's no guarantee it would kill her."

I scrubbed a hand over my face, ashamed that I'd questioned Violet's actions. "You're right," I admitted. I glanced at my watch. "Soon as you finish talking with Violet, I'll take care of everything."

It was going to be a very long night.

Chapter 38

VIOLET

Present day

Danger, unseen, was out there . . . nimble, mysterious, and silent as a crouching black cat. Any second it would pounce, a streak of black blending seamlessly in the night. I struggled to breathe past the fear clogging my throat.

A cool hand stroked my brow—tender and reassuring. A long-ago scent that quieted my panic—magnolias, an aromatic mixture of gardenia, honeysuckle, citrus, and spice—as fresh and sweet as lemonade. I lay in the dark, breathing in the familiar scent and vividly remembering my mother. When I was growing up, she could be distant and aloof, always racing out the door to get away from us. But there were also these moments of sweet, kind love that allowed me to glimpse a softer side of life. A memory resurfaced, a pleasant one where I was small and hurt myself and my mother comforted me, her hand pressed on my forehead as she murmured to me that all was well.

The nightmare was gone, and so was the fuzzy haze between sleep and waking.

That lingering smell should not be here.

That brush against my forehead should not have happened.

I heard nothing, but I was not alone in my bedroom. I sensed the hushed breathing of something alive, the faintest rustling of clothes.

"Delaney?" I despised the weak quiver in my voice. I couldn't let her see that these stupid games reduced me to a ball of flayed nerves. She was toying with me, intent on destroying her prey.

Had I been drugged last night? I was always so careful not to drink or eat anything I hadn't personally prepared. My hands slid across the cotton sheets, searching for the chip of sea glass or the tumbled bit of tourmaline I tucked beside me each night to ward off evil. Where had they gone? My wandering hands only brushed the smooth expanse of linen.

Stay calm. They're nearby. Have to be. I curled my fingers into my palms.

"I know you're in here, Delaney. Just cut it out."

"Shh." The whispered command scraped against my chilled flesh. A warm, soft hand slipped into mine and pressed, as if reassuring me all was well.

A childish urge to hide under the covers almost overwhelmed me. Ignoring my instincts, I squeezed onto the hand holding mine and reached for the lamp on the bedside table beside me. No slipping out for Delaney. This wasn't the first time she'd trespassed in my room and then denied doing so later, claiming that it was just my imagination.

"Gotcha!" I cried out triumphantly, gripping her hand and flipping on the lamp.

A stranger hovered above me. I blinked, taking in the intense eyes. No, not a stranger at all. I screamed and jerked my hand away from the woman's very warm hand. A very much alive hand.

The hand of my supposedly dead mother.

"Who are you? Get out!" I kicked at her body. This couldn't be my mother. Delaney had found someone with a striking resemblance to our mom and then had paid her to terrorize me. This was payback for trying to expose her fake fiancé. It had to be. Unless I really was batshit crazy and beginning to suffer hallucinations.

"Violet, hush, it's really me. I know this must be a shock, but please hear me out before—"

"Get away from me!" I scrabbled to the opposite side of the bed. "I'm calling the cops."

My eyes darted to the bedside table. Damn it. Of course, my cell phone was there beside this . . . apparition. Out of reach.

"Darling, it's okay. I would never hurt you."

Hell's bells. She even sounded like Mom. How had Delaney found this twin stranger? A random fact I'd come across on the internet flashed through my addled brain. There was actually a website that had the capability of scanning your face and finding up to six twins for you from around the world. This elaborate stunt must have cost Delaney a fortune.

I rolled off the side of the bed and backed against the wall. The woman started toward me. I couldn't get trapped here in the corner between the bed and the wall. Carefully, I moved sideways, waiting for the right moment to make a dash for the door.

"I'm alive, Violet. I wasn't in that car when it burned."

"Okay, lady. You've had your fun and games with me. Collect your money from Delaney and leave me alone."

"Remember when I took you to see *Peter Pan* in Huntsville? Or the time we went to *The Nutcracker* in Birmingham and you insisted you wanted to be a ballerina when you grew up?"

She bestowed a tender smile, and my fear gave way to anger. How dare this stranger play such a cruel act? I slow clapped and stepped away from the wall. "Quite a performance. Delaney prepared you well. But my real mother would never have let me believe she was dead and then never contacted me."

I brushed past her and grabbed my phone off the table. "I'm calling the cops now. Game's over."

"Call Detective Boone Kimbrel, then. He'll verify my story."

Shock rooted me to the ground, and I tried to tamp down the shiver that spread through my body. Boone Kimbrel. The detective who'd always seemed way too interested in my case, who'd been way too gentle in his interviews, and who also had happened to be with my mom when she'd found me That Night. What did he have to do with this? I shook off my misgivings. All of that was coincidence. "You're crazy. Either that, or you think I am."

"Don't ever say that. You suffered a trauma—that's all."

"Delaney?" I raised my voice, loud enough to carry down the hall. This charade had to end. "Where are you? If I call the cops, you're going down with this actress you hired."

"Delaney's not here," the woman said calmly. "And Parker is out of it for the night. Go on and call Boone. We thought you might have trouble believing the truth. He's waiting outside."

There were more than one of them. I was in deep trouble if there really was a second person waiting to pounce on me.

"How did you get in here?" I asked past dry lips. I'd locked all the doors and windows before coming to bed. Was this a vivid dream? A hallucination? Maybe returning home had finally unraveled my sanity.

"I let myself in the back door. The spare key was under the back-porch planter, same old place we always kept it." She pulled out a cell phone from her pants pocket and punched in some numbers. "I'm calling Boone to come inside and corroborate my story."

Boone. There was something about the familiar way she said his name that again set me on edge. "No!"

"You're frightened. I can't blame you. I'll just have him step out of the woods a moment."

She spoke into the phone. "Shine your flashlight at Violet's window."

Seconds later, a beam of light bounced through the glass french doors.

This woman wasn't acting alone. It had to be Delaney out there, but I wasn't taking any chances. These people might be dangerous—if they were even real. I ran to the dresser and grabbed my car keys.

"Boone. Shine the light on your face so she knows it's really you."

I couldn't help but look back over my shoulder. A man stepped out of the woods, a flashlight spotlighting his face. Impossible to make out the features, though.

I bolted for the door and ran down the stairs, practically taking a tumble in my desperate hurry. For a moment, I paused by Dad's shut bedroom door. Leave him and find help, or stay and wait for the trespassers to close in?

I ran to the door. Best thing to do between two awful choices was to make a compromise. I'd lock myself in the car while I called the cops. If the man outside entered the house, I'd go back in and try to protect Dad until the police arrived. And if this was all another mental breakdown . . . well, I'd have to take a chance on looking ridiculous to the cops. Outside, the crickets chirruped, and a gazillion insects buzzed. I flew down the steps and ran to the car. Almost there.

A set of strong arms gripped my shoulders. I screamed, useless since no one was within hearing distance, but it beat a silent submission to brute force. My heart jackhammered against my ribs.

"Violet, it's Detective Kimbrel. You're safe. No one's going to hurt you. We need to talk."

He released me, and I stumbled backward, gaping at the tall man. The woman in my bedroom hadn't lied. It was indeed Kimbrel. My gaze flitted to the house, where she stood in the doorway, backlit by the light within.

"Wh-what are you doing here?"

"Helping Hyacinth. I'm sorry for the scare." He loomed over me, awkward and lanky as always. *Tall like me.* Again, I tamped down the errant whispers in my mind. Kimbrel ran a hand through his hair and

273

gestured to the woman who walked toward us. "There's no good way to break the news. This really is your mother."

My body shook violently, and I took another step back. I fought facing the truth, even as it paraded itself before my very eyes. "You're in on this with Delaney," I accused.

"Why would I do that? Delaney means nothing to me. It's you I care about."

I wanted to clamp my hands over my ears. "Care about me? You don't even know me. You must be some kind of sick—"

"He's your father, Violet."

I gaped at the woman.

"Think about it," she said softly. "You remember what it was like in that house. Parker and I never got along, to put it mildly. And Delaney? We despised each other from day one. Boone and I would never help Delaney to hurt you. Never."

I continued to shiver, despite the oppressive humidity. Mom alive? Parker not my real father?

She reached a hand out toward me, palm up. "And see? I brought you this all the way from Portugal. A blue chip of sea glass, just like the one the crows gifted you so many years ago."

Who else would know that about me? Even Delaney didn't know the significance of that bit of glass. Only Mom. I stared at them, and the truth stared back.

"But . . . why?" I asked Mom in a small voice. "You just"—I raised an arm and then let it drop—"just left me all alone, believing you were dead."

"It was better this way. For both of us. I was miserable and scared, trapped in a horrible marriage, trapped in this small town. I always intended to return when you were ready."

She made it sound like she'd left me for a short vacation instead of the truth that she'd abandoned me for years. Hurt lanced my heart, shredding it into tiny pieces. The betrayal cut me to the quick. I quickly tried to force it down and focus on my outrage. Anger braced me, and the trembling was replaced by a burning resolve that tingled like an electrical burn from my scalp to my toes. "You left me," I said, each syllable steady and clear. "Left when I needed you most. Abandoned me to the mercy of Alabama's psychiatric system. Did you think you'd left me where I'd get compassionate care, *Mother*?"

She flinched, and I took a petty satisfaction in her discomfort. It wasn't a fraction of what she'd put me through. Boone regarded me with his head hung low, an apology in his eyes. My biological father? I wanted nothing to do with him.

"Honey, please." Mom held out an arm, as if she wanted to touch me, pull me into an embrace.

Fat chance. I wanted nothing to do with either of them. I picked up the car keys I'd dropped when Boone had grabbed me, and I strode toward the house, needing to distance myself from their presence. A deep desire for a sleeping pill fueled my steps. I wanted to down at least two and then burrow into my familiar bed with the covers over my head.

"We know this is a shock, but you need to hear us out," Boone said.

I whirled to face him. "You don't get to order me around. You've never been a father to me, so don't think I owe you any respect."

"Violet, hush. If you would only—"

Boone shook his head. "Might be better if you talked to her alone."

I kept walking. How could they do this to me? Lie to me all these years?

Mom caught up and walked alongside me. "I know you're angry. You have every right. But let's go back to your room and talk, okay? You're in trouble, and we can help."

She wouldn't leave me alone until she'd had her say. I stood in the doorway and spread my arms, blocking her path. "Fine. But don't you dare wake up Dad. My *real* dad. I won't have you upsetting him."

"Since when did you start caring for Parker? He was never nice to anyone but Delaney."

I kept her barred from the entrance.

"All right, then," she sighed. "I'll be quiet."

We proceeded through the kitchen and softly crept up the stairs into my bedroom. Carefully, I closed the door with a gentle click and stood in the middle of the room, arms folded. "Why are you here?"

"First, I'm truly sorry for scaring you in the middle of the night like this."

"There's no good way to break the news that you faked your death. And that you stayed away when I needed you most."

"For months, I did visit you in the hospital. Sent money to you for years as well. Boone made sure the funds were put into your own personal account."

That explained that little mystery. It hadn't been Dad or Delaney slipping me money out of guilt. It had been Mom all along.

"And when I did visit, you acted like you either didn't know who I was or didn't care that I'd come. I was depressed, honey. I couldn't live with Parker anymore."

As if it were yesterday, I recalled the screaming matches between them, which were followed by long stretches of brittle silence that could last for weeks at a time. I remembered walking on eggshells when Dad started drinking, and Mom's often-distracted air of being physically present but having her mind adrift elsewhere, somewhere I played no part in and didn't belong.

"In hindsight, there was a certain peace in the hospital that was missing at home."

Mom's eyes filled with tears. "Guess I deserve that."

"You could have divorced Dad. Instead, you cheated on him and ran away."

"But this way, I managed to hide my inheritance overseas, and now it's all mine. Yours, too, of course."

I stared at the woman I'd never really known. Mom had shown what mattered to her—and it wasn't me. "I don't care about your damn money. Where have you been all this time?"

"Portugal. It's where I got that sea glass for you." Her face glowed with a happiness I'd never witnessed before. "Algarve, to be exact. It's one hundred miles off the Atlantic coastline, complete with sandy beaches, lagoons, and jagged rock cliffs. You would love it."

"Portugal," I repeated, momentarily caught up in her description of paradise. "It's so foreign . . . do you speak Portuguese?"

"Don't need to, although I've picked up a bit. There's a huge number of expats and foreign retirees there."

Hard to imagine that all these years I'd been hospitalized, she'd been lying on an exotic beach and having a grand ole time. The anger returned, doubled.

Mom continued on, oblivious to my feelings. "It's paradise without the heavy price tag. I live comfortably on fifteen hundred dollars a month. I want you to go there with me. Leave this place behind."

"Sounds like you haven't been suffering the last few years. Congratulations."

Mom reached out a hand for me, a silent plea for forgiveness. I jerked my body away to avoid her touch.

"How did you pull it off?" I asked, remembering the crushed, burnt frame of the car that I'd seen in photographs. "There was a body . . ."

"Boone helped me. He knew how desperate I was." I tuned her out. I was sick of all her words. All her lies.

Enough. I'd had it. I'd forgotten how selfish she could be. How she wanted everyone to bow to her own wants and needs. Death and time did that—altered perception and put a rosy haze on a person's past behavior.

"Stop talking and listen to me!" My voice rang through the room, and Mom clamped her mouth shut, finally. I drew a deep breath. "Why did Detective Kimbrel"—I refused to call him my father—"help you fake your death? Why would he put his career on the line?"

Now that I wanted her to talk, she'd gone quiet.

"Because he loved me. Still does."

I gazed at her stupidly. Love? So it had been more than just an affair. Random bits and snippets of memory floating through the ether of my mind fell neatly into place—Dad's constant jealousy and Mom's dreamy, distracted retreats inside her head, no doubt thinking of her lover.

Needing space, I stood and paced the room, rubbing my temples. I suddenly stopped and stared at the woman who had birthed me, whose death I had mourned for so long. Shouldn't I be ecstatic at the unexpected reunion? Where was the joy?

Honestly, I wished she'd stayed dead.

"Why did you come back?" I asked abruptly. "Why now after all these years?"

"You need me."

"No, I needed you years ago. Not now. What's the sudden urgency?"

"Delaney. She went to Boone two days ago." Mom cocked her head to the side and regarded me quizzically. "With Ainsley's bracelet."

I sucked in my breath. I was too late, had postponed running away for too long. Libby's detour of confronting and trying to force my sister into telling the truth and revealing all she knew about that night was for naught. Delaney had made good on her threats, and I was screwed. I sat on the bed and put my head in my hands. How long now until I returned to the state hospital—or worse, the Tutwiler Prison for Women?

"Anything else incriminating that Delaney might have found?" Mom asked.

I marched out to the balcony, careful of the missing planks, and retrieved the necklace from beneath the bird feeder. "One more thing,"

I said, returning to my bedroom. "Here's a necklace that belonged to Ainsley."

"It's okay, hon. We'll take care of this."

"We?" I gave a bitter laugh. "I can't count on you. For all I know, you'll disappear again. Having a grand time on some beach in Portugal."

"Boone will fix it."

Her absolute confidence gave me pause. "I forgot. He's a dirty cop. What's he going to do—destroy all the evidence?"

"He's not dirty. And he's not just any detective. He's your father."

"Excuse me for not entirely trusting either of you. Are you saying he's going to get rid of the bracelet Delaney turned in?"

"Of course. But we need to know how Delaney got ahold of Ainsley's jewelry in the first place."

"Haven't a clue."

Mom tapped an index finger against her lips, like she used to do when in deep thought. Like she had done back when I was a little girl and loved her so much. Back when her touch would obliterate any sadness or disappointment and I'd feel secure in her embrace. My chest burned, and a scalding blurriness crumbled my vision into puddles of indistinct form.

Her arms were around me, and I held on to her, sobbing into her shoulders like a baby.

"Shh," she whispered in my ear. "Everything's going to be all right."

I got myself together and pulled away. Mom's comfort was too little, too late now. I wanted her out of my bedroom, out of my life. The easiest way to get her out immediately was to fabricate a half-truth. "I need some time to be alone. Tonight's been a shock."

"I understand." She squeezed my shoulder. "Don't worry. I won't let any harm come to you ever again."

How I wished I could believe that fairy tale.

She held out a hand, palm up. "But first, I need that necklace."

Chapter 39

VIOLET

Present day

Room 429. My least favorite place in all of Normal. I rolled out my shoulders and raised my chin, determined to leave Emmeline Upchurch's dinner tray with as little conversation as possible and end this long, tiresome day. My sleep had been fitful last night after Mom's presence had exploded the world as I'd previously understood it.

Another thirty minutes, and I could leave Whispering Oaks. No, make that five minutes. For once, I was sneaking out early. The smell of cafeteria roast beef, spilled milk, and the ever-present, pervasive pine-cleaner odor had my stomach churning so bad I couldn't even eat today. That, combined with no sleep—thanks, Mom—had me cranky and on edge.

I kept imagining Mom holding Ainsley's necklace, and my future, in the palm of her hand. Even scarier, I wondered what Detective Kimbrel was going to do with the bracelet. Mom seemed to think he had some sense of loyalty or honor to me. Nope. Let's see: he'd cheated on his wife, he'd committed a crime by falsifying a death, and he lied to his superiors at work. I didn't trust him one damn bit.

On the other hand, with a long list of sins like that, why doubt he'd trash evidence in a murder case? Mom had no doubts he would, and she knew him lots better than I did.

I draped fresh linen on my right arm and pulled out the last tray from the cart. With a little luck, the old bag would be asleep and not even notice me when I set the tray on her bedside table. Wouldn't have to change her bedsheets either. I could leave that for the night shift, claiming I didn't want to disturb her sleep.

I entered Emmeline Upchurch's room and stifled a sigh. Of course, she was awake.

"About time you got here," Emmeline snapped. "You're late."

"Yes, ma'am."

I set down the tray and spread open the fitted mattress sheet. Without prompting, Emmeline rolled on her side. Through the thin cotton gown her spine stood out like corded rope. Her bare arms and legs were covered with sun spots and skin so transparent medical students could study her live body to observe the inner machinations of a human's vascular system. With practiced efficiency, I unrolled the top of the dirty sheet from the mattress and fitted the clean sheet in at one corner, stretching it all the way to the bottom.

"Hurry up. My dinner's getting cold."

I snatched up the second layer of bed linen and tucked it under one side of the mattress. Biting my tongue, I went around the bed to the opposite side, and Emmeline rolled onto the clean linen so I could finish the job.

What if I accidentally pushed her a little too hard? That brittle body would splat onto the hard linoleum floor.

My hands started shaking at the casual violence of my sleep-deprived thoughts. It took me twice as long to complete the task as it normally did.

"Your shady past is bad enough; don't add incompetence to the list." Emmeline sat up and handed me her pillow.

I couldn't even look at her, sure my anger would scorch her. I changed her pillowcase and placed the pillow under her head. Emmeline's chin jutted forward, her sunken chest rising and falling, her breath rattling around in her old lungs. *What if I pressed the pillow against her mouth? It would only take seconds.* Quickly, I finished my tasks, horrified at the direction of my thoughts.

Longingly, I pictured Portugal. Days from now, I could be lying on the beach beside Mom, not a care in the world. Was it really possible?

I wasn't sure how much longer I could live at home. Whether or not Detective Kimbrel covered for me, Delaney was a threat. My sister wouldn't be satisfied until I was put away and Dad was dead. She wanted everything for herself. Not to mention she hated me. I'd never be safe as long as I lived with her.

Emmeline called out to me as I left her room, but I pretended not to hear. I pushed the empty cart down the hall, pausing when I heard Ainsley's name. Heart thundering, I stood in a patient's doorway and watched the TV news.

"—and it's been confirmed by Police Chief Daniel Thornell. Gerald 'Dinky' Stedmyer has been arrested for the 2007 murder of fifteen-year-old Ainsley Dalfred. Police obtained a key piece of physical evidence tying the convicted sex offender to the crime. In a raid of Stedmyer's home, police found jewelry that the victim was wearing at the time of her death."

They cut from the news desk to footage of a short, scruffy man in handcuffs entering the county jail.

I slumped against the wall and drew several deep breaths. There was only one way that jewelry could have ended up in that poor, innocent man's possession. What the hell was Delaney going to think when she heard the news? She was bound to think I was responsible for framing that man. Maybe it was time to take Libby up on her offer after all. I wanted out of that house before something else terrible happened. I glanced at the clock at the end of the hallway. If I hurried, maybe I could go home, rush in, and pack a suitcase and gather my crow-gift boxes, all before Delaney got wind of it. Right about now, she'd be occupied cooking supper, ready to slip out the door as soon as I got home from work.

Screw the cart. I left it in the middle of the hall and ran.

Chapter 40

DELANEY

Present day

Excitement built in my body with every tick of the grandfather clock. Detective Kimbrel should arrive within the next fifteen minutes, and then Violet about thirty minutes later. Wouldn't *she* be surprised when she spotted his sedan outside. And not in a good way. My lips involuntarily curled upward, and my right leg violently swung back and forth. I was like a wired-up cat with a twitchy tail, ready to pounce. From my position, seated in a high-backed chair by the living room window, I'd know the second he got here. I drew back the curtain an inch, once again checking the road and anticipating the county sedan's arrival.

"You expectin' company?"

I dropped my hand to my side and eyed Dad. He could be observant at times, too mentally sharp for my liking. The raspberry glow of his herbal iced tea, heavily laced with valerian, was mostly untouched in his hand.

"Drink up," I ordered.

The tea, along with his nighttime sedative medication, should keep him knocked out for a few hours. By the time he awoke, Violet would be gone, carted away in handcuffs, never to return again. I could hardly wait.

Obligingly, Dad lifted the glass to his lips, and I turned my attention to the window once more. Detective Kimbrel had asked that I keep Dad calm while he made the arrest. I'd do whatever it took to ensure Violet's speedy arrest. Did she really think she could just show up on my doorstep, and I'd have to take her in? Apparently, yes. And then she'd had the gall to complain about the spent trust fund money and wanting to claim part of her mom's inheritance.

That money was mine.

I jumped up and paced the room, needing to release more pent-up energy.

"Who you got coming over here?" Dad demanded.

"Just a friend. It's got nothing to do with you." I checked, happy to see the tea was almost gone. He'd downed that quick.

"I don't want strangers in my house." Dad's eyes fluttered, and he leaned his head back against the sofa cushion.

This wouldn't do. I wanted him in bed in his room, not lazing on the couch, where he might awaken when the detective made the arrest.

"Looks like you're ready to call it a night." I moved his TV tray out of the way and held out a hand. "Time for bed."

"My western isn't over yet."

"Too bad." Him and his western movies. It was all he ever watched. Once he was finally gone, I never wanted to see or hear another one of them.

He scowled. "Seems like bedtime gets earlier and earlier every day," he mumbled. But Dad offered no resistance as I led him to his room and then shut the door.

Five more minutes. I poured myself a vodka tonic and downed it quickly. A little something to take off the edge. After Violet was sent packing, I'd break out the good stuff, the Grey Goose, mix it with chocolate and caramel liqueur, and then get smashed on chocolate martinis.

Now that was a celebration well worth the resulting hangover the next morning.

The old-fashioned clock struck the hour. Five deep chimes that vibrated in the pit of my churning gut. The unmistakable crunch of tire on gravel sounded from the front yard, and I scurried to the window.

Detective Kimbrel's black sedan rolled into the driveway, a hearse of doom for my sister. I opened the door as he walked up the porch steps, tall and lumbering, jaw set in determination.

"Right on time," I commented, holding the screen door open. "Come in."

He nodded and stepped across the threshold, looking around the den and kitchen with curious eyes.

I stayed at the door and frowned at the conspicuous sight of his vehicle. "Maybe you should park in the backyard," I suggested. "In case Violet sees your car and gets scared off."

"She won't."

At my raised brow, he shrugged. "She seems to trust me."

"Okay, if you say so." I shut the door and wondered if it was appropriate to ask if he wanted a drink. I'd never entertained a cop in my house before.

"Where's your father?" he asked, strolling through the den and acting as if he owned the place. He switched off the television set as the evening news was about to begin.

"Dad's asleep. Would you like something to—"

"Good. Before your sister gets here, I want to take a look around her room. Since you never found that necklace, maybe I can. Or I might find some other piece of evidence that could help solidify a case against her."

I was taken aback. Shouldn't he be presenting me with a subpoena or something? But hey, it wasn't my civil rights he was trampling on.

"Sure. If you'd like. It's upstairs."

I started up the wooden staircase, conscious of Detective Kimbrel directly behind me, watching my every move. My spine prickled with foreboding. So ridiculous—Violet was the one in trouble, not me. The detective wasn't searching *my* room.

At the top of the stairs, I gestured down the hallway. "Last room on the right."

"After you." Kimbrel swept his hand across his body, motioning me to continue.

"Why? You don't need me, do you?"

"It would be best. In case there are any questions later. You understand."

Not really, but I quelled my misgivings and led him into Violet's ridiculous pink-and-lavender bedroom that looked as though it belonged to a preadolescent girl. I edged near the dresser as Kimbrel brushed past me. He surveyed the room and, unexpectedly, strode to Violet's nightstand and picked up the framed photograph of Violet and her mother mugging for the camera. It'd been snapped in a rare happy moment when we'd all vacationed in Gatlinburg, Tennessee. Of course, Dad and I had been excluded from that touching Hallmark moment. Mom and Violet had been so tight there was no room to edge into their relationship.

Not that I cared.

I studied the detective's face as he examined the photograph. Something in the hungry look of his eyes and the intent stare as he gripped the frame sent bells ringing in my head. His preoccupation with the photograph was off, but I couldn't explain how or why. It made me uneasy. I should have downed two vodka tonics instead of one.

Finally, he carefully returned the photo to the nightstand and set about opening drawers and making a cursory search. I'd expected him to practically upend furniture as he looked for clues, but he merely swished his hand in a couple of drawers. Hell, I'd searched more thoroughly than that.

The detective ambled to the french doors and opened them. "Nice view."

Irritation replaced my unease. That balcony was a sticking point. Violet had gotten the best bedroom growing up—Mom had seen to that—and I'd considered claiming it as my own years ago. But in the end, I'd chosen the master suite.

"Yes, but my room's bigger and has a private bath."

He ignored that, frowning as he surveyed the balcony deck. "What's all out there?"

"Nothing but a chair and a bird feeder. My sister is obsessed with crows. You remember. People around here used to call her the crow girl after that write-up in the *Birmingham News*. I don't see the big deal myself. Just because—"

"Someone's sitting out there."

"What?" A tingling shot through my veins. "That's impossible."

I'd been home for more than an hour, cooking an early supper for Dad and then preparing for the detective's visit. No one else had been in the house with me, not even a damn ghost. What was this foolishness? I brushed past him and walked onto the deck.

A woman stood at the far end, casually leaning against the railing, her back to us. There was something familiar about the slender curve of her shoulders. She slowly turned and stared at me. Her Mona Lisa smile was calm and mysterious, as though she owned this place and all its secrets. The air in my lungs collapsed. I couldn't suck in enough oxygen; every breath burned.

"Hello, Delaney."

It's really her. Mom. Impossible. "It can't be. You're supposed to be—"

"Dead?"

Her crimson lips curled, and her smile turned sardonic. She had the upper hand here. All collected and powerful. I felt battered and confused. Utterly crushed. Black splinters crashed inside me, their sharp edges spiking my panicked mind. Bits and pieces of the past needled my brain . . . the ruined body charred from the fire of the car crash, too burnt for proper identification . . . her horrible fights with Dad . . .

"How? Why?" I stumbled to the iron baluster and clutched it as though it were an anchor and I were drowning. "I-I don't understand."

"What *I* don't understand is how you came into possession of this." Mom held up the cross-pendant necklace. Ainsley's necklace.

Chills prickled my flesh, and I swirled around, seeking Detective Kimbrel. Were they both ganging up on me? He stood not three feet behind me. His face was grim, even malevolent; not a trace of the detective-bureaucrat remained in his dark eyes. I'd been set up. He came toward me, and I involuntarily stepped back. There was a threat of danger in his measured gait and calculating eyes. He jabbed a finger at me. "Violet didn't kill Ainsley. You did."

"Whaa . . . no. Violet pushed Ainsley off the cliff. I saw her do it."

"You admit you were there that night?"

Too late, I realized my slip. Must have poured too much vodka in my vodka tonic. "Maybe." I chewed the inside of my mouth, drawing the tang of blood. How had they guessed? I glanced back and forth between the two, my neck whiplashing. "You two know each other," I reasoned aloud, trying to crystallize information with each new bombshell that detonated. "You're lovers."

"Always knew you were a smart girl," Mom said with a smirk.

Same old Hyacinth, same old hatred. I turned back to the detective. "You helped Mom fake her death. Why? There must be money behind . . ." I shook my head. "Of course! Bet you squirreled away money from your parents' inheritance. We were surprised how little there was when we collected. How did you manage to pull it off?"

"Never mind that," Kimbrel answered for her.

I snorted. "Yeah, y'all wouldn't want to discuss your illegal activities, would you? Didn't figure you for a dirty cop, Kimbrel. *Her*—" I cast Mom a scathing look. "Her I could see orchestrating a stunt like this. But she needed your help to make it work."

"She had her reasons. Let's stick to the present."

He still protected Mom, I noticed. The man must still be in love. "The present. After scamming Dad and me from our money, you want to move on to a more serious criminal act. Like covering up Violet's murder. You didn't come here to arrest her. You came here to threaten me with blackmail."

His silence and implacable gaze confirmed everything.

"It's not going to work. I could turn you both in for what you've done."

"And who do you think they're going to believe—the tramp of Normal with her wild tale of the dead coming back to life? Or me, a respected detective with over twenty-five years' service?"

I let the tramp remark go. "But why?" I cocked my head at Mom. "Why risk everything? You're doing all this for *her*?"

"Not entirely," Mom answered. I switched my gaze her way. "He's doing it for his daughter."

My thoughts had slowed to poured-molasses stage, and it took me several seconds to catch her drift.

"Fuck," I whispered softly. I was so screwed. Blood was blood, and once again, Violet had won. Unless I could turn this whole thing around. And quick.

"How did you get Ainsley's bracelet and necklace?" Detective Kimbrel asked. "You weren't just there that night. You stole the jewelry off a dead girl, didn't you?"

I pursed my lips. He wasn't the only one who could keep his mouth shut.

"You killed Ainsley Dalfred," he continued. "There's no other explanation. Confess now, and it will go easier on you."

"Violet killed her, not me! They were arguing, and after Violet pushed her off the cliff, I rushed down to the river to see if Ainsley was okay."

"Go on," the detective urged. "What happened next? Why were you even there?"

I licked my dry lips and swallowed hard, forming the rest of my story.

"Okay, I was spying on them," I admitted slowly. "Only because I was worried about Violet. She'd been acting strange and was all obsessed with Ainsley. When she sneaked out of the house that night, I followed. I was concerned she was in some kind of trouble, and I wanted to help."

Mom snickered, but I ignored her.

"I saw them together. They were doing . . . you know, naughty stuff. Kissing and fondling."

There, did they really want that tidbit about their daughter to become public knowledge?

"Go on," Detective Kimbrel grumbled.

"I hid, intending to follow Violet home and talk sense into her before they got caught, and hell broke loose. After Ainsley fell, I called out to Violet, but she ignored me and ran into the woods. I found Ainsley in the water. She'd landed on a rock and injured her head." I managed a little sob. "She was dead before I got to her."

"Again, how did you get her jewelry?" the detective asked.

I brought my hands to my face and swiped at imaginary tears, buying time as I thought fast. "Their clothes and shoes were at the riverbank. Ainsley had tucked her bracelet and necklace inside her T-shirt."

"Liar," Mom said, her voice lashing with scorn. "I'd bet that you pushed Ainsley off that cliff. Then you took her jewelry as a sick trophy."

Her uncanny guess about the jewelry stabbed fear in my gut. That bitch had figured out my number almost from the start, before she'd even married Dad. Attempting to fool her was a waste of time.

"It will come down to my story versus Violet's story," I told the detective, hoping to sway him with reason. I turned Kimbrel's earlier question back on him. "Who do you think people will believe? A woman long suspected of murder and who was recently released from psychiatric care—or me? If you really love your daughter, maybe you should convince her to leave town and never come back. That way, we can all have what we want."

"We're not here about Ainsley Dalfred's murder. Richard 'Dinky' Stedmyer was arrested and charged with her murder less than an hour ago."

My world shifted, and my thoughts were out of kilter. "What are you talking about?"

The detective's eyes gleamed with satisfaction. "Thanks to an anonymous tip, Stedmyer's house was searched, and cops found a bracelet belonging to the victim. Violet's name has finally been cleared."

I gaped at him, horrified. "You took that bracelet and planted it on someone else."

"A sex offender who admitted being at the scene that night."

All my plans, destroyed by a dirty cop. If only I'd brought the evidence to someone else, anyone but this detective. It wasn't fair. I was stuck with Violet now.

"What's your game?" I asked, narrowing my eyes. "Why are you here?"

"We want you to leave Normal and stay out of Violet's life. Parker's as well."

"Gladly. If the price is right."

"I'm not giving you a dime," Mom said quickly. "You have as much to lose as we do if the truth comes out."

"You're bluffing. Both of you get out of my house, before I call a *real* cop."

"Told you she wouldn't listen to reason," Mom said, looking past me to Kimbrel. "And there's no appealing to her sense of decency. She has none."

"You've no right to talk like that," I scoffed. "Not after the things you've done, *Mother*."

Mom's face flushed, and she took a step toward me. "You know nothing of love. Nothing of honor. And stop calling me *Mom*. You were never my *real* daughter—now were you, Delaney?"

Lava-hot rage burned and blistered my veins. Violet was the only one she'd ever loved. Growing up, it was always about Violet, never me.

Mom's vitriol continued. Her eyes hardened even more. "You killed Ainsley and then tried to blame my Violet."

"Ainsley was already nearly dead from a fall when I found her and finished the job. Call it a mercy killing."

"You don't know the meaning of mercy." Mom stepped closer, jabbing a finger toward my chest. "I've heard about your father's drastic mental and physical decline, and I suspect you might be behind that as well. Not that I care what happens to Parker."

"But . . . how could you possibly . . . I mean, that's not true. I'd never hurt—"

"You're evil. I'd put nothing past you, Delaney. You have no conscience. Not even with your own family."

"Oh yeah? No one would ever nominate you for the Mother of the Year award."

"What's all the ruckus?" Dad stood in the doorway—wearing only boxer shorts and a T-shirt, silver hair disheveled and eyes bloodshot. His gaze locked on Mom. He lifted a shaky hand to his wrinkled face, scrubbed, and looked again. "Hyacinth?"

The controlled tightness in her face loosened, and she cocked her head to the side. "Parker. You don't look well."

"You're not dead?" His face crumpled like a whipped child's. "This can't be. It can't . . ." He looked at me, seeking help.

"What a bitch, Dad! She and her lover think they can just waltz into *your* house. After all these years of deceiving you."

He appeared to notice Detective Kimbrel for the first time. Red mottled Dad's cheeks. "I remember you."

That made two of us now aware Hyacinth was alive and that Kimbrel must have helped fake her death. Surely I could swing this fact to my advantage. I egged Dad on, welcoming the diversion from Kimbrel's grilling.

"Did you know this man is Violet's real father? Mom was cheating on you. She's been lying to you for years."

"What? I'd suspected, but . . . is that true?"

Mom nodded.

Dad stumbled from the doorway, an arm raised at Kimbrel.

The detective caught it midair, as effortlessly as though he were swatting flies.

"How dare you come in my home? First you fuck my wife, and then you trespass."

Kimbrel dropped his arm. "Go back to bed, Parker. And forget you ever saw Hyacinth again."

"You and that slut don't tell me what to do. This is *my*—"

"Shut up, Parker," Mom interrupted. "I put up with your abuse for way too long. I won't tolerate it anymore."

I'd seen Dad plenty drunk and pretty mad over the years, but drugged or no, his temper flared as it had in the old days. His eyes dilated, and his hands formed fists at his sides. With surprising speed, he lunged forward. "I'll teach you . . . you . . ."

He shoved against me in his zeal to reach Mom, and I lost my balance. A creaking noise sounded, and something beneath my feet shifted.

I was falling, tumbling through the open cracks. The deck opened, and my legs, then waist, fell through. Instinctively, I grabbed onto a plank. I dangled in the air, only four fingers curled over a rotten board. Far below was a wide expanse of cement. This couldn't be happening. Not to me. Nobody defeated my plans. My gaze swept over my beautiful gardens and the empty backyard.

A crow dive-bombed my head, beating its ugly black wings about my face, and I started to lose my tenuous hold.

Chapter 41

VIOLET

Present day

I was in the grips of the worst nightmare of my life. How else to explain the sight before me? Delaney dangled by an arm from my balcony. Several crows darted and flitted at her, cawing in a raucous cacophony that must surely be the symphony of hell. Mom, Boone, and Dad stood above, frozen figures, watching in horror.

I ran to her, out of breath in no time, as though my lungs were full of punctures. Her blonde hair blew in the breeze.

Boone was the first to act. He got on his knees and reached a hand out for Delaney. Dad quickly did the same.

I bent over double, exhausted and wheezing. My crows, those naughty birds, escaped to the trees, as if they'd been caught in the act of wrongdoing. I felt my mother's eyes on me.

Silence stretched and warped time as the setting sun beat down on my numb face and arms. The rasp of my labored breathing gusted my ears like the roar of an advancing hurricane. My sister's blonde hair transformed to black, and I was at the river once more. A scream rent the air.

Ainsley!

I hurtled down a rabbit hole with frightening speed. The wormhole in my memory burst, revealing the lost hours of that night, complete and uncompromised. I'd landed again in that moment when I had pushed Ainsley.

~

Ainsley's eyes widen, and her mouth forms an O of surprise. Her body topples backward, and her arms windmill uselessly to break the fall, while her heels fail to dig into the ground. Her legs churn as if peddling a broken unicycle. A tragic clown stumbling to her doom.

Her eyes lock on to mine, stunned. I cannot move.

And then, with a sharp outcry of fear, Ainsley falls from the cliff. My paralysis shatters, and I run to the edge. Naked arms and legs thrash in the air.

Until the splash.

A cannonball of black river water geysers up like a fountain. Of course, the water. Ainsley will be okay, will emerge from the water angry as a wet hen, but alive. I wait as the splash settles and the river is again a smooth black mirror.

One second, two, then three . . . and yet Ainsley doesn't resurface from the mysterious depths. She must be playing a trick on me, trying to scare me. How many times have we jumped down to the river from this very spot? I stare hard at the scene below. Ainsley must be swimming underwater and heading for the opposite shore.

I wait.

As the seconds tick by, the oppressive humidity grows so heavy it feels like a blanket of heat smothering me. And still no Ainsley.

Something is very wrong.

"Ainsley?" I call out to the darkness. My cry is weak and tentative, quickly absorbed by the night. I take a deep breath. "Ainsley? Where are you?" This time my voice is louder, but there's still no answer. The still water and unmoving trees seem to mock my pleas.

I race down the cliff, partly sliding most of the way on my naked butt. I barely note the sand abrading my skin. At the river's edge, I call again. "Ainsley?"

Water licks the shoreline by my toes, and my brain scrambles, fighting the inevitable conclusion.

I killed her.

No, no, no.

I run away. As fast and far as I can until only the pain in my chest and legs consumes me. Inhale, exhale, keep going, keep moving.

The trees whisper, taunting me.

You killed her.

You killed her.

You're in trouble now.

~

Another high-pitched scream from Delaney, and the past dissolved. How could I save her?

Her hold broke, and she fell, screaming on the descent. I couldn't look away, not even when she landed with a sickening thump on the patio cement and the scream abruptly stopped. Her lifeless body lay twisted and broken. Blood pooled under her head, tinting her blonde hair crimson.

I thought I should go over, check to see if she was still alive.

My legs couldn't obey my brain's logic. I couldn't and wouldn't do it. I had enough horrifying memories rattling in my mind without adding Delaney's dead face to the list. And what if her eyes were still open? Everyone knew that if a dead person's eyes remained open, they were in search of someone to return with them to the grave.

I dropped to my knees and shut my eyes. From a great distance, I heard the front door bang open and footsteps pound down the porch and then the side of the house.

Dad wailed. A long, mournful cry that I'd never forget. "No! Oh my God, no!"

The scent of magnolias enveloped me as Mom's arms wrapped around my shoulders. I stepped away from her embrace.

"It's over, honey. She'll never hurt you again."

"What happened?"

"Boone and I were having a little conversation with her about how she was treating you. Parker walked in on us, and things got . . . heated. Parker came at me, and Delaney happened to be in his way. She lost her footing and—"

"You two have to go," Kimbrel urged, patting the top of my head as if I were a child. "You weren't supposed to be home for another half an hour, Violet. We'd wanted to be finished speaking with Delaney before you arrived. The police are on their way now."

I stared at him, trying to process his words past the blizzard of thoughts in my mind. I still resented that he thought he had the right to order me around. "I don't see why I have to leave."

Kimbrel turned to my mom. "Get her out of here. I'll strike a deal with Parker. Everything's going to be fine."

Just as she had when I was only fourteen years old, Mom led me away from the danger, whisking me to my car. "Drive to Wesson's General Store. Once you see the police cars go by, wait a minute; then buy something inside before getting back on the road and returning home. You never saw any of us, and you never witnessed Delaney's fall. It was an accident."

"Then let me tell that to the police."

"No. I don't want the shadow of suspicion to fall on you again. Just do it. I'll explain everything later."

"But Mom, I don't believe—"

"Do it." She practically shoved me in my car. "We'll meet in the morning. I promise."

I regarded her suspiciously. "What about you? Where are you going?"

"My car's hidden nearby. Go on now!"

I obeyed, not because I entirely trusted Boone or Mom but out of sheer fear. I didn't want to face the cops or have people connecting me to another death. I tried not to think about my sister or Ainsley. But as the miles slipped past, I replayed the fall over and over in my mind. Now that my memory had returned, it refused to be silenced any longer.

This was what I'd wanted, right? The purpose behind years of endless therapy sessions that had mined the dark recesses of my mind for the answer to this question: *What happened the night Ainsley died?*

Now I knew, and I didn't like the answer. I'd pushed Ainsley off the cliff, and the river had claimed her.

And I'd left her there.

For years, the twin demons of guilt and fear had suppressed the memory of what I'd done. They were the monsters under the bed, the beasts in the basement, the spooks in the attic. Occasionally, I'd recall that push, but the old memory was like a ghost, and I could only catch brief glimpses of it in my peripheral vision. I'd known it was bad, but you couldn't touch a ghost, only feel a whisper of air tickle the fine hairs of your neck and arms. I couldn't smell it, only a faint whiff of an unnamable scent. I couldn't taste it, either, only the dry, sticky roof of my mouth after the memory had floated away once more.

I had pushed Ainsley off the cliff.

I was that monster.

But I hadn't done it on purpose either. There was at least that truth. Somehow, I'd have to move on from all this, to find comfort and strength and beauty in whatever the future held. And I'd have to do it alone. I couldn't count on anyone else; they had all let me down in both big and subtle ways.

I pulled myself together and walked into the store, hoping that Mom's instruction to do so was part of a well-constructed plan. I assumed a mask of indifference as I randomly picked up a pack of gum and a bag of chips, giving a small nod to several shoppers. Dutifully, I returned to my car and waited. I didn't have to tarry long.

A row of blue lights strobed the twilight, streaking past me. I straightened my shoulders and pulled onto the road, heading home.

Chapter 42

VIOLET

Present day

I half expected Mom not to show up today. If last night hadn't been goodbye, this morning surely would be. I'd called in sick today, and Cora had been very understanding, insisting that I take the rest of the week off work. News had quickly spread about Delaney's accident. Willie had agreed to sit with Dad this morning when I'd explained I needed to run errands, and so I was free.

I arrived for our meeting—at a Huntsville truck stop thirty miles away—feeling bruised and exhausted.

The borrowed Ford pickup truck was already at the far end of the parking lot when I arrived, dark blue in color with the license plate ALA934589. I pulled in alongside it and then slipped through its unlocked passenger door.

"Morning, hon. Coffee?" She pointed at the extra cup in the console and took a sip of her own. "One cream and two sugars."

I paused, the Styrofoam cup poised halfway to my lips. "How did you know what I like?"

"I've been keeping tabs." Mom pulled off her dark sunglasses but kept a baseball cap pulled low on her forehead.

"Through Boone?" I guessed.

"Among others."

"Like who?"

"Mostly Luanne Smithers."

I flinched as though slapped. "Should have known it. One of the few kind people I trusted over the years, and she was only nice because you paid her to provide updates on me."

"That's not true. Well, only for the first month. After that, Luanne refused to accept any more money, saying that she liked you. She and Boone even lobbied to make sure you went to the nearest halfway house as soon as an opening could be arranged once you were eligible."

I closed my eyes and let the sudden bitterness at the news wash out of my heart. At least my biological father had actually tried to help me, even if I hadn't been aware of it at the time. And what would I have done without Luanne and . . . "Hey, what about Seth Goodson? Was he on your payroll?"

"Nope." Mom eyed me curiously. "At first, I wasn't sure men were your thing." Her voice rose at the end of the sentence, turning it into a question. "You know, after your obsession with Ainsley."

I carefully set my coffee back in the console cup holder. It had taken me a while, but I'd finally realized Ainsley had most likely been a girl-hood experiment and one that had accidentally ended in disaster. My attraction to her had been real, though I'd never since felt the same pull toward another female. But that was none of Mom's business.

"You don't have the right to ask me about my sexuality. You lost that right years ago when you let me believe you were dead."

"So we're back to that. Not that I blame you, of course."

"It will always come back to that. Your desertion will always be between us."

"Fair enough."

The sadness in her voice and eyes got to me for a second, but I hardened my heart. Bottom line: Mom cared more about her money and herself than she did me. Maybe one day we could form a relationship of sorts, but not now. Not for a long time.

"I don't expect you to believe me, but I left Normal because I wanted to provide a safe, secure haven for that day you'd be able to live in the real world again. A place far from here, away from dangerous suspicion. A place where I could protect you."

"But believing you were dead . . ." I had to catch my breath a moment before continuing. I'd suffered so much at the news. Had felt so alone for so long. I cleared my throat and said simply, "It was too high a price to pay."

She didn't speak for several long, painful moments. "I see that now. Maybe I should have stayed and fought it out with Parker. Maybe I wasn't thinking clearly. I was depressed and scared. Out of my mind with grief."

If anyone understood what that felt like, it was me. I'd lived through plenty of the same emotions.

Mom gripped the steering wheel with pale, bony hands. "The least I can do for you now is tell you the truth about that night," she said.

"I know what happened. My memory returned last night when Delaney fell. I pushed Ainsley from the cliff. I'm the reason she's dead."

"That's not the whole story."

The back of my neck prickled. "What do you mean?"

"Delaney killed her. She admitted as much last night on the balcony. She'd followed you down to the river that night. Witnessed the two of you arguing and then Ainsley's fall. After you ran off into the woods, Delaney searched for Ainsley. Once she found her, she killed her—probably bashed her head in with a rock—and stole her jewelry."

My gut clenched, and my eyes filled with tears. "Why?"

"I believe Delaney was a true sociopath, a narcissist at the very least. She didn't care about anyone but herself. My theory? She saw an opportunity to get you in trouble, to punish us for not making her the center of our world like Parker did."

Poor Ainsley. I hoped she hadn't been conscious when Delaney had lifted the rock to kill her. I closed my eyes and leaned back in the seat.

"Hadn't you ever wondered how she got Ainsley's jewelry?"

"Delaney told me that I'd confessed to the murder and had the jewelry on me when I returned home."

"Such an evil woman," Mom muttered.

Truthfully, I couldn't argue with Mom's pronouncement, not after the horrible things Delaney had done trying to convince me I was crazy.

"Thanks for telling me the truth, Mom." I hadn't even thought about the jewelry last night. I'd been drained after the police visit and had taken my anxiety pills and gone to bed. But eventually I'd have wondered about the bracelet and necklace. "I feel bad about the guy they arrested, though. Detective Kimbrel must have set him up."

Mom snorted. "Don't waste a moment of guilt and sympathy on that monster. He's got a long rap sheet of child molestation. And he was there in the woods that night. Watching the two of you. The man's back in jail, which is no less than he deserves."

I shuddered, remembering the unexplained noises in the woods. "We did hear something. I'd wondered if it was Irma, searching for her long-dead lover."

A fleeting smile chased across her features. "You always were a sucker for a good ghost tale."

We didn't speak for several long moments.

"How's Parker holding up this morning?" she finally asked. "Couldn't help but feel sorry for him last night."

Dad had claimed responsibility for the accident, saying he'd been doing repair work on the deck and had neglected to tell Delaney of the danger. Supposedly, she'd gone on the deck to feed the crows for me. As if Delaney would have done such a thing. But the police had bought the story. What else could they prove? I shifted in my seat, remembering my conversation with Dad. It had been awkward, the truth about my parentage lying between us unspoken. And we'd both been laden with guilt and sorrow over lost lives. Mainly, we'd spoken of how we were going to explain last night's events.

"Dad feels guilty about stumbling into her," I told Mom. "But he also knew Delaney had been drugging him with her teas and over-medicating him with prescription pills. Whenever possible, he'd dump out the tea and spit out the medicine behind her back. It probably prolonged his life."

"So he'll survive the little bit of guilt," Mom commented dryly. "Boone worked out an arrangement with him. The price of his silence about my fake death is for me to provide him a modest allowance for whatever time he has left."

"Sounds fair."

She shot me a warning glance. "Watch out for Parker. I wonder just how much he really is suffering from dementia. The man was pretty damn sharp in his negotiations with Boone."

Paranoid. Mom had always believed the worst about him. Not that Dad didn't deserve much of her hatred. I let her warning go without comment.

The silence weighed on us again. I really had nothing more to say to my mother. I opened the door a crack.

"Wait." Her hand was on my forearm. "Remember Portugal? I'd love for you to come live with me. We can be a family again."

I stared into her eyes—the same dark-blue hue of my own—and shook my head. "No. It's too late."

"I know you feel that way now, but darling, please, think about it, okay? Give it time. At least come to visit once in a while?"

I shrugged from her grasp and stepped onto the parking lot asphalt. I'd have made a clean exit, too, if I hadn't heard her sniffle. No matter what, she was still my mom. There was no escaping that fact. And I knew what it was like to live without hope.

I leaned back into the truck and gave her a brief, fierce hug. "Maybe one day, Mom. Just maybe."

Chapter 43

BOONE

Present day

At last, the official incident report was finished. I'd no sooner attached it in an email to my supervisor than, as I expected, Dan called me into his office. Josh scowled as I passed him by. The little twerp would never forgive me for stealing the glory of Dinky's arrest.

Dan regarded me, unsmiling. "Shut the door and take a seat."

I obeyed without comment. I'd expected this as well.

Dan slowly straightened in his chair, hitting the red record button on a large 1970s vintage tape recorder. He folded his hands and leaned forward, eyeing me gravely. "Mighty convenient that you happened to be at the Henderson house when Delaney Henderson accidentally fell to her death."

Had he just stressed the word *accidentally*, or had I gone paranoid? "Like I explained yesterday, I had an anonymous call to check suspected elder abuse taking place with Parker Henderson. It's all in the report I just emailed you."

"If Henderson's daughter had been abusing him, maybe that was no accident. Could be he wanted her dead."

"You've seen the man. He's physically weak and mentally impaired." I needed to convince Dan that Delaney's fall had been accidental. "Parker Henderson doesn't have the strength to have thrown his grown daughter from a balcony, or the wits to set a trap for her."

"So now you consider yourself a doctor too?"

"Hardly. It's common sense. You have his statement."

Dan drummed his fingers on his desk, a sign that he was perturbed. I'd witnessed it many times over the course of my career. I didn't speak, preferring to wait him out and let him say his piece.

"What is it with you and the Hendersons? Every time there's a tragedy involving them, there you are, hovering in the background."

"Two events over the span of ten-plus years with a dysfunctional family. I hardly call that surprising."

"Three events," Dan insisted. "You were also the investigator in the Hyacinth Henderson death."

Perspiration collected on my palms and forehead. "Are you kidding me? Get real," I bluffed with a bravado I was far from feeling. "I was the only investigator in the county at the time. Now you're suggesting that my old car-accident report is suspicious?"

"Maybe I am."

He eyed me with open mistrust, staring me down. I didn't look away. That old police tactic of drawing out a confession through prolonged silence wasn't going to work on me. If you had something to hide—and I had plenty of secrets—talking was lethal.

Dan was the first to speak. "And you were wrong about Gerald Stedmyer's guilt in the Dalfred case. Even after Josh believed him guilty and asked you to pursue that lead further, you refused to do so. It took another anonymous call about searching the man's place for Ainsley Dalfred's jewelry before we could make an arrest. Very strange."

I shrugged. "If you say so."

Again with the drumming fingers on his desk. "Andy Bushnell mentioned to me that Delaney recently came to see you while Josh and I weren't in the office. What was that all about?"

Now that I hadn't expected. Still, I was prepared.

"Miss Henderson claimed someone was stalking her, but she couldn't prove it. I advised her to be careful."

"And yet you never thought to mention any of this to me when the woman *accidentally* dies a short time later?"

Oh yeah, he'd definitely emphasized *accidentally*. My boss had a boatload of doubts.

"My apologies, sir."

"This all doesn't add up. Why don't you tell me what's really been going on?"

"If you're questioning my official report, perhaps I should hire an attorney before answering any further questions."

Dan's pale face mottled red with anger. He flicked off the record switch. "After all these years of working together, this is what it comes down to between us? Recorded conversations and legal threats?"

"The tape recording was your doing. And my hiring an attorney isn't a legal threat. We're talking protecting my basic civil rights here if you're suggesting I've falsified reports."

"I'm suggesting a lot more than falsified reports." His voice rose, loud enough that I wondered if employees on the first floor could hear him. He stood up from his chair and jabbed his index finger at me. "I don't trust you. Not a damn bit. I might not be able to prove you've done anything improper, but everything you've done connected with the Henderson and Dalfred cases is mighty questionable. You're unfit for this office."

"That's unfortunate you feel that way," I said with a poker face of calm. "I don't plan on leaving. You and your nephew can't make me either. Not until I'm good and ready."

"I want you out of here. Effective immediately." He sat back down abruptly and pressed record on the tape recorder again. "Sign this resignation I've prepared. It's a fairly generous retirement incentive."

He shoved paperwork at me, and I barely restrained myself from giving a low whistle of surprise as I read the figures. The incentive was generous. Very generous. Seemed I was "good and ready" to leave after all.

I rose to my feet and waved the papers in my hand. "The terms appear to meet with my approval. As soon as my attorney reviews it, I'll sign. I'll get back to you within the week. You and Josh just have to wait a little longer, and you can have this damn place to yourselves."

Dan's mouth twisted. "You've turned into a real bastard, Kimbrel. Take leave without pay until you sign those papers. And don't wait too long, or I'll have the offer nulled and voided."

"Thank you for your kind offer, *sir.* And by the way, you might want to delete your final words. The upstanding citizens at your civic groups and church might be surprised at your language. *Bastard.*"

Dan came out from around his desk with surprising speed and grabbed the collar of my shirt. "Don't get too cocky there, Boone. Get those papers back in one week or else."

I pushed him away from me. "Or else what?"

"I'll subpoena to have Hyacinth Henderson's ashes collected. If there are large enough bone or teeth fragments, we can run a DNA test."

I felt the blood drain from my face. Had the Hendersons ever scattered her ashes as Hyacinth had requested in her will? I'd never thought to check on that loose end.

Dan's lips curled knowingly.

"You have no grounds to get a subpoena."

"You really want to bet your life on that? The judge happens to be a good friend."

Take the money and run. I gave Dan a grim nod and looked past him to the wall of fame behind his desk, plastered with various written commendations from politicians stretching all the way up to the Alabama governor's office. My boss held a full house of aces and kings, but I played my one good card.

"Sounds like it's in both our interests for me to retire. After all, you wouldn't want a public stink about your lead investigator's integrity. Not after all these years of your direct supervision."

I made a slow exit and slammed the door behind me, half expecting Dan to make another threat. He didn't. I strolled to my desk and packed what few items remained there into an empty cardboard box I'd been keeping for this very moment.

Josh smirked, watching my every move.

"Problems?" he asked.

"Fuck you." I tucked the box up under my arm and walked out.

In the parking lot, I tossed my jacket and the box in the back seat and pulled out of there for the last time. I'd expected to be sad and nostalgic, but instead, a feeling of relief washed over me.

In many ways, I was finally free. Violet was cleared of any scandal, a sex offender was back in prison where he should be, and I finally had enough money to survive without working in the rat race. But more than any of that, my deadly secrets would now go to my grave. The only other person who knew my sin was just as guilty as me and never wanted our secrets revealed. It bound Hyacinth and me yet deeper in a complex web of passion and love and lies.

The weight of my crimes was still there, and at the oddest moments of the day—grilling in my backyard, picking up milk at the grocery store, watching football—I was decimated, remembering the sound of water splashing as Ainsley's body dropped into a watery grave, meeting the same fate as Irma had decades earlier.

At least I no longer had to worry about those secrets coming to light.

Violet and Hyacinth consumed my thoughts during the drive home.

My daughter had humbled me when we'd spoken late last night after everyone had left and Parker had gone to bed. She hadn't been planning to kill Delaney at all. How foolish of me to assume the worse just because she'd been working on the deck. Violet had explained that her only intent was to replace the rotten boards before she moved out. She wanted Parker to move into her old room and feed the crows in her absence.

Only my own sin blinded me to innocence. Violet was a better person than Hyacinth and me combined. Even if she doubted her own essential goodness, my daughter was kind and compassionate. One day, she'd realize that her doubt and her struggle were what made her a decent human being. Sociopaths like Delaney were the ones who went to their grave with no regrets.

I crossed the bridge over Hatchet Lake. Sunlight sparkled on the vast expanse of water already starting to fill the drained lake, and I took it as a reassuring sign that my life in Normal would soon return to normal.

Only one question remained now.

Stay with Ellie in Normal, or move to Portugal with Hyacinth? I imagined the warm, sandy beaches of Portugal. Hell, I'd even looked up her foreign town online and viewed the picturesque village where Hy had started life over. Hyacinth still dreamed about the three of us finally living together. A real family. But recent events had proved to me that we only brought out the worst in one another. I'd always wonder if Hy had gone to that balcony in hopes of Delaney accidentally falling. Initially, we'd agreed she'd sneak into the house minutes after I arrived and we'd confront Delaney together. Instead, she'd arrived ahead of me and hidden on the balcony.

I dug out the slip of paper from my shirt pocket that Hy had slipped to me last night. It had her Algarve address scribbled on the printed receipt of a one-way plane ticket.

I only hesitated a moment, then rolled down the car window. I tossed it out, watching as it fluttered in the wind a moment and then disappeared.

Time to take Ellie on the vacation of her dreams. Anywhere but Portugal.

Chapter 44

VIOLET

Three weeks later

I hold the peanut in my palm and will Tux with all my soul to take this final treat. Each day, he's drawn inches closer, but he's never been bold enough to feed directly from my hand. He cocks his head and regards me. The blue gray of his baby-crow eyes from our first meeting has darkened to a midnight hue that matches his plumage. His mouth has also deepened from red to black, transforming Tux into a perfect creature of the shadows. His talons grip the railing, and he sidles forward, one foot and then the other, making cautious progress.

"You know you want it," I say in my best crow-whisperer voice. "I won't hurt you, little buddy. Promise. We're friends."

In a burst of flapping wings, he descends on my palm and scoops the peanut into his beak, one eye on me all the while. Too soon, he flies off to his usual perch, crunching his treat.

My throat constricts painfully. "Thank you, Tux."

I can't believe I'm leaving him again. I thought about Tux often while away, imagined that he was a friend waiting for me to return home. It brought me comfort during dark times.

Willie Crenshaw pulls into the drive, and I reluctantly cross to my bedroom door.

"Dad's going to take good care of you," I tell Tux. "Same treat, same time, same place."

I walk through the old bedroom of my youth. Already, the construction crew has painted the old lavender walls a sage green, and tomorrow Dad's new furniture will arrive. At the closet door, I pause, eyeing the crow-gift boxes on the top shelf. Should I take them with me? I've had them since elementary school, and the sight and feel of them always comfort me when I'm lonely.

"They're fine where they are," I mumble aloud. They'll be here waiting for me if I need them again. But halfway down the steps I stop, turn around, and return to the closet. I gather up most of the bits and baubles—marbles, buttons, string—anything that happened to catch their fancy. My cupped hands throb with their warmth as I carry them to the balcony. Tux has already flown the coop, but I feel him watching me from afar. I lay out the gifts on the small wicker table. "For you," I explain.

Somehow, I know he'll remember these. The pretty colored objects will catch his eye and make him curious and happy all at once. A crow smorgasbord of treasure.

Downstairs, Cora, Dad, and Willie sit at the table drinking coffee. She and Willie seem happy with our arrangement. They'll stay here in the house with Dad, looking after him and overseeing the home renovation crew as they spruce up the place. I'm paying Cora double her Whispering Oaks salary, plus throwing in free room and board for the two of them.

"You sure you can afford this?" they asked when I first made the proposition.

If they knew the huge sum of money Mom had deposited in my banking account, they wouldn't have worried.

"Yes," I assured them. "Keep me updated if he needs anything, or if his health suddenly worsens."

Not even one week after seeing the new doctor, Dad's mental improvement has been significant. One of the first things I did after Delaney's death was have a locksmith open the safe behind her beauty queen photo. As I'd suspected, that was where Dad's prescriptions were hidden. Doctors analyzed the medication and concluded he'd been taking way too many sedatives.

Without the herbal teas and excessive medication dosages from Delaney, he seems happier and more coherent most of the time, although dementia and cirrhosis are surely taking their slow, inevitable toll. He continues to randomly dig in the yard, and Willie promised to record a video when Dad uses the new metal detector and discovers the hidden treasure I strategically buried—enough Confederate coins and memorabilia to provide entertainment for whatever time he has left. It was a blast setting that up and marking the treasure locations on a map for Willie. He'll subtly guide Dad in the right directions.

Dad rises from the kitchen table and walks toward me. For a second, I stiffen, worrying he will hug me goodbye. We've never done so before, and I don't want to start now. It is not our way.

Thankfully, he does not. Instead, Dad stuffs his hands in his pockets. "You're coming again to visit one day," he says gruffly. "Right?"

"Of course. And I'm leaving you in good hands."

"Oh, yeah, yeah. Sure thing," he mumbles, staring down at the floor.

"Okay, then," I say in my no-nonsense tone, eyeing my other suitcase by the front door. Awkwardly, I pat his shoulder. "Don't forget to feed the crows."

"Don't you worry about them birds," Cora assures me.

Dad leans in and whispers in my ear. "Always considered you my own daughter, you know. Sorry I was such a mean son of a—"

I pull away. "It's okay. It's over." I draw a long breath and add, "Dad." My vision blurs, taking me by surprise. Never thought leaving this old house would make me sad. It's not like Dad and I have ever been close, but we formed our own unlikely friendship of sorts in the wake of Delaney's cruelty. Quickly, I nod at Willie, and he helps me with the luggage. We carry our burdens out to the car, and I avert my gaze from the patio where Delaney died.

The crew has been instructed to jackhammer up all the cement and haul it away. Within days, new sod will be laid over the disrupted soil, erasing all physical reminders of Delaney's fall.

Willie and I set off, only making one pit stop at the florist's before reaching the graveyard. I said my goodbyes to Libby and Calvin last night, and Libby promised to visit once I've settled down in my own place.

Willie stays behind as I get out of the car and cross the cemetery, carrying a posy of flowers. Only a handful of folks is scattered about the grounds—all absorbed in their own loss and grief. Even though my name's been cleared, I still hear the townspeople's whispers everywhere I go. I'm relieved no one's close by as I visit this grave. No probing eyes and gossiping lips to chronicle my actions.

Under a copse of sweet gums near the river, I find the square plot of freshly turned earth. Aggressive shoots of bermuda grass snake across churned red clay. Soon, nature will take its course and blanket this patch of land covering her bones. The etched marble tombstone is modest and to the point: AINSLEY DALFRED, OUR BELOVED ANGEL, MARCH 15, 1992–JULY 2, 2007.

Kneeling, I lay the brightly colored flowers below the marker. A quick glance over my shoulder—yes, no one can see or hear me—and I trace the cold, imprinted letters.

"I'm sorry, Ainsley," I whisper. "It was an accident. I didn't mean to hurt you. If I could take it back . . ."

But of course, there's no going back to that night. Everyone in Normal might believe me innocent now, and legally, I'm off the hook, but in my own heart, I know better. Mom and Detective Kimbrel explained that Delaney had bashed Ainsley's head, stolen her jewelry, and left her for dead, and Dinky Stedmyer had done the rest.

Ainsley and I really did hear something that night. Dinky was watching us in the woods. Once Delaney had left, he took advantage of Ainsley's weakened state, assaulted her, loaded her in his boat, and then disposed of her body.

That's what I've been told, anyway. But I would never 100 percent trust Mom or Kimbrel. I sense they each have their own agendas and secrets to preserve. As for me, technically, I might not have committed murder—but the real fault is mine and mine alone.

That moment of rage, that one angry push, set in motion the chain of events that led to Ainsley's death. I have to live with that. And live I will. I'm leaving the ghosts of my past behind here in a place that is Normal in name only.

I brush the tips of my fingers against my lips and then touch the cold marble slab. "Goodbye, my friend."

You'll always be my best friend.

I close my eyes a moment, picturing Ainsley as she fell—her long dark hair a black cloud; pale, moonlit arms and legs flailing uselessly; wide, beseeching eyes—and the shrill scream that will echo in my mind until I, too, am laid to rest one day. I accept responsibility for that.

Another memory—another fall. Delaney tumbling from my bedroom balcony, blonde hair whipping in the wind. But that accident isn't on me.

One death that I regret and mourn; one death that is a relief. Neither woman can now bear witness against me, whether their words be true or false. For the first time in my life, I feel free.

A single flower remains in my hand. I stroll to Delaney's grave and toss a lily of the valley at the foot of her tombstone, careful to hold my breath lest her recently departed spirit enter my body. She wasn't my real sister, not biologically, and not of the heart either. I try to conjure some emotion, some grief at her passing, but I'm numb. *Too bad we couldn't be closer*, I finally manage. It's the best I can do.

There's only one thing left.

I wander down by the river and reach into the pocket of my jeans, pulling out the chip of blue glass that the crows gifted me so long ago. I toss it into the water. It was a part of the past. My mind and my memories are whole now; I don't need magical talismans.

I stroll back across the cemetery, wondering how Mom is getting along back in Portugal. And Kimbrel isn't all bad, as I've come to discover. A decent man who made mistakes. He offered to drive me to the bus station, but I declined. Maybe one day we'll talk more. Not now, though.

Willie stands by the Plymouth Duster. He jingles the keys. "Ready to go?" he asks.

I nod, slipping into the passenger seat. He starts the car and slants me a curious look. "You sure you want to go? It's never too late to change your mind. Cora's heartsick you're leaving Whispering Oaks, and I'm sure yer daddy wants you to stay on."

"Positive. I'm leaving."

The question is, Where to? My hand involuntarily slips into the front flap of my purse, and I run a finger along the edges of the passport and bank account card Mom has given me, but I still have no desire to live with her. Portugal sounds like another planet, an exotic hodgepodge of culture and beauty. It's all . . . too much for me. And living with Mom, at least for now, doesn't sound like a good idea. In my heart, she's been dead to me for years. No, it's time for me to strike out on my own.

"You have my number," I remind Willie. "We'll stay in touch."

"I'll let you know the minute he can't live at home no more."

We say nothing as he crosses the bridge, but Willie lifts his right hand, curling all his fingers and thumb into his palm, except for his pinkie. I laugh and hook the pinkie of my right hand in his. Everyone knows that crossing a bridge like this means you are friends forever. There are bits and pieces of Normal that will stay with me after all, but I'll choose only happier memories like this one.

River water gleams under the glaring sun—cold and deep and mysterious. We cross the railroad tracks, and Willie grins, lifting his feet and arms. I play along for old times' sake.

As we near the white oak's canopy, he shoots me a grin. "I knew writing you that letter to come home was a good thing. I told my Cora you'd set everything right. And you did. For yer dad and for yerself." His grin fades. "As far as yer sister, well, it's not up to me to judge."

I'm never sure how much Willie knows about what went on with my family. I suspect he knows a great deal. My own feelings about Delaney aren't quite so charitable as his. But she's dead now, and I refuse to let her memory rob me of another single day of peace.

We pass under the tree's shade. "Now make a wish," Willie reminds me.

I close my eyes. *I wish . . .* the answer materializes in a blink as I recall the flash of my blue glass chip as it disappeared into the muddy water . . . *I wish for a beach cottage on the Gulf.* I've still never seen the ocean, but I envision its blue waves and sandy shores. That's where I'm heading. I'll buy a little place and a car, maybe go back to school and figure out the future. Seth lives in Mobile and still works the oil rigs. Maybe I'll look him up one day, see how he's really coping in the outside world.

At the loud honk, I open my eyes, smiling as we leave the tree's shadow and emerge into sunlight.

ACKNOWLEDGMENTS

Many thanks to my editors, Megha Parekh and Charlotte Herscher, and to my agent, Ann Leslie Tuttle, with the Dystel, Goderich & Bourret LLC literary agency.

ABOUT THE AUTHOR

Photo © 2013 One Six Photography

Debbie Herbert is a *USA Today* and *Publishers Weekly* bestselling author who's always been fascinated by magic, romance, and gothic stories. Married and living in Alabama, she roots for the Crimson Tide football team. Debbie enjoys recumbent bicycling and Jet Skiing with her husband. She has two grown sons, and the oldest has autism. Characters with autism frequently appear in her works—even when she doesn't plan on it.

For more information, visit www.DebbieHerbert.com and sign up for her newsletter to receive a free short story. Connect with her on Facebook at Debbie Herbert Author or Debbie Herbert's Readers and on Twitter @debherbertwrit.